INNOCENT GUILT

REMI KONE

QUERCUS

First published in Great Britain in 2025 by

QUERCUS

Quercus Editions Ltd
Carmelite House
50 Victoria Embankment
London EC4Y 0DZ

An Hachette UK company

The authorised representative in the EEA is Hachette Ireland,
8 Castlecourt Centre, Dublin 15, D15 XTP3, Ireland (email: info@hbgi.ie)

Copyright © 2025 Remi Kone

The moral right of Remi Kone to be
identified as the author of this work has been
asserted in accordance with the Copyright,
Designs and Patents Act, 1988.

All rights reserved. No part of this publication
may be reproduced or transmitted in any form
or by any means, electronic or mechanical,
including photocopy, recording, or any
information storage and retrieval system,
without permission in writing from the publisher.

A CIP catalogue record for this book is available
from the British Library

HB ISBN 978 1 52944 132 1
TPB ISBN 978 1 52944 133 8
EBOOK ISBN 978 1 52944 135 2

This book is a work of fiction. Names, characters,
businesses, organizations, places and events are
either the product of the author's imagination
or used fictitiously. Any resemblance to
actual persons, living or dead, events or
locales is entirely coincidental.

1

Typeset in Bembo by CC Book Production
Printed and bound in Great Britain by Clays Ltd, Elcograf S.p.A.

Papers used by Quercus Editions Ltd are from well-managed forests and other responsible sources.

For my mother and my sister,
and in memory of my late father
who loved books

Chapter One

Leah

Margaretta rarely laughed, but she died with a smile on her face. She was halfway through a book about birds, wearing fruit print pyjamas too tight around the thigh. She fell into a coma without warning and hours later she was gone, her soul sent to the God she loved, her body left for me to bury. I had thought about Margaretta dying before. Everybody does. Not Margaretta, but someone close: mother, father, husband, wife. Most people could take their pick but for me, there was only her.

My parents had been killed in a car accident when I was five, their instant death leaving me stranded in the wreckage. I was too young to remember, let alone say goodbye, but life has a curious habit of giving you the second chances you don't want and, staring at the body of the woman who had adopted and raised me, I was saying goodbye to my entire family. Again.

Growing up, I had assumed Margaretta had been unable to have children, but when I was eighteen, she told me she had a son. She didn't tell me his name, and she rarely mentioned him after that. When she did, it was always in the past tense: she *had* a son; he *had* been sent to prison; she didn't want to talk about him and that was that. No regret, no hint of sadness or shame, just information she thought I should know because I was the family she had chosen. Now Margaretta was gone, and I was alone in the world. Again.

I got off the bus before it reached the river and walked over the bridge into Battersea, from the north side of London to the south. Margaretta had always hated being south of the river, and I smiled as I remembered her irrational dislike. It was past lunchtime, but there were surprisingly few people around, and I was conscious of the sound of cars rattling along the tarmac. The fog was starting to clear as I turned the corner, and I could see the station in the distance, silhouetted against the late autumn sky. I knew Randle was watching me even though I couldn't see his face. Benjamin Randle often watched me when he thought I wasn't looking. I had no idea what he found so fascinating. Maybe he didn't know many police officers who looked like me; maybe he had never worked closely with a woman before; maybe he didn't know himself. I could tell I made him nervous even though he hid it well. It was surprising, considering how confident he was with everyone else. Confident without being cocky, charming without being sleazy; it was a skill which came with entitlement, and Randle was nothing if not entitled. He expected great things to happen to him and they probably would, if he stopped idealising the job and just focused on results. There were no perfect detectives and the sooner Benjamin Randle learned that, the sooner he would stand a chance at becoming halfway good.

I strode through the gloom towards him, following the motion of the lit cigarette as it travelled to and from his mouth. He was standing outside smoking, drawing deeply on the cigarette, as if each shot of nicotine gave him a deeper insight into the mysteries of the world. It was a wonder that he didn't feel the cold, standing there in just his shirtsleeves, brown leather boots buffed hard to hide the scuffs. I pulled my coat tighter around me and kept moving forwards. The coat was more business chic than detective casual, but Margaretta had brought me up to value classic essentials, and the high collar shielded my neck from the wind.

Randle inhaled again, watching me through half-closed eyes. Finally, he spoke.

'I've been trying to call you, ma'am . . .' He was trying not to sound aggressive, but there was a hint of accusation in his voice.

'I'm here now.'

I hadn't told him about Margaretta; I hadn't told anyone. It had been three weeks since her death, but I never alluded to my private life.

Randle let out a short laugh, observing me as he exhaled.

'So you are, ma'am. So you are.'

His mouth crept into a half-smile, slowly at first, his lips pushing against the creases on either side until they turned up at the corners. He couldn't help himself – he liked to smile and, if it were a skill, Randle had undoubtedly perfected it. I seldom paid attention to looks, but there was a symmetry to Randle's features which you noticed, and a warmth which drew people in. Fair hair, slightly longer at the front, light stubble that was neither messy nor neat, long nose, slightly broken at the bridge; his face felt familiar yet distinctive, and I was aware of the appeal, even though I didn't succumb to it myself. We stood like that for a moment, with Randle silently trying to coax a reaction and me refusing to engage. He must have known he was fighting a losing battle, but it was a habit he found hard to kick.

'Let's get to it, then,' I said.

I began to move past him into the grey brick building, my mind already focused on the afternoon ahead. I expected him to fall in behind me, and I stopped when he didn't. He stubbed out his cigarette, relaxed but deliberate, to show he wasn't trying to waste my time. He was still smiling when he looked up – then his expression changed completely, his gaze fixed beyond me. I knew something was wrong, before I even turned to look.

Over the years, I had learned to expect the worst, but I wasn't prepared for what I saw next. A figure walked towards us with slow, cautious steps. Her brown hair was slick with sweat in spite of the cold, and her body trembled visibly. She wore a pale blue shirt buttoned to the top and a dark, plain, knee-length skirt. She didn't make a sound, and the closer she came, the slower she seemed to move. She looked helpless and afraid, and there was something about her movements that seemed erratic. I reached for my handcuffs, never for one moment taking my eyes off the woman approaching the police station, soaked in blood.

She was facing us, her hand wrapped tightly around a baseball bat. Her skin was drained of all colour, and her body was lopsided, as if the weight of the bat was pulling her down. She was still some distance away, too far to hurt us but close enough to see us clearly. I pulled out my badge, carefully holding it up. The woman seemed to register it, but her expression barely changed, a veil of terror and shock. She wasn't out of control, but she didn't appear to be in control either. Her neck was stooped, her arm dangling beside her so the bat thumped against the ground with a low, rhythmic thud. She didn't hesitate as she passed Randle, then me, her eyes staring directly ahead. She just kept walking, through the doors of the police station, surrendering herself to the mercy of the law.

Chapter Two

Leah

I stared at the dark brown liquid, watching coffee from the machine trickle into the paper cup. The woman was being examined by a doctor, and we couldn't question her until he was done. I jabbed the orange button for another shot of espresso, frustrated that we didn't even know her name. There were hours of CCTV footage to sift through, a task I had never cared for, even in the lower ranks. Waiting for an update was tedious, and the slow drip of caffeine did little to lift my mood. DC Akosua Owusu hovered beside me, the novelty of becoming a detective pasting a perpetual grin on her face. Her afro was in neat cornrows, drawing attention to her wide cheekbones and almond-shaped eyes. She liked to be noticed and nature was on her side.

'Let me know as soon as you find something on the CCTV,' I said. 'We need to know who she is and where she came from.'

'Yes, ma'am. Anything you need.'

Her deep Scottish voice had surprised me at first, but I was slowly getting used to it. She had bounded up to me on her first day, shiny afro teased into a perfect crown.

'I just want to say how excited I am to work for another woman of colour . . .'

I hated the phrase and had been tempted to tell her I preferred mixed race or black, but there was something endearing about her enthusiasm, and I'd been surprised by my restraint. She had called me a role model, and I had cringed at the label; my mistakes and triumphs were mine alone, and Akosua would have to fail or succeed on her own.

Now I watched her scurry away to review the CCTV, so eager to please me that she almost looked back. The sun had disappeared, and the afternoon sky was dark. I glanced through the window at the city with all its secrets. Two hours had passed since I had sent a team to search for possible victims, and I had heard nothing back. I caught sight of my reflection in the metal drinks machine. I had never been a fan of being called 'fresh-faced', but those days were long gone. A small line dug its way into my forehead between my eyebrows, giving the appearance of a slight scowl. It used to be a conscious decision to frown, but now there was a permanence to my irritation. A tiny smudge of blood marked my shirt where the woman had brushed past me on her way in. She had been covered in the stench of death. I had smelt it before – damp mixed with sweat and blood. I hated how it clung to me now, seeping through my pores.

'Ma'am?'

Randle appeared behind me; his reflection dwarfed mine in the scratched metal casing.

'The doctor says the woman hasn't sustained any noticeable injuries and there's no indication she's the victim of assault.'

'Then she's either the attacker or a witness,' I said. 'We need to know which one.'

Chapter Three

Leah

I had led so many interviews, I had to resist the urge not to categorise each suspect: the ones who talked, the ones who refused to talk; the ones who cried, the ones who refused to cry; the ones who lied, the ones who didn't know how to. On the surface, it seemed simple, but dig a couple of inches and all theories went out the window, because every police interview was different, and the most helpful categories only ever had one person in them. The woman sitting opposite me was impossible to read. Her lips were slightly parted, but no words came out of her mouth. Her clothes had been taken for testing, but a whiff of blood still lingered. The smell hit the back of my nostrils, and I recoiled in my chair. Stripped of her skirt and shirt, swamped by the white paper suit, she looked smaller and more vulnerable in the stark interview room. My fingers rested lightly on the edge of the table, my glass of water untouched.

'Can you explain the blood on your clothes? We want to help you, but you need to talk to us.'

It was the fifth time I had asked the question; the fifth time she hadn't replied.

The woman's eyes were wide with panic, and she was clearly in a state of shock. I watched her, registering every movement, conscious that the tiniest gesture – a flick of the hair or a clenched fist – could say a lot. Her eyes were both frightened and frightening, seeming to say something without telling me anything at all.

She didn't blink as I flipped my notebook shut.

'Let's take a break,' I said.

I expected her to look relieved, but her expression didn't change. The rhythm of her breath stayed constant, and she looked through me when I pushed my chair back. I nodded to Randle to stop the recording, welcoming the release in my hips as I stood up.

I hadn't realised how thirsty I was until I stepped out of the room, and my mouth felt dry and heavy as I bent over the water fountain. It was too low, even for me, and the water came out in an uneven trickle. The mute woman wasn't ready to talk, so I had to work with what I could see: the blood on her clothes had been relatively fresh, so if a crime had taken place, it was fairly recent, and the fact she was still in shock told a similar story. I let the water flow for a few seconds. It was a pointless exercise as the temperature was regulated by the machine, but there was something relaxing about the sound. Randle's footsteps disrupted the calm.

'It's all yours.' I released the button and wiped the drip from my lips. 'Any news on the blood on her clothes?'

Randle leant against the wall, dislodging flakes of peeling paint.

'It isn't hers, ma'am,' he said. 'D'you think she's hurt someone?'

'I don't know. Walking in here was either a cry for help, an admission of guilt, or both, but we haven't found a body and, unless you know something I don't, she still hasn't opened her mouth.'

'What if she doesn't tell us anything?'

His eyes were tired, and there was a film of sweat gathering between his neck and collar.

'We find another way,' I said. 'If she speaks, great, but we don't even know we can trust what she says. Someone's dead to this world or fighting to stay in it, and standing around won't do them much good.'

I strode down the corridor, re-energised. Pausing outside the interview room, I observed the woman for a moment, hoping the blankness had been an act. She had barely moved since we left her. Her chin was dipped towards her chest so her head sagged on top of her neck; her hands were clasped tightly on the table in front of her, leaving faint red marks where her nails dug in. She looked even more distant, withdrawing entirely into herself, seemingly unaware of her surroundings. She would have been fascinating to watch if another person's life wasn't potentially at stake. A pathetic figure, hunched and afraid. If it wasn't genuine, she was giving the performance of a lifetime.

'How are we going to find the victim if we don't have a lead, ma'am?'

I didn't answer. The clock was ticking, and we would either find them in time or we wouldn't. It was as simple as that.

Chapter Four

Alistair Cowan. Forty-four. Divorced. Two children. Alistair Cowan. Forty-four. Divorced. Two children.

He kept repeating the facts over and over to himself, because as long as he could say the words, he knew he was still alive. It hurt to make the sounds, and his voice came out as a thin rasp, barely audible above the hum of the wind, but he had to keep saying the words, because he was desperate to cling on to his life.

Alistair James Cowan. Forty-four and three months. Married for five years. Two legitimate children and a third child his ex-wife didn't know about. Partner at Rossan Brown Meyer Management Consultants. The youngest man to make partner in a generation. Houses in London, Suffolk and the south of France . . .

He tried to think of more facts, but he kept drifting in and out of consciousness, struggling to make sense of the blur of information in his head: his name, his age, his family; it was all beginning to sound unfamiliar. He had no sense of time, but with every passing moment, he felt he was losing his grasp on the world. He couldn't remember when he became partner. It had once seemed so important, but he couldn't remember the date or even the year, so he went back to his name and his age, formulating the words again and again.

Alistair James Cowan, forty-four, divorced, two children. Alistair James Cowan, forty-four, divorced, two children. Alistair James Cowan, forty-four and three months, almost dead.

Chapter Five

Odie

Odie Reid hadn't been called a pest and manhandled off a crime scene for quite some time. Even though it annoyed her when it happened, she missed feeling like she was doing her job. Odie could talk long and hard about how journalism had gone to the dogs, if anyone cared to listen. Kids these days didn't know what journalism was, but it didn't stop them getting all the good stories because they were hotwired into social media. Gone were the days of digging into a story, getting doors slammed in your face – now everything was out there at the click of a mouse. There was no adrenaline rush or thrill of the chase, just the glare of a Google search page or the flash of an 'X' feed – and everyone had access to that. She felt like a walking, talking cliché, bemoaning days gone by when journalism actually counted for something, but she was proud to be a cliché because that was the kind of journalism she loved and she would fight for it as long as she had the energy which, at fifty-four, wouldn't be forever.

Odie wasn't a fool. She had been around for long enough to know she was taking up space, only there because her name still carried a certain cachet in circles where she was praised for her no-holds-barred exposés in the nineties. People still remembered that she was supposed to be good, but there was only so long she could rely on her bullishness and former glory to keep her job; newspapers were struggling, and Odie needed a story to remind people she was still worth having around.

She opened her browser and brought up YouTube. You had to look hard to find a story, but she needed all the inspiration she could get. Taking a gulp of coffee, she sank down into her chair, only to be jolted by her phone vibrating next to her hand. It rang once – short, sharp, then silence. It had to be Ross.

It was still strange seeing Ross Calhoun's name on the door. Odie had recruited him straight out of university. He had prided himself on being the only black man from a provincial Irish town whose name she could neither remember nor pronounce. Determined to prove himself to his racist neighbours, he had come to London as soon as he could afford it, making up for lost time in hipster bars in Bow. He had looked so young that first day in the office, Odie had doubted whether she was doing the right thing, hoisting him out of his twenty-something fog of weed and rollies and hurtling him into a life of words and half-truths. Almost fifteen years on, Ross Calhoun didn't look much older – only the odd line of grey in his hair and slight pinching of skin around his eyes betrayed a new maturity. He was also now her boss.

Ross was reading when she entered, toying with a cigarette he never intended to smoke.

'I see you've graduated to the real thing,' Odie observed.

'Roll-ups are for kids.' He flashed her a boyish smile.

'How long's it been?'

'Three days. A few hours. Not as many minutes. Being in the office helps. Means I'm safe to hold them. Can't trust myself outside.'

'You make it sound like we're in prison.'

'Only of our own making . . .' He smiled again, amused by his corniness. It might have been endearing if he didn't have all the power. At that moment, Odie wished she had never given him his first job and had left him philosophising about the state of the nation in that dingy East End bar. Sometimes she doubted he remembered the debt of gratitude he owed her. It wasn't that he was patronising or smug, but he had never been uncomfortable with his superiority and that was something Odie could never forgive.

'Good story last week.' It was a conversation starter rather than a compliment, and they both knew it. The story had been average, and Odie had been bored writing it. She decided to play along anyway.

'Thanks.'

'So . . .'

'So what?'

'What next?'

'I'm following a few leads. I'll have something later.'

Her comment was met with total silence. She hated it when Ross did this, but she knew better than to fill the void with pointless words. Besides, she had nothing to say. He looked at her for a moment, and she stared straight back. After a while, he got up and crushed the cigarette in his palm, idling towards the bin to dispose of the tobacco. As he turned back to face her, Odie was struck by how he managed to walk away from something so addictive; she wondered how tempted he really was by the packet of cigarettes on his desk.

'A few leads,' he finally said. It felt like minutes since she had uttered the words, and Odie almost didn't recognise them as her own.

'Yes.'

'Do you actually have a story, Odie?'

There was an uncomfortable pause as he sat back down. Time was, Odie said she had a story, and they would hold the front page for her, or close. Now the pressure to justify her existence left her feeling mentally exhausted.

'I need time, Ross.'

'Fine . . . but while you're waiting for your muse to visit, you can take care of this.' He pushed a piece of paper across the table. More history. 'Rebecca Stanton's pregnant. I want you to get the story.'

Odie let out an involuntary sigh. Seven years ago, television golden girl Rebecca Stanton had been arrested for the murder of her two-year-old son who had tragically drowned in the bath. Hysterical, Rebecca had broken down and ranted about killing her son as she was dragged screaming from her house by police. Hours later her confession had been retracted, excused as the raving of a distressed mother who didn't know what she was saying. Odie was convinced of Rebecca's innocence. She strongly believed there were good people and there were bad, and she decided Rebecca Stanton was good. As a mother herself, and not a great one at that, Odie knew what it was like to hate your child momentarily, but it was a big leap to kill your baby, and Rebecca Stanton, with her sheltered life and smiling face, was no murderer. Rebecca had been acquitted and Odie's 'Is this the face of a child killer?' piece had done wonders for the paper and bought her a stay of execution at a time when she was close to getting fired. The nation rallied round Rebecca; Rebecca's grateful family gave endless exclusives to the paper, and sales soared. Seven years on, Rebecca had the chance of happiness again with a new child on the way. The story was almost writing itself and, while Odie knew she was mad not to milk the Stanton case for all it was worth, the truth of the matter was that it bored her. The original murder trial had been news, but she felt this latest tale of hope triumphing over adversity was beneath her – tabloid treacle which any hack could write. It was almost as if Ross was taunting her with her past glory, reminding her of her current inability to perform. She hated him for not believing in her, but he didn't seem to care.

'Why can't Jack Hunter do it?'

'Jack Hunter's contribution isn't in question.'

'Is that a threat or a warning?' She squared up to him. The ease with which he brushed her aside wound her up even more.

'I don't want to fight with you, Odie. Just do it.'

Definitely a threat. She helped herself to a cigarette and left.

Chapter Six

Leah

It had been six months since I had moved back to London from Leeds, but my flat still looked like a stranger's. I prided myself on interior design, but I had done nothing to make it feel like home. Poetic in name only, the World's End Estate was a taste of the real world in one of the most rarefied areas of London. Drugs were sometimes a problem, but I had wanted to find somewhere near work, and I needed a place fast. I had no 'significant other'; I was too old to have a flatmate and too sane to have a cat, so it was just me. I had been warned against buying on the ground floor, but I wanted to be close to the communal courtyard, and everyone knew I was police. I let myself in, squinting at my mobile in the darkness to see if I'd missed a call about the search. I fumbled with the light switch, ignoring the flickering bulb as I read a message from Margaretta's lawyer. He had sent a curt order to ring him, but it was late. Selwyn Peterson would have to wait.

It was raining slightly but nothing torrential. I had left the curtains open, and shallow puddles of water shone in the dark outside. My skipping rope was in its usual place behind the door. I needed to let off steam, so I decided to brave it. Changing into a pair of trainers, I tucked in my shirt and slipped out into the open air. I don't know how long I skipped for but, by the time I had finished, I was drenched with sweat and rain, listening to my breathing as if it belonged to someone else. My calves were knotted with cramp and fatigue, but the discomfort was strangely soothing, all thoughts of Margaretta and the mute woman briefly erased from my mind. I almost didn't hear my phone, and reached for it just before my voicemail kicked in.

'Any news?' My shirt clung to my ribs, and I was still out of breath.

'Nothing. I was just checking in, ma'am. Checking everything's OK.'

'Why wouldn't it be?' I said.

'These last couple of weeks, you've seemed . . .'

I let his words linger, daring him to finish the thought. Seconds passed, then I heard his breath fill the silence between us.

'You don't need to score brownie points, Randle. Doing the job will be fine.'

I made no apologies for being hard on Randle – my job was to make him a better detective, not to be his friend – but after I hung up, I was struck by my solitude. I had had friends at university, but you get to a certain age when the effort outweighs the benefit, and you don't have time to keep up with them anyway. Alone in my flat with no distractions, I had plenty of time to think, and the various compartments I had pushed to the back of my mind came to the fore.

Margaretta's funeral had been a peculiar affair – a random gathering of individuals insisting how much Margaretta had meant, even though she had never once mentioned any of them. The living have an annoying habit of laying claim to the dead, and if I could have banned all well-wishers from the service, I would have done. Margaretta had always kept herself to herself; it wasn't that she didn't like people or that people didn't like her, she just had no real close friends. I had never stopped to think about it before, but now I realised it had been a deliberate choice. It had often been just the two of us – the family she had chosen after her son was locked away. I had never felt close to her emotionally, but she had been a big part of my life, and London without her felt strange and incomplete.

Margaretta had left her house to me, an act of surprising generosity after a lifetime of frugal gifts. I had meant to go there earlier but I didn't want to miss anything, and I was hoping for a lead. I showered, changed and waited, but there was still no news of the woman with the blood-soaked hands. I made my way to Margaretta's, taking a shortcut down the side streets. London had lost the gloss I remembered growing up, and I thought back to the times I had trotted excitedly behind her as she told me stories about the landmarks we passed. It was the closest I ever felt to her, and the city was charged with memories.

I was assaulted by familiar smells and vivid images the moment I stepped inside her house – the acidity of homemade cleaning products mixed with the faint odour of varnished wood; hours spent at the huge oak table learning my times tables while Margaretta patiently looked on. For someone who had died without warning, Margaretta had been well prepared: everything was neat and tidy as always, and there were only a few loose ends left in a box at the foot of her bed. Rifling through the contents, I wondered why I had put off looking through it until now. It contained very little: a few letters to post, a short list of bills to pay, a ceramic dish to return to the next-door neighbour. I flicked through the letters, unsurprised that each one already bore a stamp. None of the names meant anything to me, but there was one address Margaretta must have known I wouldn't miss. I stared at her black scrawl, transfixed by the information she had so casually allowed me to see. It wasn't a prison I knew well, but there was only one person she could be contacting in a place like that: 'ELI CARSON', the son whose identity she had left me to discover for myself. I typed his name slowly into the search box on my phone, waiting for the internet to tell me what Margaretta had not.

Thirty-one years ago, Detective Eli Carson had shocked polite society when he killed his wife, Elizabeth, and her alleged lover, David Francis. Rising rapidly through the ranks, Eli had spent his career hunting for killers in the shadows of society, which made his fall from grace all the more unexpected. Eli's barrister had argued that his client was suffering from a psychiatric disorder at the time and didn't know what he was doing, but the jury had convicted him of murder – Eli Carson had meant to kill his wife and her lover.

I'd never had high expectations when it came to people; I had learned that from Margaretta. But whereas she talked as a Christian who saw sinners in need of salvation, I spoke as a cynic who saw the world for what it was. We both believed in justice, but she was prepared to leave it up to God, while I relied on the rule of law. Honour, loyalty, integrity, trust – characteristics I had witnessed since I was a child – characteristics she would have been sad not to have passed on to her own child, Eli Carson, the son she had hidden but never forgotten.

The sound of my mobile cut through my thoughts. I rummaged to retrieve it from the bed behind me, crumpling Margaretta's immaculately pressed sheets.

'You better have news, Randle. Now isn't a good time.'

There was a pause, then his voice, deep and clear down the phone.

'We know who she is, ma'am. We have a name.'

Chapter Seven

Leah

I rolled the blue latex over my fingers, slipping a rubber glove over my right hand. A handbag had been found not far from the station, its contents scattered like a trail of breadcrumbs. Bank card, keys, security pass, purse, pencil, now laid out on a table in front of me, a patchwork of clues about the woman covered in blood. There was no phone, but we finally had a name and the beginning of a profile: Fiona Garvey. White. Single. Forty. No previous convictions, records or even parking offences. Nothing to raise alarm bells until the bloody baseball bat.

I held the security pass up to the fluorescent light. The rest of the station was quiet, and a buzz echoed around the small room. The photograph on the pass was slightly blurred. Fiona's face looked fuller, her eyes more animated.

'Rossan Brown Meyer Management Consultants. Corporate secretary. Makes sense from her clothes,' I said.

Randle scanned a message on his phone, squinting as he glanced at the screen.

'Her bank card hasn't been used since morning, ma'am. We can't get much more detail until tomorrow, but she probably used it to get to work. She must have travelled on foot at the end of the day, or she could have taken a taxi and paid cash.'

'Is this hers?'

I lifted what looked like a red canvas yoga bag.

'It was found near the handbag, ma'am. Looks likely but we don't know for sure.'

He handed me a printout with an address.

'She lives in Clapham. Maybe something happened in her flat when she got home?'

'. . . and she walked here, covered in blood?'

Randle dipped his hands into his pockets, shifting his weight to the balls of his feet.

'I don't know, ma'am. But there could be something there.'

If there had been a body in the flat, Fiona had hidden it well. There was no trace of disinfectant, no trail of blood. Her flat was neat and small without feeling cramped. Fiona had obviously mastered the art of storage, and everything seemed to have a place. I opened the cupboards, wondering whether she was the kind of woman who projected an image of tidiness to hide a life of disarray, but everything was in order. Matching crockery and glasses stacked according to size, pots and pans tucked away out of sight. Tidy without being spotless, nothing sinister or out of the ordinary. The only hint of disorder came from an odd assortment of mugs crammed into one corner – mementos collected over a period of years from conferences, shows and unexciting holiday destinations. Fiona Garvey had captured her memories with the most practical of souvenirs. Standing in the kitchen with its hidden pots and pans, I had a slightly clearer sense of the mute woman. I had braced myself for the possibility of finding a body, but the lack of one didn't faze me. There was a version of events where Fiona had walked home after work and been surprised by an intruder whom she had pounded to death, but no disturbances had been reported in the block and people seldom die quietly. There was no sign of an intruder, and I sensed that Fiona hadn't been home since morning, and I was glimpsing a snapshot of her life before it changed forever.

'Not exactly the home of a keen sports fan.'

I hadn't heard Randle come up behind me, and I stiffened at the sound of his voice. He stood in the doorway, head to one side, making the room seem smaller.

'Just doesn't strike me as the home of someone who loves baseball.'

'Grown-ups in pyjamas playing rounders. I've never seen the appeal myself,' I said.

He shook his head as if I were a lost cause, eyes laughing at my response.

'I played a few times with my dad when I went to see him in the States, ma'am. Guess it has a sentimental place in my heart.'

I turned away and pulled open a drawer – plain silver cutlery, arranged according to size, larger utensils in a small tray to the left.

'I'm glad you have fond memories, Randle, but you don't need to be a fan to own a bat. There's a special class of criminal that buys them to hurt people, not to play a game.'

His mouth tilted into a slight smile.

'Am I missing a joke?' The drawer was stiff when I tried to close it, and there was a sharp bang when I slammed it shut.

'No, ma'am.' Randle shrugged. 'Makes sense. I used to play cricket at school. Broke a lot of bats. My dad had a baseball bat from his dad; it was still in pretty good shape when he gave it to me. You think Fiona Garvey bought the bat because she wanted to do harm?'

'We don't have a body and we don't know much about her. Spare yourself the energy making it up.'

I moved into the narrow corridor, my plastic overshoes creaking on the thin carpet. There were no paintings or posters, no clutter to give Fiona away. The doors on either side of me were open; the door at the end firmly shut. It sprang back when I pushed down the handle, and the air felt warm as I stepped inside.

Judging by the tiny room, Fiona Garvey didn't read for fun. There was one bookshelf, empty except for a selection of management consultancy books with uninspiring titles that could barely fit along the spines. Like the kitchen, everything about the shelf looked orderly. The books were arranged alphabetically, pushed to the front so they sat evenly along the ledge. Organised without being obsessive, structured without appearing alarming. If you could tell anything about a person from their décor, Fiona wasn't a woman who liked to live life on the edge. I pictured her at home, swotting up on a profession no one understood. Then I saw her outside the police station, bloody and numb. My eyes roamed the room, resting on a photograph of Fiona smiling with a woman who must have been her mother. She looked happy, relaxed and unremarkable. My thoughts flitted back to the mute woman in the police station once again. *What did you do, Fiona? What did you do?*

Chapter Eight

Alistair Cowan couldn't tell whether he was dead or alive. He had never given much thought to what happens after you die, but he hoped it wasn't this – excruciating pain and a crippling sense of fear. He could scarcely breathe now, and he was scared to try too hard, in case he died with the effort, if he wasn't already dead. The vision in his left eye was obscured by a thin sheen of something he suspected must be blood, and his right eyelid was swollen around his other eye, the added weight pressing heavily on the eyeball. His head exploded with every thought, so he tried desperately not to think, but he had to concentrate to stay alive, assuming he still was. He didn't know what had happened to him, and the agony he felt was so acute, he was no longer sure whether it was better to live or to die.

At first, the distant murmur was so muffled he couldn't tell whether it was the sound of his own thoughts. His ears were clogged with blood from the gash on his head, and he could only see a few feet ahead through his left eye. As the sound grew louder, he could tell someone was approaching, and he could make out several pairs of trainers shuffling towards him. Gradually he heard the voices more clearly, arguing or talking loudly, he couldn't be sure which.

The group had stopped nearby, and he didn't know whether they had seen him. He tried to make a sound, but he found he couldn't, the words circling round his brain. He was about to give up when he sensed one figure break away from the others, coming closer. The flood of relief was overwhelming, and he would have smiled if any of the muscles in his face still worked. He had been found; he had been given another chance, and it was all going to be OK. He could see an outstretched arm, and he braced himself to be hauled up and restored to the realm of the living. The moment never came. Instead, a hand swept down, reaching into his pocket. He heard the gentle rustle of bank notes being extracted, then folded. Then there were more voices and murmurs as the group drifted further away, and Alistair was left alone once again.

He hadn't been sure whether he preferred death to life but, lying in the dirt with the hope of rescue gone, he knew what he wanted without a doubt in his mind: Alistair Cowan wanted to live.

Chapter Nine

Leah

'Alistair Cowan. Forty-four. Fiona covered as his secretary when Alistair's assistant was away.'

Randle placed an iPad on my desk, nudging aside my morning coffee. Alistair Cowan looked back at me from behind the cracked screen: he was a handsome man nearing middle age who made an obvious effort to look young. Boyish hairstyle with surprising flecks of grey, and a tanned, smooth face with barely a wrinkle in sight. He almost passed for a man in his thirties, but his eyes gave him away – serious beneath the glint, betraying years of hard work and uncompromising ambition. His smile hadn't come easily, that much I could tell.

'Good-looking guy.'

I raised an eyebrow at Randle's words, but I couldn't disagree. Alistair was the kind of man you would notice if he walked into a room; you had to give him that.

'He was due back from an out-of-town meeting, but he never made it home. His ex-wife lives in Boston with their two children. He missed a call with his kids. She phoned his office when she couldn't get hold of him, but they hadn't heard from him either. He definitely got on the plane from Scotland, so he's been reported missing.'

'Did you speak to her?'

He nodded. 'Nothing else of note.'

'Fiona covered as his assistant?' I took a hit of my coffee.

'Yes,' Randle said. 'It started as a one-off but then became more regular. She took over when Alistair's PA went on sick leave. Pretty much managed his life. He kept her on even when the old PA came back.'

'You think they were having a relationship.' We hadn't been working together for long, but it was obvious what Randle thought.

'They spent a lot of time together.'

'Doesn't mean she was sleeping with him.'

I had worked closely with Mark, my detective inspector in Leeds, and I had never thought of him in that way.

'It wouldn't be the first time, ma'am.' Randle pushed his point gently. 'Boss hits on secretary, secretary looks up to boss.'

The thought of Mark made me irritable. 'And that doesn't sound remotely sexist or old-fashioned to you?'

'Just because it's sexist doesn't make it untrue. Rumour has it, Alistair Cowan was a bit of a player.'

I drained my cup, setting it down on the dull wooden surface. 'Let's test the rumours and see.'

Rossan Brown Meyer stood proudly in the heart of the city, a characterless mixture of concrete and glass. We were shown round by a partner who looked bored by our questions, her eyelids drooping further with each introduction she made. Everyone had their favourite Alistair sleaze anecdote, but there was more to him than the arch seducer, and he had earned his place at the top of the firm. The youngest person ever to make partner, he had built a reputation as a fierce negotiator and trusted advisor, modelling himself on the fat cats of the eighties who didn't see materialism as a dirty word. His colleagues respected him, even if they didn't like him, and he had billed millions of pounds for the company over the years. Hero or villain, Alistair was seen as a survivor and, although no one actually said it, it was as if everyone expected him to turn up in his own good time. Maybe the stress of work had finally got to him, and Alistair had shipped himself off for some R & R. It was plausible, but I knew it wasn't true. Alistair Cowan was either dead or in danger, but his colleagues didn't need to know that yet.

While everyone had a lot to say about Alistair, they had little to say about Fiona beyond how 'nice', 'sweet' or 'polite' she was. She often worked from home, so her absence wasn't questioned and no one said anything remotely negative, except for Alistair's former assistant, Mayanna Duncan. She sat opposite us in a windowless meeting room, coiling and uncoiling the same strand of hair. She talked in half sentences like a bored teenager. I forced my face to look interested and waited for something useful to come out of her mouth. She was dressed to be noticed, and her outfit bordered on inappropriate without crossing the line. Suggestive but professional, Mayanna's brand of trashy respectability wasn't an easy look to pull off, but somehow, she managed. She stared at Randle through false eyelashes, trying to look demure.

'I have nothing against her personally,' Mayanna said. 'Everyone knows I have more experience, but you know what Alistair's like . . .' She trailed off.

'What is he like?' I asked.

'Charming. You know . . . I never fell for it, but Fiona, you know . . .'

'No. I don't.' I flicked my eyes to my watch.

'Fiona wasn't used to attention. Alistair was . . . he was nice to her, and she liked him. I could tell. She was . . . committed to her job. She'd do anything for him. You know . . .'

'Are you implying Alistair and Fiona's relationship went beyond the professional?'

She looked at me coyly. 'I'm not implying anything, Inspector. I'm just saying she was dedicated. It's easy to get overlooked in this firm if you don't have a champion, and you could say Alistair was Fiona's champion.'

I looked across at Randle, wondering what he made of her. He was sitting forwards in his chair, but his eyes gave nothing away. Mayanna watched us both closely, a slight frown hardening her face.

'I know what you're thinking,' she said. 'You think I'm jealous. You're thinking she took my job and I'm trying to get even.'

'Are you?'

Randle's tone was so unassuming, she answered without hesitating.

'Yes, I was jealous. So what? It doesn't make me a liar. Something was going on between them. You don't have to believe me, but it's still the truth.'

Randle walked beside me as we made our way back to the car. He was almost a foot taller, but we were perfectly in stride.

'They had a thing. It ended badly. She wanted to get back at him. It got out of hand,' he said.

'Based on what?'

'Human nature. Our basic desire for some kind of justice.'

He was so at ease with his looks and his opinion that having to justify himself still came as a surprise. I rolled my eyes involuntarily.

'Did you read that in a book? Firstly, we don't know there was an injustice and secondly, work relationships are never straightforward.'

Randle raised an eyebrow in interest.

'What do we know about Fiona?' I said.

'Didn't stand out in a crowd. Kept herself to herself, rarely went out with her colleagues, behaved at office parties and was always the first in the next day.'

'So, why pick her? She doesn't seem his type.'

I remembered the photograph on Fiona's security pass; I had never used the word plain to describe anyone, but if you had to choose an adjective for Fiona, that would be it. She wasn't unattractive, just unremarkable, with a face which worked hard to be neutral and blend in with the surroundings. Alistair, by contrast, was flash and showy – his suits were made to measure; his shoes were handmade. He kept a hairbrush at the office so his hair remained sleek throughout the day, and the prevailing view was that he collected beautiful people as if they were accessories.

'She's not exactly an obvious candidate for an office romance.'

'Maybe he liked a challenge,' Randle said.

There was something about his tone which made me glance up at him. His eyes were focused on the building opposite, but I was certain he had been looking at me.

We had hit the lunchtime rush, and the city was packed with people, programmed to walk in a straight line. A woman bulldozed her way between us, and I imagined Fiona, anonymous in the throng.

'What about Fiona now?' I asked.

'Still not speaking, ma'am. The magistrate's extended detention.'

'Whom did she talk to last? Anything from her phone?'

'We haven't found her mobile yet, but she's got a contract. We've requested her phone records.'

'The sooner the better.'

The crowd had thinned as we turned the corner; Randle's pace slowed, waiting for me to react.

'What?'

'The general consensus is that Fiona Garvey is the most reliable person you'll ever meet. She's never late, and she never misses an appointment.'

'So?' I didn't mask the impatience in my voice.

'So, I checked her office calendar. Turns out she missed an appointment yesterday . . . with her psychotherapist.'

I stopped, blocking the path of an anxious courier.

'What could Fiona Garvey possibly have to say to a psychotherapist?'

Chapter Ten

Odie

Odie was toying with the idea of whether to call Rebecca Stanton. She had wasted most of the day searching for leads, and the sky looked heavy and oppressive without the sun. She had given up on her internet trawl, clicking through her emails, sipping lukewarm coffee. She hated the taste, but it kept her from smoking, and it seemed like an acceptable vice. There were a couple of emails from her ex-husband which she ignored. Bored, she glanced down at the series of videos playing on a loop in the corner of her screen. She was about to call it a day when an email flashed up.

She didn't recognise the address, but that was often the case. Her contact details were published at the bottom of each article, inviting members of the public to comment or vent. She knew Ross expected her to 'engage', but it just wasn't worth her time. She was about to shut down her computer when another email popped up from the same address, a seemingly random assortment of letters before the @. This time there was a subject line:

'You should read this.'

Short, clear. No exclamation marks, no caps, just a simple suggestion. Odie stopped for a second. It was probably a virus sent by some bored teenager rebelling against 'the system', but there was a fraction of a chance that it could be something worth pursuing, and that fraction made it worth the risk. She opened the email to find just a link. She flicked back to the first email – the same link, no other text. She clicked and sat back, waiting for the file to load.

She couldn't be certain whether the prostrate figure in the clip was dead or alive. The footage from the mobile phone was blurry but, judging by the pool of red liquid by their head, she didn't fancy their chances. It could have been anyone, anywhere, at any time. There was nothing to go on, and she didn't even know if it was real. She was about to forward it to the police when she noticed something. She had briefly lived south of the river when her mother was dying. It was a time she tried to forget, in a part of London she disliked, but she had spent many mornings jogging round Battersea Park to shake off her hangovers, using landmarks to navigate her way around. It was barely visible in the corner of the screen, but she was pretty sure she recognised one of the signs. She froze the image, annoyed she had no clue how to enlarge it. It was a long shot, but if the video was authentic, she knew she didn't have much time before the clip was taken down, or the police got involved. She grabbed her coat and headed for the door.

Chapter Eleven

Leah

'Judging by Fiona's calendar, she's been seeing a psychotherapist called Sonya Waugh for coming up to a year.'

The light was fading, and Randle squinted at the pages in his leather notebook. I knew he preferred to drive, but I had done my time riding shotgun to my superior officer. There was a rhythm to driving which helped me think, but every time I tried to focus on the case, thoughts of Margaretta and her relationship with Eli crowded Fiona Garvey out.

'You OK, ma'am?'

I realised he had been waiting for a response.

'You don't need to worry about me,' I said, not unkindly. 'Just help me find Alistair Cowan before it's too late.'

In the six months we had been working together, he kept trying to get me to open up. I had to admire his tenacity; every attempt to find out more was met with monosyllables or simple evasion, and yet he persisted. I couldn't tell whether he was genuinely curious or uncomfortable with the formality of knowing nothing about me. Apart from the incident with Mark, there wasn't much to know – no dark perversions or hidden addictions, nothing to support the image of the damaged, maverick mentor he hoped I would be. I wasn't sure I believed in the label anyway. There were people who took responsibility for their actions and people who didn't; 'maverick' was just an excuse to do as you pleased without heeding the consequences. Eli Carson had been hailed as a maverick, and he had ended up in jail.

Randle rolled his shoulders, grimacing as he dropped his hand to his knee.

'Are *you* OK?' I asked.

He pulled a thin canvas strap from his jacket pocket, wrapping it tightly around his wrist.

'I came off my bike in a race last weekend. It gets a bit stiff when I forget to wear the support.'

'Brompton?'

He smiled. 'Suzuki. I fix them up and race them, when I get the time.'

He watched as I re-formed my impression of him.

'Pegged you for more of a golf man,' I said.

He laughed, relaxing back into his seat, pushing the lever so his legs extended with less of a bend.

'How often did Fiona see the therapist?'

'Once a week at first.' He rubbed his jaw with the side of his thumb. 'Sometimes more as time went on.'

'Why was she seeing her?'

'We don't know. She did it privately. Akosua spoke to her mother. Even *she* didn't know,' he said.

'D'you tell your mother everything?'

'I'm not a fan of secrets, ma'am. If someone asks, I'll tell.'

I wasn't sure he was being serious, but I saw no hint of a smile. We were moving out of the centre into something resembling suburbia – the houses were uniform, and the air seemed to linger the further out we drove.

'Any history of mental illness? Depression?' I asked.

Randle consulted his pad again, though there was barely anything written on the tiny pages. 'None, as far as we know, and there were no pills in Fiona's flat, other than standard-issue paracetamol and ibuprofen. Nothing strong enough to numb any kind of pain.'

'And you'd know about that, would you?' I asked the question without thinking, surprised when it made him blush. I concentrated on the road, allowing the colour in his cheeks to subside.

'I dated someone who struggled with depression. Sertraline, fluoxetine, citalopram. Every time I went looking for toothpaste, I found a different drug.'

He was trying to make light of it, but I could tell it was difficult for him to talk about.

'I used to think depression was a made-up disease to make privileged people feel less guilty about having things good in life.'

'And then?' I surprised myself by wanting to know the answer.

'I met Sarah.'

'And where's Sarah now?' I asked.

'I don't know.'

For a moment he looked different – more battle-worn, lost in his memories. I wondered why he had suddenly felt the desire to say something personal, and when he spoke again, it made sense.

'I don't think Fiona Garvey was depressed, ma'am.'

'OK . . .'

'It's just . . . I've been with someone who's depressed, and there was nothing Fiona's colleagues said and nothing in her flat to suggest that.'

Sonya Waugh's practice was in a semi-detached house on a quiet residential street deep in North London. We were let in by a timid receptionist who took our names and pointed us up a narrow set of uncarpeted stairs. Sonya's office was behind a huge oak door designed to block out noise. My first knock was met with silence. Randle's fist made more of an impact on the wood and after a while we heard footsteps approaching from the other side, clipped and fast.

'I wasn't expecting you until later. I don't like being disturbed.' Sonya's tone was clear.

'This won't take a moment of your time.' I flashed my smile and my badge, realising that charm alone was never going to work. 'Can we come in?'

There was a moment's hesitation and then Sonya Waugh did what every law-abiding citizen usually did and stepped aside for us to enter.

'I'm Detective Inspector Hutch; this is Detective Sergeant Randle . . .'

'What's this about?' Sonya stopped abruptly, as if surprised by her own rudeness. 'I'm sorry. I've only got . . .'

'. . . twenty-five minutes until your next appointment. Yes, we know.'

I smiled first, and it was only then that Sonya followed suit, raising her hands in mock defeat.

'Of course. You are, after all, detectives.'

'Yes, we are.' Maybe charm wasn't off the table.

'So, what is this about?'

Sonya was sitting down now, her long legs stretched out in front of her. She was elegantly dressed, with a well-tailored jacket over broad shoulders, and flat shoes which kept her under six foot. The office was lined with floor-to-ceiling shelves of books on psychotherapy, except for one shelf dedicated to triathlon trophies. She may have been an amateur athlete, but she was clearly a disciplined one.

'What can I say? I like sport.' She said it with an imperceptible shrug that was almost apologetic. My brief recce of the office had been subtle, but Sonya's eyes hadn't left me since we entered the room.

'So, what's this about?' Sonya repeated her question.

I took the seat diagonally opposite, leaving Randle to sit facing Sonya. It was a conscious decision, designed to appear unthreatening. Being a therapist, Sonya probably knew all my tricks, but it was still worth a try.

'You have a patient by the name of Fiona Garvey,' I said.

'I have a lot of patients. Both you and I know I'm not at liberty to tell you much about any of them.'

'You want to help your patients,' I continued, undeterred.

'Is that a statement or a question?'

'I hope it's a statement.'

'Thank you. Your confidence in my integrity is . . . flattering, but I still can't change my position.'

I stood up, moving slowly around the room to shift the dynamic.

'Fiona Garvey needs your help.'

It was a cheap ploy, but Sonya looked up sharply.

'Why? What's happened to her?'

'I'm not at liberty to say.'

I half expected her to shut down the conversation and usher us out, but she leant forwards in her chair, giving me her full attention. When she spoke, her voice was softer and less formal.

'I don't know if I can help if you don't tell me anything.' She took a breath before asking her next question, as though she dreaded what I might say. 'Is she OK?'

'No.' I saw no reason not to be honest. 'We think she might be a danger to herself and to others.'

'Why?' Sonya asked the question as if the thought had never crossed her mind.

'That's all we can tell you just now.'

'Look, Inspector, I'm not trying to be difficult, but my patients have to come first. You know how this works.'

'Yes, and I also know that someone's at risk and anything you can tell me about Fiona Garvey could make a difference.'

'I don't know what you want me to say,' Sonya said. 'I've worked with people who are at risk and people who are said to pose a risk – seemingly dangerous predators convicted of horrific crimes. Are you trying to tell me Fiona is one of them?'

'I'm trying to tell you that I don't know but I need to find out.'

She held my gaze for the briefest of moments, but I couldn't decipher the expression in her eyes. Finally, she spoke, and her words were chosen carefully.

'I haven't seen her for a couple of weeks, but I've been treating her for almost a year, and there's nothing in her behaviour which makes me believe that she's a risk to herself or anyone else.'

'Why did she need to see you?'

'You'd have to ask her that.'

Chapter Twelve

Odie

It had been a while since Odie had done any exercise. In the brief periods when she had got into the habit of running, she had hated every second. The sound of her own breathing unsettled her, and dragging her body around the great outdoors to the thump of her rapidly pounding heart was both humiliating and unnerving. She ran to shake off the fug of alcohol. There was something about the cold air which alleviated the pain in her head and made the world bearable again. She ran because she had to, and when her knee gave way, she stopped and took painkillers instead.

Driven by necessity, Odie's visits to the park had been irregular. She didn't know the place well and, replaying the image from the internet in her mind, she began to doubt what she had seen. The closer she got to the park, the less familiar it felt, and she began to question her ability to recognise what it looked like from the inside. It was easy to miss the pedestrian gate in the dark. Winter was threatening to take over from autumn, and she struggled with the shorter days. She parked on a side street nearby and, as she made her way along the path, she felt completely isolated but strangely at ease. She hadn't told anyone where she was going. The sensible side of her knew that was unwise, but the investigative journalist in her preferred to keep it that way until she knew more. If anything happened, she just hoped she could remember how to run.

The park was bigger than she remembered. She had always thought of it as an open expanse which helped to calm the chaos in her mind. Now, free from the influence of alcohol, she saw it for what it really was: a patchwork of shrubbery and grass with a haphazard beauty of its own. It was entirely unfamiliar in the darkness. The faint glow from the gas lamps hit the ground in little puddles, and she couldn't see much ahead. She was about to turn back when she remembered the signs. Every time she had jogged round the park, she had no idea how she would find her way out, but she had followed the signposts until she emerged with a clearer head. Now, at a loss once again, she followed the signs and tentatively moved forwards.

As she made her way further into the undergrowth, she felt like everything was closing in on her. Not an anxious person by nature, she had tried to ignore the fact that she had been on edge for months. It was only now, as she got closer to her destination, that she realised she was depending on someone else's pain to make her feel better. There was something perverse about wanting to find another human being dead to improve her day. She wondered whether she should feel bad about it, but she told herself she was searching for a story not a person, and that somehow made it OK.

She felt faintly nostalgic when she saw it – the dark green sign faded to an odd shade of yellow, consonants blacked out like an incomplete crossword. It had marked halfway when she used to go running, and she recognised it in the image she had been sent. She took a moment to find her bearings, reorientating herself so her perspective was similar to the one on her computer. The figure had been lying in the bottom right-hand corner, partially obscured by the thicket bordering the area. She made her way towards it, fearing there would be nobody there.

She saw the feet first, polished leather shoes streaked with mud and dirt. Her eyes travelled slowly up the body, appalled by the bloody mess in front of her: the face battered beyond recognition, destroyed by another person's rage, the body coiled and swollen, skin split open by a brutal force. For a moment, she wondered about the mother, wife, children and friends who would never see this man alive again, whose lives would be forever changed once they knew what had happened. Then she forgot about them and took her first photograph.

She was conscious she had to report the crime, but she needed to make sure she was one step ahead. This was a story she couldn't lose, and when the police came crashing in, there would be no room for a middle-aged journalist with an attitude problem and a point to prove. Her fingers worked fast, capturing each detail with a series of clicks.

Chapter Thirteen

Leah

My mobile rang as I made my way back to the car.

'Hutch?' It was Frank, the duty sergeant. 'Call came through for you. Said it was urgent.'

'Thanks, Frank. Put them through.' It was probably a complete waste of time, but you only had to ignore one genuine cry for help to lead to a lifetime of guilt and regret.

The voice at the other end of the line was high and childlike, the speech artificial.

'To whom am I speaking?'

The precise grammar sounded awkward in such a young voice.

'Detective Inspector Hutch. You asked for me.'

'Yes. That's right. I want to report a crime.'

Chapter Fourteen

Odie

Odie listened intently as the boy described the location of the body. She had rehearsed him well. His delivery was a bit stilted, but he served his purpose. She handed over a twenty-pound note and watched him hold it up to the light. She could have been insulted, but she would have done the same if a complete stranger paid her to pretend she had found a dead body. She could have called the police herself but then she would be a key witness. This way, she was just the irritating journalist who arrived at the scene early. Calling Leah Hutch made it all the more satisfying.

By the time Leah got there, Odie had been in the park for close to forty minutes. From the moment Leah saw her shock of white-blonde hair, she knew they had no chance of controlling the press – the story was already out there; Odie Reid would make sure of that.

Chapter Fifteen

Leah

'You took your time, Hutch.'

Ever since I'd been a junior reporter working under her, Odie had spent too much time trying to get under my skin. It felt like wasted energy, but sometimes she succeeded, and I suppose that made it worth it in her mind. She felt I thought I was too good for journalism, and she hated the fact I had left before it was too late, while she was stuck in a world where all the rules had changed.

It was impossible to miss her trademark hair, but I ignored her, moving towards the body lying in the thicket. Tall trees blocked out the moonlight, and I steeled myself for what lay ahead. Randle followed closely, intrigued by the tension between me and Odie. I could tell he wanted to know more, but it was easy enough to find out our history, and I wasn't going to be the one to fill him in. I turned to him, shooting off instructions.

'Get the area sealed off and make sure forensics are on their way.'

He hovered for a moment before moving off; front-row tickets to the Reid/Hutch show would have to wait.

I had seen the baseball bat and the blood on Fiona's clothes, so I knew the attack had been brutal, but I wasn't expecting the body to be so distorted or the face so disfigured. Someone had meant to kill this man and the murder had been savage and merciless. His face was a blur of flesh and blood, framed by filthy, matted hair, and his features were indistinguishable except for his eyes, which were fixed in an expression of horror and amazement. This hadn't been an easy death, and whatever he had seen just before he died had scared and surprised him in equal measure. His head had been smashed repeatedly, and it was almost impossible to recognise the groomed image of Alistair Cowan we had seen so many times. I closed my eyes and tried to rearrange his blunted features into some semblance of a face. Opening them again, there was something almost artistic about the way he had been reconfigured, and I couldn't look away. I had almost forgotten Odie was there until her flash went off.

'This is a crime scene, Odie. You know that.'

'Wasn't when I got here. Just a couple of police constables trying not to throw up.'

'Let's not play games.'

'I wouldn't know how.'

She lowered the camera slowly to give me the full benefit of her smirk. We had been together for barely five minutes, and we were already back in the playground.

'How did you know the body was here?'

A pointless question, but I had to ask.

'How did I know?' Her eyes were almost mocking as she waved a hand at the green expanse behind her. 'I've always been a fan of nature, Hutch. I was taking a walk, saw the ambulance pulling up . . . saw the police. Stuck around.'

The camera was back in front of her face, muffling her words as she spoke. The flash beamed in the dark, highlighting the blood against the grass. I was already tired of the exchange, but Odie was clearly just warming up. She took another picture; one more, and I would have no qualms smashing her camera. Luckily for Odie, I didn't have the patience for the paperwork, and she was an unnecessary distraction.

'Put that away, or I can always arrest you,' I said.

'You could, but where's the fun in that? Besides,' Odie slipped her camera into its case, 'I've finished now.'

There was no point arguing; the less I had to do with Odie the better. She was the poster girl for the life I could have had, back when Odie Reid's name meant something in the world of journalism, and I was the protégée she had graciously taken under her wing. The life of a journalist would have been easier than dancing around dead bodies looking for answers that didn't exist, but there was nothing appealing about the life of a journalistic has-been, and that was what Odie had become. Desperation had never sat well with me and, looking at the woman in front of me, I knew I had made the right choice when I walked away from her job. I had seen that look in Odie's eyes before – the hunger for the story, the all-consuming desire to get there first at all costs. The stench of desperation was nauseating, and I felt an almost irrational dislike for her rise up inside me and then quickly fade. I didn't have the time to waste thinking about Odie; I just needed to get rid of her before she became a problem.

'I don't want his name in the news tomorrow, Odie,' I called as she walked away.

'You'd have to give me a name for that to happen.'

'I'm serious,' I said. 'We'll release the name when it's the right time. Have some respect for the victim's family.'

The dig at Odie's integrity was designed to sting. It worked, as I knew it would.

'I've been doing this for over thirty years. I know how to treat a victim's family.'

'Would be a shame if you suddenly forgot.'

The threat wasn't lost on her, but she shook it off. Our encounters always went the same way – she tried to get the better of me, I tried not to let her. I'd love to say I wasn't keeping score.

'Dare I ask if you've got any suspects?' She knew the answer before she asked the question but that was part of the fun for her.

'No. You can't.'

'You know I'll find out.'

'I'm sure you will, but right now, this is my crime scene, and I don't want you on it.'

Odie smiled. She enjoyed our confrontations, predictable though they were.

'A pleasure as always, Hutch.' And she was gone.

Randle was grinning as he approached, collar up to repel the cold.

'Wasn't sure if I'd find one body or two, ma'am.'

'Funny.' So, he did have a sense of humour. 'Any news on forensics?' I said.

'They're on their way.' His eyes wandered down to the body. He drew a sharp intake of breath. 'Wow . . . Fiona Garvey did that . . .'

'We don't know *what* she did yet.'

We didn't, but things weren't looking good for her. Chances were this was the missing Alistair Cowan, and by the time Odie had spun the story, the public would be baying for Fiona's blood.

Chapter Sixteen

Odie

Driving away from the crime scene, Odie felt a sudden rush of anticipation she hadn't experienced in a long time. She wondered who had sent the link. Someone involved in the crime or an innocent bystander carrying out their civic duty? But why didn't they go straight to the police? Did they know she would be able to recognise the park, or had they left it to chance? Was she the only journalist who had been sent the tip-off? Was she the only one to pass the test? She might never know, but it didn't matter for now. What mattered was that she had the beginnings of a story. If she followed the trail, she might end up with something worthwhile, which would be all the more satisfying if it came at Hutch's expense. She pushed down on the accelerator, exhilarated by the hum of the engine as the car struggled to shift into a higher gear. She was surprised it had lasted this long, but there was something strangely comforting about the battered BMW refusing to go down without a fight. It wasn't over. Nothing was over yet.

She focused on the road ahead, but the image she kept seeing was the body in the park, bloodied and lifeless. She replayed her conversation with Hutch – another round of sparring to add to the list of pointless encounters they had had since Hutch had left the paper, damaging Odie's reputation on her way out. She had accused Odie of fabricating sources, without listening to her side of the story. Odie had been protecting the vulnerable, and lives had been at stake. The time would come to pay Hutch back for what she had done, but it was too early to know whether this was the case that would settle the score. Sometimes talking to Hutch was like warming up for a race she knew she was never going to run. It would be a modern miracle if she identified the victim before the police did. His face was a swollen mass of distorted features and, even if it had been vaguely recognisable, there were probably a couple of million men in the city who fitted the profile. And yet, as always, Hutch went through the motions of warning her off. It would have been tedious, if it weren't one of the few things which kept Odie sharp. When it came down to it, it didn't matter if the police identified the body first; what captured Odie's imagination was the story behind the crime, the story of the killer who could bludgeon another human being's face beyond recognition, who had carried out an attack which went beyond simple murder. That was what piqued the interest of the public. She already had the images; she just needed the right words, and she was confident she could find them. Once a suspect was charged, the media would effectively be gagged. She was at the mercy of Hutch's investigation, and the more she thought about it, the more her need to discover the truth intensified. She was nothing without her job, and the dead body in the park offered the best lifeline she had been thrown for a long time.

Odie always knew where to find him; she was just never sure when he would be there. He had been sitting at the same table for the past fifteen years, strategically chosen so that he was far enough away so the barman couldn't see him drift into drunken oblivion, yet close enough to ensure he didn't lose precious drinking time stumbling back and forth for a refill. She was disappointed to find his table empty. She hovered by the door in case he had sloped off to the bathroom, but when he didn't materialise after a few minutes, she knew he wasn't there. Odie toyed with the idea of getting a drink herself. She sensed it would make her day feel better, but she wasn't in the mood for limits, and she knew she would ignore the internal voice telling her when to stop. The last thing she needed was for things to get out of control and news to get back to Ross. She tucked herself in a discreet corner with a glass of Coke and waited, swirling the liquid around in her mouth so the sugar gnawed away at her teeth.

It was a while before Steve Baber showed up, slinking his way towards the bar, head down, shoulders hunched. Everything about him exuded thirst but not a thirst which could be quenched; Baber was more like a dying plant which, try as you might to revive it, always looked on the cusp of death. He was on autopilot as he paid for his drink and he watched the whiskey fall into the glass, silently willing the barman to pour in that little bit more. His eyes were dead until he'd had the first sip and even then, the spark of life was soon lost in a haze of nothingness.

'Stevie!' Odie slid into the seat next to him, pinning him between her body and the wall. Ten years ago, she might have resorted to mild flirtation, but now she couldn't be bothered to brush her hair, let alone seduce the pathetic excuse of a man beside her. She sat back in her seat, making it clear she was in no hurry. Baber downed his drink, making no attempt to look at her.

'I was just leaving.'

'You only just got here.' She pushed a fresh whiskey towards him. 'One drink, Baber. Don't be a disappointment all your life.'

'Let's not do this, Odie. We both know I'm very little use to you.' He looked as tired as Odie felt, but she didn't care.

'I'll be the judge of that.' She pushed the glass closer towards him. 'My treat.'

He finally looked at her, barely concealing his disdain. 'Cheap.'

'They were out of champagne.'

'Don't know who's more desperate, you or me.' If she didn't know him better, she would have thought he was smiling.

Practically the same age, their careers had followed a similar trajectory, but Odie had earned her success because she was good, whereas Baber was simply privileged. He was a certain kind of man from a certain kind of background, and the younger, hungrier Baber had taken advantage of that to progress. It worked for a while, but mediocrity had eventually caught up with him. Insecurity led to mistakes, mistakes led to self-pity, self-pity led to drink. Baber had become a shadow of a policeman, waiting for his pension. There was a time when they used to drink together, but Odie grew to resent the desperate way he knocked back each shot because she sensed the same desperation in herself, and she loathed Steve Baber for acting as a reminder of how far she had fallen. She may not have been as pitiful as him, but they occupied the same pit.

'Make it quick, Odie. I prefer to drink alone.'

'So do I, but I need to know about the body in Battersea Park.'

'Nobody tells me anything. You of all people should know that.'

'Names. Suspects. Don't waste my time making me ask questions.'

He finished his drink, opening his throat with practised efficiency. 'Hutch's case. I barely know a thing.'

'So, tell me the little you *do* know, and I'll leave you in peace.'

Baber suddenly looked very tired, and there was emotion in his face Odie hadn't seen for years. Sometimes it was easy to forget that Baber was a living, breathing human being with feelings.

'Buy me another drink first.' It wasn't an order, more of a plea, as if he were mustering up the courage to tell her something. Odie got up without questioning and made her way to the bar. She placed the whiskey in front of him, almost kindly. Baber acknowledged the gesture with a nod, and Odie watched patiently as he poured the liquid down his throat, oblivious to the burn. He didn't say anything for a while, but she knew better than to interrupt his thoughts. His mind was far away when he finally spoke, and she sensed he was picturing the image he was describing, wishing he could forget.

'I can't stop thinking about her hands.'

'Whose hands, Steve?'

'*Her* hands,' he repeated numbly.

'Tell me whose hands.' Odie's voice was almost gentle now.

'She just walked into the station and her hands . . .' He stopped, staring at his empty glass.

'Do you want another?'

She wasn't sure he had heard her.

'Tell me about the hands, Steve.'

He looked at her blankly, haunted by the memory.

'They were soaked so deep; it was like her skin was red. It didn't even look like blood.'

'Did you get her name?'

He shook his head. 'All I can see is her face and her hands.'

'What *about* her face?'

He was silent for a while, staring into the space ahead. Odie was ready to give up but, just when she decided to leave, he spoke again.

'It was the face of a victim.' Baber finally turned to look at her, his eyes begging for answers. 'They didn't match, Odie. The face . . . the face didn't match the hands.'

Chapter Seventeen

Odie

Getting information out of Baber had been slow and painful, but Odie had lined drinks down the table so every memory was rewarded with the sting of alcohol. Baber wasn't the best of sources, but he was all Odie had. Or almost all she had. He didn't know who the woman was, but a few calls to old acquaintances and Odie soon had a name – Fiona Garvey – not that it meant much, yet.

Hutch was obviously playing the case close to her chest, and police station gossip was patchy and inconclusive. The internet did little to fill in the gaps. In an age when privacy was something you had to fight for, there was precious little about Fiona online. The only people she followed were environmentalists and life coaches, and there was no evidence of a social life. Odie searched for Fiona's name in connection with the murder, but found nothing about the body in the park. She was buoyed by the dearth of coverage – the story was there for the taking.

She had no concrete facts linking Fiona to the crime, but it wasn't her job to connect the dots. That was the beauty of the English language, it could be so evocative without saying much at all. All she had to do was present the facts she knew and leave the readers to draw their own conclusions: *Woman turns herself in to police station covered in blood; hours later, battered corpse found in nearby park. Who is Fiona Garvey and what did she do?* Odie opened a blank document and started to type. The words came easily for the first time in months. Odie finally had her story.

Chapter Eighteen

Leah

'No one deserves to die like that.' The tiredness had caught up with him, and Randle looked older and wearier as he stared at images of the body.

'No,' I said.

I had seen worse, but there was something particularly chilling about the crime when I thought about our one and only suspect.

'Do you think she did it?' he said.

The sky was an inky black, and the office felt brighter when he tugged down the blind. It hovered above the base of the window, and I could see the gleam from the glass.

'DNA results will be back soon.' I suppressed a yawn. 'Let's try not to guess if we don't have to. Any sign of the informant?'

'Not a thing. What else do you need me to do, ma'am?'

'It's been a long day. Go home. Get some sleep. Come back fresh. Nothing's going to happen until the results come in.'

'I'm fine to stay.' There was something defiant in his tone. 'I'll just be awake thinking about all this, ma'am.'

'I can't help you there,' I said, and I couldn't. Randle would have to find his own way to shut out the images of death; no one could teach him how. I gave him something close to a smile. 'Go home, Randle. You're more use to me fresh.'

He didn't try to fight me, but I could tell he wasn't happy. Most detectives would have welcomed the chance to rest, and I couldn't work out whether his insistence on staying was out of genuine commitment, the desire to prove something, or both. I had given up on trying to prove myself a long time ago. There would always be those who thought my success in the force was nothing more than an exercise in box-ticking. Maybe it was, but I hadn't become a police officer to be considered a success, so it didn't matter either way. People were killed, and I tried to catch the killer. It was a purpose worth having and not everyone had that privilege. But what of Fiona Garvey? Turning herself in with a baseball bat stained with another person's blood. Hearsay and deduction got us to a place where she had had an affair which had led to a man's tragic death, but these weren't facts, and Fiona had said nothing to help or hinder her case. She was as much use to us as the silent, unidentified corpse which now lay on a slab.

DC Akosua Owusu was full of nervous energy as she approached. She was small and compact, her smooth oiled complexion covered by a sheen of sweat.

'What is it?'

I could hear her panting as she drew closer.

'I've been going through Fiona's emails, like you asked, ma'am.' She handed me a file.

'Anything interesting?'

'Nothing apart from the usual work admin between her and Alistair . . . but . . .'

The inevitable 'but'.

'But what, Akosua?'

'Fiona Garvey is pretty efficient. Files all her emails, always replies the same day. To every single one . . .'

'Except?'

Akosua's face darkened as the blood rushed to her cheeks. She recovered, speaking with confidence I didn't see in her eyes.

'Except for one email from Alistair which went unanswered.'

'What did it say?' I asked.

'*Are you OK?*' Akosua pronounced each word carefully.

'Maybe she replied in person?' Randle said. He was fiddling with the zip of his jacket, taking his time to leave.

'What were their exchanges generally like?' I said. 'Did he ask about her welfare? Her weekend? Were they on friendly terms?'

'Not particularly. Their emails are purely functional. Exchanges of information. Sometimes a thanks for a job well done.'

'It doesn't necessarily mean anything, but maybe something *did* happen between them, and Fiona wasn't OK.'

Scanning the pages in the file, I thought back to something Sonya Waugh had said.

I haven't seen her for a couple of weeks, but I've been treating her for almost a year, and there's nothing in her behaviour which makes me believe that she's a risk to herself or anyone else.

I had thought nothing of it at the time but now it seemed important. Sonya hadn't seen Fiona for two weeks; the email had been written ten days ago, a few days after that final appointment. Maybe Fiona wasn't a risk when Sonya had seen her, but something had changed after that. Something could have happened between Fiona and Alistair and, if Fiona had killed him, that something could be the reason why.

No one deserves to die like that. Randle's words came back to me as I sat down at my desk. I thought of Margaretta's son and the couple he had killed in cold blood. Their deaths had been painful and gruesome and, even though his victims meant nothing to me, I felt a sudden flash of anger.

No one deserves to die like that.

Randle was right. It was time for Fiona Garvey to speak.

Fiona's face was blank, and her eyes had lost their wildness. Bored of the endless questions which had received no answers, I let the images speak for themselves. Very slowly, I placed the photographs in front of Fiona, flipping them over like cards on a poker table. I paused after each one so she could grasp the full horror of what had been done to the man in the park. Her face remained impassive, and I couldn't be certain she was focusing on what was in front of her, even though she was looking down. Exasperated by my inability to get through to her, I had started putting them away when I finally got a reaction. Fiona Garvey opened her mouth and screamed.

Chapter Nineteen

Leah

The sound of Fiona screaming was still ringing in my ears when I woke up the next morning. For the first time, I had seen something in her other than fear. I had seen someone reminded of scenes they wanted to forget and, in that moment, Fiona Garvey had gone from mute woman inexplicably covered in another human being's blood, to viable suspect running from an atrocity she may have committed herself. I lay still, turning over everything in my mind – Fiona, the body, Eli, Margaretta. It had been almost two weeks since Margaretta's funeral, and I still hadn't cried. It's hard to grieve for someone who never said they loved you, but Margaretta had cared for me in her own way, and I felt an enormous sense of gratitude to her for taking me in. I rolled over and reached under my pillow for my mobile. An email from Margaretta's lawyer stating that he couldn't get through by phone; he had a packed schedule but could see me before he started his day. I showered and dressed in ten minutes, gulping down yesterday's coffee. He didn't say it explicitly, but I knew he wouldn't contact me again.

Selwyn Peterson was cut from the same cloth as old-school academics and headmasters. He kept me waiting for twelve minutes before I was shown in. Tall, he hid his heft beneath a well-cut suit, giving the illusion of being slim. He was the kind of man who was born to be a certain age, wearing his superiority effortlessly. We never had any reason to meet before Margaretta died, but I had been aware of his existence and, the moment I stood in his oak-panelled office, I understood I was dealing with a man who had known her for years. It was something in the way he looked at me, as if I were the one who needed to be introduced.

'I'm glad you were able to come in,' he began without apology. His grip was practised and firm, applying just the right amount of pressure. 'In the event of her death, Margaretta asked me to contact you.' He paused for some sort of response; I waited to hear what he had to say.

'You're aware Margaretta had a son?'

'Yes. She was Eli Carson's mother. I already know.'

A short intake of breath, a shuffle of paper, then two words: 'I see.'

He didn't ask how I knew or when I had found out.

'I see,' he said again.

'Why didn't she tell me? I wouldn't have cared.'

He regarded me for a moment, then pulled an envelope from his desk drawer and slid it towards me. 'Open it.' It was more of an order than an invitation.

Inside was an old photograph, the colour faded, the edges curled and frayed. The image was blurred, but I could make out a much younger Margaretta squinting into the sunlight, smiling in a way I had never seen before. She looked more relaxed and at ease than I ever remembered. Next to her stood a man I recognised from the internet to be Eli, handsome in an unchallenging way, with pale ivory skin and intelligent, searching blue eyes. In front of them was a beautiful woman with a clear mahogany complexion, sitting on a chair with a baby in her arms, Eli's hand resting on her shoulder. I held the photograph up to the light to get a better look. The image was small and difficult to make out at first but, as I tilted the picture towards the lamp, I was in no doubt that the face of the infant staring back at me was a younger version of my own. I turned the photograph over, and there, in Margaretta's distinctive handwriting, was the date of my second birthday. I left the room and threw up.

'I don't understand.'

Minutes later, I was sitting opposite Selwyn again, suppressing my quiet fury. My memories were incomplete, and there was nothing to connect my life as I knew it to that of the child in the photograph.

'I think you do.' There was neither sympathy nor cruelty in Selwyn's voice; this was just another obligation.

'Why am I in this picture?'

'I think that's fairly obvious.'

'But why show me this now?'

He almost shrugged, but I sensed he would have found the gesture crass. He resorted to cliché instead. 'I'm just the messenger.'

'Then please, Mr Peterson . . . explain the message.' I tried to keep the aggression out of my voice.

His eyes softened, but his manner was still brusque. 'Miss Hutch, I appreciate you've experienced a big shock, but it's not my job to take you for a trip down memory lane.'

'I'm not asking you to.'

'Very well.' He took a file out of a drawer and placed it in front of me. 'Margaretta left this for you.'

'What is it?'

'Personal documents. Notes. Information from the lawyer she hired to defend her son. It's all in there.'

There was something unsettling about seeing another person's name on a piece of paper and knowing it was referring to me: thirty-six years before, Rachel Sarah Carson had been born to Elizabeth and Eli Carson. After the murder of Elizabeth Carson and her alleged lover, David Francis, full custody had been granted to Eli's mother, Margaretta Carson, née Johnson. Margaretta had moved south, changed my name to Leah, and reverted to her maiden name. And so began life as I knew it.

'My name's Rachel?'

'Leah, Rachel. Sisters – the Bible. She wanted there to be some link.'

'Where did my surname come from?' It seemed easier to start with the small things.

'Nickname of an old teammate from Margaretta's sporting days.'

'You must have known her well to know that.'

'Don't test me, Leah. Neither of us have the time for that.'

'OK.' I flicked through the pieces of paper, resisting my instinct to attack. 'It says here that my mother's body was never found. Why?'

'Because it wasn't.'

'What happened to her?'

'You'll have to ask Eli that.'

'You want me to ask the man who killed my mother to tell me something he hasn't told anyone for over thirty years?' I stared at him, incredulous.

Selwyn sat back in his chair, slowly removing his glasses. It was a practised move, designed to intimidate.

'He didn't tell anyone then; he hasn't told anyone since. If you want to know more, Miss Hutch, I suggest you lose your patience with someone who can actually provide you with answers.'

I got up before I said anything I regretted.

'Thank you for your time.'

Selwyn watched me gather my things before he spoke again. He wasn't smiling, but his voice had lost its earlier sharpness.

'Read the file, Leah.'

It was all he said. Then, as if I wasn't there, he put his glasses back on, making clear the meeting was over.

Chapter Twenty

Leah

I was acutely aware of the file in my bag as I slipped onto the crowded tube. It was morning rush hour – the one time I wished I were tall – and I was trapped between strangers who had turned the avoidance of eye contact into an art form. I crossed one arm in front of me to claim a slither of space. Wedged between three people and a metal pole, I could barely turn my head without brushing lips with the man next to me. I hated it when people read over my shoulder, but I found myself staring at Odie's article on his iPad. There was an image of the body in the park and above it the words: 'What kind of a monster does this?' followed by the account of the bloodied Fiona Garvey turning herself in. I didn't have time to read much but it was enough to know the damage had been done. I got off at the next stop.

I hadn't spoken to Ross Calhoun in a long time. We had worked together briefly early on in his career, long before he became Odie's boss. There had been a moment when something could have happened between us, but I had left; Ross got married, and we hadn't stayed in touch socially. Our paths had crossed professionally a number of times, mostly concerning Odie, and the moment he had agreed to go ahead with Odie's article, he must have been expecting my call.

'What the hell are you playing at, Ross?'

'I'm fine, thank you. How are you?' Cool as always. I had once found it attractive; now it was irritating.

'You're jeopardising a police enquiry.'

'And you're overreacting. A body was found. A woman walked into your police station covered in blood. It was our duty to report on it.'

'You printed her name.'

'It was in the public domain.'

I had never heard Ross apologise in all the time I had known him; I knew he had no intention of saying sorry now.

'You virtually accused her of killing that man,' I said.

'Did we?' he asked innocently. 'Last time I checked, we published a story about two separate incidents which occurred within twenty-four hours of each other. Are you confirming the two are related?'

'I'm not having this conversation.'

'Hutch. Please . . .'

'No. Put your dog on a leash, Ross. She does any damage, it's on you.' I hung up.

Randle was already at work when I entered the building. His bloodshot eyes had the slightly dissipated look of someone who had been out partying the night before, but there was a distinct sharpness to them, and I could tell he had been at his desk for at least a couple of hours. I headed towards the kitchen, ignoring what I assumed was a greeting. I thought about calling Odie but there was no point. The case had already become a story, and the more fuss I made, the more pleasure Odie would have spinning it out. The DNA results were due in any moment, and I needed to see the report. Almost on cue, Randle poked his head round the door, waving a folder. There was a click as the kettle came to a boil. I reached for it, watching a teabag shrink under the weight of hot water.

'You look like you haven't slept,' I said.

'I went out with some friends, ma'am. Needed to get the image of the body out of my mind.'

'Do you need to talk to someone?'

Anyone but me.

'No, ma'am. Nothing I can't handle.' He kept his tone light. 'This just came in.'

He was halfway across the room with a single stride.

'And?'

He held out the folder. 'It's not Alistair's blood.'

'So, she didn't do it?'

'No. I don't know, ma'am. The body in the park isn't Alistair Cowan. They checked the DNA against a sample from his hairbrush. It isn't his blood, and Fiona Garvey's DNA wasn't present at the scene.'

'What about the blood on her body and the bat?' I could sense Randle's thoughts were racing; I needed him to focus on the facts.

'There was a match. The blood on Fiona is Alistair Cowan's.'

'So, Alistair Cowan is still out there, dead or alive.'

'Yes, ma'am, but who's the guy on the slab?'

'I have absolutely no idea.'

Chapter Twenty-One

Leah

The last thing Kenny O'Sullivan wanted was a slew of dead bodies panicking the public. It scared people unnecessarily, and it reflected badly on him. It was the cliché many police officers feared: serve your time without issue, then get stung for something on your way out. Kenny was determined to go out on a high and somewhere along the line, he had started to care more about perception than policing. 'Policing *is* perception,' he would say. 'If the public don't feel safe, then we might as well not be here.' Where some people saw facts, Kenny saw headlines – headlines generated by the police to help a case and headlines created by the press to drag down the force to which he had dedicated his life. One white man pummelled to death; another, at worst, murdered – at best, seriously at risk. My investigation had become Kenny's PR nightmare, and I found myself in the spotlight, the last place I wanted to be.

I had worked under Kenny before I went to Leeds, and I expected a lecture the moment the DNA results arrived.

'You need to change the headline, Leah.'

He was a big man with an annoying habit of taking over my space when we spoke. He stood, legs akimbo, deliberately filling the narrow doorway of my office. His button nose was hidden in a disproportionately large face, and he had a habit of sucking in his nostrils when he was angry or frustrated.

'We're trying, sir.' My shoulders tensed as I looked up from behind my desk.

'You're trying, are you?' He chuckled softly, but there was no trace of humour in the sound. He took a step towards me, his voice a low rumble so his words stayed in the room. 'Did I just *try* when you told me you wanted – sorry, *needed* – to transfer back? Did I just *try*, or did I actually *do* something?'

'I'm grateful for everything you've done, sir.'

Grateful and resentful – I hated having to turn to him to get away from Mark.

'I'm not asking you to thank me, Leah. I'm just asking you to answer the question.'

'You actually did something.' I forced the words out.

'I did,' he said. 'And all I ask in return is that you do the same.'

'Yes, sir.'

He squeezed the tip of his nose, moulding the flesh into a small point.

'Look, Leah, I don't know what happened in Leeds and I don't need to know. Just don't make me regret helping you.'

And there it was, I owed him. I had to get out of Leeds with my career intact, and Kenny was the only person who could make it happen. He suspected it was because of a relationship gone wrong, an ill-advised affair with a superior officer which had blown up in my face. Humiliating as that was, I let him believe it because it was better than the truth. I didn't tell him about Mark's unwanted advances, because Kenny would have asked why I hadn't made a formal complaint, and I would have had to confront my shame.

'Any news on the identity of the body?' Kenny's eyes bored through me.

'Owusu and Randle are looking into it, sir,' I said. 'I think we're finally getting somewhere with Fiona Garvey.'

'Am I missing something?'

He jutted his neck forwards so his breath warmed my face.

'I'm not sure I know what you mean?'

'I watched the interview, Leah. You're getting nowhere.'

'We finally got a reaction, sir,' I insisted.

'You put her in distress, and she's still not talking to you. She has an exemplary personal record, no criminal record, and we have no idea what she's done, if anything. She could have *found* that bat; Alistair Cowan could be alive.'

'She was covered in blood,' I said.

'Do you have enough to charge her?'

I shook my head. The simple answer was *not yet*.

'Exactly.' He took a step back. The room felt brighter and less oppressive; I realised he had been blocking the light. 'You're getting nowhere, Leah, and if you can't see that, God help us all. I want Fiona Garvey released. When you find Alistair Cowan's body, you can bring her back in. Let's not run down the clock if we don't have to . . . What?'

'I didn't say anything.'

His nostrils flared in amusement. 'You haven't changed, Leah. You think you have to talk to speak?'

We stared at each other, locked in a silent battle he had already won.

'I'll ask you again: do you think you have enough to charge Fiona Garvey?'

'Not yet, sir.'

It stung to admit it out loud. For the first time, I felt I could get her to talk, but I was going to have to let her go.

'We've got a dead man and a killer on the loose. Focus on identifying the body you've got and get me some good news to give to the public. If Fiona Garvey is worth talking to, trust me, her time will come.'

My silence was enough to satisfy him, and it was a relief when he finally left.

I marched to Randle's desk, looming over him until he pulled his eyes away from his computer. His forehead was creased in concentration as he destroyed a banana in two bites.

'The boss was looking for you, ma'am,' he said.

He frisbeed the banana skin into a nearby bin, looking at me expectantly.

'Well, he found me.'

'You worked with him before?'

'Yes. A long time ago.'

'It must be good to be back?'

'Terrific,' I said without smiling. 'Any news on the body from the park?'

Randle looked at me, trying to interpret my expression, but I was practised at giving nothing away. He gestured at a screen of text too small to read.

'He's not one of ours, ma'am. No prints on the system.'

'What about his phone?'

Randle hesitated.

'Don't tell me we can't find that either?'

'About that, ma'am . . .'

His smile was disarming; I glimpsed the charm that must have got him out of trouble countless times before.

'We got Fiona's phone records. There were several calls to Alistair Cowan.'

'She was his PA, Randle. I'm sure she called him a lot. Doesn't tell us anything if we don't know what was said.'

I twisted the strap on my watch. Every hour that passed decreased our chances of finding Alistair alive.

'What about the new guy?' I asked.

'We have his phone, but it's damaged – waterlogged from the rain. They're trying to fix it.'

'So, what *have* you got?' I needed results.

Randle pushed aside a stack of papers, revealing a plastic evidence bag.

'This . . .'

At first, I wasn't sure what he was showing me. I seldom bought anything which needed to be ironed, let alone professionally laundered, so it took me a moment to realise I was looking at a dry-cleaning tag.

'And?'

'It was safety-pinned to the lining of the man's suit jacket, protected from the rain,' Randle explained. 'We checked it out. It's a family-owned dry-cleaners. He was a regular and he paid by card.'

'Have you got a name?'

'C. E. Walker. Charles. Albert Bridge Road.'

Chapter Twenty-Two

Odie

Odie's phone shrieked loudly in her pocket, snapping her out of her reverie. She had escaped the office for an afternoon walk and had only just started to relax. She knew the voice instantly; she had been married to its owner for seventeen years, drawn to his promise of stability after a childhood of chaos and disappointment. The marriage had been over for a long time, but they shared a son.

'Richard, I'm busy. Can I—'

'Daniel got the job.' Richard Reid had mastered the art of interrupting her, conscious that when he got Odie's attention, he only had a small window to make his point.

'Oh. That's good.' Odie wished she could sound more thrilled, but she had always found it hard to be happy about someone else's success, even if it was her son's. When Richard had told her Daniel had decided to become a journalist, she had actively encouraged it, hoping it might bring them closer. If anything, it just gave Daniel a public forum to tell the world he wanted nothing to do with her.

'I thought you'd want to know,' Richard was saying.

She didn't, but she knew she should. 'Of course. Thanks, Richard. I appreciate it.' And she did, in her own way. She had never been a contender for Mother of the Year. She was young when she got pregnant, and she hadn't felt ready. Richard was thrilled to become a father and assured her her nurturing instincts would grow, but they never did and, much as she loved her son, Odie found it hard to get excited about his accomplishments. She didn't understand him, and she feared she never would.

'You should give him a call. I'm sure he'd like that,' Richard said.

For a moment, she allowed herself the illusion that maybe that were true, but somehow she doubted it. She hadn't been there when Daniel needed her as a child, and he had stopped seeking her approval a long time ago.

'OK. I will. Richard, look, I've got to go. I've got Ross on the other line.'

It was a lie, and they both knew it.

'Call him, Odie. Please.'

She hung up, staring dumbly at her phone. *Please.* In one word, Richard had managed to crush her with the weight of his hope. Pointless, senseless hope, as he yearned for a mother and son to rebuild a relationship they had never had. *Call him.* She thought through her options: call Daniel and inflict an awkward conversation on them both when he would be at work and her mind was elsewhere, or send him a gift and put off the mother/son bonding until she had more presence of mind. She chose the coward's way out and sent him a bottle of champagne, as impersonal as it was expensive.

She could feel everyone looking at her when she entered the office, conscious of the creak of chairs as they strained to see her face. Ross flung open his door and stood staring at her across the room, his eyes dark and expressionless. After a moment, he turned and went back to his desk. She had been summoned, and he made sure everyone knew it.

Odie closed the door carefully behind her. 'That was a bit melodramatic, don't you think?'

'No more than your story.'

It wasn't the response she had expected, and the voice was unfamiliar. Scanning the room, she realised they were not alone. A petite, neatly dressed woman sat in the corner, regarding her with something close to hatred. For a second, Odie wondered if she was from HR, but her instincts told her otherwise – the dress was too homely, the dark hair in a long thin plait.

'You had no right.' The woman's voice was quiet with rage.

Confused, Odie turned to Ross, trying to work out if he was on her side.

'This is Mary Garvey. Fiona Garvey is her daughter,' he said.

Odie hated Ross for putting her on the spot, and she refused to give him the satisfaction of witnessing her discomfort.

'Mrs Garvey, this must be a distressing time for you and your family, but—'

'Is that all you can say?' Mary Garvey cut her off mid-sentence. 'Why did you have to mention her name?'

Odie continued, as if she hadn't been interrupted. '. . . I simply reported the events as they were presented to me.'

'Can you even hear yourself? "The events as they were presented"?! What events?' Mary asked, incredulous. 'My daughter went to the police because she was traumatised. She needs help, not hate. Do you know what it's been like? What people have started saying about her? People who don't even know her?'

'That's unfortunate, but I'm not responsible for that. I only write the facts.' Odie's words sounded hollow, even as she said them.

'And what about the fact that *that* body had nothing to do with her?' The woman was standing now. 'She's been released. This morning. Do you even know that?' Mary Garvey was almost shouting – whether it was in anger or desperation, it was hard to tell.

'Mrs Garvey . . .' Ross interceded before the situation escalated. 'We understand how you could have found Odie's piece misleading, and we shall make clear that the police have confirmed that Fiona had nothing to do with the body in the park.'

Mary Garvey's eyes expressed her relief, but the distrust was still there. Ross turned to Odie, his voice firm.

'I think it would be better if you left us. We'll continue this later.'

Odie had been dismissed by a man nearly twenty years her junior. Furious, she made her way back to her desk.

Chapter Twenty-Three

Leah

Charles Walker had hidden his wealth well. Red-brick exterior, not a caretaker in sight, simple white blinds obscuring the view of Battersea Park. We could hear Vivi Walker shouting at her maid on the other side of the door. From the moment she opened it, I knew the Walkers had money to burn. The epitome of cash-rich/time-poor, Vivi didn't even have the patience to wait for us to introduce ourselves. She gave us the once-over, made an unintelligible sound, then turned back into the house, expecting us to follow, her ash-blonde bob keeping its perfect shape.

She led us into a large room with a high ceiling and polished mahogany floor. She never once looked over her shoulder, walking steadily ahead as if our presence made no difference to her one way or another. The room was plainly decorated with simple, clean furniture that looked Scandinavian. Once again, the Walkers had made an effort to play down their wealth, but the paintings gave them away. Nothing too showy or recognisable, but I had been around enough art to know a collector's piece when I saw one, and the Walkers had both good taste and the means to enjoy it.

Vivi Walker's voice was clipped and bored, at odds with her

surprisingly gentle face. 'What has he done now?' Her green eyes were slightly too far apart, her eyebrows waxed into a flawless arch.

I didn't know it then, but the 'he' in question was Anthony Charles Walker, heir apparent and general waste of space. He had been in his fair share of trouble, proof money could buy neither discipline nor obedience, and from the tone of his mother's voice, her son had exhausted her patience long ago.

'I'm afraid there's been an incident,' I said.

It wasn't the word I had planned to use, but her nonchalance threw me off script.

The look of boredom disappeared instantly. Her eyes became strangely alert.

'Is it Charles?'

People have a nose for tragedy, and Vivi Walker sensed she was a widow before I even said the words. I did most of the talking while Randle looked on sympathetically. She felt he was on her side, and he probably was. Vivi was surprisingly calm, her large eyes focused and still. She didn't cry or break down; she just stared at us, absorbing the facts with silent dignity.

'It's not what I would have wished for him,' she said when I had finished. Understated like her décor, this was a woman who found being expressive vulgar. I wondered whether she had loved her husband. It was impossible to tell.

'What's going on?'

The voice came from the doorway. I turned to see a man I assumed to be Anthony Walker slouched against the frame. Long and angular, he had the same bored manner as his mother. He directed his question at her, as if we weren't even there.

'What's going on, Mother?' he repeated. His green eyes were

sunk deep into his face, and he had thin brown hair, too long at the back.

'Your father's dead,' Vivi said. No warning jab, just a crippling blow to the gut. It was an unkind way to deliver the news and she must have known it, but she seemed in no hurry to comfort her son. She caught me looking and despised me for judging her.

'What, Inspector? You want me to pretend he's alive?'

I didn't bother with a response. I had met her type before – cold, sophisticated, sometimes cruel. Anthony was on his knees, sobbing uncontrollably by the door. Vivi didn't move or even look at him. Randle shifted uncomfortably, waiting for me to say something. When I didn't, he walked up to Anthony, gently pulling him to his feet. I watched in silence as Randle settled him in a chair, murmuring under his breath as if soothing a small child.

'I'm sorry,' Randle finally said out loud.

He directed the words at Vivi, and I knew he meant them. Her face softened, and she smiled at his sincerity like it was the last thing she expected from him. I should have been the one to say it, but the truth was, I wasn't sorry. I was finding it hard to sympathise with Vivi Walker and she knew it.

'Do you know who killed him, Inspector?' She lit a cigarette as she said it, walking across the room to open the door that led to the veranda.

'We're not sure yet whether it was a random attack or someone known to him,' I replied. 'We're looking into everything. Family, friends, associates. Is there anybody in Charles's life whom we should be aware of?'

'Like whom?' Her eyes were alert again, more suspicious than concerned.

'I don't know, Mrs Walker. It would be helpful to hear whether you have any thoughts.'

'He spent a lot of time away from home.' She didn't elaborate.

'Did he work away from home?' I asked.

'He was away a lot. I presume he was working,' she said.

'And did you have any reason to believe he wasn't?'

'Why would she?' Anthony's voice was strained after the tears.

'I don't know. Did you, Mrs Walker?' Even as I asked the question, I knew she wouldn't say.

'No.'

She had been hinting at something, but Anthony's words had changed her mind. I tried one last time.

'Is there anything you can tell us which might help us find who did this to your husband?'

'No, Inspector. I don't think there is.'

'If you think of anything at all . . .' Randle handed her a card.

She took it politely, slipping it into a pocket I hadn't noticed. 'Of course. I'll show you out.'

Chapter Twenty-Four

Odie

Odie forced herself to call Rebecca Stanton and conduct a quick interview, determined to get Ross off her back. Relieved the day was finally over, she stopped for a drink after work. She chose a run-down pub, close enough to walk from the office but sufficiently hidden to deter colleagues from dropping in on their way home. As she made her way past the curved wooden bar towards the furthermost table, she saw the woman out of the corner of her eye. She couldn't mistake the tiny physique, and there was something tragic about Mary Garvey now she had no one to attack. Sitting at a table by the window, her white wine barely touched, she looked unbelievably sad.

'Are you OK?'

It had been a while since anyone had asked Mary Garvey how she was. She looked up blankly, taking a moment to place Odie from the meeting with Ross. Odie wondered whether to leave her in peace, but she recognised loneliness in another human being, and something made her pull up a chair. She watched Mary Garvey cry for ten minutes, not knowing what to say and hoping that the other woman would take the lead. After a while, Mary took a sip, observing Odie over the rim of her glass.

'You bring them up and do everything you can to keep them safe, but you can't protect them, not in the long run.' Stripped of its earlier intensity, her voice was much softer than it had been in Ross's office.

'How is she?' Odie wasn't sure she had the right to ask.

Mary shrugged, her voice hollow and distant. 'She always used to talk to me, but she's barely said a word since I picked her up. Went straight to her room; said she needed some space. So I'm giving her that . . . I guess.'

Her pain was palpable, but her eyes were empty.

'Do you have children?' she asked.

'I have a son.'

'What's he like?'

'I don't really know.' Odie had never admitted this to anyone before, but she couldn't lie to this woman.

'That's a shame.'

'I don't think I've ever known.'

Mary glanced down at her wine, swilling the liquid around in the glass. 'Sometimes I think the only reason I know Fiona so well is because she didn't have many friends at school. She was a shy child. Her teachers always complained they could barely get a word out of her, but when she came home, she told me everything, described them all in detail – the chemistry teacher who scratched his bum when he thought no one was looking; the maths teacher who hid a calculator in his drawer because he couldn't do mental arithmetic. She saw everything, watched everyone, but no one took much notice of her. At least not at school. She's a hard person to get to know, always has been . . . but I know her.'

'What's she like?'

'Kind. Gentle. Normal. Nothing extraordinary, but I love her.'

Odie couldn't help but be touched by the description.

'Everyone liked her. She never lied. Always kept her promises. Never bothered anybody. Before the piece you wrote, no one had a bad word to say about her, but now she's being ripped apart online.'

'I didn't accuse her of anything.'

'No. You let everyone else do that.'

'I'm sorry.' Odie hadn't meant to apologise, but the words came out before she had time to think.

Mary looked at her, sighing softly into the silence. 'You know, I believe you are.'

They sat for a moment, nursing their respective drinks. Odie had so many questions, she wasn't sure where to begin, but Mary spoke first, her gentle tone taking the sting out of her words.

'When I read your article, I was convinced you didn't have children.'

'Why would you think that?'

'Because no mother would have done what you did.'

It was said without any hint of accusation, but it made Odie defensive.

'I just did my job. Being a mother has nothing to do with it.'

'Being a mother has everything to do with everything.'

'Maybe we're just different mothers.'

'Maybe.'

There was an uncomfortable pause. Mary looked down at her hands.

'Do you think your son could rip another human being to pieces?' she asked.

'He doesn't have it in him.'

'How can you be so sure?'

'I just know.'

Odie racked her brains trying to remember if Daniel had ever been in a fight, but she couldn't remember even a scrape or punch from childhood. His sensitivity had always fascinated her. He was so different from her that she often wondered how he could possibly be her child; she knew it was a question he often asked himself. Wrapped up in her thoughts, she forgot where she was for a moment, but the sudden pressure on her hand pulled her back to reality. She looked down to find Mary's fingers tightly clasped around hers, squeezing her flesh with each word.

'I know my daughter. She wouldn't hurt anyone.'

'Don't you wonder whose blood was on her?'

'Of course I wonder.'

'Then how can you be so sure?'

'How can you be sure about your son?'

'My son didn't walk into a police station with blood on his hands.'

'I know my daughter.' Mary let go of Odie's hand, their short-lived friendship forgotten. When she spoke again, her voice was hard and accusing. 'I don't care if you were doing your job. You threw an innocent girl to the wolves for the sake of a cheap story. I hope you can live with that.'

Mary Garvey downed her drink and left.

Chapter Twenty-Five

Leah

The day felt long, and I was happy to put it behind me. I opened my front door and stepped back into my life. Disappointment came with the job, but frustration was harder to take. Vivi and Anthony Walker had credible alibis, and we had no other suspects in the frame. I reached for the light switch, cursing myself when it didn't turn on for forgetting to buy bulbs. There was a Co-op round the corner, but I didn't have the energy to go out again, and it seemed fitting to end the day in darkness.

I navigated my way to my bedroom, tripping over a bag of clothes I had been meaning to donate to a charity shop. Kicking off my shoes, I listened out for the dull thud. I contemplated my options for the evening. I had told very few people I was back in London – I was terrible at keeping in touch and, after ten years in Leeds, there weren't many people to tell. An ex-boyfriend lived nearby but it had been eight years since we had spoken, and history had never been my favourite subject; I thought about skipping, but my Achilles was sore and I wasn't in the mood for pain; then there was Eli's file in my bag, waiting to be read.

It was like being sliced open after local anaesthetic – aware of the impact but conscious the pain would be deferred. The first thing I saw was my birth certificate, the black and white proof that bound me to the man who had killed my mother. The paper had yellowed over the years, and it was missing a corner on one side. Beneath it was the thin rectangle of an old newspaper article. It almost tore when I lifted it up to the light. It seemed that no one knew what had really happened. Eli had never disputed the evidence, but he hadn't helped the police to fill in the gaps either. My thoughts moved to Margaretta and the day someone had asked what I did for a living. Her answer had been simple: *she puts evil people away*. I wasn't sure what to make of it at the time because she had said it without pride or feeling. Now I knew Eli had been a detective, her response started to make sense. She hadn't wanted to feel proud because she had wanted us to be different.

I stared at my birth certificate, concentrating on the names: Father – Eli Ruben Carson; mother – Elizabeth Afia Carson; parents I never knew I had and never felt I needed. I put the birth certificate to one side and leafed through the rest of the file. Selwyn had called it a file, but it was more of a scrapbook – photographs, reports, more newspaper cuttings, letters – a patchwork of information bound together by tragedy. I was familiar with the basic facts but, as I looked through the pages in front of me, the past came to life and the horror of what Eli had done began to sink in.

Thirty-one years ago, on the 5th of May, the police were called to a remote country cottage belonging to one David Francis, after a putrid smell was noticed by a passer-by. The house was some distance away from the road, hidden by a mini wilderness of long grass and forget-me-nots. The land was public property, but it led to nowhere, and David Francis had enjoyed the delights of nature in relative peace, disturbed only by the occasional rambler and teenage couples mistaking sex for romance. A secluded Eden, it was the chosen location for seventeen-year-old Ron Kirwan to propose to his girlfriend, Amy Pritchard. It was supposed to be the most important night of his life; it became the most memorable for all the wrong reasons.

A copy of Ron's statement to the police lay sandwiched between two newspaper articles. His shock and despair were evident, transporting me back to the night he had lost his innocence.

'It was public land. Everyone knew that. We weren't doing anything wrong. Amy and me had gone there before to . . . you know. I thought it would make it special to go back. She liked it. She always said she liked it. There's this dog . . . She likes the dog . . . Reminds her of one her parents had when we were kids. It was because of the dog, how she knew something wasn't right. She's grown up with dogs. She's always said that if we ever get married, we have to get a dog. Prefers them to people. Like friends to her. It's weird but that's Amy . . . She knew something was wrong from the barking. I was going to ask her to marry me, but it wouldn't stop. I could have killed the dog for spoiling things. I tried to carry on, but something was wrong. I don't know anything about dogs, but I knew it was wrong. It didn't sound right. There was something about it. Like it was panicking. You could hear it inside you, like a vibration. I didn't want to be there, but Amy thought the dog was in pain. I wanted to leave it, but she wouldn't. She couldn't.

'The sound was coming from the house. I'd never been that close before. Didn't want to get done for trespassing and get it in the neck from my dad . . . The dog kept barking, and there was this smell. We could smell it, the closer we got. It was . . . I don't know . . . like rotting. Like old meat and bananas when you forget to throw them out. The closer we got, the stronger it got. It made me feel sick. I wanted to go home, but Amy was bothered about the stupid dog.

'The door was slightly open. I didn't want to go in. It was trespassing, but there's no stopping Amy when she's got an idea in her head. I love that about her. We called out but no one answered. I told her we shouldn't be there, but she just kept saying she hated people being cruel to animals and you can't leave a dog like that. She just wanted to make sure it was OK.

'It was easy to find the dog. It had been locked in the cupboard by the door. We could hear it scraping against the wood, like it was desperate to get out. We let it out and it just ran, like it was running for its life. We could have left then, we should of, but it was too late. I'd already gone in the bedroom and seen it and it was too late.

'There was a hand poking out from under the bed, covered in blood. It looked like a man's hand, but I wasn't sure. I shouted something but no one answered. Now Amy wanted to leave but I didn't know what to do. It was too late to leave . . . It was a person . . . We couldn't just go and leave a person under the bed. Someone had been hurt. You can't just leave a person. I thought they needed help. I just wanted to help. So, I knelt down by the bed, even though the smell made me feel sick. The floor was slippery, and I could feel something wet on my knees, like water but stickier. I didn't let it bother me, even though I was wearing my good trousers and my mum would kill me . . . I just wanted to help the person get out of there, but there was no person . . . only a hand . . .'

Ron Kirwan and Amy Pritchard had been the first to the scene, the first to witness the horror Eli Carson had left behind. Blood, human remains, discarded clothes – a scene of life interrupted and then abruptly ended. The hand was later identified as belonging to David Francis, a successful solicitor who used the cottage as a weekend retreat. The rest of his remains were found buried in a field not far from the house. The grave had been shallow and haphazard, as if Eli had been more concerned with making a hasty exit than covering his tracks. It was initially assumed that the butchered remains of David Francis and Elizabeth Carson had been buried together as lovers, bodies entwined in a sadistic punchline to Eli's cruel joke. But the joke was that Elizabeth wasn't even there. Her blood and clothing had been found at the scene, but there was no sign of her body. Elizabeth Carson was missing, and so it was to remain for over thirty years.

Originally cast as the grieving widower, Eli played the role of the doting husband to perfection. He missed his wife and mourned her loss, and everyone interviewed spoke of the intense bond between the couple. He never actually lied, and the more I read, the more I realised that the reason it took the police so long to work out he was guilty was because they didn't ask the right questions. Eli was one of them, and they never questioned his innocence. Or maybe the mess at the crime scene had quieted their doubts – Eli would have known better than to leave incriminating evidence; if he were guilty, they would never have found the hand. Hidden in plain sight, he taunted and manipulated them, saying very little and relying on middle-class respectability and inside knowledge to evade capture. For a while, it looked like the murders would never be solved. A tenuous case against Ron Kirwan and Amy Pritchard was dropped due to lack of credible motive; no other likely suspects were found, and the investigation began to wind down. The killing of David Francis and Elizabeth Carson came to be seen as a random atrocity, attributable to a force of pure evil which might forever remain faceless. Then a bloody axe was found with Eli's fingerprints, and a version of the truth began to emerge.

Eli was arrested shortly afterwards. At first, he refused to comment, then he suddenly confessed to both murders. He gave an in-depth account of how he had disposed of David Francis, but he never revealed where Elizabeth was buried. It was his way of staying in control, and he didn't care about the pain it caused those who loved her.

The file contained a handful of letters Eli had sent to Margaretta over the years. I skimmed a couple, then put them to one side. They were polite and uninteresting, mostly concerning the mundane details of Eli's time in prison. I was struck by the tone: there was no hint of apology, no glimmer of contrition, just the musings of a man getting on with his life. As I gathered up the pages, I spotted an unfinished letter at the bottom of the pile. Margaretta's writing was unmistakable – elaborate and unrestrained in a way Margaretta had never been. I moved to the kitchen, delaying the inevitable as I spooned grains of coffee into a cafetière. Caffeine made me bolder, and I savoured the sting as it rushed to my brain. I downed another cup, then another. Then, pumped full of toxins, I began to read, imagining Margaretta's clear, distinctive voice.

Dear Eli,
The years roll on, and we press on regardless. I know you have no relationship with Jesus, but I continue to pray that you will ask God for forgiveness so you can know true peace, even as you serve your time behind bars. I was reading my Bible this morning and I was reminded of these verses which I want to share with you. I read them to you as a child and, as the apostle Paul wrote to the Philippians all those years ago, so I write to you now to encourage you.
    '. . . whatever is true, whatever is noble, whatever is right, whatever is pure, whatever is lovely, whatever is admirable – if anything is excellent or praiseworthy – think about such things.'

I know it's hard but think on these things in your darker moments.
Love as always,
M

PS . . .

She never finished it.

'. . . whatever is true, whatever is noble, whatever is right, whatever is pure, whatever is lovely, whatever is admirable – if anything is excellent or praiseworthy – think about such things.'

Margaretta had read those same words to me as a child but, until that moment, I had completely forgotten them. I put the letter away. There was a faint breeze coming through the window, and my limbs ached in the cold air. I wrapped my arms around my torso, rubbing my biceps with the balls of my thumbs. I had gone as far as I was prepared to go in one night. Thinking about Margaretta made me feel unbearably sad and returning my thoughts to Eli was somehow less painful. Most of his letters were in envelopes, neatly sawn open with Margaretta's silver letter opener, but one lay loose, folded unevenly into two. I reached across the table, flicking it towards me with the edge of my nail. It was dated before Eli had been convicted. His other letters had been relatively short, but this one was brief to the point of being aggressive. Three sentences in capitals, full stops marked with gusto. I read it out loud, even though no one was there to hear.

'YOU WIN. I'LL TALK. BUT YOU'LL NEVER KNOW WHERE SHE IS.'

I wondered what had made him change his mind and decide to confess, but with Margaretta gone, only Eli could answer that.

Chapter Twenty-Six

Odie

Odie remained in the pub long after Mary had left. She kept replaying Mary's words over in her mind:

You threw an innocent girl to the wolves for the sake of a cheap story.

It wasn't the first time she'd been called a hack. She recalled Hutch's parting words to her when she left the paper. She hadn't raised her voice, but she made sure everyone heard:

You're worse than the people you judge so harshly. Winning doesn't count if you cheated to get the prize.

She had accused Odie of letting her desperation for a story get in the way of the truth, leaving a question mark over her integrity from which Odie had never fully escaped. She detested Hutch's moral superiority and the way Hutch had stood in the doorway, accusing her of inventing sources, as if Odie's brand of journalism only existed in the gutter. Over the years, she had convinced herself that Leah Hutch's opinion didn't matter, and it annoyed her that at a time like this, Hutch's words had returned to the forefront of her mind. She pushed her drink aside, conscious the alcohol was making her sensitive and paranoid, and decided to call it a day.

The rain hit her hard as she emerged into the night. Cold, wet and without an umbrella, she paused for a minute under the street lamp as the water soaked her jacket. She replayed the recent run of events: an anonymous tip-off, a dead body, a woman covered in blood. It should have been a good week, but she was finding it hard to stay optimistic. She had put in a call to the IT guy at work to see if he could trace her anonymous source. She had low expectations, but it was still frustrating when he emailed her back to say that the IP address was hidden, so her best hope was to contact the police. Moments later, he messaged her off the record — for a price, he might be able to help her further, but there were no guarantees. Uncertain and illegal, the worst possible combination. She hadn't bothered replying.

She hadn't heard back from Daniel. He rarely initiated contact, but she had hoped he would bother to acknowledge the bottle of champagne, even if he didn't thank her for it. It was disappointing but not entirely surprising. The years had passed but, in many senses, Daniel was still a fourteen-year-old boy who hated his mother for abandoning his father. Daniel, Ross, Mary Garvey — they all had something against her and thinking about them was exhausting. She needed a shower, a cigarette and a change of scene.

She started to undress the moment she entered her house, stepping over the doormat of unopened mail. Discarding her clothes haphazardly en route to the bathroom, she paused in front of the mirror, surprised by how old she looked. It had been so gradual, she had become a different woman without even noticing. It was a relief to let the water run over her — hot almost to the point of scalding, soothing away the day. She thought about the body in the park — the nameless, faceless man whom someone had battered to death for reasons she might never understand. Then she thought about

Fiona Garvey, a woman she had never met, whose story intrigued her in a way nothing else had for a long time.

Odie was so caught up in her thoughts that she didn't hear the sound at first, a faint rattling, like a door shaking in the breeze. She dismissed it as nothing, but the noise persisted, growing louder and more urgent, as if someone was trying to get her attention. She switched off the shower, hoping she was overreacting. The sound had moved from the back of the house to the front. Wrapping a towel tightly around her, she grabbed the closest object which could double as a weapon and crept down the stairs, armed with a broken umbrella. The sound had stopped, and she was faced with an eerie, unsettling silence. She paused, listening out for a possible intruder, but there was nothing. She was alone. She exhaled slowly to release the tension, unsure whether to feel relieved or unnerved. Someone had been there. She was almost certain of that. As she turned back towards the stairs, she noticed something resting in front of the door. She had barely looked down when she entered the house, but she vaguely remembered stepping over a mound of entirely white envelopes. The brown paper rectangle hadn't been there before, yet there it was now, on top of the other letters. She looked through the peephole, searching for a retreating figure, but there was no one there. Tentatively flipping the latch, she ventured a couple of steps, looking out into the darkness. The street was entirely silent; if someone was watching her, they were keeping themselves hidden. She shut the door, her heart beating fast in her chest.

The envelope was unmarked, apart from her name printed neatly on the front. Her heart rate had slowed, and she felt calmer and more in control. Carefully peeling the envelope open, she pulled out three sheets of white A4 paper covered in small, typed print. The title on the first sheet read 'Fiona Garvey: the Life of a Monster'. Below it was a photograph of Fiona, unassuming and unthreatening. She skimmed the text, but there was nothing particularly interesting. She started from the beginning, reading more carefully. She reached the same conclusion. Someone had sent her a blow-by-blow account of the unremarkable life of Fiona Garvey – what she did each day, how she spent her time, whom she spent it with. Nothing untoward, nothing alarming, except for the ironic title. The anonymous tip-off and now this; she couldn't rule out the possibility that the two were related or even sent by the same person, but who? She pulled out her phone and brought up the anonymous email, searching for clues. There were so many questions she wanted to ask, but she couldn't find the right words to respond to her nameless, faceless source. After five attempts, she finally decided what to write. One word: 'Why?' She pressed send before she could change her mind.

Lying on her bed, she tried to make sense of it all. Nothing in Fiona's past hinted at a tendency towards violent behaviour, but every time Odie was swayed by the thought of the quiet, unassuming secretary, she was reminded of the woman coated in another person's blood. The image disturbed and intrigued her, and her thoughts were so focused on Fiona, she barely registered the sound of the engine humming outside. Her first thought was that whoever had delivered the envelope had returned. She raced down the stairs, hoping to catch a glimpse of them slipping away, but outside there was stillness once again, and at her feet stood the bottle of champagne she had sent Daniel, unopened.

Chapter Twenty-Seven

Caroline Gordon hated riding a bike in London. She didn't belong to the green-juice-drinking hipster brigade who navigated roundabouts as if they were driving cars and cycled home after all-night raves without a helmet; she did it because it was convenient and cheaper than public transport. But every time she climbed onto her battered leather saddle, she felt she was taking her life into her own hands. She had had numerous accidents and shattered many bones, working through the various parts of her body in almost systematic order. Each time, she swore never to get back on a bike, yet here she was once again.

Now on her journey home, she felt more relaxed, cycling across Wandsworth Common, away from the temperamental drivers and packs of Lycra-clad men. It was late, and she veered off into the foliage, keen to shave time off her commute. She heard the crunch first – duller than the snap of a twig, but sharp enough to know something was wrong. Then her bike pulled away from under her, and she fell. *Not again*, she thought. *Not again*. Lying flat on the ground, she gently moved each limb, carefully checking she hadn't broken anything. She was sure she had heard a crunch, but everything felt intact, and nothing hurt too much. She tried to get to her feet, but she stumbled and fell, landing on something both hard and soft. She felt her way across the surface, terrified by what she would find. Her hand slid across something warm and wet. It was hard to see, but somehow she knew what it was — bone covered by skin, skin covered by blood; another human being, dying beneath her. Alistair James Cowan, forty-four and three months, barely alive.

Chapter Twenty-Eight

Leah

Alistair Cowan was in a coma. Not much use to me but at least he had survived the night. I added an extra shot of espresso to my morning coffee. The machine had been serviced and the liquid came out faster, but it still had the same bitter taste. I drank quickly as I turned the corner. Kenny O'Sullivan had been right. Fiona Garvey's time had finally come. There was nothing to place her at the scene of Charles Walker's murder, but we were looking into possible links all the same. Two professional white men attacked in parks around the same time; it was a question I knew I had to ask. Moments later, Fiona sat across from me in the interview room – flanked by her lawyer, his ridiculously long torso making her look shrunken and cowed. The more I probed about the attack, the more I felt I was losing her. I took a sip of water and tried a different approach.

'When did you last see Sonya Waugh?'

It wasn't what Fiona had been expecting, and her eyes snapped to attention.

'What?'

It was the first word I had heard her say, and I allowed myself a small internal celebration.

'Sonya Waugh,' I said. 'The therapist you were seeing.'

Fiona's lawyer tried to shut down the question, but she ignored him.

'I know who she is.' Her voice was soft but clear.

'When did you last see her?'

Her eyes had begun to dart. She stared at me, confused. 'I don't know.'

'Why did you need to see a therapist?'

I fired the next question, barely giving her time to think.

Her lawyer advised her not to answer, and I was surprised when she spoke again.

'I thought it would help,' she said. 'A girl at work had seen someone. I heard her talking about it, and I thought it might be a good idea.'

'Was there a reason for you to see Sonya Waugh?'

'I was worried.' The frown between her eyes dissolved, making her face appear more open. 'I fainted at work. A couple of times. It wasn't serious, but I didn't want it to become a problem. It's happened before . . . once when I was stressed. I just black out for a bit.'

'And were you stressed at work?'

'No. Not really.' The words came out too fast. 'My boss had been focused on a big deal. I had been working hard, but I was fine. I went to see my GP. He said there was nothing wrong, but I thought it would help to speak to someone.'

'And did it?'

'Yes. For a while.'

Her face was strained again, and I sensed her mind had drifted to the night of the assault.

'When was the last time you blacked out?' I said.

Fiona just looked at me, her eyes pleading with me to stop.

'When was the last time you blacked out, Fiona? Was it the night Alistair Cowan was attacked?'

Her lawyer pushed her not to comment, but she barely noticed he was there. She nodded slowly, looking straight at me.

'I need you to say it,' I said, indicating the machine.

'Yes.'

Neither of us spoke for a moment, and I searched her face for the details I knew she would never give. Her lower lip was caught between her teeth, her arms folded carefully on her lap.

'Why did you show me that picture when I was here before?'

'Why do you think?'

'You think I had something to do with that?'

'Did you?'

Her pupils dilated. She shook her head so hard, I heard a crack.

'No,' she said. 'I didn't hurt that man. I didn't hurt anybody. I wouldn't do that.'

I placed a photograph of Charles Walker on the table. Unharmed, he smiled half-heartedly at the camera.

'Are you sure?' I asked.

'Yes. I don't know who that is.'

I pulled the photograph back towards me, leaving the image face up.

'You understand why you're here?'

Fiona nodded.

'You walked into a police station, covered in Alistair Cowan's blood, carrying a baseball bat also covered in his blood. How do you explain that?'

Fiona shook her head, and I pressed on before her lawyer could interject.

'How do you explain that, Fiona?'

'I can't.'

'He was beaten so badly, it's a miracle he's still alive. You were carrying a bat covered—'

'I didn't do anything. I wouldn't.' She cut me off, her voice urgent and shrill.

'Then explain to me what happened, Fiona. Let me help you.'

'It wasn't me.'

'Who was it, then?'

'I don't know.'

'But you were there.'

'I know.'

'Fiona,' I began gently. 'You've got to help me. You walked into a station with a weapon. To the outside world, it looks like you were giving yourself up. What were you doing if you weren't the one who hurt Alistair Cowan?'

Her eyes flitted from side to side. There was a low hum coming from the overhead light, and she glanced up, distracted.

'OK. Let's go back a step,' I said. 'Were you with Alistair Cowan the night he was attacked?'

'Yes.' Barely audible but it was a 'yes'.

'Why?'

She bit into her lower lip, staring at the light to avoid my eyes.

'Alistair asked me to meet him. He liked to go to this greasy spoon near Wandsworth Common. Said it kept him down to earth. He liked the way they fried their eggs. We were supposed to meet there. There's a shortcut he showed me, through the common.'

'And you just so happened to bump into him in that large expanse?'

'I don't know. I can't remember. We always check in before meetings. I must have called his phone. It has a distinctive ring.'

'You think you called, or you know you did?' I said.

'I must have done. I don't know.'

'OK. So, let's say you called him. What happened when you found him?'

Fiona's face looked blank. Her eyes settled on the panel of opaque glass in the door behind me as she picked at the base of her nail. I softened my tone, trying to draw her back.

'What happened, Fiona?'

'I don't know,' she said eventually. 'I just remember him on the ground, hurt. Screaming . . . On and on . . . like . . . I'd never heard anything like it. I didn't know what to do.'

'Then what?'

'I don't know. I didn't hurt him.'

'Did you see the person who did?'

'No. I don't remember what happened. I blacked out, and when I woke up, all I saw was blood.'

'Was there blood before you blacked out?'

'I can't remember. I don't know. All I remember was him screaming and screaming.'

'What happened, Fiona? Try to remember what happened before you blacked out.'

She was still for a moment. The light above her flickered and died, so her eyes were in shadow when she finally shook her head. She sighed, her whole body quivering with the exhalation.

'I tried to save him, but there was too much blood. It was everywhere. Like he was drowning . . .'

Her voice trailed off as she relived the horror, or pretended to.

'Why did you leave him?'

No answer.

'Why, Fiona?'

She looked distraught and tired, like a child on the verge of tears.

'I don't know,' she whispered. 'I had to get out of there. There was nothing more I could do. It was bigger than me.'

'What was bigger than you, Fiona?'

She leant across the table so her face was only a foot away from mine. Up close, I thought I could smell the faint residue of blood clinging to her skin. I was probably imagining it, but it reminded me of the first time I saw her, walking towards me, painted red.

'I had his life in my hands. What was I supposed to do? What was I supposed to do?'

I finished the interview and made my way back to my office, using the stairs so I had more time to think. Randle had checked Fiona's records – a call had indeed been made, but somehow Fiona's story didn't add up. There were too many coincidences, and the blackout felt convenient. I spotted Kenny O'Sullivan long before he saw me but, even with my head start, he managed to pin me into a corner.

'How did it go?'

His nostrils flared with each word, and I had to concentrate hard to focus on his eyes.

'Nothing conclusive but at least she spoke.'

'Have you got enough to charge?'

I stared past him down the long corridor, making him wait for what he wanted to hear.

'Yes, sir. I think so.'

Kenny's smile travelled to his eyes.

'Progress at last.'

Chapter Twenty-Nine

Odie

Odie checked her email, but there was still no response from her mysterious source. She wasn't surprised, but she couldn't help feeling disappointed. Even though she knew the anonymous email was probably an innocent tip-off, her mind had already raced ahead to disembodied voices and cryptic clues guiding her to the truth.

Fiona's alleged victim had been found, bloody and half-dead. Odie's first instinct had been to go to the hospital but according to Baber, the man was in a coma and even Hutch hadn't managed to get an audience. The police finally had enough to charge Fiona, and the case was off limits unless the charges were dropped, but Odie couldn't let the story go. She had to get to the victim. She trawled through her recent past, sifting through acquaintances for a possible way in. Although she didn't have many friends, Odie had met a lot of people over the years. She had a mental file for everyone, and it didn't take her long to think of someone who could help; she just wasn't sure he would want to.

Phil had been more than an acquaintance but never a friend. They had been introduced through an ex-colleague of Odie's years before and bumped into each other a week later. Phil had been an unlikely candidate for a nurse, impatient with life and people, terrible with small talk and superficialities. His career choice had intrigued her, then he had intrigued her. They had had a brief relationship which ended after a few months when he confronted her with a list of her shortcomings. She hadn't spoken to him since, but it wasn't difficult to track him down. They were beyond favours, but they had never cared enough about each other to hold grudges, and Phil was happy to take the 200 pounds she offered in exchange for calling her the moment Alistair woke up. The money also bought her a photograph of the comatose man. It wasn't the best image, as it had been taken and sent in haste, but it left Odie in no doubt about the amount of force that would have been needed to do such damage to another human being.

She turned her thoughts back to the only real lead she had – the pages she had been sent about Fiona Garvey. They were both dull and enlightening: few hobbies, even fewer friends. While Fiona didn't have many substantial relationships, she seemed to know or be known by a lot of people. Odie listed all Fiona's named associates on a piece of paper and started to contact them one by one. Everyone painted a similar picture, and she found it increasingly difficult to match the Fiona Garvey she was learning about with the violent maniac who had tried to kill her boss. She was working her way down the list when her phone rang.

She was surprised Daniel wanted to see her after the previous night. The returned bottle of champagne was such a deliberate act of rejection, she thought Richard was joking when he rang to tell her Daniel was coming round and wouldn't mind if she was there. It was a long way from an actual invitation, but it was better than nothing. Richard had said Daniel had met someone, and she wondered whether being in love had softened him. She was tired of tiptoeing around him, and she had to keep hoping that they could resolve things and move forwards.

Seeing Daniel always felt like seeing someone you had known as a child, grown-up for the first time. She couldn't get used to the angry bearded man sitting opposite her, but then again, she didn't see him often enough for his face to become familiar. Richard flapped around in the background, trying to give them space, but conscious he needed to be present to keep the peace when they inevitably started arguing. She could hear him clattering around in the kitchen, putting the finishing touches to a meal he had finished preparing long before they arrived.

'Congratulations.' She was on safe enough ground with that.

'Thanks,' Daniel said.

He had always been a boy, then a man, of few words when it came to her. Odie wondered whether he spoke much in the rest of his life; somehow she couldn't imagine it. She knew her next question was provocative, but it annoyed her that she had made an effort, only to have it thrown back in her face.

'So, you don't like champagne, then?'

He just looked at her as if there was nothing to say. He had perfected that look at the age of fourteen. Then, it had seemed petulant, now it was faintly intimidating.

'I don't drink. But I wouldn't expect you to know that.'

There was always a dig. She should have let it go, but she kept on pushing.

'Since when?'

'Since forever.' He had resorted to the role of surly teenager, making up for the years when he had blotted her out of his life.

'OK.' She didn't understand it, but everyone was entitled to make their own choices.

'You don't even know why, do you?'

He looked at her in disgust, daring her to find an answer, but she didn't know how to respond. How could she know when they hadn't had a proper conversation for years? It wasn't the first time Daniel had misconstrued something she had said, and these exchanges always ended the same way. She convinced herself Daniel was being his usual unreasonable self. It was only when she caught a glimpse of Richard, his eyes trying to hide the pain, that she realised why her son didn't drink.

Odie would never forget his fourteen-year-old face, blotched with tears, silently accusing her in the hospital waiting room. He felt she was responsible, and she knew he was right. She had had an affair. It hadn't meant anything, and she could barely remember what the man looked like now. It had been a tricky time in her marriage, and Richard was trying so hard to please that he had lost all sense of who he was. She found herself pulling further away from him, hating his weakness, seeing him as less of a man. She hadn't meant to be unfaithful; she hated the idea of infidelity on principle, and she was determined to end it almost as soon as it began, but Richard found out before she had a chance. She wished he had confronted her and told her how much she had hurt him, but he didn't. Instead, he poured two litres of good whiskey down his throat, took an overdose of painkillers and wrote her a beautiful, heartfelt letter. Daniel found him, half-dead, when he came home from school, and although Richard appeared to have forgiven her, she knew Daniel never would. Much as she wanted him to, she didn't blame him. No child should have to see what Daniel had seen that night. He would always have that image in his head, however hard he tried to erase it, and Odie knew it was her fault.

The atmosphere cooled significantly. Daniel answered her questions in adolescent monosyllables, giving little away. It was clear he didn't want Odie in his life, but she couldn't give up on him, so she stayed for longer than she wanted and suffered his hate. As she walked to her car, she thought about Mary Garvey, so sure of her child, when Odie barely knew hers. She wondered at Mary's sense of certainty, envied it even. Odie had immersed herself in the life of Fiona Garvey, and the more she found out about her, the more she began to doubt that the woman was capable of attempted murder. Maybe Mary was right, and Fiona was innocent, in the wrong place at the wrong time, trying to save the man she was accused of trying to kill. She recalled Baber's words and his haunted expression.

The face didn't match the hands.

It was so out of character it didn't make sense. Odie opened up the gallery on her phone, searching for the image Phil had sent of Alistair Cowan. There was a close-up of his face, taken without a flash, and she initially mistook him for the man she had found in the park. She flicked through the images – first the dead man in the park with his tailored suit, then Alistair Cowan lying still in his hospital bed, his head sinking into the bleached white pillow. Two mounds of pulpy, pale flesh. Close-up it was hard to differentiate between them. White professional men, brutally attacked in parks – one beaten to death, the other bludgeoned into a coma, both barely recognisable after their assaults. Odie's mind started to whirr, the question involuntarily lodging itself in her brain. What if it wasn't a coincidence and it was the same attacker, preying on privileged white men? But where did that leave Fiona with her blood-soaked hands? It didn't make any sense.

Chapter Thirty

Jake Munro prided himself on being in good shape for his age. He ran four times a week and spent two mornings at the gym with a personal trainer. The effort paid off, which was just as well as he had always been a vain man. He didn't usually run at night, but it had been a difficult week at work, and his wife was driving him mad; he needed to get out of the house to let off some steam. His career was finally where he wanted it to be, but with success came added stress. Two years ago, he had bought a third stationery company. There had been several waves of redundancies as he consolidated the companies, and it was only now that he felt he had a team in place that could deliver his aggressive plan for growth. It hadn't been easy, and the need to micromanage was starting to take its toll.

He ran for what seemed like hours, pushing his legs as hard as he could through Richmond Park. The trees cast a shadow on the path – strange silhouettes that moved beneath him as he pounded the ground with heavy thuds. He had never mastered the art of graceful running, but what did that matter as long as he kept going, working his body to relieve his mind? There were other joggers around to begin with, noticeably slower and often in his way, but with each circuit he made of the park, his run became more solitary. There was a point towards the end of each lap when he emerged from the wooded area onto the road that bordered the green. He hadn't reached it yet, but he knew it was coming, and he enjoyed the sense of anticipation. His legs ached after a couple of hours of extreme exertion and, much as he wanted to complete the circuit, he couldn't run any more, his limbs seizing up with cramp. He made a mental note to increase the amount of salt in his diet as he slowed to a walk, shuffling his way through the leaves as he made his way out of the wood. He was aware of footsteps behind him, but he thought nothing of them. The path had narrowed, so he paused to allow the other jogger to move past him, but no one came. The footsteps had stopped, and there was no one there, just a maze of trees fading into the darkness and the soft hum of the wind. He carried on down the path, heading for the exit. Like an echo, he heard footsteps again, the rhythm slightly off, mimicking his pace but not quite matching it. He quickened his steps, suddenly paranoid he was being followed. He was fit and relatively strong, but he had never been a big man, and he didn't fancy his chances if it came to a fight.

The footsteps became faster behind him, his pursuer gaining on him with each second. His legs were still burning, but a sudden fear pushed him to run, forgetting the cramp. He was on the road now, and he could see the way out ahead of him, some 400 metres in the distance. He drove his arms through the air, clawing through the darkness in an effort to move faster. He was sprinting, the pain a distant memory as he raced for the exit. He could hear the footsteps behind him, closer and closer. The sound became so loud, he couldn't tell whether it was in his head, but he was too scared to look over his shoulder; he had to keep going. He didn't stop until he was out of the park. Standing in the middle of the street, surrounded by cars, he struggled to catch his breath. It was only then that he glanced behind him to reassure himself he wasn't going mad, but there was no one there.

Chapter Thirty-One

Leah

Once Fiona was charged, Eli slipped to the forefront of my mind. I knew I had to see him, and there would never be a good time. The team was still checking for links between Fiona and Charles Walker. So far they had found nothing, and it felt like we were ticking a box to appease Kenny. It was possible Fiona had a vendetta against affluent white men, but the bodies told the wrong story: Alistair Cowan had been covered in Fiona's DNA; Charles Walker was found without a trace. I thought of Eli with his brilliant professional record and the gruesome scene he had left behind. He would have known how to hide his tracks, so why didn't he? Why leave himself so exposed?

I had been to countless prisons over the years, but the closer I got to the building, the less confident I felt. The woman beside me flinched as the prison gate slammed shut. Her jumpiness irritated me, and I tried to stay focused, slowing the flow of air through my nostrils to avoid the smell. I hadn't rehearsed a speech or planned an agenda. The moment I saw Eli, I wished I had.

It was easy to see that Eli Carson was once an extremely handsome man. Thirty years in prison hadn't entirely robbed him of his looks, but it hadn't done them any favours either. His skin was paler than it should have been, crinkling into deep folds around his eyes so he looked older than his fifty-nine years. His fair hair was thinning, and he was too slight for his frame, but his bone structure was immaculate, and there was an intelligence to his face. I had seen many inmates over the years. After a while, they all started to blur into one – individuals to be sure, but with the same look that came from knowing society didn't want them and they might turn out to be one of prison's inevitable casualties. Eli was different. He sat opposite me, in no hurry to start a conversation or put me at ease. I stared at him, searching for my face in his and was relieved when I couldn't see it. We looked nothing alike, but he seemed familiar, like someone I knew from the past but couldn't quite place. We stayed silent for a moment, getting used to each other. He spoke first.

'You've come a long way not to say anything.'

'Don't worry, I've got plenty to say,' I said.

'I'm not worried.' He sat back in his chair. 'One thing I have is time.'

We were surrounded by the great and the good of the criminal world – some innocent, all condemned. My eyes rested on a skinhead with a ring of devil's horns tattooed around his neck, the muscles so thick and gnarled they merged into each trapezius. He had to fill his days somehow, and there were worse ways a man could spend his time than in the gym. Endless hours locked up with nothing to do but reinvent yourself, get into more trouble or pump iron. A man like Eli Carson could go insane in here.

'Leah Hutch.' He said my name like it amused him. 'Interesting choice of name; Margaretta always was . . . creative.'

The implied familiarity hit a nerve. I thought of Margaretta lying in her bed, dressed in fruit print pyjamas, exhausting her mind counting bananas and pears. It would have been easier to take pills for her insomnia, but Margaretta didn't do pills.

'You miss her.' Eli's words were more of a statement than a question. He wasn't looking in my direction, but I knew he had been watching me. 'You're smaller than I thought,' he said.

'I wanted to be five foot ten, but the gene pool said no.'

He laughed at that. 'Funnier. And prettier. Your photographs don't do you justice.'

'Please don't.' Obsequiousness didn't suit him, and I'd never been a fan of flattery.

He closed his eyes then opened them after a few seconds, as if wiping an idea from his mind. There was a coldness to them that made him seem indefatigable, like he could watch the world without sleeping. I was the first to look away.

'So, you followed in my footsteps,' he said. 'Margaretta must have hated that.'

'She did, but not because of you. She hated detectives. She didn't trust the lack of uniform.'

'She didn't trust anyone.'

'She trusted you once.'

'Possibly.' His smile faded quickly as he tired of small talk. 'And how is work? Perhaps I can offer some fatherly advice.'

'I'm not going to discuss my job with you.' My voice was calm.

'Of course. I respect that. So . . .' He gestured expansively, and I noticed how long and thin his fingers were, just like mine. 'So, what exactly do you know, Leah?'

'You're my father. I had a mother. You killed her.' Our family history in three short sentences. 'I want to know what happened to her.'

'Are you asking me a question?'

'Well, I'm not reciting a poem . . .'

'A sense of humour.' His tone was mocking. 'I'm afraid I don't have an answer for you, so if that's your only question, you might as well go now.'

'I don't have to be here.'

'And yet you are.'

I wasn't sure when it had happened, but the balance of power had definitely shifted, and we both knew I wouldn't leave until my time was up. My gaze shifted to a young inmate in the far corner, flesh dripping with tattoos so no patch of skin remained unmarked. Eli stood out, his porcelain skin untouched by ink or sun – so white, compared to my dark skin, so unlike me, I was glad.

'This isn't going to work if you don't answer my questions, Eli.'

'Fine, but I'm not talking about what happened to my wife's body.'

'And I'm not talking about myself.'

'Fine.'

It was either a stalemate or a truce; I wasn't sure which.

'I'm glad you're here,' he said after a pause. 'I don't often get visitors.'

He looked me straight in the eye, and I realised that although he appeared frail, there was nothing weak about him. His eyes were sharp and steady, the challenge laid out before me; this wasn't an offer of friendship. A small part of me suspected he genuinely wanted company, separated from the intellectual stimulation he craved, but I could tell he was toying with me, bored of solitary games with no one to beat.

'Did you think of me when you killed my mother?'

'It had nothing to do with you, and it had nothing to do with Margaretta, but she was never herself after what happened.'

'And whose fault was that?'

He had ruined Margaretta for me, blunting her emotions so she could cope with the tragedy he had caused.

'You know nothing about it!'

His voice rose slightly, and I saw a sudden flash of anger which quickly disappeared.

'Who was he? My mother's alleged lover? Was she having an affair?'

Eli lowered his eyes, and I watched the memories play out across his face.

'Yes,' he said, and I believed him.

'Why? Had she done it before?'

Eli almost didn't answer. Then he gave a slight shake of the head.

I had thought about my parents when I was a child – tiny tableaus of domestic harmony, their features never defined. The fact that my mother had had an affair caused unexpected sadness. Then I remembered how she died.

'Did you hate her so much for cheating, you wiped her out without a trace?'

Eli rocked back in his chair so his toes lifted upwards and his heels gripped the floor.

'Is that what you think?'

There was a slight lilt to his voice.

'I *think* you were punishing her by making sure she was never found, but you needed to cover your tracks, so you sprinkled her lover at the scene. No one would suspect *Detective* Eli Carson of leaving such a mess. Clever and cruel at the same time.'

Eli looked at me, emotionless, his arms folded across his chest. His ribcage was narrow, despite the width of his shoulders. He seemed taller than I had originally thought.

'Why did you decide to confess?'

Eli's head snapped up. He observed me with an intensity that would have been frightening, if I frightened easily. 'What makes you say that?'

'You refused to comment, then you suddenly confessed to both murders. Why?'

'Does it matter?' His eyes didn't leave my face. I had given numerous suspects that same look, and it felt strange being on the receiving end.

'Yes. It does.'

'Why?'

'*You win. I'll talk. But you'll never know where she is.*' I let the words hang between us. His words to Margaretta, all those years ago.

'Where did you hear that?' His voice had lost all expression.

'Why did you change your mind and confess?'

He looked directly at me, pale eyes nothing like mine. 'How can you be forgiven, if you don't confess?'

'Eli,' I said. 'Don't play games.'

'I'm not. You grew up with Margaretta. You must have heard her say those words.'

'I want to know why you confessed.'

His lips curled up – a hint of a sneer hidden in a smile.

'Because Margaretta was right,' he said.

'About forgiveness?'

'No. I don't care about that.'

'Then what, Eli?' I inched forwards. 'What was Margaretta right about?'

He uncoiled his body, sitting straighter in his chair.

'It doesn't matter now. It's in the past. Let it stay there,' he said.

I walked away, wondering what Margaretta had been right about. She was gone now, guarding Eli's secrets in death as in life. I thought of Ron Kirwan and Amy Pritchard, falsely accused of my mother's murder. I doubted they had forgotten the nightmare they experienced, and I wondered what they remembered about the events of that night. I googled their names when I emerged from the Underground – Amy had died five years before from alcohol poisoning, and I found a moving tribute by their daughter, Debbie Kirwan. There was little trace of Ron from an initial search, and I needed to take my time to have any chance of finding him.

I stood on Albert Bridge and watched the water shift slowly beneath me, snaking its way around the city. It was my favourite bridge in London, pale pink and majestic, arched over the Thames. I thought about my mother and the affair which had led to her death. It was one of the few things I knew about her, and it saddened me that the one person who could tell me more was the man who had ended her life. Then I thought about Margaretta with her lifetime of secrets and the past she had tried to erase. There were so many memories which now had new meaning, so many questions I wished I could ask. I pulled out a photograph which had found a home in my wallet on the day she died. There was nothing special about it – I looked cross-eyed and Margaretta wasn't looking at the camera – but it was one of the few pictures I had of the two of us together with me as an adult. It was taken on my birthday a few years before, and Margaretta had her arm around me in a rare show of affection. I rummaged in my bag for the packet of cigarettes I kept for the times when there wasn't a skipping rope to hand. I stared at the solitary cigarette with its companion lighter nestling beside it. I didn't feel like smoking, so I just flicked the lighter on and off, watching the flame bounce silently in the breeze. Then, without thinking, I put the flame to the photograph and watched the image burn until there was nothing left. Afterwards, I felt better – unsentimental and strangely focused. Dwelling on my relationship with Margaretta wasn't going to solve anything. She was dead so there was no one to confront. I needed to find out what had happened to my mother. I wouldn't stop until I knew.

Chapter Thirty-Two

Leah

I fell asleep searching online for Ron Kirwan, and my body jerked at the sound of my phone. As the light fought its way through my lashes, it took me a moment to recognise Randle's voice.

'Did I wake you, ma'am?'

'No.' My eyes were still closed, and I was glad he couldn't see me. 'What's up, Randle?' I said.

'I think I've got something on Charles Walker. Vivi called. She wants to talk. I said I'd meet her at the station.'

'And where is she now?'

'On her way. I know it's early, but I thought you'd want to be here. She doesn't want an interview. Just to talk. I told her that was OK.' I could hear the uncertainty in his voice. 'Is that OK, ma'am?'

'It's going to have to be.' It didn't seem like I had a choice.

Vivi Walker was already there when I arrived. She was sitting at Randle's desk, a mug of tea balanced awkwardly in her hands. She was unsure whether to grip the handle or treat it like a teacup. She gave up and put it down. Her face was drawn, without make-up except for a dash of red lipstick, adding a sense of drama to her grief. Randle was perched on the desk, comfortingly close without invading her personal space. He had judged it well; Vivi looked at ease, guarded but ready to talk. When she looked up, I could feel her noticeably withdrawing into herself.

'It's OK, Vivi. I asked Inspector Hutch to come,' Randle said.

'Why?' She didn't hide her disdain.

'Tell the inspector what you told me.'

'I don't want people to know.' Her voice was firm, but she hesitated before she spoke, more vulnerable than the woman we had first met.

'We're not people, we're police. Different species altogether,' Randle said.

Vivi didn't strike me as a laugher, so I was surprised to see a slight smile.

'I don't want people to know.' Vivi repeated herself, but her tone had lost its edge.

I kept a respectful distance, observing every detail without appearing to look closely at all. It was a skill I had perfected as a child without much family, fascinated by other people and the quirks that gave them away. Vivi was staring at me with naked dislike.

'This was a mistake,' she said.

In seconds, she was across the room. I hung back, letting Randle go after her.

'Wait. Please . . .' He dropped his voice so I could just about make out what he said. 'There's nothing to be ashamed about. What he did doesn't reflect badly on *you*.'

'Easy for you to say. You're not the one he humiliated.' Vivi turned to me, raising her chin defiantly. 'Yes, Inspector, my husband was unfaithful. Gold star for you.'

I ignored the jibe, uninterested in feeling smug because another woman's marriage had been exposed as a sham.

'How do you know he was having an affair?'

Vivi stared at me in furious silence. 'I thought you would gloat, but you don't even believe me. I'm not sure which is worse.'

She wasn't the first woman to assume her husband was having an affair. Mark's wife had come to see me after he had tried to kiss me. She said she knew how he felt and wanted to know if I felt the same way. I felt disgusted and indignant, but I still didn't report him.

'What makes you think your husband was having an affair?' I asked again.

She looked at me, stubborn and unblinking – Vivi Walker wasn't going anywhere until she had shown I was a fool to doubt her, and that was fine by me. I took a seat opposite, gesturing to her to sit back down.

'You've said it now, so let's start from the beginning. It will come out anyway. Things usually do.'

She still hadn't taken off her coat, and she fiddled with the collar, flicking it up and down with her manicured forefinger. Randle knew better than to speak, so he stood nearby, reassuring her with his presence. She looked from me to him, then back to me. Then she smiled, as though agreeing to talk had been the easiest decision in the world.

'I'd like some more tea,' she said. 'With a cup and a saucer this time.'

I had to hand it to her, Vivi Walker was a pro.

'I never loved him, and he never loved me,' she began.

'Why did you marry him?' Randle asked. He seemed genuinely interested, and his idealism surprised me.

'Why does anyone marry anyone? It took me a while to realise I didn't love him; I think he always knew I didn't.' She took a sip of her tea, savouring the burning liquid. 'You know he had nothing when I met him? He had nothing and he came from nothing. Some would say he *was* nothing, but I believed in him. A council estate boy with a talent for making money. I gave him capital for his business; he gave me affection. It worked for a while until he didn't need me. Imagine . . .' Another sip. 'He married me for *my* money then had the audacity to cheat on *me*.'

Her hand gripped the Tiffany pendant around her neck, angry with a man she could never confront.

'He spent a long time talking on the phone. At different times of the day. The phone would ring, and he would go off into another room so I couldn't hear him.'

'And he never said who it was?'

'Never. One day I asked him. He said it was work, but it couldn't have been. His work mobile was on the table in the sitting room, and they always called on that phone. I didn't say anything, but he knew I wasn't stupid. After that he was more careful. He said he had started smoking again, and he would go out into the garden "for a cigarette" because he didn't want to ruin the furniture with the smell. He never used the veranda, and when he came back in, his clothes barely smelt. He always took that phone.'

She had lost some of her composure, nervously watching our reaction. 'I know what you're thinking,' she said. 'I thought I was being paranoid too. Believe me. But then I checked his phone. Lots of calls from one number. Late at night, during the day, all the time.'

'What did you do?' I asked. 'Did you confront him?'

It was the first time Vivi didn't hold eye contact with either of us. She looked down, playing with the arm of the chair like a distracted teenager being told off by their parents.

'No. I didn't. I didn't see the point. He would just lie anyway. No . . . I decided to ring her instead.'

I smiled inwardly, impressed by her resilience.

'Who was she?' Randle's tone was gentle, fearful of appearing too keen.

'I don't know.' Vivi shook her head sadly. 'I couldn't bring myself to make the call.'

'Where's the phone now?' I asked.

'I already told you. He always took it out with him, so if he didn't have it on him when you found him, I don't know where it is.'

I could see the disappointment on Randle's face. I sympathised because I had been drawn in by Vivi too.

'It's OK. We appreciate you coming in. We're doing everything we can to solve your husband's murder.'

I offered Vivi my hand, waiting as she let it dangle between us.

'I didn't come here for him. I came here for me. I want to know with whom my husband was having an affair.'

She sat rigid in her chair, determined to make her point, but it wasn't our job to play private investigator.

'I'm afraid we can't help you with that,' I said.

'I can help *you* though.' Vivi waited until she had my full attention. 'I took down her number.'

'Do you still have it?'

'Yes.' She opened her bag and pulled out a folded piece of paper.

I stared at it for a moment, wary of a false start. 'Thank you, Mrs Walker.'

'I don't want your thanks, Inspector,' she said. 'When you find out her name, I want you to promise you'll tell me.'

Chapter Thirty-Three

Leah

We traced the number Vivi Walker gave us to Clare and Gary Traynor in a council estate in South London. It had been a while since a case had taken me to Stockwell, but I was familiar with the mishmash of concrete tower blocks and large houses, and I knew my way around. The Traynors lived on the eleventh floor of a nondescript block of flats. The lift reeked of urine, but it was quicker than the stairs. We stopped on the seventh floor, shunted to the back as a man forced a sofa into the small space. He had short dreadlocks, greying at the roots, and his beard was dyed black.

'Going up?' Randle asked.

He ignored him, avoiding eye contact as the lift began to climb. We had reached the ninth floor when he turned to me, his eyes full of contempt.

'You're a disgrace, working with them.'

I sensed Randle tense beside me; I reached for his arm to stop him getting involved.

'You're a disgrace,' the man repeated, but I said nothing, holding his gaze until the doors eased open as we arrived on the eleventh floor.

'He had no right.' Randle was indignant.

'Nothing I haven't heard before,' I said.

'It doesn't make it OK.'

It didn't, but it wasn't his battle to fight, and it wasn't a fight I wanted to have.

Clare Traynor answered the door immediately, ushering us in before her neighbours had a chance to gawp. Her flat was small and unmodernised but impeccably kept. The décor looked straight out of a middle-of-the-road interiors magazine, but I liked that she had made the effort. There was a cloying smell of scented air freshener tinged with potpourri. Blue and white china knick-knacks and oversized candles were carefully arranged around the room.

'Do you like it?' She assumed we did and carried on. 'I moved things around when my husband finally left me – useless piece of trash.'

'Where is your husband now?' I asked.

'Ex.'

'Sorry. Ex.'

'Somewhere in Spain with the rest of the Brits – I know . . . he's never had an original thought in his head. What's happened now?'

'A man called Charles Walker was found dead in Battersea Park,' Randle said. 'In the months before his death, several calls were made to his mobile phone from a landline. Your landline.'

My eyes flicked down to her hands, often the biggest giveaway when a person was lying.

'I don't know a Charles Walker,' she said, her hands unmoving on her lap.

I watched as Randle handed her a printout of Charles Walker's call history, studying her face as she turned the pages blankly.

'Can you confirm that's your number?'

'Yes.'

'And you still maintain you didn't know Charles Walker?' I asked.

'I didn't make those calls. Look . . .' She ran a hand through her hair, dislodging the comb that kept it in place. 'I'm hardly ever here. I work shifts at Guy's Hospital. You can check the schedule.'

I glanced around the room, freed of all trace of Gary Traynor. 'When did your husband leave?'

'What? You think Gary made those calls?' She sighed, pitying our ignorance. 'It could have been anyone. He ran card games most days. Couldn't be arsed to get a proper job. Half the block were in and out of this flat. I've only just got rid of the stink of beer.'

'Do you have an address for Gary, Mrs Traynor?'

'It's Ms. And your guess is as good as mine.'

We took the stairs this time. Randle was unusually quiet as he bounded down the steps. I wondered if something had unsettled him, but he was grinning as he waited by the car.

'Why the rush? An extra twenty seconds won't solve the case.'

'Sorry, ma'am. Force of habit. I used to live in a block like this. We used to race each other to the bottom.'

My face must have betrayed my surprise. Randle squeezed his knuckles against his lips, suppressing a smile.

'I'm sorry,' I said.

'What? Did the accent throw you off, ma'am?'

'I guess it did.'

He dug his hands into his pockets, scuffing the road with the toe of his shoe.

'My mother got pregnant young. My dad left before I was born. My granddad kicked her out.'

He spoke in emotionless bullet points.

'I'm sorry,' I said again.

'Why? His loss. My mum's an incredible woman.'

Randle angled his body away from me, his face hidden in the dim light.

'We lived in a council flat like Clare Traynor's until my granddad took us back. He said he'd pay for my secondary education, if my mother "made better choices" in her life.'

He shifted his gaze to the maze of concrete towers, his face still turned away.

'Some of the kids in my school wound up in jail. My mum didn't want that for me. So, we moved back to Hampstead. Private school, Oxford, an accent that would make my granddad proud.'

I could hear a hint of melancholy, but he covered it with a laugh.

'And what – you miss the simplicity of your misspent youth?'

'No, ma'am. Being poor sucks. Too much energy trying to survive.' He turned to face me. 'What did you make of Clare Traynor?'

'I think she was telling the truth.' I was relieved to be back on professional ground.

'So do I.'

He leant against the car, holding a cigarette in the space between us. 'Do you mind?'

'No. You're alright.'

He curled his hand around the match to protect the flame as I watched the stream of residents going in and out of the tower.

'What now?' he asked, following my eyes.

'We ask Akosua to look into frequent visitors to the Traynor flat in the last six months, and we track down Gary Traynor. Clare's right. Anyone could have made those calls . . .'

We drove back in silence, manoeuvring down narrow streets to avoid the traffic. Several times, it felt like Randle was about to speak, but he turned the words into a cough or a yawn and said nothing. We arrived at the station; he hovered for a second as I moved towards the doors.

'Thanks.' It hadn't been a particularly hard day, but I felt I needed to say something.

'No problem, ma'am.'

He paused, hands in pockets, glancing up and down the street. It was getting dark, and a handful of officers were already making their way to the pub around the corner, picking up the pace at the thought of a pint with a whiskey chaser to wash away the taste of crime. Randle nodded in their direction.

'How come I never see you in there, ma'am?'

'I'm not a big drinker.'

'I hear pubs serve soft drinks these days.' His face had relaxed, and I sensed he was already transitioning out of work mode, anticipating his first beer. I could tell he wanted to talk, but I didn't go to work looking for friends.

'Good night, Randle. See you tomorrow.'

'Good night, ma'am.' A moment, then he turned and walked away.

The office had sunk into the gloom of evening. The daytime buzz had disappeared, and the sound of my mobile cut through the silence. Alistair Cowan was stable but still in a coma; his doctor promised to call me the moment there was any change. I thought about going home, but I felt wired and restless. There was little I could do about Alistair, and my mother's death was never far from my mind. I needed to find Ron Kirwan to ask him about that night.

I kicked off my shoes, rolling the balls of my feet against the hard floor. Ron didn't have a criminal record and, apart from his arrest thirty-one years ago, there was no sign of him on any database. He wasn't active on social media, and he didn't have the kind of job which broadcast his achievements online. Frustrated, I googled Amy Kirwan, née Pritchard, rereading the tribute her daughter had written when she died. Debbie Kirwan – I tried searching for her, chiding myself for not thinking about it before. Instagram, X, LinkedIn – she had them all. There was even a company address. The email I wrote bounced back, so I sent her direct messages. I didn't say much, but I felt totally exposed. Eli still held all the cards. Finding Ron Kirwan was my only hope.

Chapter Thirty-Four

Odie

Odie had expected to wait longer for news about Alistair, so she was surprised when she got the call from Phil – Alistair had woken from his coma that morning, but he was in a fragile state and Odie didn't have much time before the police descended to stake their claim. She chewed slowly as she listened, abandoning the stale croissant that served as her breakfast. She was almost out of the door when she remembered she had left her phone by the sink. She found it rattling against the ceramic, flashing as a notification came through. For a second, she thought it was Phil telling her not to come, then she clocked the email address, and she knew she had seen it before. She hesitated, suddenly nervous. She had asked the question 'why', but she wasn't sure she was ready for the answer. She took a breath and opened the message – a single attachment with a line of text underneath. She clicked on the file and waited. The reception was patchy, and an image of Fiona Garvey appeared slowly on her screen. It was the same photograph as the one in the pages she had been sent. Intrigued, she flicked to the line of text.

Because people deserve to know the truth . . .

There was nothing more, but it was enough – a connection between the first anonymous email and the envelope delivered to her house. Proof the same person had sent both. Her phone beeped and she held her breath, but it was only a text from Phil.

If you're late, I'm gone, but you still owe me. Don't mess me around. P.

She headed out, buoyed by the idea of a source. Someone was feeding her information. They wanted Fiona Garvey's story to be hers.

There was nothing good about hospitals – just the smell of sickness and the sense of her own mortality. Nothing positive had ever come out of a hospital for Odie, only the obvious or the downright depressing. If she thought someone was going to die, they usually did; if she knew they were sick, they normally got worse. Except for Richard. She had to keep reminding herself that if there were a God, he had spared Richard – and saved her from the guilt of being responsible for his death. Walking down the brightly lit corridor, the stench of disinfectant clogging her nostrils, she wondered whether Alistair Cowan would prove to be the exception or the rule. He had every reason to die, but she needed him to live.

She hovered by the entrance to the ward, masked by a vast bunch of flowers. She wondered whether they were too conspicuous, but they helped shield her face, and it was a thoughtful gesture from a well-wisher of sorts. Phil led her to Alistair's room, slipping away before she could ask how long she had. She hesitated, slowing her steps to dull the sound of her feet. Alistair was lying slightly propped up in his bed, his eyes closed. His battered face had regained some of its original structure, but the features which had once made him handsome were flattened and barely recognisable. His eyes flashed open as she approached.

'Who are you?' He struggled to sit up, but the effort was too much for him, and his upper body slid slowly down the plastic headboard, crumpling against his pillow.

'My name is Odie Reid. I'm a journalist. I'm sorry for what happened to you and I'm trying to find out the truth. The police have arrested a woman and I want to make sure they've got the right person.'

She spoke fast, determined to make her case before she was ejected from the room.

Alistair closed his eyes again. She wasn't sure he had heard her, so she tried again.

'Mr Cowan...'

'I heard you, Ms Reid. It just hurts to keep them open. It's better like this. I hope you don't think I'm being rude.' Even in pain, his manners were impeccable.

Intrigued, Odie sat down, pulling her chair closer to the bed. She had formed an impression of him in her mind, based on a CV of historical facts. Meeting him threw up new questions, and she needed to know how Fiona Garvey fitted into his story.

'What happened that night?' Odie's voice was soft but insistent.

Alistair turned his head away, physical pain overtaken by horrific memories.

'What woman?' he asked in a half whisper.

'What?' For a second, she wasn't sure what he was talking about. It was as if he was conducting the conversation at a completely different pace.

'What woman did they arrest?' he asked, pushing for an answer.

'Fiona Garvey. She works with you.'

'I know who she is,' he said flatly. She could tell he was tiring, but he continued to speak, his voice quieter. 'Why?'

'She turned herself in at the police station. She was covered in blood.'

'What did she say?' He sounded distressed.

'I don't know. As far as I know, she can't remember what happened. Her mother is convinced she didn't do it.'

'What does *she* say?'

'Not much, but it's not looking good for her. Who did this to you, Alistair? Was it Fiona?'

'No.' He didn't hesitate.

'Then who?'

'I don't know.'

'Then how do you know she didn't do this?'

He opened his eyes and reached for Odie's hand, surprising her with the strength of his grip. 'You have to get her out. What happened wasn't her fault.'

'What happened?' she asked again.

Alistair didn't reply, but his eyes became manic as his fingers tightened around her wrist. The door opened, calling time on their brief conversation. Odie's head snapped round abruptly. It was too soon; she wasn't ready to leave, but it wasn't her decision to make.

'The police are here. You have to go.' Phil loomed nervously in the doorway.

'Give me a second . . .'

'I could lose my job, Odie. You have to leave. Now.'

Odie looked at the injured man staring back at her from the bed. She opened her mouth to say something, but Alistair got there first.

'Help her. Please,' he pleaded. 'You have to help her.' Then he closed his eyes.

'Come on, Odie.' Phil's voice was insistent.

Making no promises, she squeezed Alistair's hand and left.

Chapter Thirty-Five

Leah

I heard the commotion before we reached the corridor – the thud of a body crashing to the ground, then a sudden cry of agony drowned out by an alarm. Instinctively I broke into a run, my leather soles sliding along the hard white floor. I pushed Alistair's door open, the momentum from my body slamming it against the wall. I scanned the room, registering the empty bed with its plain headboard. The top sheet had snaked its way onto the floor, one corner twisted around a swollen white ankle. Alistair was crouched low, trying to crawl towards the door, slowed down by pain and the weight of the material pulling him back towards the bed. It was a pathetic sight: a grown man wrapped in a bed sheet, utterly defeated before he had even begun his escape. Randle moved to help him, but he was pushed aside by the team of nurses armed with syringes, swooping in with military efficiency. Voices piled on top of voices – a jumble of words as Alistair fought to get out. His arms flailed unsteadily as the nurses effortlessly subdued him.

'I need to go . . . to work. I need to . . .' I never got to hear what else he needed; he was cut off mid-sentence as the sedative kicked in.

*

'He's not dying any time soon.' It was the first thing Randle said as we reached the escalator.

'What makes you say that?'

'He can't walk, but he tried to discharge himself. There's something keeping him alive.'

I hadn't been a hundred per cent sure of Alistair's words at the time, but Randle had heard them too. My mind flicked back to that day at Rossan Brown Meyer, with its interchangeable employees with their pinstriped armour and preppy ruthlessness. One person had stood out.

'What was the name of that secretary at Alistair's firm?'

Outside, the air was cool and heavy as the revolving doors spat us out.

'Mayanna Duncan.' Randle didn't hesitate. 'Do you want me to get in touch?'

He looked at me expectantly as the wind pushed his hair off his face.

'Get her to check Alistair's calendar. We need to know why he was so desperate to get back.'

Chapter Thirty-Six

Odie

Odie sat in her car watching the mass of children escape from the school across the road. She tried to think back to a moment when she had seen her life stretch before her, promising possibilities for the future, but every memory was coloured by the present, and she couldn't remember a time when she had felt entirely hopeful. She hadn't heard from Richard since the night with Daniel. She had expected him to call, but he hadn't, and she was surprised by the strength of her disappointment. He usually called to apologise for things which weren't his fault, but she suspected the other night had dredged up memories he preferred to keep buried, memories she wanted to bury too. She checked her phone again. Still no message. She put Richard out of her mind and focused on Fiona Garvey and work.

Something told her there was a link between the attacks on Alistair Cowan and the man who had now been identified as Charles Walker — the similarities between the assaults, the demographic of the victims. The same person who killed Charles Walker could have tried to kill Alistair Cowan. She was increasingly sure they were connected, but she couldn't get her head around unassuming Fiona Garvey — dangerous predator, or innocent woman who had witnessed a horrific crime? Now Fiona had been charged, there were limits to what Odie could say about her case, but she was determined to pursue the story. If she found evidence that proved Fiona was innocent and Hutch was wrong, Hutch would have to drop the charges. First, she needed to get Mary Garvey on side.

She scanned the crowd for a small adult amidst the sea of uniforms. Mary Garvey was one of the last teachers to leave, her long woollen coat clinging to her delicate frame. Odie could just about make out the petite figure forging a path through the adolescent bodies, her tidy plait swinging behind her. Mary was almost at the bus stop when Odie caught up.

'Hanging around school gates. People have got in trouble for less.'

Although there was no hint of friendliness in her voice, Odie could tell Mary Garvey didn't have the energy to fight. Her neck had slumped deep between her shoulders, and her eyes were duller than the last time they had met. A more sensitive person would have let Mary be, but after years of invading people's privacy, Odie tried not to let other people's feelings get in the way of her job.

'If you answered my calls, I wouldn't have to come here. Trust me, this is the last place I want to be. I hated school.'

'Let me guess. Attitude problem?'

'Something like that.'

'Too smart for your teachers? All that brain power fizzing over into bad behaviour and a need for destruction?'

'ADHD hadn't been invented back then. There were no excuses, only suspension.'

'What do you want, Odie? Haven't you done enough?'

'I think I can help you.'

'And why would you want to do that?'

'Because I want to help me too.'

A glimmer of life appeared in Mary's eyes. Odie wouldn't call it hope, but Fiona's mother had thawed.

'Five minutes,' Mary said.

It was all Odie needed for now.

They walked for a couple of minutes before Mary stopped and perched on the curb. Odie was taken aback, but she hid it as best she could.

'There's a café over the road.'

'You said five minutes. No point getting comfortable.'

Odie lowered herself down onto the pavement, looking up at the neighbourhood around them with its characterless buildings and soulless suburban streets. Mary followed her gaze, sensing her disapproval.

'I chose here because it was safe. I was fed up having things thrown at me on the way to school. You bring your kid up in this city and that's all you ever think of: is she safe? Can I protect her? And now, thanks to you, people think my daughter is someone they have to be protected from. My daughter . . .' The emotion rose in her voice.

'I don't think she did it.'

'What difference does that make? They've charged her and our lawyer says you're not allowed to report on the details of the case.'

'Not now, but it's not about now. I know you don't want to think about this but, whether she's convicted or acquitted, a journalist on your side can make all the difference.'

'I don't want to think about her being convicted. If you can't help now, you're no use to me.'

'Remember Rebecca Stanton? The woman wrongfully accused of killing her baby?'

Mary nodded wearily. 'What's she got to do with me?'

'I helped her. I know I can help you.'

'How?'

Odie thought about Rebecca Stanton, vilified even though she was found not guilty. She had seemed irredeemable, but the power of Odie's words had turned her fate around. Mary Garvey should be thanking her for her help. Odie kept her voice even.

'Your daughter turned up at a police station covered in blood. If Alistair Cowan dies, she'll be charged with murder. She'll be facing a very long jail sentence. She's scared and confused, and she needs someone to think about all the options.'

'And let me guess, that someone is you?'

'No. It's you.' Odie took a moment to let her words register. 'I'm just here to help you find out the truth.'

'And that's *your* job, is it? Not the police? Not the lawyers?'

'Mary. Please. As far as the police are concerned, Fiona is guilty. All they want now is a conviction. They aren't interested in Fiona's innocence.'

'And you are?' Mary's stare was unflinching.

'I'm interested in the truth, and I don't think she did it. But she was there, and she knows what happened.'

Mary gave a hollow laugh, her patience evaporating with each exhalation. She stood up, smoothing the front of her trousers. 'Well, that must be five minutes.'

'I think your daughter is worth more than that.'

'Don't you dare tell me what my daughter is worth.'

'Mary, please . . .'

'I have nothing more to say to you.'

Mary had already begun to walk, and Odie felt the story slipping away once again.

'She won't survive in prison. *You* know that, and *I* know that.'

Odie waited for the full impact of her words to sink in. She could see Mary's pace slow, her shoulders slouched in defeat.

'Look, I'm not allowed to report on the case now anyway, so I have nothing to gain in the short-term. What have you got to lose? I could help you find something which could help Fiona. There's a chance we could even get the charges dropped. If I can't make a difference, you're in no worse a position than you are now. You don't have to be powerless in all this.'

She let her words hang between them. When Mary didn't react, she played the only trump card she had.

'I saw Alistair Cowan.'

Mary stopped walking, her back rigid with expectation.

'He said Fiona didn't do it.'

Odie waited for a response. Mary didn't turn around when she spoke.

'What do you want, Odie?'

It was simple.

'I want to speak to Fiona.'

Chapter Thirty-Seven

Jake Munro wasn't in the mood to run. He told his wife it was because of the rain, but he had never allowed the weather to bother him before. He tried to forget the incident in the park, but he couldn't. There had been no one behind him, but he couldn't shake the thought that someone had been following him. He felt foolish – foolish for being paranoid and foolish for feeling scared. They weren't feelings he was used to, and they wouldn't go away.

He usually enjoyed the fight to get to work, jostling with other city workers for the straightest path through the crowd. Today it irritated him, and the lack of space made him claustrophobic and bad-tempered. He couldn't bear it. Deciding to take another route, he turned down a long side alley, accepting that the detour would inevitably make him late. There were a couple of people ahead of him, but they disappeared around the corner as he moved forwards. Soon it was just him.

He was alone for about thirty seconds, then, as he neared the turning, he sensed a presence behind him. His headphones prevented him from hearing anything beyond the sound of music pounding in his ears. He stopped and waited, but no one overtook him. He glanced back, but there was no one there. Annoyed that he had let his nerves get the better of him, he continued down the alley. He felt the presence again, bearing down on him from behind. This time he didn't turn around. He strode down the alley, looking straight ahead, moving as fast as he could without running. He didn't stop until he arrived at his office, and it was only when he took off his headphones that he heard his heart pounding uncontrollably.

Chapter Thirty-Eight

Odie

Odie insisted on meeting at Mary's house first. She had read about Fiona, but she wanted to know the woman Fiona once was. Few people were made for prison – some grew accustomed to it, most learned to survive. Everything Odie had discovered about Fiona put her in another category, and that category never recovered.

'Why are you doing this?'

Mary had asked the question countless times, and Odie was getting tired of reassuring her.

'I told you,' Odie said, 'I want to put things right.'

'And the real reason?' There was no hostility in Mary's voice. 'You're in my home; I'm not going to throw you out now.'

Odie shrugged. 'It's a good story *and* I want to put things right.'

'How noble of you,' Mary responded bitterly. 'I'll show you her old room.'

It was the perfect haven for a young girl, without the usual pink clichés: photo collages of Fiona with Mary; black and white Athena posters of beautiful people posing in front of landmarks; shelves full of books Odie recognised from Daniel's childhood; charcoal sketches of animals Blu-Tacked to the wall; cuddly toys stored lovingly in a corner. A comforting refuge for a child with few friends and an adoring mother; a scene of innocence frozen in time.

'What happened to my little girl?' Mary's voice was hollow and searching.

Odie wondered the same thing.

And so it began, the endless waiting – waiting for the bus to take them to the prison, waiting for the guard to escort them to the anteroom, waiting to be searched, waiting for the prisoners to be called into the visits hall, waiting to see Fiona. Mary barely said a word, but her eyes never stopped moving. They scanned everything, looked everywhere, as she familiarised herself with the world her daughter now inhabited. She didn't flinch when the sniffer dog was paraded in front of them, scurrying back and forth sucking air in and out in short, sharp bursts. Her mind was elsewhere, trapped in its own hell but ready to endure it for Fiona's sake.

Odie forgot about Mary for a second, methodically removing her personal effects for the security scan: shoes, belt, phone, coins, laid out in a shallow tray. It was like they were going on holiday, except they weren't. The full search on the other side destroyed the illusion that there was anything pleasant about the world they were entering. It was designed to make you feel guilty, to make you think twice before breaking the law. Looking over her shoulder, Odie watched Mary suffering the intrusion, the tough façade starting to crack as she was prodded and patted like an inanimate object. It was then that she started to feel bad, because she knew the worst part was yet to come. Seeing your daughter as a prisoner for the first time could crush a person. Nothing could prepare you for that, but Odie should at least have tried.

The room was much like the others Odie had seen in the past:

thirty or so metal tables arranged in formation, each with four matching chairs screwed into the shabby linoleum floor. In one corner of the room was a pile of toys, a depressing reminder of all the children growing up without mothers. She looked away as a brother and sister fought over a plastic car. Then the doors opened and in they came, a line of inmates, each face telling a different story. That's when the waiting really began, sitting on the cold, hard chairs, eyes searching for Fiona. The minutes stretched out as the room filled with chatter, and still Fiona didn't come. They waited and waited, and when Odie saw the guard heading towards them, she knew something was very wrong.

Chapter Thirty-Nine

Odie

Fiona had bled for almost twenty minutes before they found her. She was still alive, but only just. Her note was simple and desperate, written in smudged pencil on a sheet of grubby toilet paper.

'It wasn't me. I can't do this any more. Sorry.'

Mary sat staring at the words, gripping the tissue so tightly it almost ripped. Odie gently took it from her, carefully laying it on the table in front of them. *It wasn't me. I can't do this any more. Sorry.* Mary started to cry – ugly, uncontrollable tears. Odie felt powerless watching her.

'She's still alive.' Odie tried to comfort her.

'But for how long? She won't survive much longer in there. You said it yourself.'

She had. It had been rhetoric then, emotive language to get what she wanted; now she feared it was true. It was one of the few times Odie wished she had been wrong. She couldn't look at Mary, so she took her home without making eye contact once. Fiona Garvey wasn't built for prison and she didn't deserve to be there, but Odie had needed a story so badly, it hadn't mattered at whose expense. She felt a deep sense of shame and guilt. In her job, collateral damage was often the price of success, and she had never minded who paid it. People had got hurt in the past, but no one had ever died except one, and he had deserved everything he got. Fiona was different, even though Odie didn't know why.

Chapter Forty

Leah

It was practically the end of the day, and I had forgotten to eat. I searched for an apple in my bag and ate slowly, jotting notes in a pad. Gary Traynor had run a card game from late afternoon into the night most days. Sometimes he ran several, and there was a long list of visitors who frequented the flat. So far no one had admitted to making the calls to Charles Walker, and we were running out of names. I had a sudden desire to skip to work off my frustration. I clenched and unclenched my fists, waiting for the urge to wear off.

'Ma'am?'

I glanced up to see Randle hovering in my doorway. I pulled my hands down into my lap.

'Mayanna Duncan came back on Alistair Cowan. She couldn't get full access to his calendar, but she did some digging.'

'And?' I felt my fingers unfurl as I refocused my mind.

'There was supposed to be a kick-off dinner with a big client the day we went to see him in hospital. Alistair was a known workaholic, and he'd worked on the deal for months.'

'Didn't want to miss his moment of glory?'

'Would have crushed him. According to Mayanna, the man lived for the job.'

My phone vibrated with an incoming text. I felt my face twist into a scowl.

I'm outside.

No name, but she knew I would go.

Odie was waiting across the road. She fiddled with her ring as she watched the entrance to the station, unremarkable compared to the buildings on either side. I couldn't see her eyes, but I could feel them lock on me as I emerged. Her hair was wilder than usual, and she hammered the pavement with the heel of her foot.

'You need to get Fiona Garvey out of there,' she said. 'She tried to kill herself today, and if you keep her in there, she may not survive.'

The thought of anyone being so desperate pained me, but it didn't change the facts.

'I'm sorry to hear that, but the courts will decide when and if Fiona gets out. You know that, Odie.'

'She tried to kill herself.' Odie repeated the phrase as if it equated to Fiona's innocence.

'That's sad and I wouldn't wish that on anybody, but trying to take her own life doesn't prove anything. It's not up to you to decide who's innocent and who's guilty.'

'What's that supposed to mean?' There was a flash of aggression in her eyes. 'It doesn't take a genius to know that Fiona Garvey didn't attack Alistair Cowan.'

'And yet, that was the first conclusion you came to yourself.'

'This isn't about being right or wrong. This is about a woman's life.'

I almost laughed, but I could see the irony was totally lost on her – Odie Reid, who had once falsified sources to secure a story, standing outside my police station, lecturing me on morality. We had worked on an investigation into the abuse of power when I was a journalist – a prominent man whose politics Odie despised. There had been rumours but never anything concrete, and when our main source lost her nerve, Odie had invented others to take her place. Now her eyes bulged with conviction; I recognised the same obsessive energy that had compromised her morals all those years before.

'Fiona's been set up. We need to do something,' she said.

'No. *We* don't, Odie. I don't take orders from you any more.'

'Stop being so stubborn, Hutch, and listen to me! I have sources . . .'

She grabbed my elbow too hard, and her fingers pinched against the bone.

'Forgive me if I'm sceptical about your sources, Odie,' I said.

Her hand fell away as if she had been stung. The indignation and desperation had gone, and she just looked angry and hurt.

'We had enough to charge Fiona with attempted murder, and if Alistair Cowan dies, things could get worse.'

I walked away without waiting for a response.

Chapter Forty-One

Jake had arranged to run with a friend but, before he even read the text, he knew he had been stood up. He thought about not going, but he felt he was being stupid. He had run alone for years, and he wasn't going to stop now because of some middle-aged onset of paranoia. He blamed work; he had been under a lot of pressure recently, and it wasn't unheard of for stress to manifest itself in peculiar ways. Still, as he entered Richmond Park and started to stretch his body, he had to make a concerted effort to suppress his fear.

He set off down the track, faster than usual, his defiance translated into nervous energy. He ramped up the volume on his iPhone, determined to drown out everything around him. The fewer distractions, the better. It wasn't quite 8 p.m. and there weren't many joggers around. His confidence grew after the first lap and, as he approached the wooded area at the end of his second circuit, he felt comfortable and relaxed, settling into an even rhythm. Stumbling on a stray branch hidden under the leaves, he momentarily lost his balance, twisting his wrist as he put out his arm to steady himself. His phone fell and as the music cut out, he heard the sound of the park, soft yet sharp, staking its claim on the city. He didn't hear the footsteps at first, then when he did, he ignored them, convincing himself he was imagining things. He put his headphones back on but, as the ambient noise faded into the background, he was aware of another presence slowly moving into his space. He turned around, unsurprised to find no one behind him. He cried out in frustration, looking around him for his unseen pursuer.

'Who are you? Why are you doing this?'

Nothing.

His instincts told him to run, but he couldn't bear the constant feeling of discomfort suffocating him when he was alone. He hated cowardice, and if there was someone there, they needed to know he wouldn't put up with this any longer.

'Who are you?'

Still nothing.

Jake was turning in circles now, throwing punches frantically in the dark. 'What kind of person does this? If you're trying to scare me, it's not working. You can't scare me. I'm not—'

The word caught in his throat as he felt the first strike to the head. He tried to spin round, to catch a glimpse of his assailant, but as he attempted to pivot, he was stunned by another blow. The force sent him flying backwards and, as he started to lose consciousness, he wondered whether his head was still attached to his body. Everything ceased to make sense as his face caved in with the third blow, shuddering at the impact. Then he felt the sharp metal driving into his chest, and he knew it was all over.

Chapter Forty-Two

Leah

I lay in bed, my back flat against the mattress. Odie had got to me like she always did, pushing her way into my thoughts so they kept me up during the night. I wondered whether I should have listened to what she had to say, but I had been there before as a junior reporter, trusting her blindly like a fool. I would never apologise for exposing her – in an industry where integrity should be important, Odie had lied even to me.

My phone vibrated beneath my pillow. I reached under, fumbling until I felt the glass screen. I half expected it to be Odie, but it wasn't her number. Ron and Amy Kirwan's daughter had finally got in touch.

Got your message and have passed it on. None of my business, but if I were you, I'd steer well clear. That night destroyed any chance my parents had of happiness. Whatever you want to know, is it really worth it? Debbie Kirwan

Her warning caught me off guard. I had never stopped to consider the effect the truth might have on me, and I could feel the anxiety starting to rise up inside.

It was raining heavily, and it wasn't yet light. I couldn't face going outside to skip, so I opted for a simple bodyweight circuit, hammering through each exercise in an effort to focus my brain.

I pushed down into the floor, letting the sweat hang off the tip of my nose as I kept going relentlessly. Up then down. Up then down. It took 120 press-ups before I decided I wanted to hear from Ron Kirwan, whatever the consequences. Exhausted and reinvigorated, I pulled myself up off the floor. I was breathing hard, and I almost didn't hear my phone. I guessed there was another body before Randle said a word.

It was the third attack on a white male in a public park in a matter of days: Jake Munro, half hidden in the foliage, undignified in death, just as Charles Walker had been. He wore a Lycra jogging kit in tasteful shades of blue – muscled legs proof that running was a long-standing habit, not a snap reaction to the creep of middle age. His face was a grotesque mess of pounded flesh just like Charles Walker's, but unlike Charles, his body had been sliced and punctured repeatedly with some sort of knife. Bludgeoned and stabbed by his merciless attacker, Jake Munro never stood a chance.

Chapter Forty-Three

Leah

Randle was behind his computer as I approached, the screen light so low, it was hard to tell if he was looking at anything at all. His morning smoothie sat untouched on his desk beside him, and he barely glanced at Akosua as she spoke. His fingertips rested heavily against his temples. He closed his eyes, willing the conversation to end. These were the kind of cases which got under your skin, burnt images in your brain and kept you questioning right until the judge passed sentence, sometimes beyond. Randle and Akosua didn't have enough flying hours not to care. The cynicism and blood-weariness hadn't kicked in, and they were too new to the job to realise that caring was a choice, not a reflex. Every time they saw a corpse, they still saw a person who had once lived and hoped. At some point they needed to choose not to see this, if they wanted to keep sane.

Akosua was speaking slowly, patronising Randle with each word. She was less eager to please when she thought I wasn't watching, and I preferred this more confident version I never got to see.

'Alistair Cowan is a separate case. We're wasting our time trying to link him to Charles Walker.'

'We can't rule out a link to Charles Walker. We can't rule anything out,' Randle said.

Akosua half opened her mouth to respond, but she stopped when she saw me. I pulled the focus back to our newest corpse.

'Where are we with Jake Munro?'

Randle swivelled to face me, grateful for an excuse to change the subject. 'Seems he was well liked, ma'am.'

'Most victims have friends. Doesn't mean they don't have enemies,' I said.

'Sure. But this guy actually had *friends*. People who *liked* him. People who care he's dead.'

'He was a popular guy,' Akosua chipped in, refusing to be outdone. 'We managed to speak to colleagues from one company earlier this morning. They were really cut up. They've closed the office out of respect.'

'One company?'

'He owned three,' Akosua clarified. 'Looks like he was building a stationery empire. Last couple of years have been good to him. He was going through a consolidation process and there was a wave of redundancies.'

I took a swig from a bottle of water, swilling the liquid around in my mouth.

'Disgruntled employees?'

Akosua reached for a strand of stray hair, pushing it tight against her bun.

'Hard to know till we do some probing, ma'am. I'm getting a list of names to follow up.'

'OK. Carry on with that. There might be something there.'

She glanced at Randle before she left, but he chose not to see. With Akosua gone, his computer screen suddenly became less interesting.

'Anything I need to know about?'
'No, ma'am.'
'Good. Keep it that way.'
They didn't need to be friends. None of us did.
'Nothing from the pathologist?' I asked.
'She said she's looking forward to seeing you.'
Georgina Harrison would have plenty to say.

Chapter Forty-Four

Odie

Odie still hadn't heard from Richard, and it unnerved her. She couldn't remember the last time *she* had called *him*, and she wasn't sure she liked the role reversal. He answered after two rings.

'Is everything OK?'

'Yes. Why wouldn't it be?' Odie said, irritated by the question. 'How's Daniel?'

'Daniel's fine.'

Richard was being unusually guarded. He normally couldn't help himself when it came to their son, filling her in on every inch of Daniel's life, from milestones to minutiae. She waited for the onslaught of trivia, but the line went silent, forcing her to speak.

'I just wondered if he was OK after last time,' she said.

'He's fine,' Richard repeated. 'Old wounds,' he added after a second.

He said it like it was meant to reassure her, but it did precisely the opposite. Some old wounds never heal, and Odie suspected that now the scab was off, Daniel would keep reliving the moment he found Richard half-dead, blaming her for what happened, again.

She had tried not to imagine the details of Richard's attempted suicide. Richard never brought it up, so it allowed her the illusion that it was right to forget. Fiona's attempt changed things. Odie started to see what Daniel had seen, and she felt terrible. Terrible because he would never forget what he had witnessed and terrible because it had taken the pain of a complete stranger for her to understand the pain of her own son.

'He's not fine, is he?'

She sensed Richard sigh, even though he barely made a sound.

'No. But he will be,' he said. 'It was a long time ago. Every now and again, something like this happens. It will pass. Usually takes a few days.'

'Should I give him a call?'

'To say what?' Richard asked, surprised.

'I don't know. To check he's OK.'

'Probably best if you just leave him be for a little bit.'

'It'll just fester. I want to clear the air.'

'Odie, I know you mean well, but I'm not sure it will help . . .'

Richard started to say something else, but she wasn't listening.

'Tell him I'll pass by his office after work. Around 6.30. Tell him to wait for me. Please, Richard. Just tell him.'

She hung up before he could protest any further.

Odie's phone rang almost immediately. She didn't recognise the number and for a moment, she thought it was her mystery informant calling with another clue. She held her breath, but it was Phil calling from the hospital.

'Oh.'

'Good to speak to you too.'

'You know I can't do small talk,' she said.

'Look, I don't have time for this. Alistair Cowan can speak.'

'And . . . ?'

'He asked me about you. He says he wants to see you.'

'Have the police been in again?'

'I don't think so. The doctors are being cautious after last time. He's not doing so well. Do you want to see him or not?'

'Of course. You know I do.' She had every intention of getting into that room, but she wasn't going to beg.

'Fine. I can sneak you in. Today. 5.30. Same arrangement as before.' Phil hung up.

Odie had never been generous with money but seeing Alistair was worth another 200 pounds. She visualised a map of Central London, superimposing the quickest route from A to B. She could be at Alistair's side by 5.30, with ample time to talk and still get to Daniel by 6.30. Alistair had been so weak the last time she had seen him, she doubted he would be able to sustain more than a five-minute conversation. She would be fine.

Chapter Forty-Five

Leah

Georgina Harrison was an exceptional forensic pathologist with bizarre taste in footwear. She wore snow boots all year round, loosening the laces in summer when her feet expanded in the heat. She insisted the boots were the only answer to poor circulation, but I had never seen her wear a jumper, and she never looked cold. She didn't have a reputation for being friendly, but I had worked alongside her as a junior officer, and that earned me a smile. She pulled out the file on Jake Munro.

'Sharp blow to the head from behind, leading to severe disorientation. Then another two from the front. Then a knife into the gut several times.' Despite the chill, her arms were bare.

'What killed him? The blows to the head or the knife?' I asked.

'Neither.'

Harrison pulled up a set of images on her computer. 'They made sure he would die, but they didn't kill him. These did.' She pointed out various wounds on his body, one indistinguishable limb blending into another.

'So, he was beaten to death like the others?' Randle asked.

'Which others?' Harrison was always precise.

'Alistair Cowan, Charles Walker.'

'Alistair Cowan isn't dead.' It was an important detail, and Harrison was a stickler for facts.

'No. But he was meant to be.'

I had to give it to Randle for holding his ground with Georgina Harrison; better men had tried, and better men had failed.

'Is there a connection?' he asked.

'Do you want there to be one?'

Harrison fixed him with her stare, intimidating but strangely unaggressive. I knew her well enough to recognise her peculiar brand of flirting. It was no secret she found Randle attractive; she had said as much in public and, recently single and available, she would be wondering why he hadn't made a move. Randle didn't have a reputation for being shy, and Harrison wasn't used to waiting for long. She let the question hang for a moment, and when he didn't answer, she continued, professional once more.

'If we take out the stabbing in the case of Jake Munro, there are definite similarities between the three attacks. Initial blow to the back of the head. Excessive violence. More force than required to kill either Charles Walker or Jake Munro. Brutal and sadistic. Personal, even.'

'Uncontrollable acts of rage.' I studied the photographs as a narrative started to form. Someone had snapped and let the monster within take control.

'It would seem that way. Look here . . .' Harrison zoomed in on an image. I had to look closely to recognise a face. 'There were twenty-seven blows to the head and arms, fracturing every bone in the face and shattering the skull. There is bruising consistent with maybe twelve to sixteen strikes to his upper body, and my guess is that Jake Munro was dead after about blow ten. He would have been unconscious after the first few strikes, and by ten or eleven, he would have been a corpse . . .'

'. . . but his assailant didn't stop.' I could see where she was going with this.

'Exactly. Uncontrolled. Excessive. A sustained attack, probably long after the victim was already dead. We're either looking at a sadist or someone driven by extreme hate. Or both.'

'And the others?' Randle was still looking for connections.

'Well, that's where it gets interesting.' Harrison pulled out two files. Charles's was thicker, but we had had his body for longer. 'You're looking for a connection between the three attacks. Correct?'

'We've already charged a suspect for Alistair Cowan's attack, and she was locked up when Jake Munro was killed,' I said.

Harrison nodded, understanding. She searched for a printout of a photograph, holding it up to the light.

'The attack on Alistair Cowan is the most haphazard. It's frenzied but somehow less fierce than the other two.'

'Is that why he survived?'

'Probably. The attack on Charles Walker is more forceful – brutal, even – and by the time we get to Jake Munro, there's a knife. Differences in style, or an evolution of the same attacker . . .'

'Increased confidence?' Randle was thinking aloud.

'Or increased confidence,' Harrison repeated, her eyes trained on his. 'You know, if you want to put words in my mouth, all you have to do is buy me dinner. I'm easily persuadable.' She laughed throatily, but Randle didn't react.

'What about the knife?'

Harrison smiled. 'I thought you'd never ask.'

Harrison had seen so many dead bodies, it was a wonder she still found joy in her work. I admired her ability to see the creative in the gruesome.

'Show or tell?'

It was obvious which answer Harrison wanted; pictures were all very well, but flesh told the real story.

'Show.' It didn't hurt to play along.

We changed into protective clothing and followed Harrison down a long, windowless corridor to the room at the back. I had been there before, but I never got used to the cold, clinical arrangement with stainless steel autopsy tables in a line down the centre and the refrigerated cabinets built into the surrounding walls. There was something schizophrenic about the meticulous cleanliness we were witnessing now and the butcher's den it became when Harrison and her team hacked into the dead.

Just under six foot in life, Jake looked smaller and more vulnerable laid out on a table. Harrison traced the wounds in the space above his body as she spoke. Her voice was different now. Gone was the playfulness of before, replaced by a more clinical tone to match our new environment. We were inside her kingdom and, like any good leader, she took the job of ruling seriously.

'Early blows to the head, then the knife, then repeated frenzied stabs, compounded by multiple strikes to the body with a blunt instrument.' She took a second to point out the impact on the skin. 'Let's discount the first attack on Alistair Cowan for now. Beyond being brutal, it doesn't fit the pattern, but if we look at the other two, the similarities are interesting. With the exception of the knife wounds, the injuries Charles and Jake sustained are very similar.

Charles Walker suffered more blows, and the force of impact was stronger.'

'It would have to be. Unless you know where to hit,' I said. 'It can take longer to kill someone without a knife.'

'Exactly,' Harrison continued. 'But the damage to the body indicates the same type of blunt instrument was used in a similar way in both attacks. You can play it either way: argue that the knife differentiates the attacks on Charles Walker and Jake Munro enough to conclude there were two different attackers, or . . .'

'Argue a progression in the same killer. Killing Charles Walker with brute force and anger was hard work, so when it came to Jake, they used the knife to speed things up.' Randle jumped in, finishing her thought.

Harrison smiled, satisfied.

'See, Ben. We *are* good together.' Lesson over; back to flirting.

I didn't say anything for a while, running over the assault in my head.

'It was personal,' I concluded. 'The way the weapons were used. If they wanted an easier kill, they could have just used the knife after the initial blow. If it were pure sadism, they could have just done a hack job, but they didn't. The knife wounds are methodical – he was stabbed to make sure he died – but the repeated blows after that: that was personal, that was hate. Both attacks were fuelled by hate.'

It seemed Alistair Cowan was a separate case, but we were looking for one killer for Charles Walker and Jake Munro.

Chapter Forty-Six

Odie

Odie got to the hospital at 5.32. Zigzagging around gurneys and nurses, she resisted the temptation to push them out of her way. Phil was waiting for her when the lift door slid open on the first floor. She had combed half a tube of gel through her hair to force it to behave, and no one gave her a second glance. Phil didn't say a word when he swiped his pass outside the door in the far corner, pulling it shut behind them even though it was electronically controlled. He looked down at her, his expression bordering on hostile.

'Don't screw this up for me, Odie.' He turned and left her in the empty corridor.

Alistair's eyes were closed when she entered his room, his body still. For a second, Odie wondered whether he was alive, then the rise and fall of his chest gave him away.

'Alistair . . .' Odie announced her presence so as not to startle him.

When he didn't react, she continued, 'Odie Reid. You agreed to see me again.'

Still no answer.

She waited, drawing a chair to the edge of the bed as she studied his bruised face. Up close, she realised he was sleeping; his breath was erratic, and tiny dots of saliva gathered under his lips. Odie looked at her watch, unsure whether to wake him. She decided against it, but the loud tick of the hospital clock reminded her she wasn't in control of time. Ten minutes passed, then twenty, then thirty. She stared at the digits on her phone as the minutes crept up. She repeated Alistair's name with greater urgency. Still no response. She was about to leave when his eyelids flickered open. He looked at her blankly, trying to remember who she was.

'Odie Reid,' she prompted him.

Alistair's face showed signs of recognition, but he didn't say anything, so she just kept talking, willing him to respond.

'Thank you for seeing me. I know it must be hard thinking about what happened, but I just want to help.'

'Do you?' He looked at her searchingly.

'Yes. I do.'

'How is she? Fiona. Is she OK?'

'I don't know. I haven't seen her.' It wasn't a lie.

'No one will tell me anything in here. The doctors don't think it's good for my recovery, and my mother just rants about justice. She'd bring back hanging, given the chance.'

It was more than he had said for days, and he spluttered with the effort so the drops of spittle around his mouth grew bigger. 'What's she being accused of?'

'Attempted murder.'

'Are you sure?'

'You almost died. What did you expect?'

'I just want to know what's going on.'

The swelling had gone down further, but his face was still distorted, and his eyes had sunk beneath folds of puffed-up skin.

'What does it feel like?' Odie asked instinctively.

Alistair paused, struggling for air or deciding whether to answer — she wasn't sure which.

'Have you ever been in a fight, Odie?' It sounded strange when he said her name, elongating the second syllable until his voice trailed off.

'Several. All verbal.'

He smiled at that. 'Think the worst, then think again.'

Odie's wit had got her out of more fights than she cared to think about. Ostensibly aggressive, she was at heart a coward. She had always known that and, luckily for her, her acid tongue prevented most people from finding out. She wouldn't have survived Alistair's savage beating. She would have begged for the first blow to be fatal, anything to avoid the pain he had endured. She admired his will to survive, wondering if something similar existed within her and hoping she would never need to know the answer.

'I'm sorry.' It was the only thing she could say.

He tilted his head to one side so it sank into the pillow, concealing his bloodshot eye.

'Would you do something for me, please?' he said. 'I need you to take a message to Fiona.'

'Why me?'

'Because I don't know whom else to ask.' He shifted in the bed, wincing as he tried to pull himself up. 'It's a stupid idea. Forget I asked.'

'I didn't say I wouldn't do it,' Odie said. 'I just need to understand what happened, first. I can't help you unless you tell me.'

He just looked at her.

'Who did this to you?'

'I don't know.'

'The police are saying it was Fiona. Was it?'

'I already told you. No.'

'How can you be sure?'

'I thought you were trying to help her.'

'I am, but I need to know the facts.'

'She didn't do it.' He was adamant.

'Then why was she there?'

Alistair closed his eyes. When he sighed, the veins in his neck bulged with the strain, and Odie noticed the film of sweat coating his stubble.

'She was just doing her job.' He sounded ashamed. 'I need her to know I'm sorry.'

Chapter Forty-Seven

Leah

We trawled through Jake Munro's past, looking for enemies, without success. Maybe Randle and Akosua were right, and everyone did like him. It was possible but unlikely; he had stripped a lot of people of their only source of income, and desperation could easily lead to hate. As the day wore on, Randle's desk, normally immaculate, disappeared beneath Jake Munro's company files. He swallowed a biscuit and reached for the packet. It was a wonder he never gained fat.

'Akosua's still out looking into what happened to the redundancies. I've checked Jake's company history. Nothing untoward so far.'

He crossed the room, pausing to study the scene-of-crime photos; his shoulders hunched as he examined each image in turn. A map of London was spread on the board next to him, two red dots indicating the locations where Jake Munro and Charles Walker had been killed.

'Neither murder seems to have had witnesses,' he said. 'The killer was able to launch a sustained attack on both Jake and Charles uninterrupted, and neither body was found immediately. Once, OK, but twice?'

It had been bothering me too, the lack of fanfare, the absence of witnesses.

'Jake was being followed. He had to be,' I said.

'And Charles?'

'I don't know.' I stared at the photographs – pale flesh stained with random swirls of blood. 'It was desperate, uncontrolled . . . like the killer didn't know what they were doing. Like . . .'

Randle turned to face me, his eyes bright and clear. '. . . like they were doing it for the first time.'

The same person who had murdered Jake Munro had probably killed Charles Walker, and we stood no chance of catching them if we couldn't understand how they thought. But beyond the conviction that both attacks were motivated by hate, we had nothing – nothing to help us get into the killer's mind and nothing to help us decipher why they had killed and whether they would kill again.

The forensic psychologist was no use whatsoever. He stared at me with rehearsed sincerity, spouting the obvious with a smugness that made me instantly dislike him. He was new to the job, and I should have been more forgiving, but sitting in his sterile office, with its fake plants and the lingering scent of body odour, was a waste of valuable time. I tuned him out, allowing my eyes to drift to the photograph of his family on the table behind him. I may have imagined it, but his wife and children looked bored. I turned my mind back to the case and the people involved: Fiona Garvey, Vivi Walker, Sonya Waugh. I paused at the thought of Fiona's therapist and her work with serious offenders. In the short time we had spent with Sonya, she had only said what was strictly necessary, careful not to compromise her client or obstruct the law. Fiona Garvey wasn't the type of woman to waste money on a quack psychologist, and I sensed Sonya Waugh was good at her job.

Chapter Forty-Eight

Leah

Sonya Waugh was working into the evening, and the residential street outside her practice filled with cars as her neighbours returned home. It was a different receptionist from the time before. Polite and efficient, she took my details and phoned up to Sonya's office. Five minutes later, I was summoned upstairs.

Sonya's door was unlocked, and she answered almost immediately.

'You don't like appointments, do you, Inspector.' She wasn't smiling, but her tone was faintly amused. 'Come in.'

The curtains were closed, and the room seemed smaller. The air smelt fresh, with no particular scent. Sonya didn't sit, so I didn't either. She obviously had somewhere to be.

'How may I help you this time? I hope you haven't come to ask me more questions about Fiona Garvey.'

'Fiona Garvey has been charged with attempted murder.' I searched her face as I said it, trying to read her reaction, but there wasn't one. 'This isn't about Fiona,' I said. 'I'm investigating two other attacks which may or may not be related to one another.'

'But you think they are.'

I didn't reply.

'Don't worry. You're not divulging confidential police information. It's obvious: if you didn't think they were related, you wouldn't have made the link for me; you'd have let me work it out for myself. You think they're related, don't you?'

'Yes.'

'So, what do you want from me?' Sonya slid into the chair in front of her desk, motioning to the seat opposite.

'Patterns of behaviour. I can't give you details, but I need to build a picture of how the killer might think. I thought you might be able to help me.'

'Why me?'

'I didn't peg you for someone who needs to be flattered.'

'That's not what I was asking. I'm just surprised you came to me.'

'Last time I was here, you mentioned you worked with violent offenders. Why?'

Sonya was quick to deflect. 'I could ask you the same question.'

'And the answer would probably be what you expect.'

She shrugged. 'They interest me. They always have. They're often vilified without any attempt to find out anything about them. My job is to understand people and to help them understand themselves. Every time I treat a patient, I understand a little bit more, and that little bit more makes me better at what I do.'

'So can you help me?'

She was more relaxed than the last time we had met. She kicked out her legs, crossing and uncrossing her feet. 'That depends. What can you tell me?'

'Two attacks. Acts of rage. Both of them. We need to know what's driving the killer.'

'I can't help you there. Every person's different. You don't need me to tell you that.'

'I don't think this killer has been killing for long.'

'How do you know?'

'The attacks lack precision. That's all I can say.' I had already said too much.

'So, what do you want from me?' The same question again.

'I want to know what drives a person who has never taken a life to take one life and then another. What makes a person suddenly flip?'

Sonya pressed her fingertips together, flexing the joints before she spoke. 'It depends. It can be for a multitude of reasons. Once again, you don't need me to tell you that.'

'Give me some possible examples. Based on your experience.'

'OK . . . but these are just scenarios.' It was the most tentative Sonya had been in our two meetings.

'Health warning heard loud and clear. I'm just looking for a starting point.'

'It's not rocket science, Inspector. Sudden recourse to extreme violence is often caused by extreme trauma, but it may not manifest itself for a while.'

'In English?'

Sonya smiled. 'People experience something terrible in their lives. They carry on trying to cope. They don't deal with certain issues, but the issues don't go away. They continue to fester until there's a trigger and then . . .' She bunched her fingers and then splayed them with sudden force – a quiet explosion.

'How far back? In your experience? How deep would we have to dig?'

Sonya shrugged. 'Depends on the person. Depends on the trauma. I can't help you there, I'm afraid.'

I had my next question ready when I felt my phone vibrate. The low buzz was almost imperceptible, but Sonya registered the sound.

'Do you need to take that?' She was unfazed, as always.

'I don't know.'

I didn't recognise the number as I slipped into the corridor outside.

'Leah Hutch . . .'

I waited for a response, but the phone immediately went dead. Confused, I called back.

'What took you so long?' The voice at the other end was gruff and hurried. 'I was about to give up.'

'Who is this?'

'Ron.'

'Ron?' It took a second for the information to click into place.

'I knew this was a bad idea.'

'No, wait. Please.'

Ron Kirwan, the man who had found my mother's dead lover. I couldn't believe he had turned up so soon.

'Debbie said you want to talk . . .'

'Yes. Can we meet?'

Silence again, then I heard his breathing, shallow and impatient at the other end of the line.

'I'd like to talk to you about the night you proposed to Amy.'

'What about it?'

'Can we talk in person? I can come and meet you,' I said.

Another silence.

'Ron?'

'Yes. I'm still here.'

'Can we meet?'

'I heard you the first time.'

His breathing slowed, and I could hear him inhale what I imagined was cigarette smoke.

'We can meet tonight. But it's going to cost you. Debbie'll tell you where and how much.'

He hung up.

I gripped my phone, unsure what to make of the conversation. Sonya was sitting behind her desk when I returned to the room, hair loosened so her face looked less severe.

'Everything OK?' She said it casually, but I had had enough experience with psychologists at work to know that every word I uttered was being studied and analysed.

'Yes. Fine. Sorry about that.'

'No need. Are you sure you're OK?'

I wondered what it would be like to talk to someone about my life since Margaretta. There were so many responses to Sonya's question, but the simplest answer was 'yes'. Sonya just looked at me, her expression disbelieving as she turned her attention to a pile of papers.

'You've been very helpful. Thank you.'

She offered me her hand. 'If you ever need to talk . . .'

The invitation was there if I wanted it, but it wasn't an offer I planned to take up. My phone beeped as I left the building. I was finally going to meet Ron Kirwan.

Chapter Forty-Nine

Odie

All Odie could think about was Alistair: his conviction that Fiona was innocent and his belief that she could somehow help him. Her arrangement with Daniel had completely slipped her mind until the inevitable text came through – Richard wondering where she had been, implicitly accusing her of letting their son down, again. She would have to make it up to Daniel. The fact that he expected so little of her made her feel less guilty. She could only improve in his eyes, and she intended to, but not now.

Odie had hoped for more from her anonymous source, but so far there had been nothing, and there was no guarantee they would ever contact her again. She was desperate for an update on Fiona's case, but she couldn't go to Hutch after their last disastrous encounter, and she sensed Baber had been avoiding her. He never relished her company, but not returning her calls was a new development and when she checked the pub, he was nowhere to be seen. Walking past the police station, she toyed with the idea of demanding a meeting, but there was no point antagonising him, and she doubted he was there. She turned to go, deciding to deal with Baber another day. She didn't recognise the voice behind her.

'Can I help you?'

She couldn't place his face at first – dishevelled fair hair and two-day-old stubble obscuring classic good looks. It was hard to determine his age, but there was something about the way he carried himself which made Odie suspect he was older than he appeared. A midnight blue motorcycle helmet dangled from one hand; with the other, he brought an unlit cigarette to rest between his lips. Odie noticed the worn leather biker boots under faded dark jeans, the battered jacket that fitted too well to be cheap. He would have looked more at home in a bar than outside a police station, but Odie could feel his eyes subtly watching her, and she knew a detective when she saw one. Besides, she had seen him before. She waited for him to speak again, buying herself time to recall a name.

'I know you . . .' he said. She sensed he was going through the same process, searching his memory for her face. 'Charles Walker's body. You were there first.'

Hutch's new protégé. He was suddenly more interesting, but Odie was in no hurry to let him know.

'Congratulations.'

He smiled at her sarcasm. 'I don't usually get congratulated for coming second.'

She was surprised by his confidence, but she liked it; it was never good for Hutch to have an easy ride.

'Well, we can't all win,' she said.

'Odie Reid?' He held out his hand. 'Ben Randle. We weren't properly introduced the last time.'

'Don't tell me – my reputation precedes me.'

'You used to work with Leah. I asked around.'

'*Leah?* You *must* get on well.'

That smile again. 'I enjoy working with her, if that's what you mean.'

'No. But thank you for clearing that up.' She was determined not to warm to his charm.

'She was in your team, wasn't she?' he asked.

'We both know you know that already, so what do you really want to know?'

Ben laughed in response, relaxing into the conversation. 'I heard it didn't end well between you.'

'Old news,' Odie said.

He was looking at her insistently, his pupils constricting under the street light.

'You're still in the honeymoon period,' Odie said. 'It won't last. You think Hutch is some kind of maverick genius leading the fight for justice, but she's not. She's self-righteous; she doesn't care about anything or anyone but herself, and you'll be just another casualty of war.'

'I can take care of myself.' He lit the cigarette but barely inhaled.

'I'm sure you can but don't ignore what's in front of you because you want to get ahead.'

'With all due respect, you don't know me.'

'No. But I know Hutch,' Odie said.

He looked away, and she sensed she had got under his skin.

'It was nice to meet you. Good night, Odie.'

'You're wrong, by the way.' Odie spoke to his back as he turned away. 'About Hutch. About Fiona. About everything.'

He pivoted to face her, so she was aware of his physicality for the first time. He was lean but broad, and she glimpsed a harder edge beneath the easy charm.

'I'm not going to discuss the case with you, Odie.'

'But it doesn't stop you from wondering whether I'm right.'

It was a punt, but from the flicker in his eyes, Odie knew she had landed on something. 'Let me guess, you've thought the same already.'

She didn't expect him to answer. Hutch would see it as a betrayal, and Odie could tell he cared what Hutch thought.

'How can you sleep at night knowing Fiona didn't do it?' she said.

'Why are you so sure she's innocent?' he shot back.

'He told me . . . Alistair Cowan.'

Her words hung between them.

Odie hadn't decided to tell him until that moment, but it had the desired effect. Benjamin Randle opened his mouth to respond, but Odie was already walking away. It had been a day of small victories and big frustrations, but on balance, she felt she was winning for the first time in a long while.

Chapter Fifty

Leah

The road was poorly lit, and my eyes strained to see in the dark. I pulled up outside a cheap hotel with a forgettable name. The entrance was up a set of battered steps – a single door in need of a coat of paint. The foyer led to a sparsely decorated lounge with a handful of mismatched chairs assembled in clusters. In one corner, a couple kissed furtively, talking in hushed tones; in another, a woman clutched the neck of a beer bottle as if she couldn't bear to be there but couldn't bring herself to leave. Otherwise, the room was empty, and there was no sign of Ron Kirwan. I checked my watch; I was still a few minutes early. I settled myself in a chair facing the entrance and ordered a soft drink. Expectation made me thirsty, and I drank quickly, barely noticing the taste. I signalled to the waitress in a half-hearted attempt to get her attention, but she showed no sign of approaching. Ron caught me off guard.

'You look like her.' His voice came from behind me.

'How long have you been watching me?'

'A while.' He was unapologetic. 'I wanted to know who I'm talking to.'

'Leah Hutch.'

I half stood as he lowered himself into the seat opposite. I noticed him wince as he made the final drop.

'Aren't you going to offer me a drink?' It wasn't a question.

'If the waitress decides to do her job, I'll buy you two.' I waved at the woman again. 'Thank you for seeing me.' I was paying for the privilege, but I wanted to get him on side. I needn't have bothered; his disinterest in me was clear.

'Why do you want to know?' It sounded like an accusation.

'She was my mother.'

'So what?' He shifted in his chair, trying to find the correct position for his hip. 'I don't think about *my* mother.'

I switched off my phone, pointedly getting rid of all distractions. 'Should we get started?'

'I'd like a drink first.'

I signalled to the waitress again. This time, I made sure she saw me.

Ron shifted in his chair again, his hip creaking as it moved through several angles. He finally settled, a little less uncomfortable, but still in obvious pain.

'You'd think I'd have stopped after Amy, but maybe she had the right idea.'

I looked at him blankly, and he laughed softly at his own joke.

'Liver failure. She drank herself to death. Took the easier way out.'

It was said almost longingly, and I was reminded that Amy Kirwan née Pritchard had once been the love of his life.

'You can't stay drunk all the time . . .'

'I know. I tried . . . Thanks.'

His first smile of the evening was for the terrible waitress as she set his drink down on the table in front of him. The woman smiled back. I wondered whether it was just me she disliked.

'I just have the odd drink these days,' Ron said. 'To take the edge off when things get . . . difficult. No more after this.' His protestations were almost convincing. 'I like to keep a clear head . . .' He trailed off, rubbing his hip gently.

'What happened?' I indicated the offending limb.

'What do they call it? Retribution. Yes. Retribution.' He chewed over the word for a moment. 'I was released when they realised they got the wrong man, but some people still thought I had something to do with it. Some lads from the village . . . One night they came for me. They jumped me. I try to forget about it, but arthritis makes it worse some days.'

'I'm sorry.'

'It doesn't matter any more. None of this does.'

'You don't sound convinced.'

'You know nothing about me.' He slurped his drink, refocusing his eyes in the gloom. 'This was a mistake. Look, nothing good happened that night. I don't want to reminisce. If you want to ask me something specific, ask me. If not, we're done here.' He shuffled to his feet, moving slower than before.

'Sit down, Ron.'

'I don't need to listen to you.'

'You're taking my money. So, sit down. Please.'

He stared at me, angry but seemingly trapped. He didn't sit down straight away.

'You said I look like her. Did you know her before that night?' I asked.

'No, but her face was everywhere afterwards. You couldn't get away from it. It was all everyone talked about. She had a nice face. Pretty. It was a shame.'

I knew it was his version of being kind, but it rankled. As if her death would have been any less tragic if she had been less attractive.

'And what about Eli Carson?'

'What about him?' Ron's eyes seemed blacker.

'What did people say about him?'

'They weren't looking for him at first. They weren't looking for anybody. We were just kids and they thought we were the ones that had done . . . that.'

I let the silence play between us, waiting for him to calm down.

'Did you see anybody else, Ron?'

He shook his head. 'The place looked deserted, but Amy said she saw skid marks – the kind a car makes when it drives away fast. She said she smelt burnt rubber but how could she? I still remember the smell of the body.'

'Did you tell the police? About the car?'

There had been no mention of it in Ron's report.

He bit down hard on the inside of his cheek, chewing the flesh as his mind travelled back.

'Amy did, but all they wanted to talk about was the hand. I didn't see tracks. By the time Amy told them, they had been washed away by the rain. There was no proof of any car. No proof anyone was there except us . . . And then he confessed.' Ron's laugh jarred. 'No one was ready for that – a police officer killing his own wife. It didn't make sense. Not the kind of sense people wanted.' He was back there, thirty-one years ago, reliving the injustice. 'No one wanted to believe it. They wanted *me* to be the killer, not some middle-class copper with money and a degree. They would have locked me up forever . . .'

He brought his mind back to the present, moving his weight to one side as he stretched his body up through the hip joint. I felt uncomfortable watching him.

'I guess Eli Carson surprised everyone,' he said. 'They kept waiting for someone to say it was a bad joke or some kind of mistake. Then when it looked like it wasn't a joke and Eli would go to jail, they turned on him, like the bunch of hypocrites they were. Everyone had something to say about Eli Carson. You couldn't shut them up.'

'What did they say?'

Ron shrugged off the question and took another hit of his drink. 'Nothing worth remembering. They said the same crap about me. You can't believe any of it. Nothing.'

'What did they say, though?' I was careful not to sound too insistent.

'I don't know . . . He'd done it before but had never been caught . . . He'd eaten his wife, which was why they couldn't find her . . . His wife was in on it with him, hiding away in the Bahamas, waiting for him to join her. There were so many Eli Carson stories, you couldn't keep track.' He flicked his glass with his forefinger. 'Eli Carson,' he grunted. 'I hate him, but I've thought about him every day for thirty-one years. I can't go to bed without seeing his face, can't sleep without waking up with the sweats.'

I searched his eyes for a glimmer of peace amidst the pain.

'What?' He took a gulp of his gin, squinting over his glass. 'You think I'm ashamed I'm scared to dream? Try seeing what I saw and see how you survive.'

He slammed the glass onto the table; a drop of liquid splattered onto the wood.

'Eli Carson stole my life. And Amy's. I'm not giving him any more of my time.'

He got up, clutching the arm of his chair to steady himself as he carefully unfurled his hip.

'I think you got your money's worth,' he said without looking at me. 'Don't contact me again.'

Chapter Fifty-One

Leah

I lay awake, staring at the wall in frustration, wanting answers but finding none. I tried to think of Margaretta and her pyjamas, counting the patterned fruit until she lulled herself to sleep, but I couldn't shake the thought of Eli driving a knife through my mother's body, or the carnage Ron and Amy witnessed that night. Violent images flooded my brain, becoming more vivid the moment I closed my eyes. Margaretta always said that her ability to sleep depended on how often she read her Bible. When she spent time reading God's word, she felt closer to Jesus and didn't worry so much. Those nights, she professed to sleep like a baby; other nights, she made do with counting fruit. I just lay there, staring at the wall. I wasn't sure when I fell asleep, but the wall slowly started to dissolve as my subconscious took over.

School was over for the day, and it was time to go home. The playground slowly emptied until there was only one little girl left. She climbed the steps to the main building and waited. Sitting at the top, she surveyed the abandoned yard: the swing, the seesaw, the hopscotch grid chalked into the tarmac. An hour before, there had been dozens of children jostling to have their turn; now there was no one else except her. She was alone, but she didn't feel scared. She just wanted to go home, so she waited for someone to come for her. Everything was completely still, and she passed the time playing with the rhythm of her breath, watching her chest rise and fall. She had been doing that for a while when she heard the hushed sound of muffled tears. She followed it, not thinking about where it might lead. Down the stairs, round the back of the building, farther and farther away. As she drew closer, the noise became louder, morphing into a piercing wail that slammed against her eardrums, refusing to stop. It was coming from behind the disused shed at the edge of the grounds, where the trees cast a shadow so it always felt dark. Everyone said there was a ghost, but no one had ever seen it. She was tense with fear and expectation, but curiosity kept her moving forwards. She followed the sound, not faltering until she came face to face with another little girl, looking back at her through the gloom. She had blonde hair and startling blue eyes. Her face was stained with tears, her mouth stretched wide with pain. The two girls were dressed in exactly the same uniform — the same pleated skirt, the same short green tie poking out from beneath the collar. But there was something different about the blonde girl behind the shed. Her white shirt was stained red, her face badly bruised around her nose and eyes, her tears the colour of dry blood. Her cries grew louder, and she wouldn't stop. Louder and louder, on and on, until her mouth stretched so wide, it swallowed her entire face.

I jolted awake, gasping for air. It wasn't the first time I had had that dream, but I hadn't had it for a while. When I was a child, there were times I couldn't sleep without screaming, but now the dreams only came at times of high stress. It was always the same, except for the colour of the tie: green, yellow, purple, pink, and now back to green. My body was rigid with tension and for a moment, I couldn't breathe. My T-shirt was smeared against my body, the sweat slowly evaporating through the material so I was left feeling cold. I moved to the cupboard, discarding the T-shirt as I went, and pulled on a fresh one. The images from the dream were still playing in my mind. I needed a distraction, and I chided myself for not skipping earlier to clear my head. I turned on the television, mechanically flicking through the channels, but I couldn't concentrate; the only picture I saw was the little girl covered in blood. I remembered the ritual Margaretta had followed when I had had the dreams as a child, and I imagined her beside me as I stood by the pan of boiling water, watching an egg crack and then burst. The smell made me nauseous. The nausea distracted me from my thoughts, and my mind felt calmer as I sat at the table and bit into the yolk.

I caught sight of Selwyn's file, waiting for me to come back to it. I hadn't gone near it since that first night. I flipped to Ron's testimony, rereading as I ate. Nothing he had told me in the bar had surprised me, except the detail about the speeding car. I visualised Eli pushing hard on the accelerator as the tyres skidded on the drive. I almost felt the pressure in the air weighing heavily as the clouds prepared for rain. The image crystallised, and I closed my eyes as a distant memory became clear in my mind: I remembered the smell of rubber as I lay crouched on the mat between the front and back seat, the pain in my spine as the car sped over the bumps in the road. I remembered squeezing my eyes shut as my hands gripped my knees, hiding in the back of Eli's car the night my mother was killed.

Chapter Fifty-Two

Leah

I was there the night my mother was killed. I needed to know what I had seen, but I couldn't remember. I scanned Eli's letters to Margaretta, arranging them in a grid across my kitchen table. It was a wonder the correspondence existed at all. It must have taken a supreme effort to keep the relationship secret, but Margaretta had hidden me too, keeping me from any acquaintances from her past. I remembered a shopping trip when I was nine, observing each stranger we passed. One woman had stopped in front of us. She had made to hug Margaretta, but Margaretta had kept her arms rigid by her side.

'And who do we have here?'

The woman had stooped until her head was level with mine, reaching out as if to pat a dog. I had waited, craving attention, but Margaretta had pulled me away.

I returned the letters to the file, angry with Margaretta for leaving me with so many unanswered questions. I couldn't remember what I had seen, and the letters didn't help. As I gathered up the last of the envelopes, I noticed a neatly folded stack of papers pressed together. Carefully separating each leaf, I laid them on the floor in a circle around me. There were pages of information with different perspectives on Eli: interviews in newspaper articles, testimonials, character references, psychiatric evaluations. I sat back on my heels, moving clockwise. Reaching for each one in turn, I mentally compared the different versions of Eli Carson – a man with many faces and a singular approach to his work. Each account captured different aspects of his character, but one thing was consistent in all of them – resounding praise for his skill as a police officer. He was universally acknowledged to be a brilliant interrogator – a detective with a unique ability to get under the skin of witnesses and suspects in order to deliver results. But results came at a price and, according to the psychological evaluation, this unique ability could have adversely shaped Eli's attitude to violence and danger.

'. . . *He has a complex history with violence, and although his experience has been, for the most part, indirect, his constant exposure to extreme acts of brutality over time has caused him to develop a higher threshold of tolerance than commonly witnessed in a police officer of his rank. Put simply, what would shock the average person, or indeed officer, has no effect on Detective Carson.*'

Colleagues who had obviously admired him before his conviction said a similar thing: the man was right for the job, but the job was wrong for the man. I recognised some of the names of officers interviewed, men and women who would have been fairly junior at the time, but who were now approaching retirement. Men who had had the type of careers Eli should have had, if the dark side of his nature hadn't won. I caught sight of Kenny O'Sullivan's name in one of the articles. It was a short interview hidden away in the corner of a newspaper page. It would have been easy to miss, but someone had helpfully scribbled a star next to the by-line. It hadn't crossed my mind that Kenny would have known Eli, but it made perfect sense – they had both trained with the Met and they were both seen as rising stars in the force. Two sides of the same coin, but while Kenny's side had landed facing upwards, Eli's had fallen facing the gutter. For a moment, I worried that Kenny knew about Eli and me, but I had never discussed my family with him, never mentioned Margaretta, or hinted at the little I knew about my past. I had been given a new name; a new start. There was no reason for Kenny to look for Eli's face in mine. I could hear Kenny's voice as I read his words. It was impossible to tell whether he was being generous or diplomatic, but I sensed he had liked Eli and, to his credit, he didn't seem interested in joining the mob baying for Eli's blood. Used to Kenny's no-nonsense pragmatism, there was a thoughtfulness to his interview which I didn't expect, but somehow seemed in keeping with a young Kenny O'Sullivan who would grow into a canny politician with the ability to read any situation. One exchange in particular caught my attention. Ignoring the questions, I mentally pasted together Kenny's answers so I could play his testimony in my mind, uninterrupted:

'. . . *You have to understand it's not a normal job. I suspect no job is easy, but this job, our job, it's not normal. We spend our days in the shadows, where the ugly becomes ordinary, and people do evil things. It's our job to find those people and put them behind bars. That was Eli's job, and he did it well. He was good at tuning into the minds of criminals. He got them in a way most police officers don't. Understood them, even. People said he was always one step ahead. Even if he wasn't, he caught up fast. It's not easy to cope with that level of violence day in, day out. It's not for everybody. It can't be. We live in the grey. The moment we stray into the black, we become lost. You've got to remember that every day. It's a real shame what's happened to Eli Carson. I can't explain it. Only Eli can. All I know is that he worked* *on some dark cases, saw some really dark ****, and maybe that didn't help. Maybe this is the worst job for someone like him. It's a great job for some of us, but maybe the job didn't help Eli . . .'*

There was something moving about Kenny's words, an eloquence that reflected his sadness at the loss of a trusted colleague. I returned to the table, looking for Margaretta's unfinished letter. I pulled it out, reading the words aloud.

'*. . . whatever is true, whatever is noble, whatever is right, whatever is pure, whatever is lovely, whatever is admirable – if anything is excellent or praiseworthy – think about such things.*'

The apostle Paul's instructions to the Philippians 2,000 years ago. Margaretta's warning to her son, which went unheeded, despite her best efforts. Eli had chosen to work in a world which strove to protect truth, nobility, righteousness and purity, but at the cost of immersing himself in the opposite. Maybe Kenny was right, and not everyone could live with that tension, but it was still no excuse.

My eyes were beginning to hurt. Suddenly tired, I had had enough of Eli. I tidied the mess on the floor and made my way back to my bedroom. I tried to take the apostle's advice and focus my attention on something good, but when I closed my eyes, all I saw was death.

I stood up in the blackness, my legs stiff from lying in a foetal position. I paced the room to shake off the cramp, rising onto the tips of my toes to snap my calves to life. I thought about going back to bed, but I knew it was pointless. I was agitated and restless, and skipping wouldn't help. I had to get out, to leave Eli and the past behind.

Chapter Fifty-Three

Leah

I hailed a cab and headed in the direction of work. I wanted to be around people, and the pub around the corner had a late licence. I hated socialising with colleagues, but it was well past midnight, and I suspected only the die-hards and stragglers would be left standing. Looking out across the city, I felt exhausted and powerless. As each layer of my life was peeled back, I dreaded what I would find at the core. The gaps in my memory made me uneasy. Even behind bars, Eli seemed to be in control. But if I could find my mother's body and give her a proper burial, perhaps I could forget him and start again.

I had imagined a traditional pub with lager-stained upholstery and the stench of stale beer. I was wrong. More of a bar than a pub, the air was clean and warm, the décor blandly inoffensive. I pulled up a stool and waited to be served. It was good to be in another world where I had more than my brain for company. I sipped my drink and soaked up my surroundings, my mind at peace for the first time in hours.

'You're here.' Randle's voice betrayed his surprise.

'Is that a welcome, or a pointless observation?' My tone was deliberately uninviting. We weren't friends, or even close, and drinking together 'after hours' opened a door to familiarity which

I wanted to keep closed. He turned to move away, and I immediately regretted my rudeness.

'Sorry . . .' He looked bemused, and I felt self-conscious. 'What?'

'I don't think I've ever heard you apologise before. At least, not to me.'

His sense of bewilderment amused me.

'You're smiling.' His body rested against the stool beside me. His shirt was untucked, and there was an ease to him that I didn't dislike.

'Now that's definitely a pointless observation,' I said, my tone lighter.

'It's just that you never smile.'

It was true. I almost felt I owed him an explanation, but it wouldn't have been an honest one.

'We deal with dead bodies and murderers every day. What's there to smile about?' I said.

'There's always something.' Randle dropped his gaze, staring at the dregs of whiskey in his glass. 'You want another drink?'

'Double vodka. No ice.'

He signalled to the barman, standing straighter so his height singled him out. Two men were waiting for attention; the barman ignored them, taking Randle's order instead.

'Is it one of those nights?'

The glass was wet when he handed me my drink.

'One of *those* nights?'

'Drowning your sorrows? Forgetting your troubles?'

'Is that why you're here?' I set the glass down on the bar, a slice of lemon balanced precariously on top. 'Cheers.'

I ditched the lemon and took a large gulp, letting the liquid slide down my throat.

'You barely tasted that.' Randle sounded impressed.

'Maybe I don't like the taste all that much.'

I looked around at the clusters of colleagues, their professional masks slipping as the alcohol took hold. 'So, this is where you come . . .'

'Sometimes,' he said.

There was an easy silence as we drank. The man opposite stared at me with interest. He got bored and ordered another shot instead.

'How do you think we're doing with the case?' Randle asked after a while.

'We, or you?'

If he was offended, he didn't show it. He took a sip of his drink, wiping his mouth with the back of his hand. 'We. The team. I think we're making progress.'

'I didn't come here to talk about work.' All dead bodies led me back to Eli, and I didn't want to think about him just then.

Randle opened his mouth to say something but decided against it.

'Can I ask you a question?' I didn't wait for an answer. 'Why do you need affirmation?'

He looked surprised. 'Is that what you think I want from you?'

'Isn't it?'

'No.'

Something stopped me from asking what he did want.

'Why do you hold everything at arm's length?' Randle's eyes never left my face.

'Everything?'

'Everyone.' He didn't hesitate.

'I do what I need to do. That's all there is to it,' I said.

He stared at his glass for a second, caught up in some internal debate. 'Can I be honest with you?' he said.

'Are you not normally?'

'You know what I mean. I need to know you won't hold any of this against me tomorrow, when we're back to being DI Hutch and DS Randle.'

'And who are we tonight?'

'Forget it.' He turned back to his drink. Off duty, he was less eager to please.

'No. I want to hear. Just say it.'

'Why didn't you say anything to that man in the lift? Back in Clare Traynor's estate, why did you let that go?'

'Is this you being honest?'

He took a sip of his drink. 'I'm working up to it.'

I smiled. 'Now that is honest.'

'Why?' he asked again.

'Because it's not my job to educate him,' I said.

'Do you know what people say about you?' Randle was still facing the bar.

'Yes, but I assume you're going to remind me.'

'You're the poster girl for a diverse police force. You got to where you are because you're black and female. You're *only* where you are because you ticked the right boxes and Kenny O'Sullivan likes you. You shouldn't have been promoted so quickly, but it helped the stats, and you work hard. Good but not great, black instead of white.'

He didn't draw breath until he had finished, searching my face for a reaction. I didn't give him one. I had heard it all before, and it wasn't worth thinking about.

'I can live with that.' I could and I did.

'Can you?'

'Yes, if "good" solves cases. Great's just about ego, and I don't care what people say.'

'I do.'

'And that, Benjamin Randle, is your biggest problem.' I had sensed it all along, but I was surprised to hear him admit it. 'I'm not interested in playing the hero. You just disappoint yourself or someone else.'

I took another swig from my glass. I did the job I had been given and got results; that was all that mattered. People wouldn't talk about me in years to come, but I would have done my job and that should be enough. Eli had been a great detective, but he had crossed the line so many times, he had forgotten where it was. There had to be some distance, or there would be no way back to the light. Randle would learn that the hard or the easy way; it wasn't my responsibility to teach him. I downed my drink and got up to leave.

'Another one?'

I thought about it for a second. It was the most open I had ever been with Randle. I could see him growing in confidence with each question and who knew where that would lead.

'Tempting, but no,' I said, making light of it. 'Thanks for the drink . . . and Ben . . .'

He looked up, almost hopeful.

'We're always DI Hutch and DS Randle.'

Chapter Fifty-Four

Leah

Randle had his back to me as I neared the building the next morning. The muscles around his shoulders tensed as he lifted the cigarette hanging from his hand. He turned as I approached and for a moment, he looked unsure of himself.

'DI Hutch.'

'DS Randle.'

'Good evening last night?' His expression was completely innocent.

'Pretty average. You?'

'Oh, me? I had a great time, ma'am.'

This time I did smile. 'You need to get out more.'

'You're telling me.' He flicked the cigarette onto the pavement, crushing it casually with his boot.

'Ready to work?'

He looked me straight in the eye. 'Always, ma'am. You never need to worry about that.'

Akosua was standing by her desk when we got upstairs. Her afro was combed out, thick and glossy around her face. Randle busied himself at his computer as Akosua filled me in on the Jake Munro redundancies.

'It's been two years and most of the casualties found other jobs or took early retirement.'

'And the exceptions?'

'Two have struggled to settle into full-time employment and have moved around a lot. One had to stop work due to cancer; one emigrated to Australia immediately; one died.'

I ditched the lid of my coffee and drained the cup, pausing to let the kick from the caffeine take hold.

'Well, we can rule out the invalid and the emigrant for now; that leaves three potentially disgruntled employees, depending on when the third one died,' I said.

'Yes, ma'am.' Akosua barely concealed her smile. 'I already emailed you their info: Chris da Silva and Robert Nathaniel, over sixty years of service between them. Neither has a criminal past or a history of violence. Eddie Adeola is the one that died.'

'Check Chris and Robert's alibis,' I said.

I pulled out my mobile and scanned Akosua's email. I noted the dates and details she hadn't thought to recount.

'Notice anything about Eddie Adeola?'

'Nothing in particular, ma'am.' She sounded uncertain. 'He was dead long before either Charles Walker or Jake Munro were killed.'

'Look at the proximity between the date he died and the date he lost his job.' I showed her her own email, but her face was blank. 'Eddie Adeola never took a sick day in his life, but he was pronounced dead by accidental overdose three months after he lost the only job he ever had.'

Akosua recovered quickly. 'I'll look into it, ma'am.'

I expected Randle to comment, but he stayed focused on his computer, staring intently at the screen.

'What's that?'

My eyes flicked to the monitor as he minimised the file. I caught Fiona Garvey's name before it disappeared from sight.

'What's going on?' I knew I was overreacting, but I had hardly slept. 'Fiona Garvey's been charged. Harrison confirmed there are two different attackers. Why are you looking at her file?'

'I . . .'

His cheeks flushed, and he looked at his hands. Akosua got up and discreetly moved away.

'You what?'

'I saw Odie Reid last night, ma'am. According to Odie, Alistair Cowan said Fiona Garvey is innocent.'

'And you were going to tell me this when?'

'You didn't want to talk about work last night.' He didn't break eye contact. 'Odie thinks we're wrong.'

'And what do *you* think?'

He hesitated. 'I think we charged Fiona Garvey and the burden of proof is against her.'

We stood there, the atmosphere charged with my hostility and his defensiveness.

'I wasn't going behind your back. I would never do that.' He waited for me to reassure him, but I was furious with Odie for trying to come between me and my team.

'Go to the hospital. Talk to Alistair. I don't care what his doctor says.'

'I didn't go to Odie. *She* approached *me*, ma'am.'

'Just go,' I said.

I knew it was a mistake to call Odie. Even after so many years, I still knew her number by heart.

'You had no right.'

'Do you want to tell me what you're talking about or is that too much trouble?' Odie's tone was cool and detached.

Over the years, we had fought many times, but I had never lost my temper. I could feel the anger creeping into my voice.

'If you have something to say to me about my case, you come to me. Leave my team out of it.'

'*Me. My.* And they say I'm the one with the ego.'

'This isn't a game, Odie. Stop wasting police time.'

'I did come to you, and you didn't listen.' The playfulness had gone; Odie's voice was hard and accusatory. 'Do your job or more people will die, and it will be your fault.'

She hung up before I could respond.

My body pulsed with a strange energy, and I needed to get rid of it fast. I made my way to the accessible bathroom, locking the door behind me. I shuffled from one foot to the other, balling my fists around an imaginary rope. I had shadow skipped before but never with the same urgency. I clenched so hard my nail sliced through the flesh of my palm, and I stared at the bloody smudge on my hand, drops of sweat forming at the base of my skull. My heart was beating fast in my chest, but I felt more like myself again.

Chapter Fifty-Five

Odie

It hadn't been easy to convince Mary to let her see Fiona. The failed suicide was still fresh in Odie's mind, and her initial concern had given way to an overwhelming sense of guilt. They were back in the same room in the Victorian prison – discarded toys in a colourful mound in the corner, pale grey walls that had lost the will to stay white. Mary had been silent since they walked through the gates, her front teeth digging into the soft flesh of her bottom lip. Odie sat, craned forwards on a rough plastic chair, fighting her fear that Fiona would never arrive. Her eyes drifted to twin boys in tracksuits, playing slap two tables down. The smaller one let out a squeal as the door was pulled open. Odie felt Mary tense as the prisoners came in.

Fiona was thinner than in her photos, eyes vacant and soulless; she barely seemed to register Odie's apology.

'I want to help you,' Odie said.

'How?' Fiona's voice was so low Odie wondered whether she had imagined it.

'I went to see Alastair.'

Fiona's breath caught in her throat.

'Is he OK?'

'Yes,' Odie said. 'He wants you to know he's sorry. He knows you didn't do it.'

Fiona looked at her blankly, and Odie feared she had lost her again. It was like coaxing a small child into a swimming pool, taking tiny steps into an expanse they couldn't control.

'Help me understand what happened, Fiona,' she pleaded.

For a second, Fiona's eyes clouded over. Odie thought she might cry, but no tears came.

'I don't remember,' she said. 'I've already told the police.'

Fiona was starting to get agitated, looking to Mary for support.

'I don't mean that night. I mean before. You and Alistair. What happened before?'

Silence.

'Tell me about Alistair.'

'What about him?' Fiona fiddled with the hem of her sleeve.

'What was your relationship like? Did you work well together?'

'I did what I was asked. He closed the deal of a lifetime. He said he couldn't have done it without me.' Her voice was flat and thin.

'And what happened afterwards?'

'What do you mean?'

There was dirt in the roots of her eyelashes, and the skin by her mouth was cracked. She stared past them at a boy laughing with his sister. She shook her head sadly at the sound.

'What does it matter?' She turned to her mother, exhaustion and frustration etched on her face. 'Why are we doing this? What's the point? I could answer a hundred of these questions, but it wouldn't matter because I can't answer the one question everybody cares about. I can't explain the attack on Alistair, but it wasn't me who hurt him . . .' She turned to face Odie. 'I appreciate you trying to help, but there's nothing you can do.'

Odie had been so intent on playing the hero that she had never stopped to think that Fiona might not want to be rescued.

Mary walked ahead as they made their way towards the exit. Her blue cotton dress dwarfed her tiny frame.

'I know you're trying to help. But I need to stop this,' she said.

'We can't give up on her now.' Odie tried to keep up.

'There is no *we*. It's about me supporting my daughter and right now I need to respect what she wants.'

'She just tried to kill herself. She doesn't know what she wants.'

The words were out before Odie could censor them; she felt Mary recoil as she stopped.

'Fiona doesn't want your help and neither do I,' Mary said.

She walked away, and Odie could do nothing but stand and watch.

Chapter Fifty-Six

Leah

'We got more information about the redundancies, ma'am.' Akosua almost kicked over her chair as she got up from behind her desk. 'Chris da Silva has an alibi, and we can't get hold of Robert Nathaniel, but . . .' She worked up to her big revelation. 'Eddie Adeola lived in the same block of council flats that the calls to Charles Walker were made from. Clare Traynor told you she didn't make those calls. What if . . .' She didn't finish her sentence, conscious she was jumping from A to D, with no idea of a B or C.

'What if what?' I could see the sun through the open window; I shifted so the rays hit my face.

'I don't know how, but what if Eddie Adeola is the link between Charles Walker and Jake Munro?'

'Who lives in Adeola's flat now?' I asked.

'His wife, Temi, and their two kids, Dele and Lola.'

She flicked through photographs of Eddie's family on an iPad, angling the screen away from the light.

'Have you spoken to her?'

Akosua shook her head. 'We're still trying to track down Robert Nathaniel. I was focusing on that.'

'Nathaniel can wait,' I said. 'Let's follow up on Temi Adeola.'

*

The stench of urine in the lift was stronger than I remembered. We emerged on Temi's floor, and each step seemed to take longer, as our shoes stuck to the film of dirt on the ground. Beside me, Akosua twitched with excitement, flicking her fingers against her thigh. The Adeolas' flat was at the end of the walkway, a hundred or so yards from the lift. The faint thud of music drifted from under the door, vibrating along the corridor. I counted eight doors before we arrived; my phone rang before we got to number three. It was Randle, never one to sit back while others embraced the limelight. I kept my voice low.

'This had better be important. Did Alistair say something?'

'Yes,' Randle said. 'Odie was telling the truth.'

'So?' Randle's timing was poor. 'Alistair was hit from behind. He may never have seen his attacker. Believing Fiona is innocent, and knowing she is, are two completely different things.'

'There was something in his eyes, ma'am. I feel like I was missing something, but I don't know what.'

'Well, when you figure it out, call me. I don't have time for this right now.'

'I know, ma'am. That's not why I phoned . . .' He paused. '*He had nothing and he came from nothing . . . a council estate boy with a talent for making money.*'

'What are you talking about, Randle?'

The words sounded familiar, but the lack of context made them hard to place.

'Vivi Walker. That's how she described Charles. He had nothing when he married her. She gave him capital, and he turned his life around.'

The music from the flat had changed, and we were close enough to be distracted by the lyrics. I pressed the phone against my ear, straining to hear Randle.

'Charles Walker grew up on the estate next door,' Randle said. 'Eddie Adeola lived in his flat with his mother until she died, then he lived there with his own family. He was there his whole life, a stone's throw from Charles Walker when they were young. It can't be a coincidence. They even went to the same school.'

'So, the two men could have known each other, but Eddie's not a suspect. He was dead before Charles and Jake were attacked.'

'Yes, but . . .' Randle sounded impatient. 'People commit suicide for a reason. What if Eddie Adeola's suicide is related to both Charles and Jake's deaths?'

And if it was, what did Temi Adeola know?

We had finally reached the front door. The music had grown increasingly louder, drowning out all signs of human life. There were no lights visible, and the flat could have been deserted or packed with a heaving crowd. Akosua knocked loudly, shouting to be heard above the din.

'Mrs Adeola, it's the police. We'd like to ask you a few questions.'

It was anybody's guess if her words cut through the racket. I nodded for her to try again. Still nothing. Akosua stepped forwards for the third time; the door swung open, and a figure rushed out screaming. Too late, Akosua saw the wooden stick Temi aimed at her head. She managed to duck, but it caught the side of her body. She fell to the ground, clutching her ribs. I couldn't see blood, but her body trembled, and she cried out in pain. I looked up, searching for Temi. Her back grew smaller the further she moved away. She was still close enough for me to catch her, and my body sprang into action before I had time to think. I grabbed my radio as I ran.

'. . . Akosua's down. I need backup. Temi fled. All eyes out for her. I'm in pursuit . . .'

I sprinted down the concrete walkway, driving my knees as my arms pumped the air. Temi was already at the stairs, flinging herself down the steps with frightening speed. I was younger and fitter, but she had a head start. She burst out onto the street and turned down an alley, skidding round the corner without slowing down. I ran faster, pushing my body until I was close enough to reach out and grab her ankle. She wasn't expecting it, and she flew forwards head first. She threw her arm out to break her fall. I approached cautiously, holding up my hands to show I was unarmed. The strength of her kick stunned me as her foot crashed against my cheekbone. I was surprised by the force, but the shock numbed the pain. I knew I had to stop her from getting away. I leapt on top of her, trying to pin her down, but she bucked beneath me, lashing out with fists and feet. She was screaming hysterically, fighting back with everything she had. I tried to control her, but she just kept attacking. I felt my lip split and the vision in my left eye blur as her hand caught me across the face. The onslaught was relentless and all I could do was react; I didn't think to reach for my baton as my knuckles made contact with her flesh. For a fraction of a second, she didn't respond, then she came back more ferocious and feral. It felt like she would never stop, so I hit her again, then again, each blow coming faster and harder.

The sound of my phone shook me out of my frenzy. Suddenly lucid, I saw my raised fist ready to strike. Temi lay bloody beneath me, and I couldn't remember when I had ceased being the victim and become the aggressor. I lowered my arm, appalled and confused, my guard temporarily down. She reached for my leg, pulling me towards her so I hit the ground with a thud as she lifted herself up. It was only then, as I watched her disappear into the distance, that I felt a sharp, crippling pain filtering through my body. I was too sore and ashamed to move. I had let Temi escape, and I had hurt her more than I had ever hurt another human being.

Chapter Fifty-Seven

Leah

Somehow, I made my way back to Temi's estate. Seconds or minutes could have passed, and I wouldn't have known the difference. The lift seemed to move faster this time, and I barely registered the smell. My brain was completely empty, and all I knew was that I needed to get back to the flat and make sure Akosua was OK. The music had stopped, but there was the faint buzz of whispers as neighbours gathered to watch the drama unfold. I searched the faces for Akosua, but she wasn't where I had left her. Tentatively, I pushed open the door to the flat, waiting for another screaming attacker, but there wasn't one – just a room in near darkness, and the sense I wasn't alone.

The flat was haphazard, without being untidy. There was a worn plastic table in the corner of the room covered with paper, and a flat-screen television bordered by a column of DVDs. On the other side, a faded sofa obscured a small wooden cot. There was an unmistakable gurgling sound and, as I drew closer, I could see a child of about three or four, peering at me through the bars. Her cheeks were pressed up against the wood, and her eyes were wide and confused. I reached out to soothe her, pulling my hand back at the last moment. I could hear Akosua's voice calling my name. I followed the sound down the hall, squinting to make out the shapes in the gloom. Akosua was standing in a doorway, shielding my view. There was an angry bump next to her eye from her fall, the faint glow of a bruise dulled by dark skin. I offered a meek smile, but there was no time to talk as she stood aside.

The smell hit me, stale sweat mixed with faeces and rotting food. A potty lay overturned a few feet from where I stood, faint brown mush soaked into the damp carpet. Beyond it was an empty water bottle nestling against a pair of pristine white trainers. The room was cluttered with magazines and a handful of plates of half-eaten food. Thick curtains blocked out the sun so there was no sense of day or night. The air was hot and oppressive, and I could hear myself breathing. My breath was so loud, I didn't hear the voice at first.

'Help me . . . help me. Please . . .'

The voice was coming from behind me. I turned to see a figure slumped on the floor. Even hunched over, I could tell he was tall. There were purple marks on his wrist where the handcuffs had started to rub. One arm was chained to the radiator, the other hung limply by his side. His face was bruised, and a thin line of blood separated his lower from his upper lip. There was a gash on his right cheek, the flesh around it discoloured where it had started to scab over. His body shivered with tension, and his eyes searched for mine in the gloom. I closed the door, aware he was struggling to acclimatise to the light from the corridor. He tried to speak again. I squatted down, ignoring the pain as my battered thighs came to rest on my calves. He had to repeat himself twice before I understood what he was saying. I didn't interrupt him, not wanting to miss a word.

'Where's she gone?' he pleaded. 'My mum. Where has she gone?'

Then he closed his eyes, knowing I didn't have the answer.

Chapter Fifty-Eight

Leah

I crouched beside the man, lowering my voice so he knew I meant no harm.

'Can you confirm your name for me?'

It seemed obvious, but I needed him to say the words.

He just looked away, drawing his knees closer to his chest. I could see dark circles of sweat staining his blue T-shirt under the arms. A wave of body odour hit the back of my nose, and I stood up, unable to bear the pain in my legs. He flinched at the sudden movement. I spoke in a whisper, trying to gain his trust.

'I'm Detective Leah Hutch.'

He made no move to engage.

I pulled out a notebook, flipping to an empty page. I printed my name in bold letters, then ripped out the sheet and slid it towards him with a pen. He barely acknowledged it, shrinking into himself, his head bent. I said nothing as I waited, allowing him to communicate in his own way. Eventually I heard the rustle of paper as he slowly started to write. His hand shook with each letter, numbed by the pressure from the handcuffs, but he persisted, spelling out his name in shaky caps: Dele Adeola, Eddie's oldest child and only son.

The cold air stung as we made our way outside. I could see

goosebumps rising on Dele's skin, and he winced in the natural light. He didn't protest when we steered him towards the waiting ambulance; he said nothing as the paramedics settled him in. I stood watching the ambulance drive off. I barely noticed Randle approach. He raised his voice when the sirens started to blare, the blue lights sharpening the colour of his eyes.

'Ma'am? Uniform are still safeguarding Lola Adeola. They said you wanted to hold off calling social services?'

He was looking at me intently. I plunged my hands into my pockets to hide the bruises I knew he had already seen.

'Now's fine. Seeing his sister taken away would have been too much.'

'That's kind, ma'am,' Randle said. 'Sparing Dele from that.'

'No. Just pragmatic. We need him to talk to us. That might have tipped him over the edge.'

Randle watched me for a moment longer. Then he turned away to make the call. I could hear the sirens receding in the distance. My mind replayed what I had done to Temi as I began the walk back to her flat. I could hear Randle speaking behind me.

'You should go to hospital, ma'am. I can look after things here.'

I continued walking, refusing to turn back. Randle didn't say anything; he just followed, but I could sense the questions forming in his mind. He wanted to know what had happened with Temi, wanted to know what I had done.

You and me both, Randle. You and me both.

The smell of damp seemed stronger when we opened the door. Nothing had been touched since we were last there: the sheets of paper spilling off the table, the faded sofa on the other side of the room. I started with the table, scanning the blanket of paper covering it like patchwork. There were printouts of Temi's bank statements, leaflets about loans from various banks; there were scratch cards and lottery tickets, always with the same numbers, on top of A4 sheets with tiny indecipherable scrawl. The plastic surface underneath was heavily scratched, faded coffee stains lining the grooves. My eye was drawn to the television in the corner opposite; it was the one extravagance in the scruffy room. The DVDs stacked next to it made me think of the films Margaretta had used to comfort me when my nightmares woke me as a small child. I recognised some classics from the nineties at the base of the pile. Above them were a few films, remarkable only for their violence, and above them, half a dozen or so cases with nothing written on the spine. I flipped one open and examined the disc, black with silver lettering: BRENDAN KLEE – MENTALIST – A JOURNEY INTO THE MIND. I opened another: BRENDAN KLEE LIVE – MENTALIST – THE POWER TO OVERCOME SELF. Each one I opened was similar, the same Brendan Klee, a different take on mentalism. My limbs were beginning to burn, and I stood up, kneading away the cramp in my leg. With every spasm I was reminded of the scene in the alley, and I felt nauseous, remembering the thud as Temi's body hit the ground.

The wooden cot against the far wall was empty, a sad reminder of the family Temi had left behind. An abandoned teddy bear was wedged between the bars, and a bundle of tiny clothes lay scrunched to one side. A dark brown notebook poked out from beneath the folds of material. Inside, the writing was hard to read, and I moved it closer to the light. Charles Walker's name had been scribbled on the first page, and below it, 'Jake Munro', followed by his address.

'Ma'am . . .'

Randle's face was obscured by a large sheet of paper, creased where it had been folded into quarters.

'You need to see this, ma'am.'

I stood next to him, peering at a map of the city, red asterisks dotted around the centre, marking various locations. They would have seemed random, if I hadn't familiarised myself with them already, acutely aware of the significance of each address: the street in Richmond where Jake Munro had once lived; the route he had run each day; the exact location where he had died.

I turned my attention back to the notebook. There were pages of notes with what looked like details of Jake's movements, brief summaries next to specific times. Then a couple of blank pages, then the name 'Paul Drayton' with what looked like a company and home address printed underneath. Randle's eyes followed mine.

'Who's Paul Drayton?'

Chapter Fifty-Nine

Leah

Paul Drayton ran a successful graphic design company with offices in LA and London. He was travelling back from California when we called, and there was nothing we could do until he returned. I sent Akosua home and watched impatiently as a nurse bandaged my hand. I was sitting on a gurney in accident and emergency, listening to junior doctors deliver bad news in whispers around me. The previous occupant must have been tall, and my legs dangled over the edge like a child's. I had a vague memory of a time years before when I was sitting in a hospital corridor waiting for Margaretta. I remembered a nurse soothing me as I sat terrified on the hard plastic chair, and Margaretta barely glancing at me when she emerged. It wasn't something I had ever recalled before, but since Margaretta had died, I found myself clutching at memories, trying to understand our shared past. I tested the movement in my hand, clenching the muscles beneath the bandage to check they still worked. The pressure from the fabric felt uncomfortable and I ripped it off the moment I stepped outside.

The buzz of St Thomas' Hospital faded behind me as the automatic doors slid shut. Randle was perched on the wall at the edge of the car park, a cigarette balanced between index finger and thumb.

'The chief said to make sure you went home, ma'am,' he called out before I could pretend I hadn't seen him.

'Well, you've done your job, so you can go.'

I carried on walking, though it was difficult to move with speed.

'He ordered me not to leave without you. At least let me give you a lift to the station, ma'am.' He didn't make any attempt to follow me.

'OK.' I was determined not to show my relief.

We drove in silence for a while, but I could see the concern on his face as he sneaked a look at my busted knuckles.

'What happened with Temi, ma'am?'

He had more courage than I had given him credit for.

'We struggled; she got away; we need to find her.'

'Are you OK? You seem . . .'

I seem what? What do I seem, Randle?

We had stopped at the lights, and he was looking directly at me. His face was in shadow; his eyes were tinged with red. I waited for him to elaborate, but he just held my gaze. Then the lights turned green, and we moved off. He never finished his sentence.

Chapter Sixty

Leah

Dele was waiting when I arrived at the station. He had been checked medically, and the doctors saw no reason to keep him in overnight. His sister remained under the care of social services, but at twenty, Dele was technically an adult. Sitting in the interview room, he looked different from the startled wreck we had found chained to the radiator, calmer but still wary. His long legs were twisted under the table; small muscles coiled tightly around his arms. He looked uncomfortable in his own body, and he was in pain, struggling to sit straight in the chair.

'We can do this later, Dele. You've had a traumatic experience.'

'No.' He didn't make eye contact. 'I want to do this now.'

'OK, but if at any point you want to stop, just tell me.'

He nodded. 'Have you found my mum?'

'We're looking for her. Do you know where she is?'

'No.' He continued to look down. 'You have to find her. Tell her we're OK. She'll be worried.'

'We're looking,' I said. 'But right now, we need to know what happened in that room. Who put you in that room, Dele? Was it Temi?'

He sucked in the air, calming his nerves.

'How did you get those bruises, Dele?'

'I box,' he replied. 'Sometimes I get hurt.'

'And the handcuffs?'

His head jerked up. 'What about them?'

'Did Temi put them on you?'

'What will you do to her if she did?'

'We just need to talk to her,' I said.

'Why? So you can lock her up?'

'Do the names Charles Walker or Jake Munro mean anything to you?' I asked.

'Yeah. Munro was my dad's boss. Charles Walker was from our ends, but he married posh, made it big. My dad was always going on about him – what you can do with focus and good grades. That's why my mum got help with Lola, so I can study. Not get distracted. Change things for us. Lola's . . .' He trailed off.

'She's what, Dele?'

'She's not like other kids. She needs more attention. My mum's working two jobs. She's trying her best.'

'I'm sure she is. We found a lot of DVDs in your flat. Can you tell us anything about them?'

'They were big in the nineties, but you don't get them so much any more.'

His voice was completely deadpan.

'Funny. Tell me about Brendan Klee.'

'He's a mentalist guy. Mum bought into all that stuff – the power of the mind; what you do with the thoughts in your head. She liked what he did, but she didn't understand how it worked.'

'So, she watched the DVDs to understand?'

'I don't know. You'd have to ask her.'

'Paul Drayton. Does that name mean anything to you? We found it in a notebook.'

He sucked his lip, the petulance of a teenager in the body of a man.

'Paul Drayton. Think, Dele. It's important.'

'I met him once. He was one of my dad's friends from way back. That's all I know.'

'Are you sure?'

'I said so, didn't I?' The teenager again.

'Might your mother know more?'

'You would have to ask her yourself but, wait a minute . . . that would mean doing your job and actually finding her.'

'Has your mother met either Charles Walker or Jake Munro?'

'Why do you want to know?'

'We're looking for the person who killed them—'

He cut me off. 'It wasn't my mum.'

'I didn't say that, Dele.'

'Good.'

'We just want to speak to her, and we need your help to—'

'To what?'

'To find out the truth,' I said.

He shook his head in disbelief, dismissing me and anything more I had to say.

'I know what you want me to say and I'm not going to say it, so you might as well stop right there. My mother loves us. Stop accusing her of something she didn't do. Do your job and find her and make sure she's safe.'

Chapter Sixty-One

Leah

I let Randle drive, rubbing my knuckles when his eyes were on the road. The pain felt sharper now the adrenaline had worn off, and I closed my eyes involuntarily as a spasm shot through my fingers.

'I can question Paul Drayton on my own, ma'am, if you want to go home.' He kept his voice casual, but his tone was insistent.

'There's no need,' I said.

We fell back into uncomfortable silence as he manoeuvred the car through the wall of vehicles tightly packed on either side.

'What happened to Akos . . .' Randle hesitated, waiting for me to stop him. 'What happened to Akos wasn't your fault.'

I stared through the window as London shifted in the rain around us. The clouds were dense, and I could barely see the water fall in the dark.

'You weren't there,' I said.

'I spoke to her. She said she would have done the same.'

I could just about make out the raindrops when they hit the tarmac; I heard the creak of the handbrake as we stopped at the lights.

'You don't get it. She looks up to me.'

I felt Randle looking at me, but I didn't turn round.

'You say that like it's a bad thing, ma'am.' He almost sounded amused. 'There aren't many women of colour in senior positions in the force.'

I stared bleakly at the rain. 'Is that all I am?'

'I'm sorry. I just mean you're a role model.'

'Role models only let you down.'

He glanced at me as the car slid forwards. 'With all due respect, that's a pretty miserable way to see the world.'

The car slowed to keep pace with the traffic. I stared at the red rectangles in front of us as the line of brake lights stretched ahead.

'You know why I transferred back?'

'It's none of my business, ma'am.'

'I'm making it your business, just for today.'

I lowered the window so the space felt less enclosed.

'My boss made unwelcome advances, and I couldn't work with him any more.'

I expected Randle to react, but he just waited. His eyelashes were so thick, they were like a ring of kohl around his eyes. I thought back to that day with Mark in the office. He had surprised me, and I remembered being annoyed at first because I hate being caught off guard. It had taken a moment for my brain to catch up with what was happening because it was so unexpected – the click of the lock sliding into place, the feel of his hand turning my face to his. Then anger and indignation kicked in as I pushed him away. I remembered the sharp sensation when my wrist struck his hand and the distressed look on his face as he opened the door. It seemed inconsequential remembering it months after the fact, but I was shaken and furious and we could never go back.

'Did he . . . ?'

We had reached Paul Drayton's office and Randle eased the car into the only free space. He manoeuvred perfectly, two fingers resting on the wheel.

'He stopped before anything happened, but he'd crossed the line. The awful thing is . . .' I paused, acutely aware of my shame. 'I didn't report it.'

'Were you scared?'

The concern in his eyes only made it worse.

'No. That's not why. He was a senior officer, and I thought we needed more black role models in the force; the police don't need a reason to go backwards. I wanted him to be better, so I let people think he was.' I turned to face Randle. 'Now do you think I'm a role model?'

He didn't hesitate. 'To some people, yes.'

I reached for the door handle, relieved to escape into the rain.

The reception was poorly done up with bright mismatched chairs arranged round a multicoloured rug. Paul Drayton's office was more sombrely decorated, except for a series of fluorescent paintings on the wall behind his desk. The man himself eschewed colour, wearing understated grey cashmere, as expensive as it was dull.

'Paul Drayton.'

He held out his hand, steering us towards a curved charcoal sofa in the corner of the room. It was too small for two, so I chose to stand. Randle settled himself to one side, glancing at the empty space beside him. I focused on Paul.

'Eddie Adeola? Does that name ring any bells?' I asked.

I looked for signs of fondness at the mention of Eddie's name, but Paul's face was disinterested, and his eyes flicked to the door.

'Yes,' Paul said. 'We went to college together.'

'What about Charles Walker and Jake Munro?'

'I've never heard of a Jake Munro. Charles I knew, but only as an acquaintance. I never saw him after college. We weren't friends.'

'And you and Eddie were?'

He didn't answer. He poured himself some water from a silver jug by the window. He made no attempt to offer us a glass.

'Had you seen Eddie recently?' I asked.

'A while ago. He showed up out of the blue.'

'What did he want?'

'What's this about, Inspector?'

I noticed his hair was almost black, but the roots at the side were grey. He reached his hand to his head, self-conscious, lowering himself into the chair behind his desk.

'He wanted a handout,' he said.

'And did you . . . ?'

'Did I what?'

'Help him?'

He made a noise resembling a snort. 'I hadn't seen the guy for fifteen years. I didn't owe him anything.'

He rested his elbows on the leather armrests, his expression unashamedly smug. A wave of his aftershave drifted towards me. I managed not to cough.

'Why did you agree to speak to him?' I asked.

He looked down at a sheet of paper, studying it intently, even though it was blank. His jumper was too snug around his shoulders. He pulled at the seams to stop it bunching around his neck.

'Because . . .' He exhaled as the fabric visibly loosened. 'Because I knew he wanted something, and I was curious. He was always so superior when we were kids . . . Why are you asking me all this?'

'He took his own life, but that's not why we're here.'

He looked up, fiddling with the cuff of his shirt.

'Since Eddie died, two of his acquaintances – Jake Munro and Charles Walker – have been found murdered. Your name was found in a notebook with their names.'

Paul remained quiet, his eyes flitting from Randle's face to mine.

'It doesn't mean you're in danger,' I said. 'But you need to be careful. We're going to schedule check-in calls with you twice a day, at 8 a.m. and 9 p.m.' I looked at the clock on the wall. It was the same shade of grey as his trousers. 'You need to make sure you answer your phone. If we don't hear from you, we'll send someone out.'

He nodded dumbly, and I couldn't be sure he heard.

'Avoid going out after dark if you can. If at any point you think you're in danger, call 999. If you have any concerns, don't hesitate to phone me.'

I was still standing, and he looked hunched and meek. He was pompous, but he didn't deserve to die. I pulled out my card, scribbling the check-in times in the top right corner.

'8 a.m. and 9 p.m.,' I repeated. 'It's just a precaution but you need to be careful.'

Chapter Sixty-Two

Odie

Odie had never considered herself to be someone who needed to be loved, but she faltered under the weight of continued rejection: Ross, Daniel, Richard – the list kept growing, and now she could add Fiona and Mary. She had left messages for Daniel, but he hadn't returned her calls. Being shunned by her son was nothing new, but now Richard had stopped looking for excuses to ring, and she felt he was punishing her, finally holding her to account for the damage she had done to their son.

She woke up with a head full of alcohol and a sense of lost time. She couldn't remember falling asleep, but two facts were immediately apparent: it was night, and she was drunk. She had always liked being drunk – decisions were easier and she felt she was never wrong. She could hear something beeping, but she couldn't focus for long enough to find her phone beneath the debris on her bed. Seconds later, it beeped again, but this time she was ready for it, feeling her way under the covers until her hand closed over the hard case. It was a message from Baber asking her to pass on his regards to Richard on his birthday. She had made the mistake of inviting him to Richard's fortieth a long time ago. He had sent a message every year since, even though he knew the likelihood of Odie being with her ex-husband was slim. She searched for Richard's number, then stopped herself. She always called him, and he was often alone. Some years Daniel had just left or was due to arrive, but the truth of the matter was that Richard generally spent his birthday on his own. *Not this year!* she found herself thinking, buoyed by the alcohol. This year she would save him from his loneliness; this year she would be kind. She thought of Richard, home alone with a cake, and the idea of being his birthday saviour amused and cheered her. He would be glad of the company, and it would make her feel good about herself. A kind deed for mankind and a shrewd way to get things back to normal. He couldn't ignore her if she was standing on his doorstep with a bottle of champagne. She was already dressed, so it was just a matter of brushing her teeth and running her fingers through her hair. She didn't dare look in the mirror, but she was satisfied with her silhouette.

Walking up to the house, something felt wrong. Her senses were dulled so she didn't register the balloons or the fairy lights. It was the sound that threw her off course – laughter mixed with the buzz of energetic conversation. She had to knock several times to be heard. Eventually Richard appeared at the door. Even though she was drunk, she could tell she wasn't welcome.

'Happy birthday! Thought you might want some company.' She held up a bottle of cheap champagne, swaying slightly as she stood.

'Thank you.' He expertly unravelled her fingers from the bottle.

'Are you not going to invite me in?' Odie was slurring her words.

He looked nervously over his shoulder. 'Now isn't the best time.'

'It's your birthday. There's no better time. I didn't want you to be alone.'

She pushed past him into the house, but he blocked her path before she got to the sitting room.

'Now isn't the best time,' Richard repeated.

It was only then that she started to see the balloons, the lights, the guests turning to look at her.

'You're having a party.' Each word came out slowly as her brain gradually caught up with her eyes.

'Yes.' Richard bit his lip guiltily.

'All these people . . . I didn't know. I thought you would be alone.' Her voice sounded hollow and pathetic.

Richard was motionless in front of her, aware of his guests watching behind him.

'Stay,' he said gently. 'Let me get you a drink.'

'I'll get it.' She stumbled towards the kitchen. 'Remember, I used to live here.'

Her hip slammed into a side table as she turned. Her body swayed dangerously, but she managed to catch herself before her legs pulled her down.

'Who knew you had so many friends.' She didn't mean to be cruel, but she hated being on the back foot.

'I think it's best if you leave.'

She knew it was Daniel's voice, even though it sounded unfamiliar.

'Why me? If anyone has a right to stay, it should be me. I owned this house. I lived here. I looked after you. Remember?'

Daniel lowered his voice so only Odie could hear. 'Don't ruin it for him. Give him at least this. You weren't invited. You're not wanted today.'

Gently, but firmly, he began to steer her towards the front

door, but she waved him off, swiping a glass of champagne from a gawping guest. She drained it quickly, even though she had never liked the taste.

'Let's celebrate . . . but . . . you don't drink, do you?' The memory of their last conversation came too late. 'I'm so sorry, Daniel. Truly sorry . . . I didn't mean . . .'

She moved towards him, but her foot got trapped under a piece of raised carpet, and she collapsed inelegantly at his feet. Her breathing quickened and her eyes began to water, but she couldn't tell if she was crying. She reached up, but Daniel was staring back at her, making no move to help. Hatred or resentment she could understand, but there was no emotion in his eyes.

'I'll call you a cab.' It wasn't an act of kindness.

The room had gone strangely quiet. Odie was unable to move, struggling to unravel her limbs. Slowly, tenderly, someone was helping her to stand. Richard didn't say a word as he lifted Odie to her feet. Embarrassed, she shook him off, determined to preserve some dignity, but she was more forceful than she intended, and her elbow smacked hard into his jaw. Richard moved away in pain, oblivious to Odie's whispered apology. She tried to get his attention, but he couldn't bring himself to look at her. Her parting words were addressed to no one in particular.

'I'm sorry for everything. Tell him I'm sorry.'

Chapter Sixty-Three

Leah

It was morning, but most of London was still asleep. I tucked my backpack by a lamp post on the Embankment, unravelling my skipping rope from its compact bag. I hadn't skipped by the river in weeks, and I craved the calm only the Thames could bring. I started slowly, quickening my pace as unwanted thoughts entered my mind – what I had done to Temi; what had happened to my mother. The faster I skipped, the clearer my mind became until there was just a white wall of nothing and the sound of my feet and breath. A couple of joggers turned as they passed me, showing their solidarity with a slight upward nod. I ignored them, shifting my weight back and forth as sweat pooled at the base of my neck. I could feel my hands start to loosen around the handles. The tension slipped away, and my body started to relax. I closed my eyes, skipping harder for ten more minutes. Finally at peace, I continued my walk to work.

It was still early when I arrived at the station. I showered quickly before my colleagues shattered the lull. The Adeola flat had been thoroughly searched overnight. I retrieved a bag of evidence and placed it on the corner of my desk. The papers from the table in the sitting room had been placed on top: loan leaflets and bank statements in plastic sleeves, chronicling the Adeolas' debt. Below them was a stack of job rejections, the pages crinkled where they had been crumpled, then smoothed. I pulled on a pair of latex gloves and picked through the paper. There were at least two dozen letters over a period of several months, addressed to Eddie Adeola. Impersonal but polite, the words varied but the message was always the same: *thanks, but no thanks; there's no position for someone like you here.*

A door slammed in the distance, followed by the sound of slow footsteps on wood. Moments later, Randle strode past my door.

'Morning, ma'am. I didn't think anyone would be in.'

His face relaxed into a smile, and I managed a small one in return.

'Is that what I think it is?' I gestured at the battered DVD player hooked under his arm. 'I'm surprised you know what one is.'

'What, *this*?' He swung the machine out in front of him. 'I saw one in a museum once, I think.'

Grinning, he rested it on the edge of my desk. His eyes were bright, and he looked like he'd actually slept.

'My mum gives me a DVD every Christmas. She's convinced they're going to die out.'

'I'm sure the world will survive.'

'I won't, ma'am,' he said seriously. 'I spent my childhood watching my mum's films from the early nineties. They're my go-to when I need to unwind.'

My thoughts drifted to Margaretta and the bookshelf of DVDs I had grown up with.

Randle misread my distracted expression. 'Sorry, ma'am. Too much information.'

He hoisted the machine back under his arm, and I pushed Margaretta back into her compartment.

'Do you think there's something in the mentalist DVDs?' I asked.

'They're pretty unusual and there're a few of them.'

'I guess it doesn't hurt to take a look.'

'No, ma'am. You got a second?'

Randle had wheeled a TV into a side room. He plugged the DVD player into the wall.

'I wasn't sure where to begin, so I closed my eyes and picked one at random.' He handed me the remote control. 'Do you want to do the honours, ma'am?'

'Not particularly. Knock yourself out,' I said.

Brendan Klee made his living out of playing with people's minds, and I was sceptical about the power he professed to hold. We watched in silence as a man's face filled the screen, slowly shrinking in size as the camera zoomed out to reveal him alone on a stage, clutching a knife. The knife looked heavy in his hands, and the weight of it pulled down his shoulders so his arms slumped by his side. His eyes closed then opened wide, devoid of expression. Then we heard a voice off-screen – a soft Irish burr, coaxing him into action so his muscles tensed, and his right hand clenched around the handle, close to the blade.

'*No hesitation, no regret, just trust your instincts . . . No hesitation, no regret, just trust . . .*'

The words played in a loop, soothing and intense, but never loud.

'*No hesitation, no regret, just trust . . .*'

The man's arms were rising slowly now, left hand over right as the mantra was repeated again and again.

'*No hesitation, no regret, just trust your instincts . . . just trust . . .*'

The words continued; the man's eyes closed once more, then the image smashed to black.

We tried another DVD, then another. Each show was the same,

as seemingly random volunteers were encouraged to submit to their basest instincts. The same voice could be heard in the background, pushing each person beyond acceptable limits. We never saw the final act of brutality; we never saw Brendan Klee's face, but he was ever-present, seductive and enticing, promising true freedom in return for giving in to self.

Randle was watching me closely. 'You don't believe it's real, do you, ma'am?'

'It doesn't matter what I believe. It matters what Temi believed — why she turned to those videos in the first place. What have we got on Brendan so far?'

'Brendan Robert Klee. Born in Ireland, 1976. Mother ran out on them when he was a child. Brought up by his father and older sister. Describes magic as his means of escape. He hasn't been on the circuit long, but he's developed some avid supporters.'

'And the DVDs?'

'That's the thing,' Randle said. 'It's pretty retro, but that's all part of his vibe. You can't buy them online or in shops; the only way you can get them is by going to one of his shows and being handed one personally. Kind of a survivor's badge of honour. Also, easier to control distribution.'

'So, Temi must have gone to at least one show.'

'Must have.'

Randle slotted a leaflet into my hand — well made and professional, without appearing too glossy or slick. *Brendan Klee: the Power of Self.* He flashed his phone in front of my face, showing me a code.

'What?'

'Two tickets for tomorrow, ma'am,' he said. 'Experience Brendan Klee first-hand. Talk to the man himself.'

Chapter Sixty-Four

Paul Drayton had no idea he was being followed, and it wasn't the first time. He had been on high alert since the detectives had come to see him, eyes flitting around every few steps, breath quickening if anyone came too close. He had never been particularly observant, and it felt too late to learn, so he just walked faster when he was out in the city, blaming Eddie Adeola for making him afraid. When Eddie had emailed him after all those years, Paul knew what the man wanted before Eddie had even asked. He should never have agreed to take the meeting, but he couldn't resist seeing Eddie's face when he said 'no'. Eddie had always acted superior at college and seeing him grovel reminded Paul how far he had come. Now his moment of triumph had been reduced to nothing. He had everything he ever wanted, but he was scared to walk down his own street.

Paul stiffened as he felt someone approach him, holding his breath until the figure moved on. He laughed nervously as he watched a woman disappear with her baby, embarrassed he had thought she meant him harm. It was broad daylight, and he was surrounded by people. He whispered affirmations from therapy, convincing himself he was safe.

The footsteps were silent, but he sensed a stride that mirrored his. His body seized up, but he didn't have the courage to turn round. He braced himself for pain he knew he would never survive.

'Not today. Please don't let me die today,' he prayed to the God he had forgotten. 'Please God, don't let me die today.'

Chapter Sixty-Five

Leah

'Come in.'

Brendan Klee's voice was harsher than in the videos. He was sitting on a stool at his dressing table, wearing a half-zipped navy velour hoody, his pale white chest with a smattering of hair on show. His back was towards the door, but he smiled at us from the reflection in the mirror. Margaretta had always said that a person has an optimum body shape and try as they might, no diet or binge could hide who they really are. She said she could always see the fat person fighting to burst through the anorexic skeleton, or the thin person's face hidden in the wider, larger shell. When I had asked her whether that meant we could never escape our true selves, she had just smiled sadly: *You can never escape who you are, and even if you think you've succeeded, the shadow of your former self is always lurking, reminding you of who you once were.*

Brendan Klee's shadow loomed large – an enormous ego to compensate for what he lacked in height.

'Thank you for helping us with our enquiries.' I nodded to Randle, and he flashed a photograph of Temi on his phone. 'Do you recognise this woman?'

'Of course,' Brendan said without hesitation. 'I don't know her name, but I never forget a face.'

'When did you first see her?'

'Over a year ago. She wanted to volunteer for one of my experiments, but she didn't have the courage. She came up to me afterwards. Introduced herself. She did that a couple of times before she opened up.'

'What did she say?'

'She said . . .' He paused, savouring the revelation. 'She said she sometimes had dark thoughts. People had hurt her family and she wanted to make them pay. Wanted to but lacked the courage.'

'So, she came to *you* for courage?'

'People come to me for all manner of things.' His eyebrows rose along with his voice.

'Courage to do what?' I said.

'She didn't specify.'

'And you didn't think to ask?'

Brendan welcomed my question in the way any true narcissist would, relishing the opportunity to talk about himself.

'That's not what my show is about. It's not what interests me as an artist or performer. If people were forced to confess their darkest desires, they might never act on them, never be true to themselves for fear of exposure and ultimately judgement.'

'What if you're enabling them to commit a violent act?'

'Not enabling, not suggesting, just empowering. What people do with that power is up to them. Ours is not to judge.'

His gaze shifted to the mirror. I could feel his eyes on me, even though it was only my reflection.

'What would you think if I told you this woman is being investigated for the murder of two individuals?'

I watched for his reaction beneath the bravado. There was no trace of emotion in his eyes.

'I would say she's come a long way from the woman who first walked into my audience.'

'Two men are dead.'

'And I'm sorry for their families, but it doesn't make that woman's increase in confidence a negative thing. Her heart's ultimate desire is not my responsibility. My work is about showing people what they have the power to do; what they do with that confidence when they leave is another matter altogether.'

He was so busy performing, he almost paused for applause.

'I make no apologies, Inspector,' he said. 'There's a darkness in us all. You need to recognise who you are and not hide behind middle-class respectability. There's no such thing as good or bad. Just experiences and people, and sometimes people aren't very nice.'

He had been practising his speech; I could tell.

'You're judging me.' He turned to face me, a spark of indignation in his eyes. 'You think I'm evil or amoral. I'm neither. I just help people see who they really are. Some people would call that kind.'

'*Some* people are dead,' I said.

'But *I* didn't tell her to kill them.'

His velour hoody clung tightly around his waist. I wanted to shake him until the pretence fell away.

'You encouraged her.'

He shrugged, one hand resting on his zip, the other wafting the air.

'She would have done something at some point anyway. Some people just do. Come tonight and see for yourselves.'

The room had grown hot from the lights, and the faint sweetness of his cologne made me nauseous.

'Did you hypnotise Temi Adeola?' I said.

'If you're asking whether I told her to kill two men, then the answer is no. I didn't. We only spoke properly the one time. But . . .'

'But what?'

He looked down, and I realised he was ashamed.

'She volunteered for one of my experiments the week after we spoke. She was the only volunteer who didn't respond. My shows are recorded. You can check.'

'You mean the experiment didn't work.'

'No.' He raised his eyes to meet mine. 'Most people respond to my work, but there's a minority who can't or won't engage. Temi Adeola was one of those people. She said she wanted to but, for some reason, she couldn't.'

'And did she come back after that?'

'I wouldn't know. I never saw her face in the audience, but that doesn't mean she wasn't there. The lights can be blinding when I'm on stage.'

There was a knock at the door, and a voice announced his fifteen-minute warning.

'The call of success. I hope you appreciate the show.' He chose the verb carefully. Then, without warning, he pulled his zip down completely, challenging us to give in to our discomfort and leave.

Outside the door, Randle spoke for the first time.

'He's right, ma'am.'

'He's a fraud,' I said.

'That's as maybe, but he's still right. You can't make someone do something they don't want to do. Not if they have a choice.'

We made our way to the auditorium. It was smaller than I imagined, with chairs arranged in concentric circles, rising up around the stage. The lights dimmed without warning, and the audience went silent as Brendan emerged from the darkness. It was difficult to see how tall he was from our seats; his clothes were cut to elongate his frame, and there was a slight heel to his shoe in the same material as his trousers. He wore thick-rimmed glasses, which I suspected were for appearances, and his voice was richer than it had been before.

'Who are you? Who are we? What are we capable of? What do we want? Deep down. Inside. Some of us choose to admit our desires. Most of us don't. Tonight I want to show you what you might be capable of, so you have the power to go after what you truly want. To be honest with yourselves, maybe for the first time.'

The woman next to me sat so far forward in her seat, her breath sent ripples through the hair of the man in front. She nodded as Brendan talked, as though he were speaking only to her. I glanced at Randle beside me – relaxed in his chair, his blond hair pushed back. We waited as volunteers were selected, placing themselves at the mercy of Brendan Klee. We were introduced to Emily, dressed completely in black. She claimed never to have met Brendan and was desperate to sing in public. She tried and failed, her throat closing up, so her voice came out in a rasp. Her eyes welled up in defeat, and she dropped her head in shame. Randle leant close, a wisp of his hair brushing against my cheek.

'Let me guess,' he whispered. 'Brendan works his magic, and she sings like an angel.'

We watched as Brendan unleashed a lengthy monologue, easing Emily into a more relaxed state. She opened her mouth, but nothing came out; she opened it again, transformed into a pseudo-celestial being. Randle grinned; I fought the urge to laugh. It was too staged, too pretentious to be real. Temi may have come looking for something, but I couldn't believe she had found it in Brendan Klee.

It was a far cry from what we had watched on DVD, but Brendan was shrewd enough to cater for a diverse audience. As the evening drew on, the mood darkened; the desires became less innocent as Brendan sought to surprise and shock. Twenty-year-old Kay told us his story. He stammered when he shared how he had been bullied all his life. He wanted to fight back but didn't have the courage. His body slumped, eyes cast down as he mumbled. Brendan stood next to him, encouraging and seductive, expensive glasses perched on the end of his nose. He signalled to a helper we couldn't see, and a foam mannequin was wheeled onto the stage. Brendan whispered in Kay's ear, and we watched as he was made to think it was the man who had ridiculed him all his life. At first, he stood limp in front of it, but Brendan continued his inaudible speech, providing gentle prompts. There was a hush, then Brendan clicked his fingers, the sound amplified in the quiet room. It was as if something snapped deep inside Kay. He pummelled the dummy with a relentless show of strength. If he was acting, he was acting well. I leant forwards in my seat to get a better look. His knuckles were bruised, and I could see the rise and fall of his chest.

I almost didn't hear Brendan calling our names. A light beamed in my eyes as he asked for more volunteers. I sat still, blocking out the murmurs around me, but Randle rose to his feet, making his way down the carpeted steps. I could feel Brendan looking, but I refused to move. Then I saw the challenge in his eyes, and I stood.

There were two other couples on the stage. I focused on the faces in the audience as Brendan spoke.

'Let's welcome our volunteers.'

He clapped theatrically, and the applause grew around us. He held up a hand to quiet the crowd.

'Three couples. What they mean to each other, only they know. One person from each pair will be hypnotised so they lose all inhibitions. When I give the prompt, they will act on whatever urge overcomes them, revealing their true self. Remember, there's no shame in being who you are. Only truth and peace.'

I rolled my eyes, not caring if he saw me. Brendan beamed at an audience who believed everything he said.

Randle chose to be hypnotised, and I was led away with two others to a cupboard-sized room with a tightly sealed door. A pair of headphones was clamped onto my ears, and I waited to be escorted back to the stage. I wasn't sure what to expect, and the uncertainty momentarily made Brendan more interesting. Minutes later, I stood facing Randle again. The lights had been turned up, and the audience was a blur as Randle stared through me, his eyes alive with an unnatural energy. No one moved; then Brendan lifted a spotted handkerchief to his nose, and the atmosphere abruptly changed. There was the sound of a slap as the man next to me was hit by his partner, and the splutter of someone choking as the woman on my other side squeezed her husband by the throat. I watched transfixed as two security guards wrestled them apart. I was so absorbed, I hardly noticed the pressure weighing down on my hand. Randle's eyes continued to look through me, but his fingers wrapped themselves around mine, his thumb gently caressing my palm. Then, before I could process what was happening, he let go. He walked off the stage in silence, leaving me to follow. I didn't need to look back; I knew Brendan was watching us, triumphant.

'Why did you go up on stage?' We were sitting in the car avoiding eye contact after the show. 'We're police officers. That's not why we were there.'

'He called our names, ma'am.' Randle still didn't look at me. 'I'm sorry. I didn't see the harm.'

'We work together. You gave me no choice. Don't put me on the spot like that again.'

He nodded, wringing his hands in his lap. I turned on the ignition, letting the engine fill the silence between us. I released the handbrake, then jerked it back up.

'What was that? On stage? What *was* that?'

'What was what, ma'am?'

'Your hand, my hand? What was *that*?'

Randle finally looked at me. I could see his eyes were dazed.

'I honestly don't know.'

'What do you mean, you don't know? Why were you holding my hand?'

I cut off the engine. I felt more exposed without the sound.

'I don't know,' Randle repeated, and his uncertainty unsettled me.

'So that was all Brendan?'

'No.' His voice was low, and he wouldn't look at me. 'That was me . . . But I didn't know I was doing it . . . It *was* me but it *wasn't*.'

Chapter Sixty-Six

Leah

The image of Brendan Klee played in my mind as I crossed the bridge the next morning – his sparkling eyes watching us leave. I shook off the memory, annoyed he had got through to Randle, quickening my pace to beat the onslaught of rain. It was just after eight, and the cars moved in a steady stream on the road beside me. I dialled the duty inspector to check Paul Drayton had answered his call.

Kenny O'Sullivan was waiting as I entered the building, blocking my path to the stairs.

'She lives!' He laughed, even though he hadn't made a joke. 'I hear you're using my budget to take in the occasional show.'

He adjusted the collar of his jacket, dark green eyes resting on my face.

'We had a lead on Temi Adeola, sir,' I said, '. . . a mentalist called Brendan Klee.'

This time Kenny's amusement was genuine; I could see him rehearsing a punchline in his head.

'Let me guess – he communed with Temi telepathically and persuaded her to turn herself in?'

He waited for me to laugh; I didn't. He drew himself up, his expression changed.

'You had her, and you lost her, Inspector. I don't care how, but you better find her again.'

I shut the door to my office and eased into my chair, my final moments of peace ruined by my encounter with Kenny. The plastic bag must have been on my desk before I sat down, but it was only then that I noticed it, heavily crinkled from multiple use, a dark blue envelope balanced on top. Inside was a note, folded carefully to fit:

'Apologies for any offence caused. DS Ben Randle.'

Short and appropriate; I threw the note away. The gift felt unnecessary, and my first thought when I opened the bag was that I hated mugs. They were ugly and unwieldy, and I never drank out of them if I could help it. Then I saw Brendan Klee's face emblazoned on the side, with the words: *Have the courage to be yourself* in gold italics just below his chin, and I realised it was a memento from the show. It was tacky and ridiculous. I smiled at Randle's attempt to lighten the mood. It was only when I reached for the bin that I realised I had seen the mug before.

I hadn't seen Akosua since Temi's flat, and it was a relief to hear her voice when I walked into the main office.

'Printouts of the photos you asked for, ma'am.'

She placed them on the table in front of us. She had a slight bruise hiding under a layer of foundation — a grim reminder of her fall. She looked tired and more pensive than normal.

'I'm sorry,' I said. 'For what happened.'

My words sounded stilted and insincere.

'No, *I'm* sorry,' she said. 'I wanted to help, and I couldn't.'

'Akosua . . .' I took her elbow, steering her away from the others.

'You have nothing to apologise for. There was nothing more you could have done.'

She let out a slow exhalation, looking younger and more vulnerable.

'Thank you. That means a lot. I thought I had let you down.'

She rubbed her ribs absentmindedly, and I felt a pang of guilt. I could see Randle watching, offering a tentative smile.

I followed Akosua back into the centre of the room. Images of Fiona Garvey's immaculate flat were spread out on a table; Randle had arranged them in a grid so the edges completely aligned.

'What are we looking for, ma'am?' Akosua asked, trying to make sense of the order.

I placed Randle's mug on the faux-wooden surface so it landed with a small thud. For a second, he looked embarrassed, unsure what I was about to say. Then he saw my look of concentration, and his body relaxed. There was no sign of the mug in any of the photos, but the more I was reminded of the contents of Fiona's flat, the more I became convinced that I had seen Brendan Klee's face in miniature once before.

'Where are the pictures of the kitchen?' I asked.

'Here, ma'am.' Akosua directed me towards a cluster of photographs I had so far ignored.

The pristine work surfaces and bleached floors had been captured as evidence, but no one had thought to open the cupboards. I reimagined myself standing in Fiona's kitchen, forming an impression of the woman before she had spoken to me: the sterile sense of order; the meticulous attention to detail; the lack of a personal touch. Everything had had its place . . . everything except for the collection of mugs in the cupboard above the hob. Each one had told a story, representing a piece of history Fiona didn't want to forget – the leavers' mug from secondary school with names inscribed across the back; mementos from the various musicals she had been to over the years; merchandise from the 2012 Olympics, showing her support for the world's greatest city; and Brendan Klee, smiling broadly, right at the back. I could see it now, and I knew I hadn't imagined it. I didn't know when, but Fiona must have been to one of his shows. Fiona Garvey and Temi Adeola, two suspected killers, somehow connected by Brendan Klee.

Chapter Sixty-Seven

Odie

Odie woke up with an agonising weight bearing down on her head. The pressure was excruciating, and she turned vigorously in a vain attempt to shake it off. She slid up against the wall behind her bed, examining her reflection in the mirror opposite. There was nothing on her head except the usual bird's nest of wiry hair, but the pressure continued, squeezing her brain against her temples. She had forgotten the previous night but, staring at her pallid face and red-rimmed eyes, she realised she had drunk too much again, and the pain in her head was nothing more than the hangover threatening to ruin her day. It was almost three days since her humiliation at Richard's house, but she couldn't forget the look of loathing Daniel had made no effort to disguise. So much for the apology she had wanted to make for standing him up; now she would have to apologise for this too. She reached for her phone and dialled his number. She had tried the day before and knew he wouldn't answer, but she needed to show willing so she wasn't completely useless in his eyes.

The sound of the bell saved her from self-pity. After the initial dizziness, being upright was strangely soothing. She moved hesitantly down the stairs, but there was no one at the door by the time she got to it. She looked down to find a brown A4 envelope, her name printed neatly across the front. She stooped to open it, her brain slowed by alcohol. There was a single piece of paper, blank except for Fiona Garvey's name, with a link printed underneath. The URL was composed of a random sequence of letters. She typed it carefully into the browser on her laptop, but when she clicked 'enter', she was confronted by an error message in angry caps. She felt like she was being taunted. The one person who could answer her questions was refusing to speak to her, and Mary Garvey had turned from cooperative ally to overprotective bodyguard once again. Frustrated, Odie crushed the paper and threw it in the bin. She had lost the will to follow clues she didn't understand, and she finally accepted what had been made all too clear – Fiona Garvey's story would never be hers to tell.

Chapter Sixty-Eight

Leah

Everything about Fiona's prison reminded me of Eli – the sterile vinyl under my feet, the smell of disinfectant pumping through my nose. Even though I wasn't going to see him, his presence loomed, and I could hear his voice in my head.

So, you followed in my footsteps.

Would I, if I had known?

'Ready?'

I hadn't noticed I had stopped walking, until the guard turned to address me.

'Yes,' I said. 'I'm ready.'

Fiona looked older than I remembered, her compact torso pasted to the back of the chair. She seemed anxious and fragile, but her eyes were more alive than when I had seen her last.

'Inspector.' She made an attempt to smile, but the corners of her mouth refused to rise.

'Thank you for seeing me. I appreciate your help.'

'I haven't done anything yet, but I'll try my best.'

'Thank you.'

She looked weary, and I wondered how long I would have before she inevitably shut down.

'Remember the photographs I showed you?' I said.

Fiona's eyes widened, and the woman I had interviewed that first time threatened to return. 'I don't want to see that again.' She sounded scared.

'No. But I think you might be able to help me find the person who killed that man.'

'I had nothing to do with that . . .'

I could sense the fear returning, and I rushed to reassure her.

'I know, Fiona. I do. But we think you may be able to help us. Do you know the name Brendan Klee?'

She nodded, sensing she was on safer ground.

'How do you know him?'

'I went to one of his shows.' No hesitation this time.

'When?'

'Last year sometime . . . I only went to one.'

'Why?'

'I read an article online. I was struck by his confidence in what he could do. He was assertive, fearless. Like he had it all figured out . . .' Fiona smiled sadly. 'He claimed to be able to see into a person's soul. I thought he would have answers.'

'And did he?'

'No.' The disappointment was still there. 'He manipulated people; it's not the same thing.'

I pulled out a photograph of Temi.

'Do you know this woman?'

Barely glancing at it, Fiona shook her head.

'Are you sure? Have you ever seen her before?'

She leant closer, looking properly this time. 'No.'

'And you never saw or spoke to her at one of Brendan Klee's shows?'

'I only went once. I told you. She could have been there, but I didn't see her. No.'

I slipped the photograph back into its folder. 'Thank you, Fiona. You've been a big help.'

'Have I?'

She looked at me expectantly, and I caught a glimpse of a different Fiona, who dared to hope. I almost felt guilty knowing how hard she would have to fight to win her freedom, then I reminded myself of the image of her covered in someone else's blood. When she spoke again, her voice was quiet, but there was a force to it which caught me off guard.

'It wasn't me. What happened to Alistair . . . I need you to know it wasn't me.'

My phone rang the moment I emerged from the building. The sunlight stung after the fluorescent bulbs inside. I blinked rapidly to reacclimatise my eyes.

'You need to see the news, ma'am. I sent you a link,' Randle said.

The reception was poor, and it took a minute for the words to arrange themselves in a coherent order on screen.

'Mentalist linked to murderer. Does this man have the power to control minds?'

Next to the headline was the image Brendan Klee had used on his merchandise, cheekbones and jaw sharpened by Photoshop.

'How did they know about Brendan?' I asked.

'That's the thing; it seems he told them. His publicist put the story out.'

Chapter Sixty-Nine

Leah

Brendan Klee looked different out of his natural habitat, less cocky and much smaller. His arms were locked around his chest, and he kept looking at the door, as if he were scared we would never let him out. The navy velour hoody had been replaced by a pink one, too pale for his complexion so he looked washed-out.

'First time in a police station, Brendan?'

I wasn't trying to intimidate him, but it didn't hurt.

'Am I under arrest?' He raised himself up in his chair.

'No, you're not, but we need to ask you a few questions, and it's easier if you answer them voluntarily.'

'Fine. I have nothing to hide.'

'Good. Because we need your help, and I'd prefer it if you were honest with me.'

He didn't flinch when I showed him the headline, reading it out loud. He whispered the words as he scanned the rest of the text, chuckling at his handiwork.

'Oh look . . .' His voice was mocking. 'You got a special mention for leading the investigation. They even named your station. That's a nice touch, don't you think, Inspector?'

'Why did you give that story to the media?'

'I didn't, and even if I did . . .' he glanced at the article, 'you know you can't believe everything you read.'

Where I saw dead bodies, he saw free publicity. He ran his hands over his velour thighs.

'"My work is about showing people what they have the power to do." Remember that?' I said.

'They're my words, so I'd be embarrassed if I didn't remember. I'm surprised you do. I wasn't sure you were paying attention.'

'The human brain is an amazing thing,' I said. 'You should know that more than most. Tell me about your work.'

'This feels like a job interview or a date.'

'If either of those could land you in prison.'

Brendan's expression changed. The groove in his forehead deepened, and his eyes narrowed into a frown. I almost smiled.

'What do you want to know?' he said.

'You claim to show people what they have the power to do. How?'

'I help people get to a place where they can listen to their hidden voice and have the courage to do what it says.'

'Meaning?'

'That would be telling.'

'I'd hate to have to arrest you to get the answer.'

Our eyes locked. He realised I wasn't joking.

'It's a combination of elements — hypnosis, prior knowledge, showmanship. Not everyone can do what I do,' he said.

'You put ideas into people's heads.'

'The seeds are already there. I'm just the gardener who makes them grow.' He smiled, pleased with the cliché.

'But not everyone's susceptible?' I remembered Temi and the failed attempt.

'No. You have to commit. What are you getting at, Inspector? I already told you I had nothing to do with Temi Adeola.'

I placed a photograph of Fiona Garvey on the table.

'Do you know this woman?'

'Should I?'

'She came to one of your shows.'

He shrugged, scratching his neck.

'She's currently charged with attempted murder for an attack much like the ones allegedly committed by Temi Adeola.'

I paused to let the information sink in, watching the different emotions flash across Brendan's face. He glanced up at the window, too high for him to see outside. I hoped he was imagining being trapped in prison, and I took my time to let the image land.

'Two women come to your show at different times and go on to commit heinous acts,' I said.

'And you think I had something to do with that?'

'You put the message out there yourself.'

'PR, Inspector. I'm creating a brand, not a stable of killers. I've never told anyone to murder someone.'

'You "unlock things", "speed up the process".'

'I can *suggest* things, but I don't have that kind of power. Look at me; do you honestly believe I can make someone kill?'

I looked at the man opposite, slumped in the plastic chair.

'I honestly don't know.'

Chapter Seventy

Paul Drayton hadn't been out for two days. It was the longest he had been alone since he had got divorced, and the sound of his thoughts was driving him crazy. If whoever had committed those murders didn't kill him, the solitude would finish him off. He knew it was stupid to think like that, but he had never been good with his own company, and video calls for work didn't count. He moved to a different room every couple of hours, but it didn't make much difference – the same bare cream walls, the same inoffensive designer furniture. His ex-wife had always said that he couldn't buy taste, but he could pay people to save him from vulgarity. She'd been right but, alone in his empty house, he would have given anything for colours and texture, anything to distract him from his fear. He couldn't bear the paranoia when he was out, the queasy sensation when he sensed someone behind him, but he couldn't stay isolated forever. He needed to have his ego massaged so he felt less like a shell of a man. He hit the remote control and watched the blinds roll up. It was still light outside, and the street lamps had yet to come on. Plenty of time to venture out and get home before dark. He would call a taxi; he wouldn't take risks.

He stood in his garden and took a drag from his cigarette, using his finger to chase the puffs of smoke away from his face. Flicking through his mental address book, he wished he had been less careless with friends. He had never been good at keeping them, and he found he didn't need them when he was married. Now he would have given anything for someone to confide in, to hand him a drink and tell him everything would be OK. He pulled out his phone and clicked on a dating app. He needed a companion to remember why it was good to be alive.

The front gate was open when he headed out. He always closed it, but he'd been so preoccupied of late, it could have slipped his mind. He stared back at his garden, in shadow under the sinking sun. It had started to drizzle and, for the first time in days, he enjoyed a moment of peace. As his fingers reached for the latch, he realised he had been holding his breath. He exhaled slowly as the gate swung shut.

Chapter Seventy-One

Leah

'You let Brendan Klee go?'

Kenny O'Sullivan was a master at making accusations sound like questions. I stood facing him in his hot office, trying not to look at the clock. The light was fading through the only open window, and he reached to turn on a lamp.

'There are no grounds to charge him, sir.'

He punched some letters on his keyboard, but what he was typing was anybody's guess. 'And his article?'

'Empty bragging to boost his audience.'

'An audience you wasted taxpayers' money to be a part of, when you didn't have a substantial lead.'

I hovered, waiting for an invitation to sit. I was glad when the offer never came. The blind had been partially lowered over the window behind him, and Kenny's shadow shifted on the canvas every time he moved.

'Any news on Temi Adeola?' His elbows rested on the edge of his desk.

'No sign as yet but she's our top priority.'

'Hutch . . .'

He rarely used my surname and when he did, I knew what followed would be a threat or a reprimand.

'Hutch,' he said again. 'A lot of people thought you weren't ready for DI.' He leant back in his chair, playing silent drums on the curve of his stomach. 'Don't make me regret bringing you onto this team.'

I had never sought Kenny's praise, but I couldn't afford to lose his support.

'You won't, sir,' I said.

The shadow behind him moved left.

'Then don't let me keep you.'

I knew he would be listening to my footsteps to see if I hesitated. I kept going until I was back on my floor. Randle was at the other end of the corridor when I turned the corner. His sleeves were rolled up, and I noticed a bruise across his lower arm. He followed my gaze, pulling his shirt down to his wrist.

'I raced my bike last night, ma'am. Took a corner too fast.'

'Maybe you should stop. Save yourself the physio bills,' I said.

He dipped his head so he was looking directly at me. 'It helps me blow off steam when I have things on my mind.'

His eyes were clear, framed by his thick lashes. He searched my face, but I kept it blank.

'Last night, when you held my hand, you seemed different. Do you think you would have done that if it hadn't been for Brendan Klee?'

'No. I would never have crossed that line . . .' He lowered his voice so the words stayed between us. 'What I did . . . I would never have done that if it hadn't been for him. It was inappropriate and I'm sorry, ma'am. I'm not trying to excuse it but . . .'

I said nothing.

'I must have wanted to do it, but I would never have dared.'

He looked at me, allowing himself to be vulnerable. His face was so open, I almost turned away.

'What did Brendan do to you?'

'I don't know.' Randle seemed lost for a moment. 'The handkerchief. His voice. I can't think what he said. I felt like I wasn't in control, but I was doing what I wanted all at the same time. Does that make sense?'

I thought back to what Fiona had said about being drawn to Brendan's confidence.

'Like he gave you courage?'

'Yes,' Randle said. 'I know he seems like a fraud, but he had an effect on me. And that's the truth.'

Chapter Seventy-Two

Leah

It was late when I started my journey home, and the bridge was lit up over the water. The rain had got heavier, and I slid a beanie over my head. Five minutes suspended above the Thames, and London changed around me. I walked along the river and turned down Beaufort Street, red-brick mansion blocks in a line on either side.

As I drew closer to my estate, I glanced at the message from the duty inspector updating me on Paul Drayton: he had answered his phone after one ring, on the dot of 9 p.m. I smiled knowing he had made it through another day.

I was struck by the silence when I opened my front door. The flat was too warm, and I made a mental note to remember to turn off the heater on my way out. I was too tired to think about cooking as I slipped my jumper over my head. I lay on my bed, exhausted, but my mind was flooded with images that kept me awake. All I could see were faces I wanted to forget – Brendan Klee, Temi Adeola, Fiona Garvey: Brendan urging a volunteer to have the courage to use a knife; Temi panting as I chased her out into the street; Fiona bloodied with her bat outside the police station. I thought back to a time I couldn't sleep as a child. It had taken me an hour to be brave enough to go to Margaretta. When I had asked to stay in her bed, she had marched me back to my little room. I was terrified she would leave me alone, but she had sat on the edge of my mattress and started counting; by the time she got to a thousand, I was fast asleep. I turned onto my side and started to count out loud. I was on 2,001 when I finally gave up. I hated the idea of sleeping pills, but I was out of options. I set my alarm, swallowed a tablet and waited for it to take effect.

I woke up groggy, long before my alarm. My phone was on silent, but the screen was flashing in the dark. I reached for it, my eyes half closed, desperate for sleep. There were two missed calls from Paul Drayton, the last made only minutes before. He sounded panicked, and I could feel the dread rising as I listened to his voice.

'*Detective Hutch. I think there's someone in my house. I was having a smoke outside and I heard something. I checked and I couldn't see anyone, but it doesn't seem right. Someone could have got in. I feel like I'm going mad. I—*'

The message cut off abruptly.

I stared at the phone lying limp in my hand. It was 2.05 a.m. Paul Drayton had made the call at 1.57. I dialled Randle's number and prayed I wasn't too late.

Chapter Seventy-Three

Leah

Ten minutes later, Randle's motorbike was outside my block of flats. I clung to his jacket as we sped off into the dark. I could smell soap tinged with lemon through the rough leather. I tightened my grip, unable to relax. The city whizzed past as we drifted through London, skidding to a halt outside Paul Drayton's house. I had called for backup, but the street was empty. His gate was open, gleaming white in the moonlight; the hinge had slipped, so the front corner dug into the ground. I was conscious of the engine revving in the silence; there was an eerie stillness when Randle switched it off. Randle heard the wail first, low and agonised like a wounded animal crying for its mother. He moved fast, disappearing round the back. I raced after him, sliding over the wet grass. I could see him ahead, black leather blending into the dark. He stopped abruptly, and I slammed into him. I stood, winded, rain seeping through my shoe. I saw the feet first, expensive trainers attached to cashmere legs. Then a torso, rigid and unmoving on the lawn. Then a mess of battered flesh attached to a neck. My eyes were drawn to a Gollum-like creature crouched near the prostrate body, bloody hands clasped as if in prayer. I was forced to look away.

Something about the scene didn't make sense. Paul Drayton was definitely dead – his shirt puckered and ripped where a knife had jabbed into his flesh. A trail of blood leaked from his side to the woman stooped next to him – Temi Adeola, collapsing towards the ground. She made no attempt to run and with every passing second, her head sagged lower. Her breath was jagged as she sank further and further down. She was struggling to get something out of her pocket. She looked to me for help, and I realised she had slit her wrist, slicing into the arteries above her hand. Randle sprang into action, stemming the flow of blood with his jacket. He gripped her hands in his, but she fought to free them. With tremendous effort she lifted her head, silently urging me to come closer, but I couldn't move, grinding my feet into the sodden grass. There was something about her expression which felt familiar. I tried to remember where I had seen it before, but my mind went blank. All I could hear was the sound of crying.

I stood back as Temi was wheeled into the ambulance. She turned to look at me, and a piece of paper fell to the ground. I picked it up, shaking off the dirt. The ink was smudged and some of the letters had been obscured, but I could understand enough to know what I held in my hand: a signed declaration of guilt, admitting to the murders of Charles Walker, Jake Munro and Paul Drayton. There were no dates or details, just a brief printed statement with Temi's name underneath. Like Fiona before her, she had turned herself in.

Chapter Seventy-Four

Leah

I could hear crying in the distance. I followed the sound towards the dilapidated shed. The little girl in school uniform was crouched in front of me, howling in agony in the dark. Her cries grew increasingly louder, then suddenly she stopped, but the sound of wailing continued. My head whipped round, but there was nothing behind me, no one else who could have made the sound. My breath caught in my throat, and I realised that I was the one crying, screaming manically into the night. I turned back, but the little girl was gone, and another figure lay lifeless in her place. Eli knelt beside it, one hand clutching a knife, the other holding mine. I wasn't sure when I had moved, but I was beside him, next to my mother's corpse. The sound of crying grew louder and louder, but when I touched my face, my eyes were dry. The sound continued, on and on, louder and louder, until the walls collapsed on top of me, and I woke up screaming my father's name.

It was well before dawn, but I couldn't sleep after my nightmare. Even though it wasn't real, I could still feel the pressure of Eli's hand. The heat from the coffee went some way towards warming me up, but the cold air still stung as I walked down the quiet street. It was at least an hour before any sensible person started work, plenty of time for me to come to my senses and go home, but I needed somewhere to clear my head and outside Sonya Waugh's practice was as good a place as any. There was a bench across the street, and I settled back against the wood. I didn't know exactly what I wanted, but I needed to process my thoughts before they got out of control. I had no idea when Sonya started work or which days she saw her clients, but it didn't matter. I hadn't decided whether I wanted to speak to her, and I liked the idea that the decision might yet be taken out of my hands. I closed my eyes and pushed my collar against my neck, trying to keep calm. The sound of hurried breaths startled me, and it took me a second to remember where I was. Sonya Waugh was bending over me. She was dressed in running gear, her arms bare despite the cold.

'You're here to see me.'

It wasn't a question.

The reception was empty as we made our way up to her office. Sonya didn't bother with the lights as she led me towards the stairs.

'Do you normally start at this hour?' I asked, genuinely curious.

'Do you make it a habit of checking?'

'Touché.'

She pushed the door open, and I caught a whiff of body odour as I passed her. It wasn't unpleasant, but I was surprised by the smell. She pushed the curtains open and turned to face me.

'Has something happened to Fiona?'

I shook my head.

'This isn't to do with the case, is it?'

Sonya gestured for me to take a seat, but I hovered near the door.

'You're welcome to stay or go, but you're here now, so you might as well talk to me. I've got some time before my first appointment.'

She made a point of sitting, rolling her shoulders against the back of the chair. The air was warm and inviting, and I was tired of wrestling with my thoughts.

'A man died earlier this morning, and I didn't stop it from happening,' I said.

'Didn't or couldn't?' There was no judgement in Sonya's voice.

'What does it matter? I was supposed to protect him, and he died. He called me for help, but he was attacked before he could get the words out.'

'Is that why you're here?'

Her question caught me off guard, and I looked at her. Her hair was in a ponytail, and she wore no make-up. She seemed in no hurry, and it made me feel calm.

'I have these dreams. I'm a small child in school uniform. I see another child in the same uniform. She's crying and she's covered in blood. She screams and then I wake up.'

'How long have you had the dream?'

'On and off as long as I can remember. I had it more as a child. Now it only comes when I'm stressed.'

'So, what's changed?'

I focused on her fingers, brushing the arm of her chair.

'Why talk about this now?' Sonya said.

'I recently met my biological father.'

'Tell me about him?' She tugged at her ponytail so her hair was less tight against her skull. She looked softer and more approachable, but her eyes were still sharp.

'There's not much to tell. He has a history of violence, and since he came back into my life, my dreams have got worse.'

'Tell me about your dreams now,' she said.

'He's in them. I wake up screaming his name.'

She had shifted her trophies so they shared their shelf with a lever arch file – prizes for excellence next to something mundane. I could hear Sonya speaking, but my eyes stayed on the shelf.

'And how do the dreams affect you?'

'They need to stop,' I said. 'I can't control my thoughts. Ever since I met him, I can't control them. And I need to. I just want to get through the days. Do my job. I don't want to think about my father.'

'And you want me to help you with that?'

I hadn't articulated it to myself before then, but I knew the answer was yes.

'What's your earliest memory?'

'I don't know how to answer that. I have snippets, but I don't know whether they're real.'

'When's your earliest complete memory? Something you can make sense of, something you can describe?'

I tried to think back to when I was four or five, but the years were blank, except in my dreams.

'There's no right or wrong answer.'

'I don't know. Maybe my eighth birthday.'

The realisation that what had happened to my mother wasn't the only thing I had forgotten unsettled me. I focused on the stripes at the base of Sonya's top.

'And does your father feature in that memory?'

'I didn't know him then. He left when I was five.' *Left, went to prison – it amounted to the same thing.*

'Do you have any idea what happened before you were eight?'

'No,' I said.

She knew I was lying; she watched as I fiddled with my ring.

'Do you *want* to know?' she asked.

'Something happened to me around the time he left. I need to understand what.'

'But you don't want to think about your father?'

The stripes had started to blur into one.

'You don't need me to tell you this, but I will if it makes it easier: your father is part of your past and until you face it, he will consume more of your thinking than you want him to.'

'So, what are you saying?'

She unravelled her legs, stretching them out in front of her. 'You have to deal with your past.'

I have to remember it first.

Chapter Seventy-Five

Leah

I was the first person Temi asked for when she opened her eyes. She didn't know my name, but she wanted to speak to the detective in charge. An officer stood guard outside her hospital room. He looked uncomfortable in his uniform, and he gave me a nervous smile as I approached. Temi seemed relieved when she saw me. Her right wrist was heavily bandaged, and her left arm rested limply across her chest. She lay on her back in the white metal bed. She had shaken off the covers, and the first thing I noticed was how small she was – thin and petite, with little muscle or fat. Her voice was deeper than I expected.

'Did you get it?'

I had no idea what she was talking about, so she said it again, louder and more intense.

'Did you get it?'

The note.

'Yes,' I said. 'How are you doing?'

'Still here.' She sounded disappointed, her entire body sinking into the bed.

'Killing yourself is never the answer, Temi.'

'What *is*?' Her voice was hollow.

I wish I knew.

'Why, Temi?' I asked.

'They deserved to die. I just want it to be over.'

'If you cooperate, the sooner that will happen, or there will be more questions, more intrusion.'

Temi's eyes glazed over. I wondered whether she was distracted or in pain. The room was gloomy, and I found the light switch. She groaned under the glare of the bulb.

'You know they won't let me see my children?' Temi said. 'Of course you do; it was probably your idea.'

'We're just trying to protect you all.'

I could see the anger in her eyes.

'I would never hurt my kids. You don't have to protect them from me. It's my job to look after them.'

'Is that why those men had to die?'

'No.' She slowly weighed up her words. 'Those men killed my husband, and there was a price.'

I stood up and walked to the window, searching for the sun behind the clouds.

'Why Jake Munro? Because of the redundancy?'

She almost laughed. 'You make it sound like nothing. That job was Eddie's life; it was our livelihood. He didn't have to take that away.'

I turned to face her, leaning back against the wall. It was cool and hard, and I pushed into it, enjoying the support. 'Plenty of people get made redundant, Temi. Most bosses aren't killed as a result.'

She pulled herself upright, straining to close the gap between us. She winced as she dropped her arm to steady herself on the bed.

'Eddie loved that job. He begged for it back. *Begged.*'

'And Charles Walker?'

'We thought he was our friend. We asked him for help. It took a lot for Eddie to ask him, and he just turned him away, like all those years meant nothing.'

I thought I saw tears in her eyes; then they were gone.

'But you didn't give up?' I remembered the calls Vivi Walker had flagged. 'Why didn't you call from your own phone?'

'I couldn't afford my mobile at the time. Gary let me use his phone. He always liked me.'

'And Paul Drayton?'

'He was the worst. Had Eddie convinced he would help. Cheated him out of the little we had left. He refused to lend Eddie money, but he let him in on a "special investment" – low risk, fast return, so he said. I told Eddie not to listen, but he was desperate. He said Paul promised it was a sure thing. Eddie trusted Paul, and I trusted Eddie.' She paused, sinking her head back into the pillow. 'We lost it all. Everything gone. Paul could have helped us, but he just watched Eddie beg, then said no. Eddie gave up after that. He said a man without hope is no man at all. I'll never forget Eddie's face when he saw Paul for who he was.'

'So, you killed him?'

She pressed down on the bandage that covered her wrist. 'Yes.'

'What did it feel like?'

She hesitated. I expected to see triumph or remorse, but she just looked sad.

'It had to be done,' she said.

Chapter Seventy-Six

Leah

'What's wrong?' Georgina Harrison was in her trademark snow boots, navy blue with a black leather trim. She was looking intently at a crime scene image, squinting under the overhead light.

'I need to talk to you about Munro, Walker and Drayton.'

She pushed a stack of files towards me. 'I know. I wanted to talk to you.'

I waited, but Harrison liked a melodramatic build-up. 'You first,' she said.

'The accused, Temi Adeola, she's petite . . .'

'So are you. And I wouldn't hang around if you had a beef, a blunt instrument and a carving knife. Would you?'

She had a point.

'But if you told me it was Temi's height, rather than her build, which bothered you, I might have said you were onto something. How tall is the suspect?'

'I don't know. Five foot. Five foot one at a push.'

'Jake Munro was slightly above average height, and Charles Walker slightly below, but Paul Drayton was well over six foot. The initial blow was almost forceful enough to kill him, which would suggest that the attacker was tall enough to transfer their full weight into the strike.'

'Hard to do if you're only five foot.'

'Hard but not impossible.' Harrison was covering her back.

'What about the stab wounds?'

'I believe the victims were on the ground, half-dead, by the time the attacker struck them with a knife. We can tell from the bruising on Paul Drayton that he was probably held down with the attacker's anchoring hand, while he was stabbed with a weapon in the attacker's right.'

'How do you know the attacker used their right hand?' I asked.

'Palm prints, patterns. The attacker would have gripped the handle of the knife when they drove the blade into the deceased. The outer edge of their palm would have hit the victim each time.' She clenched her fist for effect, striking the top of her chest. 'I can't say for certain, but chances are they would have used their dominant hand. We found the edge of a right palm print on the body.'

I imagined Temi driving the knife through another human being's flesh. The image jarred, and I realised something I implicitly knew the moment I saw her bandaged right wrist. She had cut open her flesh with the opposite hand, her stronger hand, the one which had lain limp across her chest. If she had killed those men, she would have used her left hand, but the killer hadn't, and that could only mean one thing.

Chapter Seventy-Seven

Leah

Temi sat up in her hospital bed as I entered. She looked weak but alert under the thin blanket.

'I know you didn't do it,' I said.

'What?' She blinked twice, her eyes becoming larger. 'I don't know what you're talking about.'

I moved the chair from the edge of the bed, placing it so I was level with her pillow.

'Paul Drayton was hit repeatedly with a blunt instrument. Where is it?'

Temi's nostrils flared and contracted as she tried to control her breathing, but the rapid movement of her chest gave her away.

'I told you what I did. I don't know what more you want from me, Inspector.'

'The truth would help.'

My flippancy unnerved her, but she hid it well.

'I've told you the truth. Those men needed to die, and I killed them.'

'Yes. You said. They drove your husband to his death.'

She nodded, pulling the blanket close with her good arm; her bandaged wrist lay limp over her legs.

'Eddie wasn't just a husband, though, was he? He was a father to a young daughter and a son who looked up to him.'

I could see Temi's brain catching up; she sounded anxious. 'What are you trying to say?'

'Just that when Eddie died, it wasn't only a wife losing a husband; a son lost a father, and a family – your family, to be precise – was destroyed. That's enough to make any young man angry, don't you think?'

'I don't know what you're getting at.' Her voice was small and strained.

'What was your son like when your husband died?'

'Upset. We all were.'

'Did he have a history of violence growing up?'

'No. Absolutely not.'

'Was he angry when his father died?'

'I don't see how this is relevant.'

'Rage can be triggered by trauma. It can transform a person. Drive them to do something they would never have contemplated before.'

'What's that got to do with my son?'

'The killer was right-handed; you're not, are you? When we found Dele, he wrote his name with his right hand.'

'So?'

'So . . . did Dele kill those men?'

'No.'

'Did he kill those men?' I repeated.

'No!' She hadn't meant to shout.

The sun had finally emerged like a laser through the window. Temi closed her eyes as the rays cut across her face.

'I know you're trying to protect your family,' I said gently. 'But people have died, and if you don't tell us the truth, more people could get hurt. Maybe Dele himself. The killings are brutal, and they get worse each time. What if Dele's developed a taste for it? What if he keeps doing it and more people die?'

Temi said nothing, searching for a way out. Her voice was quiet when she opened her mouth.

'I did it. I swear. *I'm* responsible for those deaths.'

'Responsible or guilty, Temi?'

'What's the difference?'

Her eyes filled with tears, and I watched her cry.

Chapter Seventy-Eight

Daniel Reid had been fantasising about going away for days. He had never spent much time outside London and, born and bred in a metropolis, he didn't have to go far to appreciate the wonders of nature. Odie had rung repeatedly since her last outburst, but he didn't want to speak to her; he no longer had the words. This weekend, away from everything, he could forget about his parents.

He turned off the road, driving up a dirt track lined by trees. It seemed to go on forever, narrowing as the foliage became denser. For a moment, he wondered whether he had misunderstood the directions, then he saw the royal blue door in the distance. It was the only house Daniel could see, and he desperately needed to use the bathroom. He parked outside the gate, slowly making his way towards the building. It was larger than it had seemed from the track, with a wide veranda bordered by a thin iron rail. There was a pile of paint tins in a neat pyramid against the wall by the front door. There was no answer when he rang the bell. He thought he heard the faint sound of footsteps approaching behind him, but when he looked over his shoulder, there was no one there. He rang the bell again, but the house appeared completely deserted. He didn't hear the footsteps again until it was too late.

The blow to the back of his head caught him by surprise. He hoped the cracking sound hadn't come from his skull, but he didn't have long to worry. As he sank to his knees in agony, he welcomed oblivion and the freedom from pain it would bring.

Chapter Seventy-Nine

Leah

'Hutch. My office. Now.'

I hated being summoned by Kenny O'Sullivan.

'So?'

Even behind his desk, Kenny managed to take up most of the room. It wasn't a clear question, so I waited for a better one.

'You knew who the next victim was and yet another man is dead.'

'I gave him my number to call in emergencies, but . . .'

'He still ended up dead. How do you think this makes us look?'

'I'm sorry, sir.' I kept my gaze even.

'I don't really care if you're sorry,' he spat. 'The public don't care if you're sorry.' He paused to gather himself. 'Do you know what they will do if more people die and they find out we were given clues?'

They'll demand your head, and you'll give them mine.

'We'll be crucified,' he said. And he was right, but it wasn't about the public or the press; Paul Drayton was dead, and I could have stopped him from being killed.

'Leah?'

I wasn't sure how long Kenny had been saying my name.

'Temi Adeola has confessed, but you think it's the son?'

'The killer was right-handed . . .'

'Yes . . . I'm capable of reading a file. But tell me this: if you're so convinced Dele Adeola is guilty, why did you let him go?'

'It wasn't evident at the time.'

'And it is now?'

His voice was softer, and I was reminded we were on the same team.

'Yes. There's no sign of Dele at their flat. We need to place a watch on Temi's daughter's foster home.'

Kenny sighed, sliding back in his chair with difficulty as his torso squeezed against the wood.

'And why would I authorise that?'

'Because he'll be back. Sir, Dele's done all this for his family. There's no way he's leaving his sister in foster care where she'll feel frightened and alone. He'll want to get her out or at least see her. He'll come back for her. I know it.'

'OK.'

Kenny swivelled his chair so his back was turned towards me. The move was surprisingly graceful. His little finger curled up and down, tapping the armrest in slow, deliberate beats. I sensed he was counting the seconds as he made me wait for his answer.

'OK.'

Exactly a minute had passed, and there was a gentle click as the digits changed on the clock.

'Forty-eight hours.' He swung back to face me. 'You better hope he shows.'

Chapter Eighty

Leah

Lola Adeola's foster parents lived in an off-white house tucked away behind Finsbury Park station. It appeared small from the front but stretched back into a tidy garden, with large French windows betraying its true size. I had filled the team in on Temi Adeola. Randle didn't say anything, but I could tell he was questioning why we were there. The street was quiet, and there was an unmarked police car parked nearby, conspicuous in its blandness. I contemplated the house where little Lola Adeola would be fast asleep under the care of well-meaning foster parents. It was strange to think that that could have been me all those years ago.

'Should I park, ma'am?'

We were approaching the turning at the end of the road, and it would have looked suspicious if we did another loop.

'No need. Can you take me home?'

We drove in silence for much of the way, meandering in and out of side streets to avoid the traffic. Randle's face was in profile beside me, the side of his mouth twitching, as if he were engaged in a private conversation.

'Are you going to let me in on the secret?'

He smiled at the question. 'It's nothing. I was just thinking about the case, ma'am.' He paused. 'Temi thought she was protecting her son, but she just let him get worse.'

'Dele was determined to kill those men. There was very little Temi could do.'

'She could have told us.' He manoeuvred the car smoothly around a sharp corner. 'When she knew he was going after Paul. Instead of following Dele and covering his tracks. If she had told us, we could have stopped him, and Paul Drayton wouldn't be dead.'

He looked at me, eyes pleading with me to agree. I recognised the feeling of self-righteousness that had led to endless disappointment when I joined the police.

'Why would she come to *us*? What have we ever done for her?' I said.

Randle pushed his hair off his forehead, exposing a small, jagged scar. I wondered if he had got it racing his bike.

'Well, it helped no one in the end,' he said. 'Her son became a killer, and she's lost the family she was trying to protect.'

His thumbs pressed hard into the steering wheel. I could tell he needed a cigarette; his thoughts streamed out, unfiltered.

'He must have really looked up to his father,' he said. 'I understand the urge to do that. I do. My dad went back to Texas when I was born. I went to find him after university. I wanted a role model, I guess, but the only thing worth looking up to was his skill at fixing engines and the way he cornered a bike. He's my father and I love him, but he's not worth a Christmas card, let alone another man's life.'

He made no attempt to hide his bitterness. I let him sit with it, turning away. Outside, a pregnant woman struggled with a pushchair. I could feel Randle's eyes on me, but when I looked back, they were focused on the road.

'What are the odds for Lola Adeola? Without a mother or brother. Do you think she stands a chance?' he asked.

'If one of them's a killer, I'd say she's better off.'

I expected him to agree, but he just shook his head. 'You can't stop a child from craving a parent. It's the way we're wired. She'll feel the loss.'

'Sometimes you need a new start,' I said. 'Trust me, I'm adopted.'

I hesitated, weighing up my desire to convince him against my need to keep my boundaries intact.

'I was brought up by my grandmother,' I said.

'What was your relationship like?'

'Fine, but we weren't close. She kept things from me. Things I should have been told. Left me with questions I would have asked.'

'She must have loved you though.' Randle spoke with feeling. 'She must have loved you very much.'

The traffic had picked up again, and the car jerked to a halt as a van muscled into the space in front of us.

'I come from a single-parent home,' Randle said. 'I know how hard it was for my mother to bring up a child and to do it alone. To do that with your grandchild, that's no small thing.'

I thought of the hours I had spent with Margaretta without really knowing her.

'She had no choice when I lost my parents.'

The windows were closed to block out the cold. There was a faint glow on Randle's face as the street lights bounced off the glass.

'We've always got a choice, ma'am,' he said, his voice solemn. 'She chose you.'

Chapter Eighty-One

Odie

Odie's letterbox snapped open and shut. She pulled the covers over her head and tried to go back to sleep, but the temptation proved too much. She dragged her body down the stairs, pretending it wasn't morning. There was a solitary brown A4 envelope propped against the door. She stooped to retrieve it, overcome by dizziness as the blood ran to her head. At first, she thought it was empty, and her anger at being toyed with stirred again; then she felt a stiff piece of paper wedged into the crease at the base. Gently easing it out, she realised it was a photograph of a young man staring straight at a camera. She didn't recognise the face.

She stumbled into the kitchen, searching for her coffee pods in the cupboard over the sink. Her laptop sat open on the table, and she would have missed the notification on her screen if it hadn't made a sound. Another anonymous email, another cryptic link. She clicked on it and a news site flashed up, various headlines competing for space. Odie's eyes were instantly drawn to the face at the bottom and an article about a young man wanted in connection with multiple murders. Something about his face stopped her from moving on from the story. It was vaguely familiar, but she couldn't place it at first. Then she saw the envelope resting on the table, and she felt a rush of adrenaline for the first time in days. The man in the photograph she had been sent had shorter hair but the same intelligent eyes. She realised he was the same man the police were searching for, and she studied each feature, surprised by how young he looked. She couldn't be sure of the connection to Fiona, but she sensed her source was trying to tell her something; it wasn't just a game.

She kicked herself for being defeatist after the last package had arrived. She should have installed a door camera, instead of wallowing and giving up, but there was no point dwelling on past mistakes; she had been given another chance. Her phone beeped as she studied the images in front of her. She was relieved Richard had just sent a text. He was fretting because Daniel hadn't been in touch for a couple of days. In Odie's mind, it was a good thing — they were too co-dependent, and it was time Daniel lived his life without constantly feeling the need to check in with his father. She didn't say all this to Richard because she didn't want to be cruel, and it took too many words to explain.

I'm sure he's OK, she typed in response. *Probably needed a break.*

Richard was agonising unnecessarily; Daniel was fine, somewhere away from them both. Odie had let him go a long time ago, and Richard would have to do the same. She turned her attention back to the photograph of the young man the article identified as Dele Adeola. He had allegedly killed three people, including Charles Walker, but the police seemed in no hurry to link him to the attack on Alistair Cowan. She stared at him, wondering whether she was looking at the man who had robbed Fiona of her freedom. Laying the clues on the table, she tried to make sense of the information. The surface was sticky, and the paper crinkled as the moisture seeped through — photographs of Charles Walker's body in the park; the account of Fiona's life on three sheets of A4; the image of the young man. She had thrown away the sheet she had been sent with the link, but she still had access to the page. She pulled up her browser, toggling through the open windows until she found it, the error message taunting her in caps. She refreshed it, and a flashing clock filled the screen:

Site under construction. Live in forty-eight hours.

Odie could feel the energy pulsing through her as she set a notification in her calendar. She pasted the link in the notes field, determined to keep it safe. When the time came, she would be ready. She flicked to the email with the news link, filing it with the others sent by her source. It was only then that she noticed the sender's address. The other messages had been sent from the same obscure account, but this one was different. It looked like it came from some kind of institution. She didn't recognise the name.

Chapter Eighty-Two

Leah

From the moment he saw me, I could tell Eli felt he had the upper hand. I didn't want to be there, but I had too many questions and, without Margaretta, there were no obvious answers.

'Why do you do this to yourself?' he said. 'Coming here. Seeing me. Wanting what I can't give?'

He'd had his hair cut since I'd last visited, and I could see traces of the professional he once was.

'Maybe I'm sentimental. You're the only family I've got.'

Behind him, a guard tried to suppress a cough. He looked self-conscious – his uniform carefully ironed as though confidence was a jacket you put on.

Eli chuckled softly to himself.

'What is it this time? Still disappointed Margaretta kept you in the dark?'

He looked smug and self-assured, as if incarceration were a minor inconvenience.

'Margaretta knew I was there that night,' I said. 'That's why she asked you to confess.'

'I don't hear a question, Leah. Have you just come here to vent?'

His eyes flashed as they caught the light. I could see he was amusing himself.

'You said Margaretta was right. Is that what you meant?'

He ran his finger along the length of the table, scraping the surface with his nail.

'Margaretta came to see me. She was convinced it was your only chance to forget. They were going to find me eventually. The longer the investigation went on, the harder it would be for you to do that.'

'You expect me to believe that you confessed because of me?'

'I don't expect anything from you, Leah.'

He smoothed his hair with the side of his hand. His cheekbones were like weapons beneath his skin.

'You should have just told me I was there,' I said.

'People forget things for a reason. It's not my job to help you remember.'

His eyes focused on my face as he calculated his next move. I pressed my palms against my knees, keeping my expression neutral.

'Did you know I was there at the time?'

'No.'

'How do I know you're telling the truth?'

'That's up to you.'

The air felt hot, and I could hear him breathing. My mother's tangled limbs flashed into my mind.

'What did I see, Eli? What did Margaretta want me to forget?'

He shifted his gaze to the seam of his trousers. When he sighed, I could see the back of his throat.

'The story ended with me in here. Why do you need to join the dots?'

'I need to know what I saw.'

'If you were there, why are you asking me? If you want to remember, remember.'

'I was five years old . . .' I tried to keep the exasperation out of my voice.

'Children can store events as memories from as early as the age of three or four. The memories are there. If you can't remember, it's because you don't want to.' He pressed his fingertips together as his eyes moved round the room. 'Do you think Fiona Garvey wants to remember?'

The surprise showed on my face before I could disguise it.

'Don't look so shocked, Inspector. You hear things in here. Read things. Your world and mine aren't that far apart. Same characters. Different location.'

'My world *was* your world. But you threw it all away.'

'A cautionary tale; make sure you don't do the same.'

'I'm nothing like you,' I said.

'You don't know me.'

'And you know nothing about Fiona Garvey.'

'I'm locked away . . . just like her. With plenty of time to reflect on life, just like her. Do you think she's better off not remembering? Maybe you should ask her. Compare notes.'

'I don't want to talk about Fiona Garvey. I don't and I can't. You of all people should know that.'

'OK. Let's talk about you. Fiona Garvey has blocked out the events of that night for good reason. You, on the other hand, want to remember something Margaretta dedicated her life to helping you forget. Believe me when I say it was for the best.'

'For you, I'm sure.'

'And for you.'

Eli's eyes had changed colour with the light, sharper and bluer; they almost didn't look real. There was a lull as we both waited for the other one to fill the silence. Eventually Eli spoke.

'You look tired.'

'I'll survive.'

'Hard work catching a killer.'

'And yet, they caught you.'

'They should have caught me sooner, but they were always one step behind. I understood people and I understood myself. You can't teach that. You either have it or you don't.' He looked at me, barely concealing the challenge in his eyes.

'Maybe you can understand too much. Blur lines you were never meant to cross.'

'That presupposes there is a line, an invisible boundary between good and evil.'

'Isn't there?'

Eli smiled, enjoying our disagreement. 'That's not what Margaretta believed.'

'What do you care what she believed?'

His eyes glinted, and I realised he didn't care and probably never had.

'I don't get it,' I said. 'Why didn't she give up on you?'

'Loyalty, love, faith.' Eli didn't hesitate for a second. 'Never underestimate the maternal instinct to protect. She wanted to forgive me, and her faith enabled her to try.'

'And did she? Forgive you?'

'No,' he said without feeling. 'But she never gave up trying. She believed I could be redeemed.'

'It's a shame she was wrong.'

'And what about you?'

'What about me?'

'That's why you're really here, isn't it? To know why she didn't give up on *you*. Why she looked after you for all those years?' He fixed me with his cold blue eyes. 'If you don't ask, you won't get, Leah, and I'd hate for this to be a wasted visit.' His gaze was penetrating.

'OK. Tell me.' I sighed.

'You scared her. Do you know that? In those months after they sent me away, you scared her.'

'Don't be ridiculous,' I bit back. 'Margaretta wasn't scared of anything, least of all a child.'

'And yet *you* managed to scare her. Quite a feat for a five-year-old.' He stared, unblinking, daring me to look away. 'She was worried you were like me. She never admitted it, but I could tell.'

I reminded myself how small his world must be and how hard he had to work to keep entertained.

'If she thought that,' I said, '. . . if I scared her, why didn't she let me go into foster care or have me adopted? Answer me that.'

'Because she loved you.'

He said it so simply, I was completely disarmed.

'Let me ask you this,' Eli continued. 'If everything you've ever done, uttered or thought was put up on four walls, would you let your family and friends enter that room? Would you even enter it yourself? What was it that Margaretta used to say? *We're more sinful than we can imagine but more loved by God than we ever dreamed.* What do you make of that, Leah Hutch? Does that comfort or anger you?' He paused for the answer he knew I would never give. 'She loved you, but she was scared of you. The two aren't mutually exclusive. She saw something in you in those months after your mother died . . .'

'. . . after you killed her, you mean.'

'She saw something in you which frightened her. Which frightens you.'

'I don't know what you're talking about.' My voice was firm.

'Don't you? Believe in your own goodness at your peril. We are none of us angels, and unless you follow Margaretta's Jesus, you're going to the same hell I am.'

He massaged the skin around his temples, waiting for me to react. It had been a mistake to see him again. I pressed my feet into the floor to stop myself from storming out.

'She never showed you the letters, did she?' he said. 'There were letters, reports from your school, concerned you were acting out your trauma. Concerned you were a danger to others. She sent them to me. She was so worried, she wanted me to see them.'

I pushed my toes against the soles of my shoes, keeping my breath even.

'You hurt people, Leah. Other children. You hurt them badly. That's why Margaretta decided to start again with new names. She didn't do that because of me; she did it because of you. She wanted you to forget, and you did, except in your dreams.'

The image of the bloodied little girl in school uniform slipped into my mind.

'What do you know about my dreams?' My voice was level, but I could feel myself shaking.

'Margaretta blamed me for your nightmares. I said you would grow out of them, but you haven't, have you? Read the letters. I sent them back to her. See the evidence for yourself.'

He smiled, but there was no affection in his eyes.

Chapter Eighty-Three

Odie

Odie's search for the institution led her to a residential care home. She snatched her keys off the kitchen table, praying it would provide the answers she craved. As she pulled up outside the maze of well-manicured gardens, she rehearsed a story about a parent who could no longer cope on their own. She imagined the helplessness that could come with old age, and she made an empty promise to drink less, to give her body a fighting chance.

The waiting area was small and brightly lit, with rubbery green plants dominating each corner. The air smelt of bottled lavender, and the receptionist had been briefed to adopt a permanent smile. Odie was shown around by Maud, a woman who could have been any age between forty and sixty. Every now and again, Maud would pause for a reaction, and Odie dutifully murmured her approval, even though she was barely listening. Her mind was focused on her anonymous source; they knew who she was, of that much she was certain and, as she walked along the corridors, she searched the face of each employee, looking for any sign of recognition. She flicked through the pages of the brochure, scanning staff biographies in the hope that a photograph would trigger a memory. There was no sudden recollection, no alleluia moment, and she began to think her visit had been in vain.

'We have an extremely low turnover of staff,' Maud was saying. 'We pride ourselves on running a happy ship and people don't tend to want to move on. Happy at work, happy in life.' She beamed, making sure Odie witnessed the trademark contentment.

'I'm sure my mother will love it here,' Odie said.

Maud beamed again. They were in the recreation room now. Maud described it as a place of refuge for the residents to relax, but all Odie saw was a vision of hell with men and women on cheap floral upholstery, staring blankly at widescreen televisions. Most people had some sort of companion or carer, but one woman sat alone, rocking in her chair. Both legs were amputated above the knee, and she had lost one of her arms. The other arm rested on her lap, her hand stroking a small toy. Odie's eyes were drawn to her, and she watched the toy slide off the woman's lap, leaving her staring, helpless as it lay out of reach. Instinctively Odie broke away from Maud, retrieving the cuddly animal and restoring it to its rightful place. The woman gave her the faintest of smiles, and Odie felt an overwhelming sense of sadness, knowing that the toy would fall again, and she wouldn't be there to pick it up.

The news played in the background, a tedious correspondent droning on about a crisis which would only get worse. Maud had started to lead Odie out of the room when Odie was stopped by a familiar voice: Leah Hutch, her tiny face magnified and stretched on the screen, pleading with the public for information. The police were still looking for the man in the photograph, and a full-scale manhunt was in motion. Maud had started speaking again, and Odie feigned interest as her thoughts shifted to Dele Adeola. It was only then that she noticed that even though some of the residents were positioned in front of the television, only one was really watching, his body rigid. Nothing moved except his eyes. They never strayed from the images in front of him, and there was something which Odie recognised, an intensity she had seen long ago. She thought she saw tears in his eyes, but she was distracted by Maud's voice.

'Can I help you with anything else?'

Yes. Tell me which of your colleagues has been sending me emails and coming to my house.

It was the question Odie most wanted to ask, but she knew there was no point. She turned back to look at the man in the wheelchair, but he was entirely focused on the news. She wondered whether she had imagined the tears.

Chapter Eighty-Four

Leah

I had been a fool to visit Eli. I pulled my thoughts back to the case. The entrance to the station was busy, and I tuned out the chatter, keeping my head down. Upstairs, I said nothing as I passed my team, and they had the wisdom to leave me alone. I closed the door to my office and slowly inhaled. There was a note on my computer, peeling off at the corner. I recognised Randle's illegible scrawl. I opened the window and pushed my head into the cold air. I breathed deeply for thirty seconds, then retreated into the warmth.

Randle sat up behind his desk when he saw me approach.

'Who's Tina?' I asked, handing over the piece of paper.

'No idea, ma'am. There was a call. A woman asking for you. She said it was to do with the case.'

'Anything useful?'

'I don't know. She insisted on speaking to you,' Randle said. 'Apparently, she made little to no sense. She wouldn't answer any questions, and she just kept saying the same thing over and over again: "It's Tina. It's Tina."'

The dregs of a protein shake sat at the bottom of his flask. He chugged it back, even though it must have been sitting there all day.

'Did she leave a surname? Any contact details?' I asked.

'Nothing, ma'am. Just the name. Do you want us to try to track the number?'

I nodded.

He balled the Post-it note in his fist, flicking it ten yards into a nearby bin. The move was slick and polished, but he didn't scan the room for praise.

'What else have we got? Any sign of Dele?'

'No, but . . .' He reached for another Post-it, crushing it in his hand. 'Temi asked to see you again.'

Chapter Eighty-Five

Leah

The officer on guard stood up straighter when he saw me. I offered a brief nod as I walked past. Temi had angled her body so she was facing the window. She was still recovering, and I wasn't sure if she looked better or worse. The agony had disappeared from her face, but she seemed defeated, and there were faint cracks visible on her skin. I had never understood or wanted children, but I respected her role as a mother, and I knew she was lost without Dele and Lola.

'How are you doing?' I was surprised to realise I cared.

She shrugged. She was so thin, her hospital gown looked like a tent hanging off her shoulders, and her forearm was barely wider than her wrist.

'You can make your life easier if you just admit it wasn't you.' My tone was harsher than I had meant it to be. 'You ran from your flat so we'd think you were guilty. Why didn't you just hand yourself in?'

She looked away so I struggled to see her features. I remembered finding her in the darkness the night Paul Drayton died.

'Paul Drayton,' I said.

Temi remained silent.

'You knew Dele was determined to kill him; you needed to be free to stop him or take the blame.'

She shook her head. 'It doesn't matter. I didn't ask you to come to talk about that.'

'Then why, Temi?'

She lowered her voice conspiratorially, as if she were worried someone might hear. 'He knows you're watching the house. There's a car. It hasn't moved. He told me.'

There was always a way to get hold of a phone in hospital, but I was surprised Temi had had the presence of mind.

'I suppose there's no point asking how you got access to a phone?' I said.

She just looked at me.

'Why did you want to talk?'

'It's Lola's birthday tomorrow . . .' She dropped her gaze. I waited for her eyes to lift before I pressed her for more. 'She's never had a birthday without us. She's all alone.'

'He's going to see her, isn't he?'

Temi wiped her eyes with her forearm, obscuring her face as she mouthed 'yes'.

'I can't hear you, Temi. Dele's going to see Lola, isn't he?'

She nodded, leaning forwards so I could see the creases of anguish lining her lips. 'He won't go to that house. Not now he's seen your people there.'

'Then where, Temi?'

'The park behind her nursery. There's a funfair there this week.'

Her whole body tensed as she whispered the words, as if Dele could somehow hear her betrayal.

'How do I know I can trust you?' I knew the answer, but I wanted to watch her eyes as she said it.

'You don't.'

'Why now, Temi? You've protected him so far. Why give him up now?'

She took a deep breath.

'I want it to stop. I need it to stop.'

Chapter Eighty-Six

Leah

The operation to ambush Dele intensified in a matter of hours. Everything had been mapped out, but I couldn't get the what ifs out of my mind: what if Temi was lying? What if she was trying to distract us while Dele went after his next target? What if the similarities between Dele and Fiona's victims were more than a coincidence? What if we made a mistake? What if? What if? Kenny had surprised me with his support, but I knew I would be the first to be sacrificed if anything went wrong.

I took my time getting home, doubtful I would get any sleep. Time was moving slowly, and there were still at least fourteen hours until Dele was supposed to appear. Too much time alone with my thoughts; too many thoughts fighting for control in my head. The rubber sheath had split on my skipping rope and the wire underneath bit into my flesh when it caught my skin. I adjusted my rhythm so my feet moved faster, dancing over the cable so it avoided the base of my calves. The rope spun loudly as it sliced through the air. I breathed steadily through my nose as my heart rate sped up. My wrists were moving so quickly, it was like they weren't moving at all – short sharp flicks as I directed the rope straight over my head. I felt weightless, my thoughts temporarily forgotten. I skipped for over an hour, my skin fizzing with sweat.

Eli's file was on the table where I had left it, a loose leaf of paper sticking out of the side. The letters were still there, tucked neatly into their individual envelopes, and I searched each one. I knew from the feel of the paper when I had found what I was looking for. The envelope felt heavier and more official, and I was conscious of the weight against my fingers as I unfolded the piece of paper inside.

'Violent', 'attack', 'blind rage' – the words were scattered on the page, and I registered each one, refusing to arrive at the same conclusion as Eli. The letter didn't go into details, but it was clear that my actions had been a step up from the usual playground squabbles. The school had been worried about the safety of the other children, and I was seen as a problem child, heading down a path of violence and exclusion. I pulled out another letter, scanning the description of a similar outburst. Again, there were no details, but the note of concern had gone, the overall tone more accusing. I read and reread the letters; the language felt excessive. Little children misbehaved all the time; it was nothing more than that. I had expected the letters from the school to be much worse, to be confronted with a monster in the mould of Eli, but all I saw was an angry child who had been through a terrible ordeal. It was no wonder I had acted out, but it was nothing a child couldn't grow out of. Then I saw the photograph, and my breath caught in my throat. It was a horrific image of a small child, her face bruised and swollen so her eyes were lost in a mound of puffy flesh, red marks around her neck. The uniform was familiar; I recognised the little girl from my dreams, and I knew Eli had been telling the truth.

Temi flashed into my mind, my fist pounding her head against the pavement. I recalled her face as she hovered over Paul Drayton's body. I had seen that same expression once before, when Margaretta had come to take me away from school, the anger still rising up inside me. It was the look of a person seeing someone they loved in a different light, a look of sorrow mixed with fear. Margaretta had protected and cared for me until the day she died; Temi would protect Dele until the bitter end. Margaretta had always been wary of me, I could see that now, but her coolness had come from a place of love. I wanted to believe she had succeeded in saving me, but there was something inside me that I couldn't explain.

She saw something in you which frightened her. Which frightens you . . .

Eli's words crept back into my mind. I tried to think of Margaretta's Bible verse, but I couldn't remember the words. As panic threatened to overwhelm me, I picked up my phone and asked for help.

Chapter Eighty-Seven

Leah

It was late, but Sonya Waugh agreed to see me straight away. The room looked different, and I wondered if she had adjusted the lighting to appear more welcoming as she prised my secrets out of me.

'I didn't think you would come back.' She said it without any hint of smugness.

'This will be the last time. I just needed . . .'

I waited for her to interject, but she just took a sip from a glass of water, adjusting the coaster as she placed it back down.

'I'm having trouble sleeping,' I said without looking at her. 'I don't want to sleep because I don't like where my mind goes.'

'Are you still having those dreams?' Another sip of water.

'Yes. But now I know what they mean.'

I looked beyond her to the triathlon trophy tucked next to the lever arch folder. It was almost too tall for the shelf, wedged against the top.

'You told me to deal with my past but what if I can't?'

Sonya leant forwards, speaking with an intensity I hadn't seen before. Her face was mostly in shadow, but I could see the deep folds around the corner of her mouth.

'There is nothing in the past we can't deal with. As long as you're physically and mentally capable, nothing is insurmountable. You just need to make sure you're equipped.'

I shook my head. 'You have no idea what happened in my past.'

'So, tell me.'

I stood up. 'This has been a mistake. There's nothing you can do. I'm sorry I wasted your time.'

When Sonya spoke, she neither rushed nor paused for breath.

'Your violent father did something horrific when you were a child. I'm guessing you were adopted to give you a chance to shake off your trauma. For years you lived as an emotionally grounded adult with no recollection of the trauma you suffered, troubled by the occasional nightmare which you struggled to understand. Then your father came back into your life, and the past started to make sense, but it scares you. Am I warm?'

I was two steps from the door.

'I didn't come here to talk about that.'

'But am I warm?'

'I said I don't want to talk about that.'

'Why not? You came here for a reason, but I can't help you if you won't tell me what's really bothering you. If you don't want to be here, you're free to leave, but if you want my help, you need to trust me. So, tell me, *am I warm?*'

My feet felt heavy on the wooden floor; the effort to leave seemed harder than the temptation to stay. The words came out in a rush of emotion before I could stop them.

'My father murdered my mother and dismembered her lover thirty-one years ago. He buried her somewhere God only knows.

I witnessed something horrific, but I don't know what. Oh, and I strangled another child and beat them to a pulp when I was five.'

The air seemed to disappear from the room. Everything was still as I waited to be judged.

'You think those events are related?' Sonya's eyes never left my face.

'The first three, yes. The fourth . . .' My eyes searched for the trophies.

'And does it matter if they are? You're talking about events which happened a long time ago. You're not that child any more. Why are you so scared about what you did over thirty years ago?'

'What if it's happening again?' I could barely say the words.

'What if *what's* happening again?'

'The violence. The rage. What if I can't control it?'

I left before she could respond.

Chapter Eighty-Eight

Odie

Odie woke early. She stared at the countdown on her computer screen – just over twenty-four hours to go until the site went live. The sense of anticipation made her uneasy and excited, and she had to stop herself from expecting too much. She had run out of coffee pods, but she needed her morning caffeine. She used two bags of tea so the kick was extra strong. Her kitchen was overrun by a mass of paper; a tsunami of Post-it notes spilled onto the floor. She opened a new window in her browser and searched for developments on Dele Adeola. There was nothing more about him in the news. She toyed with the idea of calling Baber to do some digging, but her mobile rang before she had a chance. It took several attempts to calm Richard down.

'Daniel hasn't called. Something's not right. We have to do something . . . He didn't go to work. They don't know where he is . . . Did you hear me, Odie? They don't know where he is.' He was beginning to sound hysterical.

Odie knew little about the man her son had become, but she was aware of how seriously he took his job. She tried to get more information out of Richard, but he kept repeating the same thing. In the end Odie was left with no choice. She was sure Daniel was fine, but a tiny part of her worried that Richard might be right, and she wouldn't be able to live with herself if it turned out she was wrong.

Chapter Eighty-Nine

Leah

I didn't sleep the entire night. I lingered in the shower trying to separate one day from the next. It was Lola Adeola's birthday and, if Temi was telling the truth, it was the best chance we would get to catch her son. Kenny O'Sullivan was guaranteed a scalp, and it would either be Dele's or mine.

My appetite was non-existent; I craved strong coffee, but I was wired from lack of sleep, and I knew it wasn't a good idea. Randle was waiting outside by the car, eating a banana. His dark blond hair was pushed back with minimal gel so it appeared to hold a natural shape. I could feel his eyes on me, and I lengthened my stride, keeping my head raised. I suspected he could see through the act, but he said nothing as the car pulled away.

I wondered which version of Dele Adeola would show up at the fairground. My mind flashed back to the young man in the interview room, unapologetic and unafraid. Then I remembered him crouched by the radiator. He had appeared so fragile then, but we had been wrong.

We positioned a van behind the Ferris wheel with a clear view of the rides. I had insisted on white to blend in with the other trucks, and so far, there was nothing to cause alarm. A handful of officers were strategically stationed, dressed as civilians. Randle was in the car on the opposite side of the park; I could just about make out his face, but he was too far away to read his expression. Akosua was hidden across the street from the foster parents' house, ready to report the moment the little girl emerged. I ran through her instructions for the third time. She was nervous, and I wanted to put her at ease.

'Let us know the moment anyone steps out, even if it's just the parents. When Lola appears, make it clear. OK?'

I could hear her stilted breaths down the phone.

'Akosua, are you OK? You don't have to do this.'

'I want to, ma'am.' A sharp inhalation. 'I won't let you down.'

I rolled down the window, staring at the neon playground outside. The lights fluttered against the sky, and there were faint squeals of excitement as the rollercoaster gathered speed. Margaretta had never been a fan of fairgrounds; she found the designs tacky, and she couldn't understand why people paid good money to frighten their children. The sun sent streaks of yellow and pink through the clouds, and I watched a little boy board the Ferris wheel, a terrified look on his face. I was wondering if I would have been scared at his age, when the sound of static filled the car. Akosua's voice crackled down the radio.

'Ma'am . . . Lola Adeola's on the move.'

Minutes later, I saw her, flanked by a middle-aged couple who looked more like brother and sister than husband and wife. Lola was apprehensive and unsmiling, glancing around with huge expectant eyes. I watched as her foster parents guided her around the park. She was too small for most of the rides, and they plied her with toffee apples and candy floss, eager to make the day fun. A bag of treats trailed behind her, straining against the plastic. She didn't look unhappy, but she never smiled.

There was still no sign of Dele. I scanned each face, knowing there was no guarantee he would turn up. Time passed, families came and went, and still Dele didn't appear. I kept my eyes on Lola, watching for any flicker of recognition as she looked around. Her foster parents formed a protective cocoon, steering her away from anyone who got too close – a woman with a pram, a junkie searching for a pocket to pick, a businessman taking a shortcut – but still no Dele. The crowds had thickened, and clusters of families mingled. Screams merged with laughter as adults persuaded children that fear could be fun. My eyes skimmed over them, searching for solitary men who never queued for a ride. I spotted one man, his face obscured by a hood, walking with purpose towards Lola. He was tall and lithe, moving past excited schoolchildren without colliding with a single one. I couldn't be sure it was Dele, but he was getting closer, and there was little time to think. My radio buzzed with voices demanding instructions. I fired them back, coordinating the attack. I rushed out, running hard as two officers appeared from the crowd in front of me. They seized the man, wrestling him to the ground. I was still several feet away when they slammed his body on the grass, grabbing his hands roughly behind his back. His hood fell back as he struggled to get away, but the face that turned to look at me wasn't Dele Adeola's.

That's when I saw it. As a fledgling reporter, Odie had taught me to take in the whole, as opposed to concentrating on details, because the best story could come from anywhere. Instinctively my eyes swept across the surrounding faces – the anxious, the scared, the curious – then travelled back to little Lola Adeola. She wasn't anxious; she wasn't scared; she wasn't curious. She was completely disinterested in the scene in front of her, her attention focused on something in the distance. Then her tiny face broke into a smile, and I knew she had seen her brother. I grabbed my radio and ran.

Dele Adeola was faster and more determined. But I trained hard, and I could outrun most men in my division. I screamed for backup as I pushed through the crowds. I was closing the gap with every step when Dele turned around. His hair was cropped shorter beneath his hood, and the beginnings of a beard had started to show on his chin. His eyes locked with mine. He looked so like Temi, it stopped me mid-stride. I saw my fist plunging into her flesh, and I didn't trust myself to go on. I stood, impotent, as three plainclothed officers jumped on Dele, pushing him down as he screamed his sister's name into the dust.

Chapter Ninety

Leah

Kenny O'Sullivan finally had his headline, no thanks to me. It had all happened so fast, I hoped no one had noticed me freeze. I accepted the praise silently, determined never to fail like that again.

'We got him, ma'am.'

I forced a smile as Akosua beamed at me, congratulating me again and again. I stood by the evidence board, surrounded by colleagues, open palms taking turns to shake mine. I sensed Randle looking at me from across the room. I expected him to look away, but he didn't.

'Ma'am?' He appeared in front of me. 'Can I have a word?'

'What?'

'I don't think you want the others to hear.' He had the decency to look down.

I grabbed his arm, steering him into a side room; the feel of the muscle through his shirt was unfamiliar and strange. There was an empty desk and two chairs, but I stayed standing, my back pressed against the wall.

'Well,' I said, 'you've got my attention.'

He stopped under the light. His skin glowed yellow.

'Is there something I should know? About the case. Something you want to tell me, ma'am?'

His foot pivoted on the linoleum, and I could hear a slight squeak.

'I don't know what you're talking about, Randle.' My hand tightened on the door handle.

'If there's something I should know to help me do my job, then I need you to tell me . . . ma'am.'

'You think I'm hiding something about the case?'

'No. I just . . . Is something wrong? I want to help.'

'Randle . . .'

'Yes, ma'am?' He sounded hopeful.

'We've just found Dele. Focus on that.'

His voice rose behind me as I pulled the door open.

'I saw you, ma'am. When you went after Dele. I saw you freeze.'

He took a step towards me, dropping his voice even though there was no one else there to hear. He was tall and broad across his shoulders, and the room grew darker when his body cut across the light.

'I'm not going to say anything but . . .' He trailed off. 'If there's something stopping you from doing your job, you need to talk to someone before it's too late, ma'am.'

I stared down at the linoleum, grey squares alternating with the white.

'If you don't want to work with me on this,' I kept my voice steady, 'I can ask Kenny to move you onto something else. Is that what you want?'

'No, ma'am. That won't be necessary.'

I waited for him to leave.

Standing in the empty room, I felt tired and alone. Dele Adeola was waiting to be interrogated, but I was too frustrated to face him. I made my way to the accessible toilet and locked myself in darkness. No one would think to look for me there. I closed my eyes, inhaling deeply through my nose until I felt dizzy from the swirl of blood and oxygen in my brain. I had a vague memory of a time as a child when my frustration had taken over and I had thrown myself to the ground kicking and screaming. I remembered Margaretta reaching out for me and me pushing her, catching her head with the heel of my foot as I lashed out. I couldn't remember the look on her face, just the curve of her back as she got up and calmly walked away. I remembered feeling alone then too, left by myself with my tears and rage. She barely spoke to me that night; then the next day, I came home from school to find a trampette waiting in the middle of the room, exactly where I had had my tantrum.

I had forgotten the incident until that moment, but as I thought back to it, I recalled other times I had wanted to lash out, and Margaretta gently guiding me to the little trampoline. I remember feeling free and light as I jumped higher and higher until the anger slipped away, and I focused on the memory until I was ready to open the door.

Chapter Ninety-One

Leah

I made my way towards the interview room, ignoring the footsteps behind me. The rhythm was clumsy and uneven; someone was struggling to keep up.

'Ma'am . . .'

Akosua clearly needed to work on her fitness. I stopped to let her catch her breath.

'There's a family emergency. Someone left a message for you.'

She handed me a number I didn't recognise. I waited for her to leave before I dialled.

'Don't hang up. Please.' Odie was wise to speak fast.

She had used a different number; I memorised the last three digits so I wouldn't be caught unawares again.

'I can't speak now,' I said.

'It's important . . .'

'Two minutes.'

I leant back against the wall as a surge of tiredness hit me. Further down the corridor, a door opened, and an officer emerged, rigid with exasperation.

'It's Daniel. He's missing,' Odie said.

'Have you reported him to Missing Persons?'

'I'm reporting him to you.'

'It's not my area, Odie. I don't know what you expect me to do.' My brain was crowded with dead bodies, and Daniel was a grown man who probably just needed some space.

'Please, Leah. He's my son.'

She waited for me to dismiss her.

'OK. I'll look into it,' I said.

Dele Adeola sat opposite me for the second time. He sneered at the idea of a lawyer, insisting he had nothing to hide. His eyelashes were long and thick, shielding his eyes. The room was hot, and his forehead glistened near his hairline. When he lifted his head, I was conscious of the smell of his sweat. Randle sat dutifully beside me. I sensed him stiffen, and I shifted my chair so we were further apart. I placed an image of each of Dele's victims on the table in front of us: Charles Walker, Jake Munro, Paul Drayton. Butchered and bloody, bodies prostrate on the ground. Dele glanced at each one, then he just nodded sadly.

'Who killed these men, Dele?' I said.

'I did.' He sounded relieved to say it, lifting each photograph as though seeing the men for the first time.

The hair on his chin was patchy, and I doubted he could grow a full beard. He was barely more than a teenager, and his sudden transformation from model student to multiple murderer didn't make sense. There was nothing in his history which hinted at a tendency towards sadistic or psychotic behaviour. He had no criminal record, and there was nothing in his school reports to suggest he was a danger to others. I thought of the DVDs we had found in their flat and Temi's fascination with mentalism.

'Brendan Klee . . .'

'What about him?' Dele almost looked bored. 'I already told you what I know.'

'He talks a lot about the power of the mind. You said your mother liked what he did, but she didn't understand how it worked.'

'So?' Dele kicked his leg out in front of him. 'She didn't understand a lot of things. D'you want to ask me about them too?'

'Did you ever meet him separately?'

Dele sniffed loudly. 'Why would I do that? There was nothing that man could do for me.'

'But you went to his show?'

'Once.' Dele frowned at Randle's interjection. 'It wasn't a big deal.'

'Did you volunteer to go on stage?' I said.

He nodded.

'What did he make you do?'

'There was a bowl of water, but I was made to think it was acid. He made me imagine he was someone else . . . I threw it in his face.'

'Who did you imagine he was?'

'Charles Walker,' Dele said without hesitation.

'Why?'

'He could have helped us, but he didn't. My mum and dad begged and begged, and he did nothing.'

'Did Brendan Klee inspire you to kill Charles Walker?'

Dele laughed at that. '*Inspire?* It was a trick of the mind. Brendan Klee didn't make me do anything.'

'So, what made you kill those men?'

'I had to,' he said, as though it was the only possible answer.

His body was slumped in his chair, and there was a faint whine to his voice. He leant forwards, and I was struck by the size of his palms as he gripped the table. At twenty, he hadn't finished puberty, but Dele Adeola was already a strong man.

'Have you ever done something you never realised you were capable of doing, but after you did it, you were surprised by how natural it felt?'

'Is that how it felt after you murdered Charles Walker?' I asked.

Dele's body twitched with a strange energy. 'For days I had this question in my head. *Will I? Will I? Will I?* Will I do it? Will I regret it? *Will I?* You know? Tina helped me to believe in myself, but it came from *me*. It had to come from me.'

Dele's eyes grew animated as he spoke, but I had stopped listening the moment he mentioned her name.

'Who's Tina, Dele?'

He looked at me as if I had missed the point.

'Who's Tina?' I repeated.

'We met her at the show.'

'You mean one of Brendan Klee's shows?'

'Yes.'

'Did she work with Brendan?'

'No. I don't know what she did . . . She was in the audience the night I went on stage. We met her in the car park after. She made some joke about our car.'

'Was she being aggressive?'

'Nah, man.' He almost smiled. 'I can't remember what she said, but it was the first time Mum had laughed since my dad died.' He said the words carefully, reliving a rare moment of joy.

'And did you see her after that?'

'Yes. I never went back, but Mum went to Brendan's shows with

Tina a few times. She came round one night. She was good with Lola. Lola doesn't like anyone except me and Mum, but Tina — Lola just loved her straight away. Sometimes Tina would babysit when Mum was doing shifts and I was at work, and she'd hang around when I got back so I could study without worrying about Lola. She was cool like that. Just wanted to help. Then we got chatting one day and . . .' He trailed off.

'What did you talk about, Dele?'

He shrugged noncommittally and, for a second, I wasn't sure he was going to answer me. Then he looked down.

'Everything,' he replied quietly. 'Everything made sense when I spoke to her.'

Randle seemed on edge in the corridor outside. There had been a shift since our earlier conversation.

'You think it was the same Tina who left the message, ma'am?'

'I don't know,' I said. 'But it seems like too much of a coincidence. Did you track that number?'

'They're still working on it. I'll get an ETA from Akosua.'

He hovered for a second, unsure what to do with his hands. I didn't have the energy to hold on to the tension between us.

'Spit it out, Randle. Please,' I said.

'I didn't think Dele would admit to it, ma'am.' He hesitated. 'But it was almost as if he was proud.'

I pictured Dele, bent over in his chair, wired and intense in that little room.

'Not proud, Randle. Relieved. A man without remorse or regret.'

Chapter Ninety-Two

Odie

Odie was starting to get worried. She didn't dare admit it to Richard, but she was. She convinced herself Daniel was OK, that Richard was just highly strung and overprotective, but the nagging doubt wouldn't go away. The more she tried not to think about it, the more anxious she became. She couldn't share any of this with Richard, so when she drove to Daniel's flat, she went alone. Odie wasn't sure what she was looking for, but if Daniel had left any clue as to his whereabouts, she was determined to find it.

Standing on the threshold, she realised that she had never been inside her son's flat before. Richard had given her a spare key for emergencies, but she had never had cause to use it. She had never been invited, never imposed herself on Daniel, never cared enough about his life to be curious about where or how he lived. Now, entering his home for the first time, she realised she didn't know him at all. She had always assumed he was the opposite of her: calmer, more measured. His flat told a different story, and there was something about the structured chaos Odie recognised in herself. She almost laughed at the irony – Daniel had rejected everything about her but had inherited her messiness and passion for words. He would never acknowledge it, and she would never bring it up.

The sitting room was crammed with books – fiction, non-fiction, self-help, biography. It was difficult to know where to begin with all the clutter. She searched the desk and drawers. There were Post-its everywhere, scribbled aides-memoires with spurts of inspiration, but nothing that would help her find her son. She flicked through his books, scanning the pages for Daniel's scratchy scrawl. Then she moved on to his notepads, skimming over each line. She was so immersed in the minutiae, she almost missed the sheet of paper pinned to the fridge with a typewriter magnet. It was partially obscured by a photograph of Daniel as a boy, with Richard grinning goofily at the camera. The picture caught her attention first, a visual reminder that her ex-husband and son were complete as a family without her. Odie wasn't sentimental, but her absence drew her to the image; she wondered when it had been taken and whether she had been there that day. It was only then, as her mind drifted, that she registered the small calendar, flat against the fridge. There was a name here, a number there, but one entry stuck out around the time Daniel had supposedly disappeared. There was no name or number, just an address. She had been right all along: Daniel had gone away willingly. It made perfect sense. She was prepared to leave it at that, but something stopped her. It could have been Richard's voice in her head; it could have been a maternal instinct she never thought she had, or the feeling deep down that something was wrong. She pulled the calendar off the fridge, careful to leave the photograph in the same position she had found it.

Chapter Ninety-Three

Daniel let his eyes close momentarily. It was only supposed to be for a second, but he found he didn't want to open them again. The pain in his head was so sharp, he couldn't think straight, and the fear within him made his chest tight beneath his shirt. He didn't know how he had ended up in the inky black room, but the cramp in his body told him he had been there for a while. He pushed himself up to sitting so he could rest his back against the wall. His trousers had ripped across the calf, and he could feel the rough floor grating against his skin. He blocked out the pain, focusing on what he could remember before he was locked in the room, but his mind had gone blank. He couldn't recall the last time he had eaten, and his muscles contracted around his empty belly. He felt faint and nauseous, but if he breathed through his nose and focused his thoughts, the pangs of hunger faded away.

Emotions came and went, but his mind never stopped working. Anger, fear, sadness – he had felt them all in the time he had been locked in the room. Underneath it was a growing sense of foreboding. He had been stuck between consciousness and oblivion, and his mind had been overrun with vivid memories. He opened his mouth to scream, calling out with every ounce of strength he had left. He was met by silence, and he began to wonder whether he had even made a sound. That was when he started to cry – quiet, persistent tears, seeping out slowly, then flowing more freely as his body started to convulse.

Chapter Ninety-Four

Leah

Dele's description of Tina was deliberately vague. He didn't know her surname and, from his sketchy recollection of her features, I doubted our e-fit looked anything like the woman we needed to find. All we could do was build up a pattern of behaviour. We knew Dele had spent a lot of time with her. He trusted her implicitly, and his instinct would be to try and protect her.

'It sounds like Tina helped your family a lot.' I eased my way back into the interrogation after a break.

'Yes. She made a big difference after my dad died.'

'And was it just babysitting she helped with?'

'No . . .' His eyes focused on a crack in the wall behind me. 'I was stressed from studying and I was working two jobs. I had . . .' He stopped. 'They say I had a panic attack. I don't know what happened to me. I just lashed out and then it was OK. One minute I was out of control . . . then I just felt calm.'

He kept pressing his hand against the side of the table, denting the plastic with the force of his thumb.

'I didn't hurt anyone, but I think I scared my mum. She was worried about me being around Lola, so I went to stay with Tina for a few days to get better.'

'Where?' I kept my face neutral.

'Her house,' he said. 'Some place out of town.'

'What did you do there?'

'We just talked. Can't remember about what. We just talked.'

I wondered whether there had been anything between them, whether Tina had crossed a line with her friend's son.

'I know what you're thinking.' Dele's eyes didn't leave my face. 'It wasn't like that. She just got me. Understood who I am deep down.'

'Did Tina tell you to kill those men?'

His eyes narrowed. He scratched at the scruff of his beard. 'You're not listening to me. I told you. It was me. It had to be me; it just took me some time to figure it out.'

'Did you tell your mother what you were planning?'

'No.' His voice was quiet.

'But she found out?'

That was the only time I saw something close to regret. He was silent for a moment.

'She must have followed me when I went after Jake. I don't know. She never talked about it. Just said it had to stop.'

'Is that why she restrained you? To stop you?'

Dele looked away, careful not to turn back until the shame had left his eyes. He said nothing, but I didn't need an answer. She was his mother, and she had done what she had to to protect him and to protect others. I had been too slow to understand.

'Did your mother know about Charles Walker?'

Dele shook his head.

'What happened with Paul Drayton?' There was an edge to Randle's voice as he pushed for a response.

'She knew I'd go after him,' Dele said. 'She must have followed me or been watching his house.'

The room had grown hotter, and his skin was clammy. He used his sleeve to wipe away a thin line of sweat. It left a smudge on the dark cotton, and he stared at it, fixating on the mark.

'I don't remember seeing her. It was like my mind was somewhere else until it was done.'

'Until what was done, Dele?' I asked.

'Until I knew he was dead.'

'Then what?'

'Then . . .' The shame returned to his eyes. 'Then I covered myself up and ran, and my mum took the blame for what I had done.'

He looked exhausted, sinking into the chair. I wondered how many hours he had stayed awake, running from our form of justice while he tried to carry out his.

'Did Tina help you get away?' I said.

'No.' Dele shook his head sadly. 'I don't know where she is.'

'What about her house? Could you find it again?'

He kneaded the skin under his eyes. 'I slept most of the way. It was dark.'

'Dele, I realise Tina is your friend, but we need to find her. The more you help us with our investigation, the better it will be for you in the long run. Dele . . .'

'You're not listening. I can't answer your questions because I don't remember. I just know that everything made sense after I was there. . . That's why I went back with her . . .'

'When did you go back?'

I expected another vague response, but he remembered the exact date. I didn't need to be told its significance. Ten days before Charles Walker was found dead, Dele Adeola had spent a week with a woman named Tina. He left home never having committed a crime and returned, ready to kill.

I took the back stairs to my office to avoid bumping into Kenny. The door was open, and a sheet of paper was taped to my computer, a phone number scrawled diagonally in black.

'We found her . . .' Akosua stood in the doorway, barely containing her excitement. 'The woman who left the message. We traced the number.'

She waited for some form of acknowledgement, but I was already on my phone. The voice at the end of the line sounded flustered. I waited for the woman to calm down.

'Tina?' I said.

'No.'

The word landed with a thud in my gut.

'No . . .' she said again. 'My name is Angela. But I know who Tina is.'

Chapter Ninety-Five

Leah

According to her records, Angela Pachulski's wasn't a straightforward tale: she had run away from home at fifteen, couch-surfing until her friends tired of being hospitable, and she found herself on the streets. Her father didn't see her for sixteen years. Then one day, she charged back into his life, carrying out a brutal attack which could have left him dead. A hysterical Angela insisted she had been pressured to kill him by a voice in her head, and when asked why she had wanted him dead, she couldn't or wouldn't say. She was sectioned – in a psychiatric unit for two years, before being released back into the world.

It was rush hour. I tried not to get frustrated as my foot lingered over the clutch. Randle didn't attempt to make conversation, and his face relaxed visibly when the car came to a final stop. The block of flats gave little away; it was a nondescript modern building on a trunk road heading out of London. The door was answered by a sombre-looking woman with a tired face.

'Angela?'

'No. I'm her sister, Jean – sister, carer, the only one who cares enough to pick up the pieces.'

She was well spoken, and each word was clipped and clear. She showed us into a small room at the front of the flat. There were photographs of Jean and a woman I assumed to be Angela displayed neatly on the mantelpiece. Apart from that, the room was devoid of personal effects, and there were plastic sheets stretched over every chair.

'She has accidents – ever since they let her out. Sometimes she passes out . . .' Jean said.

She followed my gaze to a photograph of Angela staring at the camera with wide impenetrable eyes.

'You're the first visitors she's had in a long time. The nurse doesn't even come any more.'

'Has she ever been visited by someone called Tina?'

It was the first and only time Jean smiled. 'You could say that,' she said. 'Tina's her alter ego. She used to talk about Tina saying things, making her do things . . .'

I could hear her mentally placing quotation marks around the name.

'What makes you think Tina isn't real?' I asked.

'You have to understand that my sister is unwell, and she says things sometimes. She talked a lot about Tina when they locked her up, but she could never remember anything about her – her surname, the colour of her eyes, what she did, where she lived . . . Angela can't remember anything specific about Tina, beyond the fact that she exists. She's a convenient scapegoat . . . an imaginary friend.'

'But why would Angela need a scapegoat when she confessed?' Randle said.

'I told you . . .' Jean sighed, pulling a hairpin out of her bun. 'Angela's not well. She's extremely fragile. You need to remember that when you speak to her. Her reliability is . . . questionable.'

'How questionable?' I asked.

She shrugged, sliding the pin back in, so it was completely concealed by hair. 'She's my sister and I love her, but you can't believe a word she says.'

Angela was standing by the window in her bedroom when we entered. The room smelt of Febreze and soap, and I noticed there was a lock on the door. Her body was charged with nervous energy, and the mania in her eyes seemed at odds with the calmness of her voice.

'You took your time. I've been trying to tell you people about Tina for years.'

'We're listening now,' I said.

She beckoned us forwards, shaking my hand with surprising vigour.

'Angela Pachulski.'

'Detective Inspector Hutch. This is Detective Sergeant Randle.'

She lowered her voice, looking around, in case someone was listening. 'Thank you for finally coming. It will be OK now. I know it will.'

'What can you tell us about Tina?'

'She's dangerous, but you know that, or you wouldn't be here. They used to think *I* was dangerous, but I'm not.' She whispered the words, as if it were a secret.

'Why would they think that?' I needed to win her trust.

'Did they tell you what I did? To my father?'

Angela circled us as she spoke. It made me dizzy watching her as she paced one way then another, trying to arrange the thoughts in her head. She abruptly changed the subject without waiting for an answer.

'I read about that man . . . Brendan. They say he has the power to control minds. Do you believe that, Detective? That one person can control another person's mind?'

'It depends on what you mean,' I said.

'Do you think you can be made to do something you don't want to?' She ran one hand over her face, becoming increasingly agitated. 'Some days, I think Jean's right and it's all in my mind. Other days, I know she's real.' She was clawing gently at her neck, her fingers digging into the flesh. 'I saw the articles, what they said online . . . and I thought, what if it *wasn't* Brendan? What if Tina made them do those things? Like she made me.' Angela's eyes were hopeful. 'That's why you're here, isn't it?'

'What makes you think it was Tina?'

I couldn't tell whether she heard me.

'Do you know what's funny?' she said. 'I don't remember it. Hurting my father. It was like I wasn't conscious, and then I woke up and I was standing there, with my dad screaming on the ground . . . I remember the sound. Like he was dying. Like a wild animal, howling in pain. I tried to help him, but he moved away. He was scared. Of me, his daughter. I had tried to kill my own father.'

'Does this have something to do with Tina?' I trod carefully, mindful of Jean's words.

Angela stared at me from under her lashes. They were too long for her face and, with her wide glassy eyes, she looked more like a doll than a person.

'Those things Brendan claims to be able to do, Tina can do that – speak to you in your dreams; remind you of your pain; make it all real. So real you have to do something . . . so real you have to act.'

Angela was completely still now, eyes far away.

'Tell me about her,' I said. 'What was Tina like?'

She turned back to look at us, her face alive with the memory. 'I thought she was nice. She used to stop and talk to me when I was on the streets. She seemed kind. She made time . . . I didn't speak much then – I used to stutter sometimes – but it was easy with her. I never felt judged.'

'What did you talk about?'

'Anything to begin with: the weather, politics, my life. Then we talked about everything. I told her things I'd never told anyone.'

'Things about your father?'

'Stop!' She almost shouted the word. 'I'm not falling for that again.'

She strode across the tiny room, scratching at her neck. I could see Jean in the doorway, ready to intervene. My cue was so subtle, I wasn't sure Randle would understand, but he knew exactly what I wanted him to do.

'It's OK. It's OK.' The soothing tone that had been absent with Dele was back. 'We're sorry, Angela. Really. You don't need to talk about anything you don't want to. Please. It's OK.' He waited.

Angela was by the window again. 'OK,' she said. 'OK . . .'

I nodded at Randle to continue.

'Did Tina ever take you anywhere? Offer you shelter for a few days?'

'Not like that, but . . .' Angela paused, remembering. 'One night she picked me up. It was raining. I was cold. She took me to her house.'

'Do you remember where she lived?'

'No. It took a while to get there. I slept most of the way. When I woke up, I remember still feeling very groggy. We were driving under an arch.'

'Can you describe it?'

'It was stone. Low. I couldn't see much in the dark.'

'And how long were you there for? At Tina's house.'

'It felt like days, but it was only twenty-four hours. I remember because of the newspaper. I always look at the date, so I don't lose track of time.'

'And what did you do out there?' I said.

'We talked. I don't remember about what. But everything felt like it made sense.' She inhaled, steeling herself to go on. 'I dreamt about my father. Except it was like I was awake. The voices in my head were so loud, it was like someone else was speaking to me. I hadn't thought about my dad in a long time, but everything he'd done to me, everything I'd tried to forget, I suddenly couldn't get it out of my mind. I just wanted it to end. Wanted him gone. The next thing I knew, he was lying there, hurt.'

'How did you get there? To your father?' Randle asked the question, but I'd had the same thought. 'Did Tina drive you to his house?'

Angela fiddled with a hole in her sleeve, pulling at the fabric so we heard it rip. 'I don't know,' she said. 'I remember getting out of a car, but I don't remember her being there.'

'Did you drive the car?' I asked.

'I can't drive.' She said it as if it were common knowledge. 'I remember Tina's voice. It felt like mine. I can remember moments before it happened, but none of it holds together. And what I did to him . . .'

She stopped, driving her nails hard into her neck so she drew blood.

'I have no memory of that. Just me standing there afterwards.'

She ran her hand across the window, watching her nails scratch the glass.

'What now? Will you find her? You need her to tell my sister I'm not crazy.' She flicked her eyes towards the door. 'Everyone thinks I made her up, but Tina's real. You believe me, don't you?'

'Did Tina tell you to hurt your father, Angela?' I asked.

'I don't know. I don't know how any of it happened. I had these thoughts . . . Then he was lying there, hurt.' She repeated the words, looking to us to make sense of it.

'Angela,' I spoke slowly, making sure she registered every word. 'If you can't remember what happened, how do you know it was Tina who made you do it?'

She shook her head, her eyes filled with tears. 'I don't. That's the worst of it. I don't.'

Chapter Ninety-Six

Leah

It had been a long day, and any goodwill had disappeared with the sun. Angela Pachulski divided the team, and I could hear Akosua and Randle arguing when I returned from updating Kenny. I hovered at a distance, watching their conversation become more animated as they sat at their desks. Randle's sleeves were pushed up to his elbows; his hair had broken free from the gel.

'What if Angela's right and there's a woman called Tina preying on people's desires?'

'Encouraging them to kill people they hate?' Akosua's voice was full of disdain.

'There are definite similarities between their accounts: the fact they can't remember details, like getting to Tina's house . . .'

'And differences,' Akosua stressed. 'Angela couldn't follow through; Dele killed three times. Angela hears Tina's voice; Dele said she didn't tell him to do it . . .'

'Maybe Tina used some form of hypnosis? Maybe Dele wasn't aware? Maybe he would never have acted if it wasn't for her?'

'Do you realise how ridiculous that sounds?'

'Does it though?' Randle said. 'What about Brendan Klee? I went to his show. I saw what he did . . .'

'But it's still a leap.'

'Neither Angela nor Dele can remember how they got to Tina's house or their final conversations with her,' Randle persisted. 'What if Tina made sure they didn't remember? How can they not remember what they spoke about? You don't just go away and come back a killer without remembering anything. Maybe Tina did something to their minds.'

'But how come Angela remembers some things, whereas Dele remembers practically nothing?' Akosua refused to back down.

'Dele's attacks took place four years after Angela's. He spent more time with Tina than Angela did. He killed. Angela didn't in the end. Maybe Tina failed with Angela, so she perfected her process. Whatever she did with Angela didn't work, so she took the time she needed to get better.'

Akosua was struggling to conceal her exasperation. Her shoulders relaxed when she saw me approach.

'OK,' I said. 'Let's assume Randle's theory has merit. Brendan Klee is a chancer who preys on other people's insecurities. Even he would say his talent is limited, and yet he managed to have an effect on Randle in a matter of minutes. This Tina, she's more intentional and . . .'

Randle caught my eye as he finished my sentence. '. . . she had more time.'

'I don't get it, ma'am.' The scowl made Akosua look older. Her hands strayed to her hips, but she pulled them down to the side, hoping I hadn't seen. 'If Tina is so intentional, why use the same name each time? Why not start again with a different one, make sure she doesn't leave a trail?'

'Maybe the name's important to her,' I said. 'Besides, neither

Angela nor Dele knew her surname, and Tina's a common enough name. Sure, it's a risk, but it's calculated. She's someone who feels in control.'

Chapter Ninety-Seven

Leah

Dele was neither hostile nor resistant, but he grew increasingly frustrated as we continued the interrogation. He rubbed his knuckles together like he was sharpening a knife, mimicking my questions in a dull, bored voice.

'*Did Tina tell me to kill Charles?* No. *Did Tina tell me to kill Jake?* No. *Paul Drayton?* No again. How many times, Inspector? I told you, no.'

He sat back in his chair, the muscle in his neck pulsing. His eyes shot around the bare interview room. He moved forwards, then sat back again, then forwards. I waited until he was still.

'Did Tina know what you were planning?'

'No one knew.' He shook his head for emphasis. 'I didn't even know at first . . .'

'What do you mean?' Randle asked. His voice was steady, but the intensity in his eyes gave him away.

Dele ran his fingers along his jaw. He closed his eyes, thinking back to the night the carnage began.

'I didn't know what I had done the first time. Not straight away. It was like it was me, but it wasn't. It was like I forgot until I heard about him on the news.'

'Heard about whom?' I asked.

'Charles Walker. When I heard, I knew it was me who had done that, and I remembered . . . It wasn't me, but it was me. You get me?' He was almost on the edge of his chair, and I could see the fine hairs bristling at the top of his cheeks. 'D'you understand?'

'I'm not sure I do, Dele.'

'It was like I didn't know that's what I wanted. Deep down. For my dad. For Mum, for Lola. I couldn't do it. Couldn't think about it. Then something happened . . . I stepped up and he was dead.'

Dele exhaled, and I saw the relief he had felt when Charles Walker finally died.

'When I heard it on the news, that's when it came back. I remembered . . . doing it . . . killing him. Not the moment I did it; I remember standing there after it was done. It was strange. Like I wasn't there but I was there. As if something inside was driving me, and I didn't have to think. I remember doing up my top because there was blood on my shirt. After that, I don't remember much.'

He leant forwards; his irises glistened as they caught the light.

'My mum says we're all conditioned to survive. It's the way we're wired as human beings. Those men broke my dad so bad he lost that basic urge. When I killed Charles Walker, that urge kicked in. It was like I was on autopilot. I can't explain it. I had to get away, and I did.'

'And you don't remember anything else?'

'I told you. No. When I woke up the next day, there was nothing.'

There was a draught in the room, and my skin tingled. I crossed my arms to keep the heat close to my chest.

'Did you regret it? When you realised what you had done?'

Dele looked at me as if I were speaking a different language.

'How can you regret being who you are?' he said. 'I needed to get back there, but I didn't know how. I had to let it out.'

'Let what out?'

Dele shrugged. 'The darkness. The anger. I kept trying to remember what I felt just before I did it. I thought about my dad, what they did to him, the time in our lives when everything went dark. But I couldn't get back there. I couldn't find the courage.' He laughed, and that sound, so unexpected, made him seem very young. 'If my mum hadn't threatened to tidy up my room, I wouldn't have found it. I don't even remember keeping it. In a bag at the back of my cupboard with my shirt.'

'Keeping what?'

'The bat,' he said simply. 'When I picked it up, it all came back. That night, how I felt, what I did, what I could do . . . It felt real, and I knew I could do it again. The knife made it quicker with Jake and Paul Drayton, but I couldn't have done it without the bat. When I held it and I saw them, I knew I could make them pay. For what they did to my dad, for what they did to us.'

'What did it feel like?'

I thought of Temi, fiddling with her bandage, unable to answer because she hadn't committed the crimes.

'Charles . . . I can't remember. I told you. But it was different with Jake and Paul. I felt more myself, but better, like I didn't have to be ashamed of who I was any more. There was something driving me, and I couldn't stop it, but I knew. I killed those men, and it felt right.'

He was completely still now, his pupils large black holes surrounded by white. Dele Adeola had been angry for a very long time. Someone had taken that anger and fed it until it exploded, but why?

Chapter Ninety-Eight

Leah

Randle looked at me intently as we stood in my office. His fair hair seemed darker in the weak light.

'The bat.' He sounded like he was delivering a punchline.

'What about it?'

'It features in every case. Dele. Fiona Garvey. Angela Pachulski too.' He handed me a folder. 'The full case file came through while we were talking to Dele – Angela almost beat her father into a coma with a baseball bat. Very similar to Fiona and Alistair Cowan. Fiona said she didn't know Temi, but what if it was Tina she met at one of Brendan Klee's shows? What if Tina manipulated Fiona as well?'

'So, what? Tina manipulates them and somehow incites them to use a baseball bat to carry out their attacks?'

'No. Not that. What if it's some kind of trigger? That's why the knife wasn't enough. Dele needed the bat to trigger the right level of emotion. He needed the bat to have the courage to act.' Randle's eyes were bright and unblinking. 'That night at the show, Brendan did something to put us under.'

I thought of the spotted handkerchief Brendan had used to trigger deep-seated emotions; Randle refusing to look at me when he explained himself in the car. My desk dug into the base of my spine as I leant against it. I relaxed into the sensation, flicking through the file.

'When you held my hand – you said it was you, but it wasn't you,' I said. 'Like you weren't completely in control.'

Randle nodded gravely, pushing his fingers through his hair. 'Angela's sister was wrong, ma'am. Tina's real, and she's dangerous.'

Chapter Ninety-Nine

Odie

Odie had five missed calls from Richard. She hadn't checked her phone, but each time it rang, she knew it was him. She had decided not to tell him where she was going; it would only worry him, and she was struggling with her own growing concern. Daylight had faded, and her headlights cut through the murk. She had been driving for a while, the smooth tarmac of the city giving way to uneven country roads. She had left suburbia behind about an hour before. She had never been a fan, but it vaguely resembled the London she knew. Now she worried about the damage to her undercarriage as her car spluttered up a steep hill. She was alone in alien territory, and Daniel might not be there when she reached her destination. She almost turned back, then she reminded herself that she didn't have a choice – she needed to do something, and this was her only lead.

Odie turned off the narrow road, shifting in her seat as she navigated the bumpy terrain. She hadn't passed a building or another human being for miles, and the sight of a blue door ahead was faintly cheering. It was set back a little way from a gate, and she pulled up, looking for a name or number. The silence was the first thing she noticed when she switched off the engine, the peculiar sound of nothing and no one. She hesitated, instinct telling her to turn around, guilt willing her to stay and look for her son. The gate was padlocked from the inside, so she knew someone must be there. There was no bell, so she tried her horn. No one came, and the low honk sounded offensive and loud. The gate wasn't particularly high. She thought about leaping over into the compound, but she was too old for heroics, and she had never been particularly agile. She stood on the bonnet of her car, slowly easing herself over. She landed badly on the other side, bashing her shin as she hit the ground. She realised that, in her haste, she had left her phone in the car, but she couldn't face the climb again, so she continued towards the house without it, looking around for signs of life. She didn't hear the footsteps until it was too late.

Chapter One Hundred

Leah

Randle bounded down the stairs, attacking them two at a time. I didn't hurry behind him; the extra seconds weren't going to help.

'We're fine to question Fiona again, ma'am. The powers that be accept the seriousness of the risk. Fiona's happy to talk to us.'

'Did you say anything about Tina?'

'No, ma'am. Fiona's never mentioned her, and I didn't want her to shut down without talking to us first.'

We had reached the enquiry desk with the usual smattering of do-gooders and victims. The main doors kept opening, and a chill lingered in the air. Heads craned to get the attention of the constable on duty, but one man was bent over his phone. His hair was cropped close to the skull, slightly thinning at the centre, wiry black strands mixed with grey. I didn't recognise Richard Reid until I had missed my chance to avoid him.

'Leah . . . Detective Inspector Hutch . . .' He approached hesitantly. 'Richard Reid.'

He held out his hand.

'I know who you are.' I looked at Randle, my mind still on Fiona.

'I appreciate you're busy, but I didn't know whom else to ask. Did Odie call you?'

I nodded, realising why he was there – Odie's son Daniel must still be missing, and I had done nothing about it. Odie would think I was being malicious, but it had completely slipped my mind.

'Listen, Richard, if it's about Daniel—'

He cut me off before the excuse came out.

'She went to look for him. She didn't tell me, but I know she did. Now he's gone and she's gone . . . and . . . something's happened to both of them; I know it has.'

He grabbed my arm and I let him; the tips of his fingers turned white as they gripped my coat.

'She always answers my calls, even if she can't speak for long . . . Ever since I . . .'

Suddenly self-conscious, he released me. For a moment, he avoided my eyes. It was common knowledge that Richard Reid had tried to kill himself. Odie had had an affair at work; she liked to think nobody had known. I doubted Richard had recovered emotionally. Anyone could see he wasn't a strong man.

'I'm sure she's fine, Richard,' I said.

'What if she isn't?'

'When was the last time you saw her?'

'I know you've had your issues with her in the past, but can't you put that aside? What if she's in trouble? What if . . .' He trailed off. 'Just come with me to her house. Please . . . see if you can find a clue. If there's nothing there, I'll leave you in peace.'

He reached his hands out towards me, and I pitied him. He had chosen the wrong person to love and had almost paid for it with his life. Odie was fine; she didn't care enough about her family to put herself in danger.

'Daniel's still missing . . .' Richard said.

Whatever I thought of Odie, their son could be at risk.

'Randle . . .'

He was standing by the door, hands in pockets, looking out into the street. I knew he had been listening, and he moved towards me before I even said his name.

'It's fine, ma'am. We've got it covered,' Randle said. 'I'll speak to Fiona about Tina. The team are on the house.'

He smiled, but it did nothing to reassure me. Richard Reid was a distraction I could have done without.

Chapter One Hundred and One

Leah

It was strange entering Odie's house without her. I knew she wouldn't want me in her home, and it felt wrong being there uninvited. Richard had a key and ushered me in before I had the chance to change my mind. The house was dark and quiet, a stark reminder of her absence. Neither Ross Calhoun nor her other colleagues had seen her, but her neighbour had spotted her car leaving. I followed Richard down the hallway to the kitchen, looking around the overstuffed room. The sink was empty and there were no dirty dishes, but the recycling bin overflowed with rinsed wine bottles, and the shelves were jammed with appliances that had never been used. The table was the obvious place to start. It was covered with pieces of paper scattered in vague attempts at piles. Whatever I thought of Odie, I had never underestimated her ability to follow a lead, and it was clear her interest in Fiona Garvey had never gone away: there were printed sheets with details of Fiona's life, a calendar annotated with Fiona's movements, scribbles on scraps of paper dotted around. There were two identical envelopes with Odie's name typed neatly on the front – no address, no other details. The first envelope was empty, its contents somewhere on the table in front of me; the second contained a photograph of

Dele Adeola. The notes on Fiona were in keeping with Odie's fascination with her case, but the photograph threw me. It wasn't the one we had released to the press, and I wondered who had sent Odie the image. Odie's mysterious source – I kicked myself for not believing her that day outside the station. She had been one step ahead from the beginning, present at the scene of Charles Walker's murder before we even knew about it, then doggedly gathering evidence in her bid to prove Fiona's innocence. Whoever had sent Odie this information had connected Fiona to Dele Adeola's case for a reason.

The table displayed all the signs of the trademark obsession I had seen in the past, and I remembered how Odie single-mindedly went after a story, forgetting about everything else. That's when I felt most sorry for Richard, consumed with concern for a woman who had never cared about her family and was unlikely to start caring now. He believed Odie was looking for his beloved son, but there was a strong possibility she was just chasing a lead, putting work ahead of family as she had always done. I looked down at the mess of paper in front of me.

'Take whatever you like.' Richard came up behind me. 'Anything you think will help you find them.'

That was the second time I felt sorry for Richard in as many minutes, handing me clues Odie would rather destroy than share. He thought I was on his side, committed to finding his son out of a sense of loyalty to a woman who had hated me for years. A text message flashed up on my screen; I read it quickly, keeping my phone low by my side.

Fiona has no recollection of Tina. Says never met. Ben.

It amused me he didn't sign his name 'Randle'. I tucked my phone discreetly away, but Richard Reid had been watching me. I sounded guiltier than I would have liked.

'I'll follow up when I get back to the station. I'll let you know if I hear anything.'

'Thank you.' Richard's face relaxed for the first time.

It was only as we were leaving that I noticed the package lying by the door – a nondescript brown envelope with Odie's name printed in the same typeface as on the envelopes in the kitchen. Richard's eyes followed mine. He acted with assertiveness Odie had alleged he didn't possess. Ripping open the envelope, he pulled out a USB stick on a plain metal key ring. There was a small white label down the side with two words: JACOB PAX.

I looked up at Richard as he handed it to me without a word. I had heard the name before, but I couldn't remember where. 'Who's Jacob Pax?'

Richard looked back at me blankly, then I saw the recognition dawn in his eyes.

'Richard,' I said. 'Who is Jacob Pax?'

'It was all over the news a long time ago. Jacob Pax: the little boy who killed another child.'

Chapter One Hundred and Two

Leah

In the six months I had been back in London, I had never learned the name of the IT guy. He never used mine, even though I was sure he knew who I was. Whenever he passed me in the corridor, there was an upward nod of recognition, silent acknowledgement that we were the same minority, united by the colour of our skin. It was late, so I went myself, counting on the combination of race and rank to get his attention fast. His office was an afterthought at the end of a series of poorly lit corridors with low ceilings and windows that hadn't been cleaned for years. The moment I crossed the threshold, I was reminded how depressing it was to be in his world. We exchanged a brief nod as I handed him the USB stick. We were on the second floor, but we might as well have been in the basement – his blinds were drawn, and a strong smell of deodorant thickened the air. I hovered by his desk as he did the routine virus check. He handed back the USB drive without a smile.

'All good?' I asked.

A brief look in my direction, but his face gave me nothing.

'My name's Thomas, by the way.'

He didn't ask for mine.

Back in my office, I inserted the USB stick into my laptop.

My body twitched with anticipation, and I pushed the stick, even though it was inserted as far as it could go. If it was a false lead, I would need to shadow skip to work off my frustration, and I prayed no one was in the accessible bathroom when I needed to make my escape. The rest of the team were sifting through the evidence from Odie's kitchen. Unsurprisingly, there had been little progress finding Tina's house. Based on Angela's recollection, we were searching for stone arches within a hundred-mile radius of London, looking at properties listed under the name 'Tina' nearby. Everyone knew it was a long shot. We didn't even have her full name.

A window popped open on my screen. I clicked on the solitary file and waited as a video started to play: it was one of those hazy summers, idealised in coming-of-age films. The footage was digitised from an old home movie, the picture blurred. I could see two figures playing in a garden – a small boy doing handstands against a tree and a girl looking on, laughing. There was about twenty minutes worth of material, all focused on the boy. In each frame, the girl sat or stood in the background as the boy vaulted and ran, full of energy and life. It was hard to imagine the same boy murdering another child.

I had a vague knowledge of the case, and it didn't take long to discover the basic facts: Jacob Pax, convicted of killing another boy in foster care over three decades ago. His story had shocked the nation because Jacob was only twelve years old at the time. What had seemed particularly disturbing was the premeditated nature of the crime: Jacob didn't kill the boy in a fit of rage; he had allegedly followed him for days, studying the boy's every move before crushing his skull with a rock. It was easier to discover more about the crime than the motive, to brand little Jacob Pax a demonic psychopath who deserved neither sympathy nor understanding, but there was a reason for what he had done. Jacob had acted out of revenge, to get rid of a boy who had bullied his sister mercilessly. He had tried to protect her, but when the attacks didn't stop, he decided to take matters into his own hands. Asked whether he thought it was worth it, his answer had been simple: he had done it for his sister; she only had him in the world, and if he didn't protect Tina, nobody else would. Tina Pax, Jacob's twin sister, the woman we had been looking for. It made too much sense to be a coincidence.

Chapter One Hundred and Three

Odie

Odie had never been blindfolded; she felt an acute feeling of claustrophobia, which slowly gave way to panic. She thought about screaming, but her throat was hoarse from crying out and she knew it would be futile. Her hands were strapped behind her and the more she tried to move her head, the more the fabric cut into her skin. She wanted to see, but she was afraid to, fearful of what she might face in the alien room. She inhaled deeply, trying to get used to the pressure around her eyes. Her breathing became steadier, her thoughts less frenzied. Then she felt the cold, dry sensation of another person's skin. She froze. She could feel a hand on either side of her temples, slowly pushing the blindfold down.

It was dark. She tried not to sound scared when she spoke, but she couldn't stop the quiver in her voice.

'Who are you?'

'That's not the question you should be asking.'

Odie didn't recognise the voice behind her, but she was pretty sure it was female.

'Why are you doing this?' She tried again.

Silence, and then just when she had given up, the woman spoke.

'Because people deserve to know the truth . . .'

Odie had heard those words before, read them in response to a question she had asked her mysterious source.

'You sent me those things,' she stuttered. 'The pages, the photograph . . .'

She heard what sounded like a laugh.

'I wasn't expecting you yet,' said the voice. 'The address was going to be the final piece of the puzzle. But you needed to see the truth first.'

'What truth?' Odie said.

She started to speak again, but the woman cut her off, her voice slow and deliberate as she enunciated each word.

'People deserve to know the truth about themselves . . . Take away fear, and we are all capable of doing terrible things.'

Chapter One Hundred and Four

Leah

Akosua had created a timeline of Tina's childhood, with bright colour-coded Post-it notes for the different stages of her life. She laid the A3 sheet across my desk, smoothing the paper so it lay flat against the wood. The bruise on her face had faded, and her skin had regained its sheen. Her voice was animated as her finger drifted over the fluorescent squares.

'Unlike her brother, Tina Pax doesn't have a criminal record, but she had a difficult childhood, moving from one foster home to another.'

'What about school?'

'It's the only thing that seems consistent in Tina's life, ma'am. She stuck with it until the end. Even stayed on for higher education.'

'Then what?'

I looked down at a trail of green Post-its.

'After that, Tina Pax dropped off the radar, popping up sporadically and then not at all.'

The yellow Post-it at the bottom of the sheet was blank, and Akosua had drawn a question mark in red ink. The lack of online history was hardly surprising, given that Tina had grown up before the social media revolution, but she seemed to have disappeared completely. Various names were printed on pink Post-its in the right-hand corner; some of them had been crossed out.

'We're trying to track down her foster parents,' Akosua said. 'A couple have passed away, and it doesn't look like Tina was good at keeping in touch.'

'Surely she kept in touch with Jacob? Get me a copy of his file, then go home.'

Akosua nodded as she rolled up her makeshift chart. Her fingers worked slowly so the Post-its stayed flat. The chart was crude and almost childlike, but I saw the look of pride as she walked out.

My muscles were cramping, and I stood on my tiptoes, rolling my shoulders to ease the strain in my back. Randle had been going through the evidence from Odie's kitchen, headphones glued to his ears as he worked. I doubted he was listening to anything, but they blocked out the sound and sent the message that he wasn't to be disturbed. He looked up as I approached.

'Do you think Fiona was telling the truth about not knowing Tina?' I asked.

He slipped the headphones down the back of his head so they rested loosely around his neck.

'As far as I could tell. She's not doing too well, ma'am.'

'It's a prison, Randle. Not summer camp. She's not supposed to be having fun. There's definitely a connection between Fiona's case and Dele's, so for the purpose of finding Tina, we need to treat Fiona as unreliable and consider the possibility that she knew Tina. Maybe she's blocked out the whole incident. She was so dazed when she turned up here.'

'Maybe Tina used another name with Fiona?'

'But why change her MO with Fiona when she used her real name with the others?'

'I don't know, ma'am,' Randle said.

I made my way to the accessible bathroom. The Jacob Pax lead seemed useful, but it had thrown up a lot of questions, and I needed to calm my mind. I locked the door behind me, slipping my shoes off so I could feel the floor against the balls of my feet. I barely flicked my wrists, shifting my weight from side to side. I imagined a long rope circling me, heavy and slow over my head. I deepened my breaths as my body relaxed.

Jacob Pax's file was waiting on my desk when I got back to my office, a blue Post-it resting on top. A plastic container of pad Thai sat next to it, obligatory takeaway to sweeten the blow of overtime. It was kind of Akosua to order it, but I wasn't hungry, and I slid the box into the bin. The file was thin and light between my fingers, and I scoured the pages, looking for clues that would lead us to Tina Pax.

Released into society as an adult, Jacob had adopted a new identity, but he struggled to adjust to life on the outside. His name was discovered by the press, and he became the victim of a vicious witch-hunt. Unable to cope, he leapt to his death on his birthday, desperate to escape the onslaught of public judgement. That was the end of Jacob Pax – notorious for a time, but ultimately forgotten. I flicked through the folder, scanning the schedule of witnesses for the list of officers involved in the case. The case had been led by a DI Timothy Barron, a high-flyer in his time, whose reputation had endured even after his death. Most of the team were retired police officers who would take too long to track down, but one name jumped out from the list: DC Eli Carson, a junior officer on the case.

Chapter One Hundred and Five

Leah

So much had happened, I had hardly thought about my father; now I had no choice. I considered sending Randle, but I needed to keep Eli separate from the rest of my life. I spent the night awake, thinking about the past. Kenny O'Sullivan's words flashed into my mind.

He was good at tuning into the minds of criminals. He got them in a way most police officers don't. Understood them, even . . .

If anyone understood Tina Pax, it would be Eli, and for that reason, I had to try.

Eli looked drawn, and the hollowness of his cheeks made his eyes even more prominent. I wondered if he had been ill, but something stopped me from asking. The room felt more crowded than before, and the conversations around us blended into a low hum.

'Did you find the reports?' Eli leant back in his chair, his mouth stretched into two thin lines resembling a smile. He watched my face for signs of shame, but I refused to give him the satisfaction. 'You're learning.' He sounded pleased. 'You give too much away. How does it feel to know what you're capable of?'

'I didn't come here to talk about me.' I kept my eyes expressionless. 'I want to know about Jacob Pax.'

'What about him?' Eli's tone changed, the playfulness gone. 'Tell me about the case.'

He stared back at me, his features settling into a scowl.

'Do you realise how ridiculous that sounds,' he said. 'I ask you a simple question which you ignore; you make an open-ended request and expect me to sing like a bird. It doesn't work that way, Leah.'

'I didn't realise there were rules.'

'There are always rules. You should know that. Answer my question . . .'

'. . . and you'll answer mine?'

His mouth twitched at the edges.

'You'll have to wait and see.' He looked down at his long, elegant fingers. I glanced at mine, so similar to his. Something passed between us.

'OK. I found the reports,' I said.

'And . . .'

'And nothing. It was a long time ago. It's forgotten.'

'Forgetting doesn't mean we change.'

He let the words hang between us. His teeth were small and white between his lips.

'What do you want to know, Leah? Are you wondering whether little Leah had a touch of Jacob Pax in her?'

'You tell me. I was too young to remember. You worked on Jacob's case. What happened to his sister?'

Eli's eyes gleamed with interest; he sat up taller but didn't reply.

'Tina Pax?' I said.

He smiled at that. 'She kept her name. Of course.'

He looked up at the cracked ceiling, and I was struck by the hard lines of his jaw.

'Of course, what?'

'The human weakness for the past when logic tells us to move forwards.'

'You don't need to speak in riddles. I get it. She wants to be connected to her brother,' I said.

'It's only natural. Tina keeps the name her brother called her in the past. I have a photograph of your mother on our honeymoon, pinned to my wall.'

'I thought you didn't like talking about her.' I fought the urge to get up and leave.

'Talking about her and about what happened are two different things. You've never asked me what she was like.'

Ever since I had seen my mother's photograph, images had flashed through my mind — a hand around mine, an adoring smile, the gentle feel of her lap; I had no idea what was real.

'I don't want to hear about her from you, Eli.'

'Who else then, Leah? Whom else are you going to ask? I knew her best. Loved her most. If you want to know about your mother, the only person you can ask is me.'

I could feel the blood pumping in my ears. I clasped my hands between my legs.

'. . . She was headstrong like you. Sure about her opinions but unsure about the world. She had a beautiful face and an infectious laugh. I hear it most nights in my sleep.'

'And what about her screams? Do you hear them too?'

Eli said nothing. I couldn't read the expression that passed across his face; then his features reset, and his voice changed.

'But you didn't come to talk about your mother. When you're ready, you know where I am.' He drew an imaginary line along the edge of the table with his finger, then pressed the tip against his mouth. 'Why do you want to know about Tina Pax, Leah?'

'I can't tell you,' I said.

'Ah . . .' There was a look of genuine glee on his face. 'Police business. Victim or perpetrator?'

'You know I can't tell you.'

'And *you* know I can't help you, unless I know the facts.'

'Then it's been a wasted visit.'

He watched me closely, lowering his eyelids so his expression was hidden under his lashes.

'You're asking the wrong question, Leah. If you want to find Tina Pax, you need to know what happened to Jacob.'

'He jumped off a building because his identity was revealed.'

'B-plus answer. You're missing the most important point. Think about *why* he jumped. Who broadcast his identity to the world?'

'You know I don't know the answer.'

'But you know the journalist. You used to work with her. Odie Reid.' He said the name slowly, elongating each syllable as the story fell into place.

'So, Tina Pax blames Odie Reid for her brother's death?'

'Close but not quite.'

'So, she doesn't blame Odie?'

'No.' Eli let out a low chuckle. 'She definitely blames her. She hates her, and hate is a very powerful emotion. Anybody can hate another person, momentarily or for a lifetime . . . You hated your mother for wanting to leave you . . .'

'I don't know what you're talking about.'

'You heard them; you told me. That's how I knew she was leaving me to be with *him*. Then you hid in the car when I went after her. That's why you were there.'

I pressed my palms against my thighs, tensing the muscles against my hands.

'We're getting off topic, Eli. I hated my maths teacher at school. Do you want to talk about her too? Tina hates Odie and blames her for her brother's death. Odie robbed Jacob of his life and ruined Tina's as a result. It's hardly rocket science.'

'You're slipping to a B minus.' His lips turned up at the corners. 'What makes you think Jacob Pax is dead?'

There it was. The important point.

'Jacob Pax. For many years now, John Pierce. Find Jacob and you find Tina.'

Chapter One Hundred and Six

Leah

A jet of water hit the back of my mouth as I hovered over the drinking fountain. I angled my face downwards so the water splashed between my eyes.

Anybody can hate another person, momentarily or for a lifetime. You hated your mother for wanting to leave you . . . You heard them; you told me. That's how I knew she was leaving . . .

I played Eli's words over and over, just as he had intended me to.

You hated your mother for wanting to leave you.

Had I? Had I gone running to my father when I found out she was leaving? I couldn't remember, but I couldn't shake his words from my mind. I remembered crawling into the back of Eli's car, burying myself in the darkness beneath the seats; I remembered the hard jolt as the car pulled away – but it was an isolated memory, and there was nothing more.

'Still no news on Tina's house, ma'am.' Randle's voice interrupted my thoughts as I walked past his desk.

Tina Pax, the woman I needed to focus on, not my mother, not Eli.

'What about Jacob?'

Akosua pulled up a report on her computer, shuffling through the multitude of windows on her screen. Her desk was cluttered with pen pots and Post-its, and there was no room for her elbow to rest. I had filled the team in on what I knew, but I didn't mention my source.

'We're still looking for the care home but have a look at this...'

She pushed a pile of paper to one side so I could perch.

'Although he changed his identity when he was released, a misdemeanour put him on the press radar, and when Odie sniffed him out, she made sure the whole world knew.'

She pointed at a section on the screen, directing my attention to one of Odie's more inflammatory paragraphs.

'In a civilised society, it is our moral duty to root out evil and expose it for what it is. We cannot let the bad corrupt the good, and we should not succumb to the fallacy that criminals can be rehabilitated. When a person commits such a heinous deed at such a young age, there's no coming back. It points to a blackness within their soul which defines them forever. They are beyond redemption, destined to commit even greater atrocities if given the opportunity. In the face of such terrible evil, it is our duty to act, to cast them out before the innocent are endangered and lives are lost. Jacob Pax killed a child in cold blood – why should he live freely when he thought nothing about taking the life of another human being? Justice must be done, even if we must be the ones to do it.'

The tone was angry and self-righteous – a vigilante call to arms in the guise of a moral crusade. Odie Reid had made it her mission to destroy Jacob Pax, 'to root out evil' and ensure he got the punishment she felt he deserved.

'Odie tracked Jacob down and exposed his identity, then left the public to decide his fate.' Akosua built up to her climax. 'People were out for his blood. He felt cornered and there was nowhere to turn, so he jumped. The police put out a statement that he had died, but Jacob Pax survived. He was in a coma for a long time, and he would never speak or walk again.'

I almost felt sorry for Jacob, living in limbo. Tina had effectively lost her brother a second time, and there was no chance of getting back the boy she knew.

'So, it was always about revenge. Always about Odie.' Randle swallowed a bite of banana. 'Tina was Odie's source. She was reeling Odie in. But why the others? Why bother to manipulate them too?'

'She was practising,' I said, considering each of Tina's targets. 'Angela, Dele, possibly Fiona. Practice runs for the big event. People who made the tragic mistake of revealing their vulnerabilities to a woman intent on exploiting them.'

'But why go to all that trouble?' Randle asked. 'Why not just deal with Odie directly?'

Akosua swivelled round to face him. 'Maybe Tina doesn't want to spend the next twenty years in prison? Maybe she'd rather keep her hands clean?'

'Maybe . . .' But I wasn't convinced. Tina's plan was too painstaking if all she wanted was simple retribution. There had to be a point to her method, a message she meant for Odie to understand. 'What's the relationship between the perpetrators and their victims?' I asked. 'Maybe the victims represent something? Maybe the similarities are more than a coincidence?'

Randle was pacing by the board, staring at the names of the victims: Alistair Cowan, Charles Walker, Jake Munro, Paul Drayton. He flicked the tip of his thumb with his forefinger as his imagination bridged the gaps our evidence had yet to fill. 'All the victims were known to their attackers. They're all white men with relatively more power. We know Dele hated his victims. He felt wronged by them in some way.'

'What else . . .'

'Angela ended up in a psychiatric unit. Dele and Fiona are facing long sentences in jail.' He paused, running his fingers across his eyelids so his eyes sprang back to life. 'Tina wants Odie locked up?'

'No.'

It was possible, but I knew he wasn't right; it lacked the grand finale I felt Tina wanted. I contemplated the images on the board, identically sized rectangles, each containing its own scene of horror: Charles Walker's body, pinstriped and bloodied, buried in a thicket; Jake Munro, face down in the dust, his skull caved in; Paul Drayton, eyes glazed in shock as he remembered the boy whose father he had let down. Three deaths prefiguring the judgement Tina believed Odie deserved. It had nothing to do with gender or race.

'Charles. Jake. Paul. Odie's like *them*.' I realised the truth as I said the words out loud. 'She's a victim. She's Tina's ultimate victim. Tina's ultimate target.'

'So, who's Odie's Dele?' Akosua asked the question they were both thinking, but I already knew the answer.

Chapter One Hundred and Seven

Leah

Richard Reid opened the door almost immediately. The hallway was dark behind him, and it was hard to see him in the gloom.

'Have you found them yet? Tell me you've found them.'

The dark patches beneath his eyes betrayed a lack of sleep.

'Richard, please can we come in?'

'Why? What's happened? Just tell me what's happened.'

'Nothing. We just need to ask you some questions,' I said. 'Does Odie have any enemies?'

'Enemies? She isn't exactly . . . easy, but "enemies", no.'

'What about Daniel?'

'What about him?' Richard was immediately defensive.

'What is his relationship like with Odie? Have you ever had any reason to think he has feelings of anger towards his mother?'

He looked anguished, then his shoulders slumped in defeat, and he invited us in.

Dele and Angela disappeared for a period of time before committing their first atrocity. According to Richard, Daniel had been missing for days. It seemed unlikely, but I had seen the unlikeliest of murderers, and we couldn't rule out the possibility that Daniel was being groomed to kill his own mother. Daniel Reid had vilified

Odie in a much-publicised article a few years before. It was no secret that they didn't get on.

We sat in Richard's front room, clutching mugs of weak tea no one wanted to drink. I looked round at the family photographs on display, noticing that Odie was absent from every one.

'He used to write diaries,' Richard said. 'When he was little. He wrote so well, I got them for him. He wrote about everything. School. His first crush. Music. I was so proud. Then, after I was in hospital, he left his diary in the kitchen one day. I know it was wrong to read it, but I hadn't read anything of his since he was really little, and I was so proud of him, you see . . .'

His cheeks flushed as he acknowledged the depth of hatred Daniel felt for his own mother. He swallowed a mouthful of tea.

'It was vicious. So unlike him. I didn't recognise my own son. I convinced myself he was just upset, and it would get better. I thought it did. I knew he hadn't forgiven Odie, but it was more indifference, not real hatred. She loves him.' He turned to face me. 'Whatever you think of her, Inspector, I know she loves our boy . . .'

He trailed off, staring at the drink in his hands.

'Richard,' I said. 'Do you think Daniel would ever harm Odie?'

I was surprised by the defiance in his eyes.

'She's his mother. He would never hurt her. Daniel would never hurt anybody.'

He covered his face with his hands, sliding them down to reveal his utter weariness. Then he got up and left the room.

Randle stared after him.

'It's OK,' I said. 'He'll be back.'

I set my mug down on the table in front of me, shifting a

photograph to make space: Daniel in his matriculation gown, Richard beaming by his side. Richard returned a few minutes later. I noticed a laptop under his arm. The lid was scratched in several places; the letters OR were printed on the back.

'I found this in Odie's bedroom when we were in her house. After you left. I thought it might help me find her.' He placed it on the table in front of us. 'She's never been good with technology. Kept the same password from when I set her first computer up.' He looked down, feeling guilty for betraying Odie's trust. 'There was a notification with a link. I didn't know what to do, so I clicked on it, in case there was some kind of clue. I was going to call you. I didn't know what to do . . .' He hesitated.

'You're not in any trouble,' I said. It wasn't a promise I should make, but I knew what he needed to hear.

He hit a few keys, and we sat in silence as a video started to play. I couldn't understand what I was looking at at first. I moved closer, peering hard at the screen: there were two shapes moving frantically as though engaged in a crazed dance. I thought they were wild animals fighting, then I recognised the sound of human screams, and I realised it was more sinister. It wasn't a noise I had ever heard before, but I knew I was listening to a man in unbelievable pain, howling for mercy as his life was beaten out of him. The attacker had their back to the camera, but I could make out the silhouette of a bat as it was raised and lowered with vicious intensity, hard wood pounding against flesh and bone. Sickened, I wanted to look away, but curiosity overcame repulsion, and my eyes stayed focused on the screen. The cries became weaker as the victim was repeatedly battered. I squinted, trying to identify the assailant before the recording came to an end, but it was too dark, and the angle of the camera made it impossible to see clearly. I had all but given up when it happened. It was so brief, I almost missed it, but once seen, it was an image I would never forget: unaware they were being watched, the attacker turned towards the camera, hands soaked with blood. Eyes manic and distant, they were barely recognisable, but it was a face I had thought about countless times before, and I didn't need to look twice to know it was Fiona Garvey.

The sound of my phone pierced through the silence.

'Ma'am?'

Fiona's face loomed deranged and bloody in my mind.

'Ma'am?' Akosua said again. 'We found Jacob Pax.' Her voice was triumphant. 'He can't speak, but we found him.'

Chapter One Hundred and Eight

Odie

Odie sat terrified, shivering in spite of the heat. She couldn't tell whether she was alone, and the sound of her breathing was so loud in her ears, she was deaf to everything else. She sensed rather than heard the footsteps behind her.

'I don't understand . . .'

'What don't you understand, Odie?' said the voice.

She hated the way the woman said her name.

'What you want.'

'Fiona Garvey – innocent or guilty?'

The question surprised Odie, confusing her in the darkness.

'What's Fiona Garvey got to do with it?'

Odie's voice sounded hollow as she repeated the name.

'Oh, I almost forgot.' That humourless voice again. 'You came before the page went live. You never got to see the truth. Fiona Garvey – innocent or guilty?'

The shivering had stopped, but Odie's skin was speckled with sweat. The damp sensation made her cold. She could no longer feel the presence behind her, but she knew the woman was still there, waiting for an answer she was afraid to give.

'Innocent . . .'

Odie wasn't sure whether she had said the word out loud. She waited, pushing against the binds that dug into the veins around her wrist.

'There you go again, Odie. Not paying attention to the facts. Seeing what you want to see. It's Rebecca Stanton all over again.'

'What has Rebecca Stanton got to do with it?'

'Everything. Nothing. It's what you do, though, isn't it? Decide who's innocent and who's guilty. Who's good and who's bad. Make excuses for some, condemn others.'

'I don't know what you're talking about.'

'Fiona wanted to hurt Alistair Cowan. Deep down, it's what she wanted. I just helped her with the courage of her own convictions.'

'I don't understand . . .' The words had become like a reflex.

'Not yet, but you will.'

Odie had been so focused on the voice, she hadn't noticed the screen in front of her. She could just about make out the shape of the television as it crackled to life, but the image was dark and hard to decipher. The camera had zoomed in artificially, making it difficult to understand the context, and she couldn't identify the shapes moving in the centre of the frame. The image was poorly lit, but Odie realised what she was watching, and she felt the bile rise up in her throat as a frenzied aggressor pummelled the life out of another human being. Odie closed her eyes, but she could still see each detail in her mind, the blows descending with alarming force. She screamed for it to stop, but it kept playing.

'Alistair said Fiona didn't do it.' It was all Odie could think to say, but she felt foolish even as she uttered the words.

'How could he know? He was hit from behind.'

'But why be so adamant? Why not just say he wasn't sure?'

'Because he owed her. What's your excuse?'

The video continued to play in the background, the incessant wailing reverberating in Odie's ears.

'I got it wrong about Fiona. Is that what you want me to say?' She would say anything to be allowed to leave the room. 'I thought she was something she's not.'

'And what was that, exactly?' The voice was still behind her.

'I thought she was innocent. I thought she was a good person.'

The woman laughed – low and unpleasant. 'So, what? She's bad one moment, good the next? Why is everything always so black and white with you, Odie? Rebecca Stanton . . . Fiona Garvey . . .'

She spoke like she knew her, but Odie still couldn't place the voice.

Chapter One Hundred and Nine

Leah

Randle cracked his knuckles, popping the joints against his palm.

'Sorry, ma'am.' He smiled wearily. 'Force of habit.'

He turned to look out of the car window, his voice muffled by the sound of the road.

'You were right to charge Fiona,' he said. 'I wasn't sure, but you were right.'

I steered sharply, almost missing the turning to Jacob Pax's care home in the dark. 'I'm not celebrating, Randle. Are you?'

We pulled up in a small driveway, bordered by well-kept hedges glistening under the headlights. Someone had tried to make the place feel homely, but they had either failed abysmally or hadn't tried hard enough. The lawn was decorated with uncomfortable-looking furniture; a statue of a cat stood guard by the front door. We were welcomed by a woman who introduced herself as Maud. She greeted us by the entrance, a wide smile plastered across her face.

'You know he can't talk to you,' she said for the third time. 'He can't communicate with anybody.'

'We understand,' I said. 'We just want to see him.'

'Of course.'

She led us down a long, nondescript corridor, describing the various rooms along the way: kitchen, dining room, laundry, post office – a self-contained world which mimicked life outside but fell short. I filtered out the sound of Maud's voice, leaving Randle to handle the small talk. He cracked jokes, reminiscing about summers with grandparents and siblings I knew he didn't have. I followed behind them, wondering how Margaretta would have coped without the order of her own home. I was almost glad she hadn't lived to find out. We entered what must have been the recreation area. Heavily starched curtains not quite covering the windows, uninspiring games scattered around the room – a board game on a table, a pack of cards on a chair. Jacob Pax was sitting in front of the television, flanked by a tall, unassuming woman in a purple nurse's uniform.

'This is Ava,' said Maud. 'She's utterly devoted and takes very good care of him.' Maud flashed us her best smile.

Ava considered us with barely concealed suspicion. Jacob continued to look straight ahead.

'Can we go somewhere quieter?' I said.

Ava spun the wheelchair around, pushing it out of the room without waiting for us to follow. She moved fast down a corridor barely wide enough for Jacob's chair. A set of sliding doors led to a small veranda.

'How much can he understand?' I asked when she finally stopped.

'Everything. Nothing. It's hard to tell sometimes.' She secured the wheelchair, gently moving him back in the seat. With her dark red hair tight against her skull, she reminded me of a teacher at school I had vaguely disliked.

'How do you communicate with him?'

She looked offended. 'We just do.' She lowered her voice as though divulging a great secret. 'He can move his eyes.'

'May I try?'

Ava stepped back, allowing me to get closer. I shifted forwards, searching Jacob's face for what remained of the boy he once was.

'I need to ask you some questions.' My eyes didn't leave his face. His hair was lank and receding; a long scar ran under his chin. 'Has Tina been to visit you recently? Blink once for yes, twice for no.'

I waited, watching Jacob as he stared through me. When he eventually blinked, I was pretty sure it had nothing to do with my question.

'Does he ever get any visitors?' I directed this at Ava.

She paused, reluctant to betray Jacob's confidence, but her curiosity got the better of her.

'Just one woman,' she said. 'She signs the register Pierce. I don't know her full name.'

'Do you use photographic passes for your visitors?' I asked.

'No. But there's CCTV at the entrance. It depends on which direction the guests are looking. Sometimes we capture their faces, sometimes not.'

'Can you show it to me?'

'You'd have to ask Maud.'

Maud was only too happy to be involved, guiding us conspiratorially to a small office at the top of the building. There were four monitors with live CCTV. She commandeered one of the screens so we could go back in time.

The woman's visits were fairly regular, always around four o'clock but on a different day each week. We cross-checked the footage against the register, scrutinising each arrival for a glimpse of her face. In one shot she wore a hat; in another, her head was tilted so her features were hidden. Each time she entered the frame, her face remained obscured.

'She knows the camera's there.' Randle's face twisted in frustration. 'She doesn't want to be seen.'

'So, let's find a day when she doesn't have a choice,' I said.

I pulled out my phone, searching for recent reports of bad weather – days when there was a deluge of rain, and the wind was particularly strong. There were two days in the past month with terrible gales; she appeared in the register on one. Maud hovered, waiting for instruction.

'Can you check this day?' I showed her the date on my phone. 'Please,' I added, so it sounded less like an order.

Randle glanced at the register for the time. 'She came at 3.52.'

Maud pushed down on a small black button, speeding up the recording so the days whizzed by. She released her finger, standing back to let us focus on the image. Jacob's sole visitor appeared on the screen. It was blustery, and the woman was shielded by a large umbrella. The wind pushed against the fabric, and she struggled to control it. Her lips moved in frustration as she muttered under her breath, bending forwards so her head was tilted down. The wind blew harder, and the umbrella suddenly shot out of her hand. She reached to reclaim it, turning towards the camera, her arm outstretched. It was only for the briefest of seconds, but in that moment, I saw her face, and I realised I had seen her before.

Chapter One Hundred and Ten

Leah

It seemed so simple, now we had all the pieces: Tina Pax had become Sonya Waugh – a witty play on words, if Russian literature was your thing. Tina Pax had been laughing at us all, plotting her revenge in plain sight. Fiona had no recollection of Tina because she thought she had never met her; she only knew Sonya Waugh, the therapist she had trusted with her secrets. She had gone to Sonya for help, and Sonya had exploited her demons. The worst of it was that I had trusted Sonya too, telling her things I hadn't shared with anyone. But it was too late for regrets.

Randle was still in shock when we walked away from the building. My mind was in pieces, and I focused on the crunch of gravel under my feet to stay calm.

'I didn't see that coming,' Randle said. 'All that time and it was her. She made fools of all of us.'

She made a fool of me . . .

The lamps on the walls had been turned on and the light bounced off the car. We had sent officers to Sonya's practice, but I knew she wouldn't be there. I had requested a search warrant, but I doubted she had left any clues. She had planned it all so carefully – an expert on human weakness, making adjustments as she went along.

'She was watching her victims,' I said after a while.

'What do you mean, ma'am?'

The wind gathered momentum, and Randle was forced to move his hair out of his eyes.

'Tina. She must have been there,' I said. 'She must have made the recording of Fiona attacking Alistair. Angela couldn't have turned up at her father's house in a car she couldn't drive. Tina followed the victims, decided when the time was right, and then she brought their attackers to them. The bats were used to trigger the right state of mind. She must have given them to all three.'

There was a soft beep as I pressed the car key. Randle nodded as he took it all in.

'The yoga bag we found near Fiona's things . . .'

'What about it?'

'Maybe it was to conceal the bat?'

I remembered the bag Dele had mentioned at the back of his cupboard.

'It's possible,' I said.

His hair fell back into his eyes; he ignored it, and the wind swept it up like a halo highlighting his face.

'But none of them recall Tina being there,' he said. 'Or anything about the actual attack. Angela has a blank in her memory; Fiona blacked out; Dele forgot. The first time, at least.'

'Tina must have been using some form of hypnosis. She could have conditioned their minds to forget.'

Randle shielded his cigarette with his coat to light it. He pulled hard on the filter so the nicotine flowed straight to his brain.

'Her own therapist.' He exhaled furiously. 'How d'you get your head around that?'

He took another drag of his cigarette, then flicked it onto the ground. My fists clenched involuntarily around an invisible skipping rope. I shook them free, but Randle had already seen.

'Are you OK, ma'am?'

I leant against the car door, staring at the sky. It didn't matter that I hadn't known it at the time – I had confessed my deepest secrets to Tina Pax.

Chapter One Hundred and Eleven

Leah

Fiona barely moved as the video played on my phone. We had been given a secure room in the prison, not much larger than a cell. A narrow desk separated us, and I could hear her breath hitch as she watched.

'That's not me,' she insisted. 'It's not me.'

I played the footage again, pausing on the final image as her face stared back at us. Fiona looked at me confused, then she looked at the screen, and her body convulsed with sobs.

'Listen to me, Fiona,' I said. 'The mind can play tricks on us and it's understandable your brain blocked this out, but this isn't about Alistair any more. There's a woman called Tina Pax, and we think she is inciting people to commit violent acts. We need to find her before someone else gets hurt.'

'I told you . . .' Fiona wiped away the tears. 'I don't know anyone called Tina.'

'Sonya Waugh is Tina Pax.'

She froze, a look of complete terror on her face.

'We believe a woman's life is in danger, and we need your help to find her,' I said. 'I can't promise you anything, but if Tina Pax did to you what we know she did to at least two other people, it could help your case.'

Fiona's head jerked up, snapping upright on her neck. 'What do you mean, what she *did* to me? Is that why I can't remember?'

'Fiona . . .' My tone was sharper than I intended. 'Is there anything she told you? Anything, however small, that could help us to find her? Please, Fiona, we need your help.'

'What happened with Alistair, I don't remember any of that . . .'

'It's OK, Fiona. I'm not here to talk about the attack.'

'Please listen . . .' she pleaded. 'I need you to understand . . .'

She looked at me desperately, and I didn't stop her. A spot of red appeared on her lip as she bit into the skin.

'Everybody thought he was great. That I was lucky to be working for the company's golden boy. I thought so too. But it was all for show. He managed big projects, but he hadn't closed a major deal in a long time, and he was worried. Really worried. Then it finally happened.' She shuffled her feet under her chair. 'I'd never seen him so happy. He said he couldn't have done it without me, that he appreciated my loyalty, and I would be rewarded. Rewarded for lying . . . for covering up for him.'

I could hear the disappointment in Fiona's voice; I remembered my own disappointment when I realised my old boss, Mark, wasn't the man I thought he was.

'He'd been bribing officials to close the deal. I was going to report it when I found out, but Alistair could be persuasive. He said if he lost his job, I'd lose mine too. He said I was his assistant, and I was complicit already. My career depended on him. People liked me, but I needed a champion. He had always been my champion. I didn't think I had a choice.

'I worked the hours he needed. Kept his secrets. And it was mostly fine. I learned how to live with it. To separate myself from what I knew was wrong. Then one night, he went too far.'

She looked directly at me for the first time – round eyes, animated and bright. Her hands were shaking, and she clasped them together until the tips went white.

'It was late when he called, but it wasn't the first time he had needed something done late. I could tell he was at a party from the noise. He had left his iPad in the office. He wanted me to take it to him.'

There was a pause, longer than before. When she spoke, the words came out in a stutter, like vinyl that had been played again and again.

'I didn't want to stay. The party had been going for a while. Alistair was drunk; they all were. One drink, he said. One drink to celebrate and then I could go. He didn't force me, but there was only one answer he wanted. So, I stayed.'

Fiona was suddenly quiet. Her knuckles dug into her thigh.

'Alistair kept giving me shots, and I didn't want to say no. He was with his two main clients. They'd finally closed the deal and they felt invincible – high on money and success. They acted like I was there for their amusement. They kept touching me; I kept pushing them off. I kept looking at Alistair to say something, but he didn't. Just stood there smiling, asking for more drinks. Then he left me with them, and it went on and on. One minute I was fighting them off, then I just froze.'

'Did Alistair put something in your drink?' Randle asked.

'I don't know. I can't prove it, but he did something, gave me something. That person, it wasn't me.'

She lowered her eyelids so they were almost shut, but I could see the glint of her irises beneath her tears.

'Afterwards I felt ashamed. I wanted to forget, but I couldn't. Every time I saw him, I remembered all over again. It was like he had offered me up as part of the deal.'

Fiona was crying openly now, letting the tears gather on her cheeks.

'Fiona . . .'

Randle's voice was so quiet I almost didn't hear it.

'Fiona,' he said with more feeling. 'If those men took advantage of you, you can press charges. You still have rights.'

'Do I?' She shook her head. 'I went to work the next day. I didn't know what else to do. He apologised for letting things go so far. Said we all do things we regret, and he was sorry. More sorry than I could know. It was his job to protect me, and he had failed. He said he would do anything to make things right. We should keep what happened between us, and he would protect me like he had always done. I didn't want to talk about it. I froze all over again. I started blacking out. But I said nothing, did nothing . . . I just felt trapped. The lies he made me a part of. The bribes. Everything that happened when he left me that night. I hated him. Really hated him. I didn't realise how much.'

She closed her eyes, and her body crumpled as she finally accepted what she had done. She had handed herself to Tina Pax. I was ashamed I had trusted Tina too.

'How much did you tell your therapist?' I asked.

'Everything.'

'And did she ever tell you anything about herself? Anything, Fiona, no matter how small?'

'I don't know. Maybe.'

The tears had stopped, but she looked drained and lost.

'We talked a lot about loneliness,' she said. 'I sensed she was lonely too. She was married once, but she's divorced. It's the only thing I know.'

Chapter One Hundred and Twelve

Odie

Odie closed her eyes, but she could still hear the screams as Alistair Cowan was attacked again and again. The video had been playing on a loop, filling the room with the glare from the screen. Then it suddenly stopped, and Fiona Garvey's image froze in front of her.

'What do you think of her now? Good person who did a bad thing? Or just a person like you and me?'

Odie hesitated, no longer sure what to say or think. She had never felt fear like this before, and she doubted whether she would have the courage to run if she were ever given the chance.

'What about him?' Fiona's face was replaced by Dele's. 'No criminal record, never been in trouble. Just studied and worked to help support his mother and sister, until he killed three men – three men he held responsible for his father's death. What about *him*, Odie? Model citizen or deranged monster? What if his father had never died? What if he had never felt wronged? Would we ever have seen the real him? Would *he*? It's not that simple, is it, Odie?'

Again, there was no time to answer, as another image flashed up on the screen – the face of a young boy Odie would never forget.

'What about him? Do you remember him, Odie?' The woman's voice had lowered to a strange whisper.

'Jacob Pax. He killed a child . . .'

'But not just any child,' the woman interrupted her. 'A bully who attacked and abused his sister. Good or bad? Bad or good, Odie?'

'I don't know . . .' Odie stammered.

'Don't lie, Odie. Yes, you do, or at least you did when you ruined his life and took away his only chance to start again.'

'I don't know . . .' Odie repeated.

'Yes. You. Do. Do you know what it was like discovering that the only person you ever loved, the brother who did everything to protect you, felt compelled to take his own life before you had a chance to say goodbye?'

This time the woman paused, waiting for a response, and in that moment, Odie realised who she was.

'My brother had paid his dues. He was trying to move on with his life, but you couldn't let him be.'

Odie imagined Tina crying over Jacob's broken body. She almost felt sorry for her, but she had to believe she had been right all those years ago.

'I'm sorry you lost your brother . . . but I didn't push him off that building. He jumped because he couldn't live with himself,' she said.

'No,' Tina spat the word out angrily. 'He jumped because you wouldn't leave him alone. You still don't get it, do you, Odie? After everything I sent you. Everything's black or white with you, but we live in the grey, and you had no right to judge!' Tina's voice was fraught with emotion, and she took a moment to calm herself before she spoke again. 'When Jacob killed that boy, I didn't know what to think. He was my twin and we had always been the same, thought the same. Yes, he had more courage and he had done a terrible thing, but everything he did, I wanted to do too. I wanted to run fast, to be funny, to stand up for myself; I wanted that boy dead too.' Her voice trailed off, and Odie strained to hear her in the darkness. 'For years I thought we were the anomaly, the evil twins who didn't fit into a society that kept us at arm's length. I read everything, studied everything, approached my psychology degree like it was a matter of life and death. I even worked with criminals convicted of the most violent offences. I did everything I could to understand why we were different. I even read the Bible, even though I don't believe in God. And the more I read, the more I realised that my brother and I were not alone. Total depravity, the sickness of the human heart. We live in a fallen world; everybody has evil thoughts – some people act on them, others don't.'

'We're not all killers.' The words were out before Odie could stop them.

'That's where you're wrong, Odie. We are all killers, but we don't all kill. Envy, hatred, anger – take any of those emotions to their extreme and who knows what we're capable of? Fiona Garvey, Dele Adeola, you, me. There's a darkness in all of us, but you took it upon yourself to demonise my brother because you decided he was worse than everybody else.'

'I don't know what you want me to say. I'm sorry about what happened to your brother . . .'

'No, you're not!'

A sharp pain radiated through Odie's back as her chair toppled to the ground. It took a second for her to realise it had been kicked over, and her hands clenched in agony as the weight of her body pressed against them. She lay in terrified silence, struggling to make sense of what was happening.

'No more hypocrisy, Odie. Let's just be ourselves.'

Odie could feel the heat of Tina's breath on her skin as she whispered in her ear. She recoiled in disgust, but she couldn't move away.

'Dele killed two men after Charles Walker. He connected with his dark side and saw it as a strength. Fiona tried to kill Alistair because she held him responsible for the worst night of her life, and she wanted revenge.' The anger had gone from Tina's voice, and she was almost gentle as she lifted the chair back to face the screen. 'We're all capable of terrible things. Fiona Garvey and Jacob Pax fit the same pattern of behaviour, yet you defended one and destroyed the other. Why?'

Odie searched for an answer, but her thoughts were jumbled, and she wasn't sure what to say.

'What about *him*?' An image of Daniel flashed up on the screen. 'What do you think *he's* capable of?'

Odie stared at the screen. She felt a rising sense of panic, and she didn't recognise her voice when she spoke. 'What have you done to my son?'

'Nothing,' came the reply. 'But what do you think he would do to you, given the chance?'

Chapter One Hundred and Thirteen

Leah

Randle drove fast, without speeding. His body was tense, but the car moved smoothly along the road. The team had found a rental property in Sonya Waugh's name on the outskirts of London. There was no stone arch nearby, but it was the best lead we had. Randle had barely said a word since we set off from the prison. I leant against the window, letting the silence build.

'It was guilt,' he said after a while. 'The look I saw in Alistair Cowan's eyes when I went back to see him. It was guilt. That's why he said Fiona didn't do it. He wasn't protecting her; he was protecting himself. Trying to keep her out of jail so she was grateful enough to keep silent.'

We were edging close to the speed limit, but he never strayed over; there was a coolness to his driving even though his anger burned. Inside the car, the air felt cold. I reached for the heater, filling the space with its hum.

'I feel sorry for Fiona,' Randle said, half to himself.

'Why? Because of Alistair or Tina Pax?'

'Tina didn't need her. She had Dele. That should have been enough.'

'She did need her,' I said. 'She needed Fiona to make a point.

Dele was just a guinea pig; she needed Fiona to teach Odie a lesson, because she was such an unlikely aggressor. She wanted to suck Odie in. Make her think Fiona was someone to save. Then show her she was wrong. Wrong about Fiona. Wrong about Jacob Pax.'

'Do you think Tina found out Fiona had been to see Brendan Klee, or do you think she introduced Fiona to the shows to see how she reacted, ma'am?'

'Does it matter?' I suddenly felt exhausted. I sank back into my seat, watching the city drift past. 'She knew Fiona was susceptible. She knew her secrets, and she knew how to use them.'

'But if it wasn't for Brendan Klee, maybe she would never have known, and Fiona would have stood a chance . . .'

'You don't need to judge or sympathise, Randle. It's not part of our job.'

His lips parted in response, but he swallowed his words before they came out.

'What?'

He paused, taking his eyes off the road for a moment as he turned to face me.

'It matters, ma'am. *How* it happened. It matters.'

He turned back to focus on the road as my phone buzzed in my pocket.

'Akosua . . .'

I put her on speakerphone; her voice echoed around the car.

'I followed up on the lead you gave me from Fiona, ma'am.' Akosua spoke quickly when she was excited. 'Fiona was telling the truth. Sonya Waugh *was* married, but she never took her married name. Her ex-husband lives abroad, but there's a house in his name.'

'Any chance you can get an address?'

'Already done. I'll send it to you now, ma'am.'

'Tell the others to proceed with the search on the rental without me. I'll check out this other address. Call for backup. I may need it.'

I turned to Randle as I hung up. 'You can join the official search, or you can come with me. It could be a wild goose chase, and it could be dangerous. Your call.'

He looked at me. His eyes filled with questions, and I could tell he was remembering the incident in the fairground when I froze.

'It's OK, Randle,' I said. 'What happened with Dele. It won't happen again.'

He pinched the sides of his mouth with his thumb and forefinger. Then he stared out into the road and slowly nodded his head.

Chapter One Hundred and Fourteen

Odie

Odie stared at the screen in front of her, confronted by the accusing face of her son.

'It's no secret there's no love lost between you and Daniel,' Tina said.

'We've had our difficulties in the past. We're moving forwards as a family.'

'Is that what you like to tell yourself?'

'Just tell me where he is!'

Odie was shouting now, anxiety and pain getting the better of her, but it was as if Tina hadn't heard.

'I've hated you for a long time, but I didn't think I could do anything about it until I saw the article.'

She didn't need to say more; Odie instantly knew what she was talking about – the damning article about mothers and sons which Daniel had written five years before. He hadn't mentioned Odie by name, but it had obviously been about her, and it had hurt.

'When I read his article, I recognised something I had seen in Jacob, something I had seen in myself: pure hatred of another human being. The moment I saw that, I knew I could use him when the time came.'

'What are you talking about?'

'Getting to know him was easy. Dating him wasn't hard. He was funny, self-deprecating – attractive, even. But he was stuck, crippled by his hatred of you. He wasn't like Dele or Fiona. His feelings had been buried, and – even though he didn't show it – the years had made him angrier. I knew it would take longer with Daniel, but I had time. Once Dele killed Charles, I knew what was possible. And I knew Daniel, and how much he hated you.'

'I'll ask you again. Where. Is. My. Son?' Odie bucked against the chair, wrestling with the restraints.

'All in good time, Odie.'

'Where is my son, Tina?' she screamed.

'Your son's not the one you should be worrying about.'

A lamp flashed on like a spotlight.

'Daniel would never hurt anybody.'

'How can you be so sure?' Tina looked Odie directly in the eye.

'I know my son.'

'Let's see, shall we?'

Tina walked over to the door and opened it. Daniel stood on the threshold, a frightening intensity in his eyes. Tina slipped out, and the door slammed shut behind her. All Odie heard was the sound of her heart beating with fear.

Chapter One Hundred and Fifteen

Leah

We parked a little way from Tina's ex-husband's house. Only one of the gate lights was working, and a short beam of orange lit up our approach. The phone signal was poor, and it got worse with each step we moved forwards. Randle spotted the car first, off to one side, obscured by a swathe of foliage. It could have belonged to anybody, but my gut told me it was Daniel's, and someone was trying to hide it. We were still far enough from the house not to be heard, but I kept my voice low as I turned to Randle.

'Run to the car and radio for an ETA on backup. I'll go on ahead.'

I moved off, but his fingers curled round my wrist. I stared at him, but he didn't let go, and I didn't shake him off.

'No,' he said. 'We go on together or we go back together.'

'Randle.' I released my arm from his grip. 'Now's not the time to make a point.'

'I'm not making one, ma'am. You said you're not interested in playing the hero. Neither am I. If we stick together, we stand a better chance.'

A mixture of defiance and loyalty blazed in his eyes. I would never tell him, but I was glad.

The house appeared unoccupied as we drew closer, but the

battered blue BMW told me something was wrong. Odie had driven that car for years, spending more to keep it on the road than it was probably worth. I spoke fast, firing off instructions as I climbed the gate. A thread from my trousers caught on the metal. I heard the material rip as I tugged my leg free.

'Give it a couple of minutes, then make a commotion outside. You need to draw her out, give me time to go round the back. Stay out of sight. And Randle . . .'

'Yes, ma'am?'

'Be careful.'

He looked at me for the briefest of seconds. 'Always.'

I had to move fast in case Tina was watching. I was sure she was acting alone, so if she came to the front door, I would have a chance to find Odie and Daniel. There was a steep stone staircase at the back of the house, leading to a basement entrance. The windows were boarded up, and the door was locked with a heavy brass padlock. It would take a couple of minutes to pick the lock, and I said a silent prayer, hoping Randle could distract Tina long enough for me to break in. I heard the clatter of a series of objects hitting the ground above me on the other side of the house. I had spotted a pile of paint tins by the front door; Randle must have disrupted them to make a noise. Seconds passed, then I heard voices, first Tina, then Randle. She had caught him; he would have to think fast to explain why he was there. I heard the slam of a door closing. I listened for footsteps retreating down the drive. The ensuing silence told me Randle was inside. He was alone with Tina, but there was no use worrying; I had to trust him to do his job. The pin shifted in the lock; I waited for the sound of metal clicking open, but it sat stiff and heavy in my hand. Gently, slowly, I pushed the pin further in, willing the padlock to twist open, until it eventually did.

The door shut behind me, and I found myself in a narrow corridor. I was surprised by how dark it was, and I could no longer hear voices – nothing above me, nothing to the side of me, just silence and darkness with no sign of Odie or Daniel. I turned to my left, moving slowly in one direction. The house was bigger than it looked from the outside, and every time I expected the corridor to end, it kept stretching out in front of me. I followed it, my eyes focused ahead. I heard a soft wailing behind me, and I spun round, running hard towards the sound. I could hear voices above me, but I couldn't see anything. My body collided with what felt like a door. I fumbled, searching for a handle. My nail snapped against a hinge. I drew my fingers slowly across the uneven surface, keeping my touch light until they found the smooth metal knob. I turned it, but there was no movement. The door was firmly locked. I pressed against it, slamming my shoulder against the wood. I could feel the resistance, but the lock was weak, and there was a low creak as it started to give way. The wailing grew louder. I pushed again.

'Odie! Daniel!' I hissed, but no one answered.

I lunged harder, out of breath. There were footsteps above me. I could hear Randle shouting, but I couldn't make sense of the words. I rushed at the door, using all my momentum. It sprang open, and I pushed Randle to the back of my mind.

The light caught me off guard after the blackness of the corridor, and my eyes took a moment to adjust. A chair was upended in the centre of the room, and a TV screen lay shattered on the floor. Daniel sat crouched in one corner, his left arm dangling in front of him, his eyes strange and wide.

'Help me!' he gasped. 'I couldn't stop it from happening.'

'Stop what?'

I inched towards him, careful to keep my distance. He was holding a baseball bat, staring with hollow eyes at a crumpled shape lying at his feet.

'Me.'

His body seemed to collapse in on itself, and the bat slid from his fingers, rattling across the floor. I grabbed his arm, pulling it behind his back. He made no attempt to resist as I slipped the cable tie over his wrists. He closed his eyes, but I saw the tears before he blinked them away.

Odie lay limp on the ground, her knuckles a raw mess of bone and blood. She had tried to fight back, but had lost, her torso folded to withstand the blows. Her chest strained against her shirt as she struggled to breathe; the material was ripped at the seams, exposing battered flesh.

'You're OK, Odie. I've got you.' I knelt beside her. 'You're safe now. Backup will be here soon.'

Daniel watched us, his eyes unmoving, silently pleading with me to help the woman he had tried to kill. The room seemed to vibrate with the sound of Odie's breathing. Daniel was still, barely making a sound. I heard a scream, and I ran.

Chapter One Hundred and Sixteen

Leah

I heard a gunshot above me. I moved through the darkness, searching for a route up, but I was hit by a series of dead ends. I turned down a corridor, sprinting blindly until my toe crashed against a rough step. I tentatively reached in front of me, feeling my way along a set of concrete stairs. Moments later, I emerged from the basement, blinking in the light. The ground floor was eerily quiet, and there was little furniture around; there was another level above me, and I gambled on Tina being at the top of the house. The stairs felt steeper as I sped up them. I found two rooms, but no one there. Rushing down to the floor below, I felt an increasing sense of panic. I shouted Randle's name, but there was no answer. I shouted his name again. I heard a creak from the kitchen and the tap of footsteps. When I entered, the back door was swinging on its hinge.

The house backed onto a small garden, which merged into a stretch of woodland. I could see Tina ahead of me, nearing a border of trees. She stopped for a moment, daring me to follow, but there was no sign of her when I reached the wood. I moved fast, and within seconds I emerged into an opening at the foot of a narrow bridge. I could hear the sound of water over rocks beneath me; a slice of moon hid under a cloud.

'You found me.'

The voice came from behind me and when I turned, she was closer than I had expected, bigger and more imposing.

'What have you done with Randle?'

'You heard the gunshot. What do you *think* I've done with him?'

'What have you done with Randle?' I repeated.

'He's dead.'

She said it without emotion, and her abruptness caught me off guard.

'I don't believe you.'

'You don't or you don't want to? It doesn't change the facts.'

'I didn't see a body . . .'

'You couldn't have had time to check every room.'

I hesitated and she saw it.

'Where is it, then?' I said.

'In the living room.'

'You're lying.'

It was the one room I hadn't checked.

'I wish I were, but it was self-defence. He attacked me, and I did what I had to.' She watched me coolly, enjoying my uncertainty. 'You shouldn't feel guilty. It was his choice to stay. Trying to impress you until the end. Why would I lie, Leah? I'm not a murderer.'

'Then why do you have so much blood on your hands?'

'One man. Self-defence. I did what anyone would have done under the circumstances.'

'What about the others?'

She didn't answer. She took a step towards me, and I moved back, closer to the bridge.

'Charles Walker, Jake Munro, Paul . . .'

'I didn't kill those men.'

She spat the words at me, and I realised she actually believed them.

'You set them up to die. What's the difference?'

'The difference, Leah . . .' Tina's voice was slow and deliberate, 'is that *I* didn't kill them. I watched the victims; I knew when they were vulnerable. But I didn't hurt them. I wasn't the one who judged.'

'You made innocent people do terrible things.'

She sniffed, incredulous. I heard Eli's laugh echoed in hers.

'Innocent? Interesting choice of word,' she said. 'I just needed to know they could do it once – to know that if the hate is strong enough, anyone can be driven to act. Dele was only supposed to kill Charles Walker, but he went on to kill two more times. Turns out Fiona had a conscience and handed herself in. She called me, you know, the day she attacked her boss. Wanted an emergency therapy session. Wasn't sure she could cope. Alistair wanted to meet in a café after hours. She said she couldn't take it any more. But she was too weak to say no. It wasn't supposed to happen that day, but she was so wound up, so full of hate.'

Her hair had fallen loose around her face, her eyes more alive than I'd seen them before.

'I only opened the Pandora's box, Leah; I'm not responsible for what was inside.'

'You really believe that?'

She looked at me without apology, her body erect in her long grey coat.

'I gave them the instrument to trigger their anger, but you can't trigger something that's not already there. Angela, Fiona, Dele,

Daniel, my brother . . . They wanted to do those things. *They* did them. Odie couldn't see that; I had to make her understand.'

'By getting her son to try to kill her?'

'By showing her what we're all capable of.'

The calmness of her hate was terrifying; her lips stretched in an ugly smile.

'You hated Odie that much, you were willing to ruin all those lives?'

'She ruined my life, my brother's . . .'

'And what? That justifies making good people commit murder?'

'Good people?'

She looked at me like I was mad.

'None of us are good. I would have thought you of all people would agree.'

'Don't try to make this about me . . .'

I could see the house through the trees behind her; I prayed Randle was still alive.

'Why? Because of the voice in your head telling you you're no different from any of them? Fiona, Dele, your father . . .'

'So what, Tina? Deep down we're all murderers?'

'Murderers, liars, hypocrites. Different degrees of imperfect. It's not our actions that make us evil, it's what's in here.' She tapped the side of her head. 'That's why your dreams frighten you so much, that's why you came to me. There's a darkness inside you that will never go away.'

'I'm not my father.'

'You haven't had to be . . . yet.'

Tina reached behind her, pulling something from under her coat. The fabric fell heavily around her body, and it was difficult to see what it was. I shifted my weight onto my toes, anticipating an attack that never came. Instead, Tina crouched low, almost kneeling on the grass. She slid a small object towards me. Looking down, I saw a gun at my feet.

'What's this?'

'Protection. Courage. Justice. Whatever you want it to be. I don't need it any more.'

I stood, waiting for her to make the first move.

'I'm sorry about your partner.'

She said it so softly, I had to strain to hear her.

'I didn't want to kill him. He left me no choice.'

'There's always a choice.' I tried to keep the emotion out of my voice.

'So, choose wisely . . .' She backed away from me as she spoke.

'I can't let you go. You know that.'

'So, shoot me, Leah. I leave here dead or free, but you're not taking me to prison; I saw what it did to my brother.'

'And so, what? You'd rather be dead than locked away?'

'My brother lost his life because I was a victim.'

'Your brother is still alive.'

'Is that what you call living?'

'He's more alive than the three men lying in the mortuary.'

She didn't seem to hear me. The water swirled behind us, beating the bridge like a drum.

'I lost him when he was sent to prison; I lost him when he was forced to start a new life; and I lost him when Odie chased him off a building. Every day I lose him a little bit more, and you tell me he's alive.'

She turned to walk away, her coat skimming across the weeds.

'Don't make me shoot you, Tina.'

'Do what you've got to do.'

She kept on walking away.

The gun felt light in my hand. Pulling the trigger would be easy, too easy. Tina was still close enough for me to catch her. I flew towards her, knocking her to the ground. She was bigger than me and stronger. She barely resisted, but I knew she would overpower me the moment she did. I could feel her chest pounding against my knee, her breathing ragged.

'What's it going to be, Leah? Dead or free?'

'I'm not going to kill you, Tina. You'll go to prison where you'll get the justice you deserve.'

'Justice . . .' She let out a low, bitter laugh. 'Whose justice? Yours, the court's? I'd rather have mine.'

Resting my full weight on her torso, I tried to reach for my handcuffs, but she was too quick. In an instant, she had flipped me over, so I landed hard on my back. The pain rocketed down my spine, but all I could think was that I had to stop her. I kicked my leg out, surprised by my strength as she fell backwards, hitting her head against the ground. I could see the blood creeping beneath her hairline, and she reached a hand up to stem the flow. Her eyes flicked to the film of red liquid covering her fingertips. I scrambled to my feet and charged at her, driving my knee into her stomach.

'Innocent people died because of you, and you need to pay for what you did.'

'No, Leah.' She was gasping for breath. 'People died who deserved to die, and people killed because they were never saints.'

'What about Randle?' I could feel the anger mounting. 'He didn't deserve to die.'

'It was me or him. What would you have done in my place?'

'I would have let him live.'

I was kneeling on her chest now, pinning her down so she struggled to get the words out.

'No. You wouldn't. Fight or flight, Leah. What would you choose? What do you always choose?'

She was straining to breathe.

'I would have let him live,' I said again.

'No. You would have lashed out the only way you know how. There's an anger inside you, just like your father.'

'I'm nothing like my father.'

I pushed down harder, trying to silence her, but she wouldn't stop.

'Then why do you hide who you are? What are you so scared of?' She paused. 'Do you know what Randle said when I told him about you? He didn't believe me. Insisted you were one of the good ones.'

I said nothing, but I could feel my body pushing down harder on her chest, and I did nothing to stop it. My brain fizzed with a strange energy, and an image of my father hunched over my mother's body flashed into my mind. I saw her limp in his arms as he carried her away, then the image faded, and I heard Tina's voice again.

'What did that child say? When you were five? What could have been so bad to make you hurt her like that? Did she see through you? Did she know?'

That child, that dream I had had so many times. It had always felt like another person's nightmare, somebody else's past. I remembered what it was like to be unmasked.

Your daddy's a killer and you're just like him.

I had been scared that the little girl's words were true, and I had wanted to hurt her to take back control. I could feel it again – the same anger I had felt that day – and I didn't realise I was holding the gun until I had it pressed against Tina's forehead.

'Pull the trigger. See if those thoughts go away,' she said. 'I dare you, Leah. Put me out of my misery. It's over anyway.'

'I'm warning you, Tina . . .'

'Go on . . . I dare you . . .'

I could feel the trigger heavy under my finger.

'Hutch!'

The sound of my name stopped me momentarily. Odie staggered towards us, collapsing with the effort of each step.

'Hutch! No!'

She was shouting now, struggling to move faster, but barely able to walk. She was too far away to hear what we were saying, but the gun in my hand told its own story.

'Does Odie know about you? About your father? Should we tell her who you are?' Tina raised her voice for Odie's benefit.

'You have no idea who I am.' I jammed the revolver into her flesh.

'You're the daughter of a killer, and there's a violence inside you which will never go away. I know it; you know it, and one day everyone will know it.'

Eli's face appeared in my mind. I saw my mother's eyes filled with fear. A flash of metal, a whirr of limbs, a rush of blood. I could hear Tina laughing softly to herself. I heard Odie's voice, frenzied and high-pitched, screaming my name. Then I heard a gunshot.

Chapter One Hundred and Seventeen

Leah

I opened my eyes, terrified by what I had done. Tina lay next to me, blood leaking from the side of her head. The life had seeped out of her eyes, and the expression on her face was frozen. She looked like she had been cut off before she could get her final words out. Odie knelt beside me, shaking me as she spoke.

'Listen to me, Hutch,' she said. 'We don't have long before they come. Leah, listen . . .' She slapped me across the face. 'You need to pull yourself together and listen to me. Tina attacked you; she had a gun; there was a scuffle; I got hurt in the fray . . .'

The preceding minutes replayed themselves in my mind: Odie flinging herself at me with the little strength she had left as my finger threatened to squeeze the trigger; her anguished scream when the gun went off; the spurt of blood where the bullet ripped through her shoulder. The images piled on top of each other as my brain scrambled to catch up.

'Did you hear me, Hutch?'

I stared at her, numb.

'Leah, did you hear what I said?'

'Odie, I . . .'

'She attacked you. There was a scuffle. I got hurt in the fray.'

'And Daniel?'

'He got hurt too. We all did, but it's over.'

I couldn't take my eyes off Tina, her head resting at an odd angle, her legs twisted underneath her in the soft grass. Odie followed my gaze.

'She went for the gun when you dropped it. It was all so quick, there was nothing you could have done.'

Tina's fingers were still clenched around the trigger, her body contorted by the force of the bullet she had fired through her skull.

I leave here dead or free, but you're not taking me to prison . . .

You're the daughter of a killer and there's a violence inside you which will never go away . . .

I inhaled deeply, shaken by how close I had come to killing her.

'Odie . . . the things she said—'

Odie cut me off again. 'It's over, Hutch. Let it be.'

I could hear the sirens in the distance. I hoisted Odie up, pinning her against my side. She had lost a lot of blood, and she struggled to hold on to me. Each time I tried to move forwards, her body dragged me towards the ground. Then I felt the weight lifted away from me, and I looked up to see Randle bundle Odie into his arms.

'Randle . . .' My voice faltered as I said his name.

'I'm sorry, ma'am. She knocked me out pretty bad.'

'But you're alive.' I was almost in tears.

'Yes, Leah. I am.'

Chapter One Hundred and Eighteen

Odie

'I'm sorry.'

They weren't the words Odie was expecting, but they were the ones she needed to hear. Fiona sat opposite her, waiting for her to respond, but with so much to say, Odie said nothing.

She felt exhausted and empty, drained of energy and emotion. Tina Pax was never far from her thoughts, and she felt an unbearable sadness about what had happened. Jacob, Tina, Fiona – lives twisted and destroyed, and her own son a victim of the events she had set in motion.

'I thought you'd come sooner,' Fiona said, '. . . then I remembered what I did to Alistair, and I thought you wouldn't come at all.'

Odie had tried to pity Fiona, but she couldn't get past the brutality of the assault and the memory of being strapped to a chair, forced to watch it again and again. But after weeks of trying to push it to the back of her mind, she knew she couldn't move on unless she saw Fiona one last time.

'I didn't lie to you,' Fiona said with a sudden intensity. 'I want you to know that.'

'I know.'

Odie looked at Fiona for the first time. She saw a woman in

turmoil, fighting to recapture the person she thought she once was. She started to speak, but Fiona got there first.

'I didn't remember what happened until I saw it, and even then, I hoped it wasn't me, but it was . . . I saw a part of me I recognise in my darkest moments, not the version of me I strive to be every day. But it was a part of me all the same.' She paused, unsure whether to continue, but she owed it to the woman who had believed in her innocence. 'I thought about killing myself again.'

There was a time Odie would have been shocked by Fiona's words, but she was past that now.

'What stopped you?' she asked.

'My cellmate,' Fiona replied. 'Something she said about everything we do being tainted by sin, but total depravity doesn't mean that we are totally depraved. We're still capable of acts of kindness, acts of love . . . Do you believe that, Odie?'

Odie wasn't sure what she believed, but she was desperate for some trace of hope.

'Maybe,' she said.

There were tears in Fiona's eyes. 'But I want to get back to being good. I need to get back to being good.'

It was then that Odie pitied Fiona.

'Maybe you never were. Maybe none of us are,' she said.

'How can you live thinking that?'

Odie smiled sadly. 'Got to be better than lying to ourselves about who we are.'

It was all she had left to say.

Fiona started to weep, silently at first, then her whole body shook, and she cried out. Odie offered no words of comfort, just sat and watched, trying to understand the feelings Fiona had kept buried for so long. She thought about Daniel in tears in the hospital all those years ago, and she remembered the anguish behind the anger as he struck the first blow. *She* had done that to him, and she was deeply sorry. She had never told him because she had never admitted it to herself, acting as if he was little more than an inconvenient reminder of a marriage doomed to fail. She hadn't pressed charges after the incident in Tina's house, but nor had she seen her son. She was a coward, and she didn't know what to say. Now the words which had eluded her were obvious.

Sorry for everything. For not being there, for being terrible when I was there. Sorry you have me as a mother, but I am your mother and I love you.

Odie couldn't run away from who she was any more than Fiona could escape what she had done, but the possibility of forgiveness made her feel hopeful for the first time in a long while.

Chapter One Hundred and Nineteen

Leah

Odie refused to press charges against Daniel, and I didn't force her to. No one apart from us knew what had happened in that room, and no one else needed to know. We didn't talk about that night, and I hoped that what was left unspoken would forever remain forgotten. There had been no phone calls or messages; no thank yous or apologies for the past. I had saved her, and she had saved me. I was grateful but ashamed. She had seen me in a way I didn't want to see myself, the way Margaretta had seen me and spent the rest of her life helping me to forget. Tina was dead, and even though she had fired the fatal shot, I couldn't shake the fact that I had pulled the trigger too.

My nightmares had become more intense, but I no longer feared them; I surrendered myself instead. Weeks later, I had another one, but this time I didn't wake up. I saw a flash of metal, a whirr of limbs, a rush of blood. Then I saw my mother, limp in Eli's arms as he carried her away. He turned into the darkness, and I followed behind.

Acknowledgements

Writing is in many ways a solitary process, but I couldn't have done this alone. There are so many people to thank, and I'm sorry I can't mention everyone.

Thank you to my wonderful agent, Camilla Bolton, for your creativity, insight and thoughtfulness. You've helped me become a better writer.

To my editor, Stef Bierwerth, for your wisdom, support and care. Thank you for being a great sounding board, for your patience and pragmatism, and for being such a fantastic advocate for the book.

Thanks to the brilliant team at Darley Anderson – Jade Kavanagh for your diligence and tenacity; Georgia Fuller, Sarah Brooks, Francesca Edwards and Ilaria Albani for being such great champions of the book. Thanks to Rosanna Bellingham, Helen Dudley and Shanika Stirling for all your support. Thanks also to Sheila David for your commitment to the book.

Thank you to everyone who worked on the book at Quercus – Kat Burdon for your amazing attention to detail; Andrew Smith for the wonderful cover; Ella Patel, Beth Wright, Katy Blott and the rest of the publicity and marketing team for working so hard to promote the book; and Lucy Rostant for posting all the proofs. Thank you also to Sharona Selby and Lorraine Green, for their careful copyedit and proofread.

To everyone who answered my questions and helped me build the world of *Innocent Guilt* – thank you. I especially want to thank Paul Ditta for the hours you spent talking to me and for sharing your knowledge so generously. I've loved our chats, and your interest in stories and TV made our conversations a joy.

I'm incredibly thankful to all of the following for your time, insight and expertise: Tony Fuller, Sammy Warnakulasuriya, Jessica Skinns, Daisy Monahan, India Ross, Patricia Rogers, Eleanore Massey, Dr David Holmes, Wesley Illingsworth, Fiona, Kate, Kwaku and David.

Thank you to Andy Curtis, Lucy Bruen and Ali King for reading at different stages and encouraging me to keep going.

Thanks to Ed Arriens and Guy Bolton for valuable advice, and to my cousin for his motorcycle expertise.

Thanks to the cheerleaders who kept me going and helped with the little things that are so important. There are too many to name everyone individually, but I particularly want to thank Kylie Hutchison, Zarene Dallas and Ned Williams. Thanks also to Lucas, Fabrizio and Yeong for all the coffees.

I'm deeply grateful to Liz and Andrew Venz for your care, support, enthusiasm and for your wonderful hospitality.

Thank you to Dominic Rose Price for being there from the start – for reading my very first draft and for being genuinely excited for me at every stage.

Thank you to my brilliant grandmother, the best storyteller I know.

Finally, I want to thank my mother and my sister for your unwavering support and for celebrating every victory, big and small.

Thank you to my sister and closest friend for reading *Innocent Guilt* in its infancy and giving helpful notes on my first draft, even though it's not her kind of book. Thank you for reading to me when we were little, and for all the childhood games we played that fuelled my imagination.

And thank you to my mother, the most inspiring person I know. Thank you for your unconditional love and for always encouraging me to tell stories – as a child, as a producer and now as an author.